In the Dark of the Moon

a novel by

SUZANNE HUDSON

In the Dark of the Moon

a novel by

SUZANNE HUDSON

Suzanne Hud[son]

09-18-05

MacAdam/Cage

MacAdam/Cage
155 Sansome Street, Suite 550
San Francisco, CA 94104
www.macadamcage.com

Library of Congress Cataloging-in-Publication Data

Hudson, Suzanne, 1953-
    In the dark of the moon : a novel / by Suzanne Hudson.
    p. cm.
    ISBN 1-931561-90-7 (alk. paper)
    1. Civil rights movements—Fiction. 2. Girls—Fiction. I. Title.
    PS3608.U348I53 2005
    813'.6–dc22

                                                    2005003687

Manufactured in the United States of America.

10 9 8 7 6 5 4 3 2 1

Book design by Dorothy Carico Smith

For my family, the Hudsons and the Johnsons

BOOK ONE
ELIZABETH LACEY
1929-1956

Elizabeth Lacey turned twenty-six in January of 1955, the same year Emmit Till was murdered in Mississippi, beaten beyond recognition, shot in the head, castrated, and dumped in the Tallahatchie River, his body tied to a cotton gin fan to weigh it down. He was killed in August, and Elizabeth's soul flinched with the quick serpent's bite of her conscience. The newspaper stories Elizabeth's mother tried to keep her from reading, and especially the photographs, smuggled into her grandparents' house, seeped into Elizabeth's spirit so deeply that the imprint left her suspecting, whenever she visited one of her brief, clearheaded moments, that she would not see twenty-seven. Then, with her grandfather's death, she knew for certain she would not. She couldn't, not after all she had done. She could not allow herself to walk through another celebration of her own life, blow out the next batch of candles, not when she was so bound up in the death of a fourteen-year-old boy, two states over, in Mississippi; and especially not with her grandfather's murder coming so close behind and at her hand.

She had always possessed an innate, unconscious awareness of the lurking jeopardy of her self, and her sense of it presented on a peripheral edge of desperation grown fierce, in her young adulthood, with misguided energy. When she was small, her thoughts sometimes raced past one another, while her words became a garble of intertwined intentions, syllables collapsing, an accordion of stumbling speech punctuated by giggles. On those occasions her mother would sigh and push a book into her hands. "Now look what you've done, Elizabeth. You've gotten yourself all twisted in knots. I declare, you're just like a worm in hot ashes. Go read a book and calm yourself." As a result, the child not only carried the visceral burden of her mother's detached disappointment, but could also read by the age of four and was reading light-years ahead of her peers by third grade. Books showed everyone that her mind could, after all, be still, but only within the context of printed words and, over time, inventions of games with words. She escaped the misery of her little-girl failings by spelling words backwards in her head, setting them to her own musical images, turning them into poems. She memorized all of her *Mother Goose* verses by age five, then proceeded to make up her own poems with the same rhyme and meter as "Jack Sprat," "Little Miss Muffet," or "Ding, Dong, Bell." Her mother, grandmother, and nursemaid taught her sayings from the Good Book, favoring Proverbs, Psalms, and Ecclesiastes; during grade school, the memorization of Bible verses became her obsession. She won for the Methodists whenever a Bible bee was held against the Baptists, garnering a semblance of approval from her mother, winning favor with Brother Stryker, keeping her age division always on the moral high ground in the hike toward spiritual victory. By the time she heard of the Mississippi lynching, though, her competitive take on salvation had been violated by a guilt that writhed through her with her mother's whispered words: *Now look what you've done.*

When she first realized what had happened, how Emmit Till's death echoed through her own acts of seeded violence, she found Eula Lura, the family's colored cook, sitting silent and aware in the kitchen, a butcher knife lying across her lap, a mound of chicken carcasses on the metal table, freshly scalded and plucked.

"Why?" Elizabeth whispered, laying her head on her folded arms, by the naked, headless birds. "How can that be?"

"Somebody wanted it to happen." Eula Lura fingered the wooden handle of the knife, ran her fingertip around the silver screw. "And somebody made it happen. That's all."

"That's all?"

"All," Eula Lura repeated, and began cutting up the chicken.

"All," Elizabeth sighed into the metal table.

"That's all," Eula Lura said. "One of them men in the newspaper, one of them white men they talked to, said it wasn't nothing to it. Said 'the Tallahatchie's full of niggers.' And that's all."

It was during the following weeks that Elizabeth heard about something more, then begged and cajoled until Eula Lura finally slipped a *Jet* magazine into her possession. Eula Lura's eyes were insistent, dark skin dropleted with sweat and condensation from the large pots of corn on the cob and turnip greens bubbling away on the gas stove. She pulled the September 15 issue of the magazine from the oversized brown handbag she brought to work every day and squinted at Elizabeth to the roar of an industrial kitchen fan sucking heat and thick scents out of the room. "Don't let nobody see this, you hear? Nobody." Then, tense and determined, she turned back to her pots and skillets and lard.

Elizabeth locked herself in her bathroom and sat on the cool, black-and-white-tiled floor, the drip-drops from the leaky showerhead echoing like a giant metronome's ticks, from wall to wall and back again. She flipped the pages and let the magazine fall open to the center, to a photograph's truth. The boy, Emmit Till, was laid out in a coffin for all to see, skin misshapen and tinted strange from its stay in the water, what was once his face now a mangled mess, the crushed forehead, the gouged-out-looking eye. Inside that moment, Elizabeth's already graying vision of the world locked into the muted shades of newsprint, the short course of the rest of her life set like boldface print, like a headline playing to her heightened senses.

In her childhood, Elizabeth's vision had been a kaleidoscope of colors, delightful trills of shades and forms. She sometimes saw the world in vivid tones and crisp shapes, like a clean-lined, black-drawn print or a deftly focused photograph. Her grandmother's chicken house might be painted hard against the sky, feathered hens setting with the fine, clean edges of an inkwell pen. Other times the colors would blur and bleed into one another, taking all form and boundaries out of focus and into an impressionist's canvas of splotched and dabbed-on blooms, and the plumage of the yard birds would haze into gradations of orange-red-brown fluff. And the sensations pulsed ever on, ebbed and flowed, until a moment would catch a passing image, a perspective-altering one, paralyzing it into still life, a snapshot filed away in her head. It was ultimately those snapshots that burrowed their way into her perceptions, beginning in color, fading to black and white, taking her further and further into their composition and out of herself. Emmit Till had become the latest in her collection of snapshots, a collection she had been building all her life, building and filing away in her head. But his was a picture she could never file away. It was the last picture, or so she thought. It was the one that would take her into a fragmented sort of vulnerability, the kind that would force her to pay for her crimes, real or imagined.

The first memory she had of her mind making a snapshot came back to her when she was six years old, revisiting the perspective of a toddler just past three, revisiting herself. Over the years, her father shot miles of home movies of her with the Kodak sixteen millimeter camera, moving pictures projected on a spider-legged screen set up in the living room several times a year. She loved watching him bring the spools of film out of round metal cases stacked like the checkers of some giant in one of her storybooks. He always read out the titles on the tin discs, all titles about her, the child, the eye of the family storm, but in reality a storm within a storm: "Elizabeth's Third Birthday," "Elizabeth and the Pony," "Elizabeth at Mayhaw Plantation," or "Elizabeth Eats a Catfish Dinner." Then he threaded the film through the projector as it ground a slow clicking into the silence, the staccato of clicks the only accompaniment to the images pulled from the guts of the machine. And she watched herself, a toddler, an infant, a four-year-old, all jump-cutty and throwing light, a pulsing flow of light, like a halo, she thought at the time, deciding then that she wanted her blonde braids wrapped around the back of her head, just like a garlanded halo, snatched from an angel.

It was at the age of six she discovered a disc of film she had never seen before: "Elizabeth at the Parade," it read. Her father threaded it through the projector, recounting the road trip the family had taken when Elizabeth

was just three years old, when they loaded up the Packard with feather pillows and lemonade-filled mason jars and fried chicken pressing grease
spots onto brown paper bags, and set out for Columbus, the sprawling textile town halfway up the state, perched on the Chattahoochee River.

They drove through the city, the biggest one Elizabeth had ever seen,
with its tall, brick buildings and wide, bricked streets. More than a few of
the stores were closed and blank-eyed, but enough remained in business to
draw some patrons, in spite of hard times. Those mills that had not shut
down in the wake of the Crash were loud with clacketing looms and big
machines throbbing a rhythm to the traffic, a dusting of cotton fluff
snowing down from open windows. She was fascinated with the place's
insistent, heartbeat cadence, however strange and triaged, the Chattahoochee slicing through town, a dark, fat snake, spinning menacing currents that would drag a man down in half a heartbeat, her daddy said. They
drove past well-heeled pedestrians, nonexistent back home in Sumner,
mingling at the storefront behind shopping bags; past hot dog vendors
wearing bow ties; past white-gloved policemen in vibrant blue uniforms;
and then the textile workers her granddaddy called "lint-heads," subdued
citizens in a city gasping for breath, struggling to stay above water, despite
what seemed to be at the surface.

They drove through neighborhoods, past parks, down avenues of oaks
and sidewalks, until they came to the road at the edge of town where some
political friends of her grandfather's lived, where the parade was to pass
after coming through the downtown. Here they joined a gathering of folks
in a mood of anticipation.

The "parade" was a presidential motorcade, knots of watchful people
lining the paved streets on the outskirts of the big city, shades of gray
motion projected onto the screen, then Elizabeth in a double-breasted
coat, pudgy hands clapping, curls spilling out from under a felt hat, curls
that looped across her forehead and brushed at deep-dimpled cheeks. The
lens found her mother, who waved it away, back to Elizabeth, who prissed
and swayed and played to the camera. Then it rested on a long convertible
touring car, where the man in the back seat waved to the crowd, the flash

of his glasses glinting a quick glare from the screen, the car drawing up even with the camera, which fell back on Elizabeth, flapping her hand with frantic, little-girl glee at President Roosevelt, on his way to Warm Springs, Georgia, just passing through on his way to the country.

"I know your granddaddy thinks FDR's some kind of a Socialist," Elizabeth's mother said as the reels were stilled, the screen a stark slab of white light. "And he *is* married to that mannish woman who's got the darkies all stirred up. But he is the President. That's why I went along with Miss Lucille's idea of going to see him ride by."

Elizabeth's grandfather made a disgusted "Hm!" sound down in his throat, near his chest. Her father chuckled and set about rewinding the film.

Miss Lucille, Elizabeth's grandmother, spoke up. "It is a bit of history, Elizabeth. Think of it. A leader of the world. You are fortunate to have seen him," her grandmother said, words growing crisp, brittle, as Elizabeth's grandfather shifted and sighed in his easy chair.

But Elizabeth was not listening, was instead transfixed by the image forming in her mind—the glare of the man's glasses, the lift of his palm, that one frame of her father's long spool of squared images. It was a black-and-white image of President Roosevelt, lifted out of the moving picture machine and frozen in a toddler's remembrance. She let the watercolor wash of her thoughts pour through the frame, filling in the deep blue sheen and sun-bouncing chrome of the car, the myriad shades of the cheering crowd. She would later think of it as a thing forever fixed in her head, like a sheet of Kodak paper laid in a stop bath. It was the first time a black-and-white image, made up of gradations of gray dots, transformed into pastels and primary colors, then back to gray, taking its place in her head, leading off the collection-to-be.

It became a secret pattern, moments in her life suspended in dull, ashen hues, a flip-chart of significant moments hanging in the gallery of her consciousness until, as she approached adulthood, they oozed their lack of color into her forced vibrancy, pulling her into a barren moonscape of lost feeling: President Roosevelt, waving from a touring car, on his way to Warm Springs, where he would one day die, leaving behind an unfinished portrait to add to her gallery; Gene Talmadge, on the stump, running for senator with evangelical fervor, inspiring her to reach for that kind of fervor; a dying dove speckled with blood, birdshot, and betrayal, pivotal, the instant she began to recognize her original sin; the eyes of a lone fisherman at midnight, the first man she would murder; then the second one, her grandfather, sprawled back in his easy chair with the hot smell of sulfur and the reverberations of a fired pistol hanging thick in the living room; Eddie Frye, the only man she loved whom she could not have, and his child, just born, slick with an amniotic glaze. Those were a few of the images she brought to the final one of Emmit Till, a child down from Chicago on summer vacation, snatched from his uncle's house in the dead of night, then beaten and mutilated before a bullet was, mercifully, Miss Lucille said, fired into his fourteen-year-old brain.

The movie projector wheel spun fast, rewinding until the loose end of film slap-slap-slapped against the machine, President Roosevelt and his touring car tucked into one of the bands of acetate on the smaller spool. Elizabeth sat up from where she had been lying on the rug, watching herself at three, one half of her present age and wisdom. "I remember," she said.

"Remember what?" her mother asked. She was filing her nails with a silver emery board. She spent a great deal of time grooming herself, was adept at conversing without looking up.

"I remember going to that parade and seeing that man."

"Oh, Elizabeth," her mother said. "You couldn't possibly remember that. You were only a baby girl."

"But I do remember," the child repeated. "I remember the lint-heads and the man in the car looking right at me and kind of smiling and lifting his hand up, like a wave."

Her mother sighed, examining the shape of the nail on her index finger. "Elizabeth, that was the President. He was waving at everybody. That's how politicians do. Just ask your granddaddy. He's been in scads of elections and he knows."

"He did look at me. And he smiled at me. And waved," Elizabeth insisted.

Her Aunt Frances, who had dropped by to look at the home movies, laughed and said, "Well I believe you, Waterbug. What I can't believe is that your daddy didn't label that film tin differently."

Jack, Elizabeth's father, answered in his steady, laid-back tone, "How else would I label it?"

"Are you kidding?" Frances said, slipping a cigarette into a tortoise-shell holder. She wore a man's wristwatch and a class ring from Judson College. "Let's wonder for a minute just how many regular old people, like us, out of thousands of regular old people, have President Roosevelt on film."

"So?" her brother said.

Frances lit her cigarette. "So why not label it 'Elizabeth Meets President Roosevelt' or 'FDR Waves at Elizabeth' or anything that would at least make reference to the President of the United States? 'Elizabeth at the Parade'? I mean, this will be a historical artifact, like Mama says."

"Because, sweet sister, Elizabeth Frances Lacey is the center of the universe to me."

Elizabeth smiled, knowing, just as they all did, that in the Lacey family her presence was much more central than FDR's. Daughter of Pearl and Jack; granddaughter of Campbell and Lucille; niece of Frances, who was the unmarried sister of Jack, who was the son of Campbell: the branches of the family tree curved their lush foliage all around Elizabeth. It was at once a place of safety and a place of suffocation, a paradox that confused her through childhood, until, at ten, eleven, twelve, she surrendered her desire to please to her desire to re-create herself.

What Elizabeth was not aware of was that, all through her growing up, she was the tap root from which her mother's emotional veins drew sustenance, the place where Miss Pearl could find the wherewithal to go through the dipping, flitting flutterings of a social butterfly. Elizabeth could not know, as a little girl, that her mother's tight giddiness at parties and teas, her obsessive attention to minutiae when it came to her appearance, her penchant for peach brandy at home, her disapproving words at her daughter's bravado, and her determination to keep unpleasantness from her only child all were mechanisms through which she held her own sanity together. Elizabeth could not know that Miss Pearl was going through the frenetic motions of a woman driven by the manic desperation to fit a mold that depression threatened to shatter—had, in fact, shattered twice before Elizabeth was born. The two breakdowns were never spoken of, the family watchful, vigilant lest a third approach, an unlikely chance, they hoped, since Miss Pearl's earlier despair had been predicated upon her inability to bear a child, to fill that part of the social requirement of a wife. Elizabeth, the saviour, had taken care of that with her gestation and birth. And Jack, relieved for his wife's relative stability, expressed that relief by thoroughly, lavishly doting on his wife's saviour child.

What Elizabeth could not comprehend was that Jack Lacey knew he had to be as vigilant toward his daughter as he was toward his wife, how he wondered whether the Lacey in his daughter would keep her on a strong track, how much he hoped she would never be as fragile as her mother, a Clayborne from Crisp County, a woman whose extended family was peppered with brawling men, pretty women, and insanity; and with suicides employing all manner of methods, from gunshots to hangings to the drinking of lye, as Miss Pearl's own mother had done when Jack Lacey took Pearl off from her family. Yet all the while he knew, down in his gut. He knew Elizabeth was different from other children even when she was an unresponsive infant, then a precocious toddler, knowing it more and more with the passing of each of her birthdays, then finally fending off his daughter's uneven ideation and aberrant rule breaking with his denial, his willingness to accommodate, make things right.

His ability to maintain the façade of normalcy was a thing he equated with strength, and Jack Lacey had a reputation for strength—physical strength as well as strength of character. A handsome man with an easy stride that commanded respect, he was a deputy under his father, the sheriff of Blackshear County, and it was simply assumed that he would take over one day, heir to that position in local politics; but it was also acknowledged that Jack Lacey would be an easy win in just about any election, personable and principled as he was. He was regarded, too, as a consummate family man, devoted to a wife who might be seen as a liability if not for his loyalty to her. He gave Miss Pearl love unconditional, kept his arm always bent at the elbow in her presence, offered over to her grasp, as if he could keep her whole and healthy with enough support.

Where Elizabeth's mother was aloof and unreachable, her father was responsive and malleable, always willing to do whatever his little girl needed to calm the chop she inevitably kicked up as she grew into a scandalously early womanhood. What all too many saw as a wide streak of stubborn independence in Elizabeth, Jack Lacey silently, and accurately, acknowledged as yet another incarnation of his wife's sharp shadows of fickle sanity, a link in the hereditary chain. But still he was vulnerable, and always, to his daughter's dimpled requests, the swoops of her dark lashes when she smiled up at him, and was the first to admit he would spoil her till the cows came home.

And so it fell to Elizabeth's grandparents, Campbell and Lucille Lacey, with whom they all lived, to be the architects of what token discipline Elizabeth ever received. Her grandmother took on the bulk of it, sending the child punished to the pastel interior of her bedroom's insistent femininity, sending her on little errands of responsibility to the post office or Taylor's Grocery, just down the street, sending her countenances of silent correction when she pushed at household rules or ignored hushed tones of veiled reprimand when she misbehaved in public, an occurrence that became more and more of a pattern as she grew toward puberty.

Miss Lucille, a self-described "renegade of the ladies' clubs," had been one of the few voices for women's suffrage in South Georgia early in her marriage, reined in by a husband who had little tolerance for such ideas but more than a little appreciation for a new base of support once it became the law; a husband who let her have her head as far as family concerns went, but became exasperated with what he called her "petticoat politics" and, later, her "New Deal-Raw Deal attitude." She was soft and bosomy, generous with her warmth but strict about manners and social scripts, consistently inconsistent. While she took pride in what she interpreted as her granddaughter's self-reliance, she felt compelled to keep her to Southern tradition at the same time. The only daughter, estranged, of a land baron, of a blooded branch of the Oglethorpe family, Lucille was steeped in the aristocratic expectations of the Velvet Corridor, brimming with courtesy, keen against making a show of money in the midst of the Depression.

Elizabeth was born the year of the Crash and spent her childhood hearing how times were hard for everybody, even though her own family seemed to be doing all right. "Crime doesn't go away just because we've all got hard times," her grandmother would say. "Be thankful your people are in law-keeping. Take pride in your people's jobs, but don't be a braggart. You remember what the Good Book says about braggarts, don't you, Precious?"

"Yes, ma'am," Elizabeth would reply. "'Whoso boasteth himself of a false gift is like clouds and wind without rain.' Proverbs 25:14." And in her mind's eye she would see white clouds thinning into silver-ribboned strands while the breeze pulled them at the horizon, squeezing them, wringing them around tree trunks wanting rain, but getting only a downy muffler of fog.

Miss Lucille oversaw the kitchen and the meals that were prepared not only for the family but also for any prisoners locked up at any given time in the Blackshear County Jail, two doors down. She made lists and plans and menus and calendars and trips to Taylor's Grocery. When the Depression's meager years forced her, periodically, to let the cook go, she herself prepared dinners of crisp-skinned fried chicken, sliced glazed ham, or juice-oozing roast beef, served with creamed or cob corn, hoecake, sliced peeled tomatoes, and snap beans topped with cucumbers soaked for hours in vinegar. She insisted that the prisoners should eat exactly what the family ate, that times were hard enough, that a man who got locked up during hard times ought to have a decent meal, guilty or no. Her husband sometimes rolled his eyes, called her a "mollycoddling Eleanor," not in a playful way, but rough, mumbled beneath his breath. She rarely took the bait, however, rarely acknowledged the slight, knowing that any political discussion with her husband would end in an argument, a notion that did not square with her idea of family decorum—not until the rise of the Nazi Party in Germany and the Japanese invitation to war, when the events of the day could no longer be avoided.

Her husband, Sheriff Campbell "Camp" Lacey, was a man of few kind words, stern and rigid in jodhpurs, high leather boots, striped silk ties against cotton shirts, and a cherished pistol at his side, his pride and joy and, ultimately, his undoing. Elizabeth was forbidden to touch the gun, had that one commandment imbedded in her brain before the age of two. And, as if to reiterate the commandment and make the pistol a source of unending terror to her, Camp fell into the habit of emptying the bullets from the six chambers into a footed pink crystal candy dish on the dining room sideboard. Then he bided his time, waiting for her to misbehave or commit even a tiny error of deportment, such as a failure to tell her grandmother she enjoyed supper.

"Oh, little girl," he would say, pulling the empty gun out of its holster, spinning the chamber. "I'm disappointed in you. I guess there's nothing left for me to do but—" and he would rest the barrel against his temple or beneath his chin or in his mouth or at his chest, his heart.

"No, Granddaddy! No!" Elizabeth screamed, at three, at six, whenever he performed his arbitrary skit.

"This is egregious," Miss Lucille always hissed.

"Goodbye, little girl," he would say.

"No, Granddaddy!"

And he would pull the trigger as the child screamed a piercing scream and her grandmother berated her husband. Miss Pearl would put a hand to her mouth while her own husband shook his head to the hollow click of the hammer striking, another snapshot, click, no explosion, no blood, no death.

"Don't you know by now, Precious, that he's joking you?" her grandmother would say. "But it's an egregious, horrid joke, Camp. Horrid."

If Aunt Frances witnessed the incident she might push her chair back from the table, throw down her napkin and say, "Daddy, this is not a thing you should do, ever. You can do untold damage to a child with that sort of trickery." As Elizabeth grew older, the joke tired and ingrained, her aunt went even further. "Hell, it's psychological facism, that's what it is," Aunt Frances would snarl, tapping her cigarette holder on the edge of a crystal ash tray.

But Elizabeth's grandfather would be all chuckles, spinning the chamber, pulling the trigger repeatedly to more impotent snaps of the hammer, while Elizabeth ran to bury her head in her daddy's lap. It was practically the only interaction between Elizabeth and the man who was her grandfather, and she feared him almost as much as she feared the gun; but unlike her grandfather, the gun also fascinated her. The thing he used to torment her was a thing that, even as a child, she sensed to be full of power, overlaid with some kind of magical glow, a force of conquest, Excalibur. She was drawn to it, and eventually managed to defy the rule against touching the gun.

There were late-night moments when Elizabeth, as young as four years of age, wandered through the big house after all the grown-ups were asleep. She listened to the thrum of the silence, heard a secret cadence of life shrouded in the rhythm of the quiet. And she visited other night noises: the tickle of insect legs against screens, the furtive groans and sighs of attic joists and piers beneath the flooring, the tinkling ping of silverware when her bare soles sent vibrations across the dining room floor, the breath of air beneath the front door carrying dusty remnants of scents from the feed store across the street. She stood before the strong leather holster hanging from the brass of an ornate coat tree and put her tiny white fingers to the handle, set with smooth pearl, studded with silver rivets, and she wished a fierce wish that she were a boy. Boys got to do things, like hold, and even shoot, their granddaddies' guns, and go on weekends in the woods with their fathers, and run and wrestle and roam farther and wider into the world than any girl ever could. She made a vow to herself, to be able to hold her own with any boy, any time, and she ran down the alleys of the town, racing to keep her vow, tangled blonde hair slung back and dancing with the quickness of her feet. She was forever dusted in street dirt, barefoot, scab-kneed, raindrops from sudden summer storms stinging her body then wriggling into muddy streaks, toes slippery with the wet as she left her small prints on the linoleum rug by the back door.

"Now look what you've done," her mother would say, putting a mop to the mess. "Little girls play with dolls and tea sets, and their mamas don't have to clean behind them till kingdom come." Then Miss Pearl would go hunt for her Jergens lotion to rub into her skin, soft flesh tainted by mop water because of Elizabeth.

At the age of six, Elizabeth set a campaign into motion, a campaign that lasted six more years until it was won and killed, a campaign lobbying her father and grandfather to take her along on their duck hunts, their dove shoots, their drives to the next county over, a wet one, to buy Early Times and beer. But her grandfather only gave a disgusted, spat-out sigh, and her father waved off her efforts, saying, "You're too pretty and sweet to be mixed up with vinegary old men and dirty little boys out in the woods."

"It just is not done, plain and simple," her grandmother said when Elizabeth complained about not being included on hunting trips. "It would be shameful to have you around such things. Men carry on in horrid ways not fit for a young lady to see. Heavens! What in the world would people say about you seeing such as that?"

"Now look what you've done, Elizabeth," her mother said. "You've gone and upset Miss Lucille. Run along now and do something productive."

So Elizabeth studied herself in mirrors with carved oak rosebuds at the edges and saw the wet midnight blue of her eyes, fringed with dark, curling lashes, the dip and curve of the waves of blonde licking her below the shoulders, too much a girl, too much a disappointment. She told her mother she wanted to wear braids all the time, thinking the two ropes of hair would tie up some of her expectations, keep her traveling down the straight and narrow paths between the buildings, cracked and sprouting small-leafed ivy. Permission was granted, and the weaving of the waves into sturdy strands of white gold became a morning ritual for her mother to perform, cinching it in, crossing it over, pulling from her daughter's repertoire of information the Bible verse Elizabeth had heard enough times to memorize with ease: "If a woman have long hair, it is a glory to her: for her hair is given her for a covering."

Her nursemaid was called "Jubil," short for "Jubilation." She was a short, spindly woman with spidery fingers the color of coffee splashed once with cream.

"She sulks too much," Miss Pearl often said. "I believe she criticizes white folks, but in a sneaky way, behind our backs."

But Elizabeth did not see Jubil that way at all. Along with Aunt Frances, Jubil was the only one who encouraged Elizabeth in her struggle to cross over into the arena of the men, with their mystique, their power, their ease of movement, their freedom. Jubil, a childless widow at thirty-three, lived alone in the little shack at the back of the Lacey property. She had cared for Elizabeth the infant and still looked after her when the family was away. She also helped tend the chickens, did the laundry and heavy housework, and kept a summer garden of corn, peppers, tomatoes, and purple hull peas. "You a child of brilliance," she said. "Got a mind touched by Jesus. He lets you see the things you see, things don't nobody else see. You belong to make something happen. Mark my words, Child. You going to make something happen in this here life."

"What will it be?"

"Don't nobody but the Lord know that. Just be you, that's all. Don't let nobody ain't got good sense tell you not to be you."

"Who ain't got good sense?"

"Never you mind. Just be you."

"But I want to be a boy."

"Say what?"

"I want to pee standing up."

Jubil let shout her baritone laugh and shook her head. "You crazy, girl. What did I tell you about that? Just what? You say it for me, Ecclesiastes 1:15."

" 'That which is crooked cannot be made straight.' "

"Unless you kiss your elbow," Jubil said. "That's guaranteed to turn you into a boy. But you better be damn sure that's what you want. I had a cousin that kissed her elbow and turned into a boy, but a ugly one with nasty habits."

"Like what?"

"Like nose picking and dog kicking and acting the twin of Cain. And he wouldn't take no bath, wouldn't keep his drawers clean. Till one day they came and arrested him for being so nasty and carried him off to prison."

Elizabeth spent the next three weeks turning her arm in its socket, aiming her lips at her elbow, coming within a half inch, wincing with determination, wishing for more than she had and more than she was, confident that she would keep her underwear spit-and-shine clean. She was not successful in her quest for boyhood, but she did succeed in conjuring up a playmate—unique and set apart from the tedious, predictable children at Sunday school—a boy called Hotshot.

Hotshot was an orphan of the Depression, picked up by her grandfather for stealing two apples and a hard candy from Taylor's Grocery. Hotshot was Bible-cover black and sickly thin, open-sided overalls revealing rib bones pushed out by hunger. He thought he was eight or nine years old, but wasn't sure, couldn't say when his birthday was, had never celebrated such a thing. Malnutrition had left gaps in his teeth and a listlessness in his eyes. He didn't have a last name, didn't know where he was from, and knew less where he was going. He had been riding the boxcars with his daddy for most of his life. But the two of them were separated in Macon, when his daddy hopped a train bound for Tallahassee, and Hotshot climbed aboard another one, the wrong one, in the Macon train yard, and ended up in Dothan, Alabama. That had been four months ago, and Hotshot had been traveling a kind of aimless meander, foraging for food on his own, being looked after by a succession of tramps and hobos who shared their sardines and potatoes and meager slabs of salt meat with him. He just happened to get caught by the law in Sumner and wound up bound for the county jail.

"You can't put a little child in jail for being hungry," Lucille said.

"I reckon I can if I want to," Camp replied.

"Good gracious, Camp, he's no more than a baby."

"He's going to be a man in a while, and a thieving nigger to boot."

"Camp, you know I don't abide that kind of language," Lucille said, "just like I don't abide putting a child in jail for trying to eat."

"All right, then, we'll do something else. He belongs at Milledgeville anyway," Elizabeth's grandfather said. "He stays quiet some of the time, like he doesn't know what's going on, then he'll bust out with sayings that don't make a bit of sense. I believe he's touched in the head."

Hotshot sat on the back porch steps at the Lacey home, devouring the pork and hoecake Miss Lucille had fixed for him. He smacked and licked his fingers, sucking up every drop of the juice from the pulled meat, licking at skillet-black fingers with his pink tongue. The cornmeal triangle crumbled as he pressed it into his mouth with the heel of his hand, leaving a yellow spackling around his mouth. Elizabeth peered at him through the screen, thinking how he needed a lesson about basic table manners, feeling full of all she could teach him.

"Milledgeville is for lunatics," Lucille said.

"I had a Nehi one time," Hotshot blurted, in spite of a mouthful of hoecake, a blast of corn meal crumbs spraying from his lips.

"You see there?" Campbell said. "Milledgeville."

"Heavens, no. Those poor crazy folks would bother him all kinds of ways. He wouldn't last a day." She looked thoughtful for a moment. "You know, the more I ponder it, the more I realize you're right."

"That a fact?"

"Yes, I think it really is best that he stay in the jail after all."

"Ten days ought to teach him a lesson," Campbell said.

"No, I mean permanently. And not locked up."

"Say what?"

"He should just stay there. Not be put there. But let him stay there, in the cell near the door, so he can come and go."

"Woman, you've lost your m—"

"Naturally you should put out an alert for his daddy," she went on. "At least try to find his daddy."

"Woman, ain't nobody got the time to go chasing down a train-riding nigger."

"Language, Camp. I do have to insist on that."

"We can't be taking in strays. There's not enough ways to support that."

"He'll earn his keep," she said. "Until his daddy turns up."

"Earn how?"

"He can sweep up, run errands, wash your car. We can spare a little food along with what I fix the prisoners."

"I had a Nehi one time," Hotshot said again.

Campbell was staring in some kind of disbelief at what he was hearing, but Miss Lucille had pulled out the tenacity that might be used when bigger issues came along if he did not let her have this concession. Campbell Lacey was a hard-nosed, ruthless officer of the law, but he rarely failed to go along with his wife's wishes when she was so insistent, as long as they did not defy convention, something she had done in the past, done even with him, before he got her good and settled down. A colored helper at the jailhouse was nothing but conventional. He sighed and went back inside, to his easy chair.

Miss Lucille tapped on the screen above Hotshot's head. "You want some tea, Sugar?"

"Yes'm, dog-gone luck."

"You want to stay next door at the jailhouse for a spell?"

"Yes'm, dog-gone luck."

Hotshot couldn't explain to Elizabeth why he sometimes ended his sentences with "dog-gone luck." It was just a habit, he reckoned, to go along with all his other odd habits.

"My daddy said I was crazier than a one-eyed dog," Hotshot said.

"Are you? Crazy?" Elizabeth asked.

"Yes'm."

"How do you know?"

"'Cause my daddy said so."

"I couldn't stand to be off away from my daddy," Elizabeth said. "Were you scared?"

"Not none."

"Did you cry?"

He thought a minute and shook his head no.

"Not any?"

He shook his head again.

"Don't you miss him?"

Hotshot licked his fingers again and wiped them on his worn overalls, thick white threads grilled across the knees. "Yes'm, I reckon. Dog-gone luck and so on and so forth."

Elizabeth took him around that very afternoon, to visit the places and folks who populated her life. Jubil showed him the henhouse and they all gathered eggs, nudging aside the birds' feathered bellies to take brown-speckled ovals into their palms, cupped and careful. One of Hotshot's eggs rolled from his unsure hands, though, cracking open, drooling albumen and yolk onto the black dirt. The boy jumped back, away from the mess. "Oh, Law," he said. "Gonna come a thunder."

"It's all right, Hotshot," Elizabeth said. "There are always more eggs. Isn't that right, Jubil?"

"Isn't that right, Jubil?" Hotshot said, in a copying-Elizabeth way more than his own.

"Yes, boy," the woman said. "You ain't got to worry about a few lost eggs, not with all these girls here spitting them out till Judgment. Ain't that so, ladies?" she said to the hens.

"I know about the Judgment," Hotshot said. "Gonna come a thunder, dog-gone luck."

Elizabeth stroked the tender shell with her fingertips and imagined the pressings of a baby chick inside, wanting to hatch free. "'God shall judge the righteous and the wicked: for there is a time there for every purpose and for every work.' That's Ecclesiastes." She put the egg to her cheek, as if to comfort the post-embryonic creature she conjured inside.

They sat on Jubil's porch drinking sweet tea while Jubil tended the zinnias in her yard, and Elizabeth talked on and on while Hotshot looked at her, grunting and nodding every so often.

"You should be nice to Miss Lucille," she said, "because she makes three-layer cakes. Yellow cakes with chocolate frosting that's so shiny you think it should stay on the cake forever. And be polite to everybody else. But don't get in my granddaddy's way. He gets irritated when he doesn't get something done at work. And if he gets mad at you, sometimes he takes out his gun and says he's going and goodbye. Going to shoot himself, I mean. But he's really just joking you."

Jubil's words were injected with sarcasm. "And he say Hotshot the one crazy in the head," she said, looking up from the flowers, her features shaded beneath a wide-brimmed straw hat, two strands of wide yellow ribbon tied beneath her chin.

Elizabeth squealed a giggle. "Jubil, you criticized Granddaddy! Mama said she thought you criticized white people, and you just then did."

"Hush that silliness, girl," Jubil hissed. "And don't you be telling your mama none of what I say."

"But why?" Elizabeth said.

"Why?" Hotshot repeated. He sat on the top step, bony knees up, skin peeking through the rips in the overalls, thighs thrown outward.

"You know damn well why, boy," Jubil snapped, then turned to Elizabeth, who was sitting on the edge of the porch, her head beneath the railing, feet swinging at the air. "If you want Jubil to stay around here, you keep quiet about what I say, you hear?"

"But, why?" Elizabeth asked again.

"Why? Why?" Hotshot echoed.

"Boy!" Jubil took the two steps up to where Hotshot sat in one nimble leap, drew back her palm, and smacked him hard on the side of the head, stinging his ear. "Don't you be smart with me!"

"I didn't. I didn't. I didn't." Hotshot was not exactly crying. Instead he was drawing his breath in with quick, short gasps, rubbing his ear, repeating "I didn't. I didn't," over and over. Every once in a while he whimpered a pathetic little moan and rocked back and forth.

For a moment Elizabeth was paralyzed with disbelief. She had never seen Jubil react in such a way. Certainly Jubil had never laid a hand on her, although she had the family's permission to take a switch to Elizabeth's legs whenever she thought it was needed, and had threatened to do so more than a few times. She would strip a small sweet olive limb of its leaves and zip it through the air. "I'm going to wear you out, now, if you don't behave," she would say. But to draw back and slap someone was something different altogether, and Elizabeth's eyes began to fill, from the shock and from seeing Hotshot, her new companion, in pain and afraid. She scrambled to her feet and sat beside him. "It's all right, Hotshot," she said.

The boy continued to rock and gasp and whimper while Elizabeth put her arm about his shoulder, patted his back, attempted to comfort him. She looked at Jubil. The woman was watching the boy, brows furrowed, forehead wrinkled in puzzlement. "Lordamighty," she said, dropping her wiry frame onto the step at his feet. "I ain't never seen such as this. This boy ain't right. Boy, you really didn't know why I got on you, did you?"

"I didn't, I didn't, I didn't," Hotshot continued to repeat, though the little breaths and whimpers were subsiding.

Jubil put her spidery fingers to his knee. "You stop it, now. Jubil ain't never going to do such as that again. You be good to Jubil and stop it. Jubil ain't going to do you bad no more."

Elizabeth continued to pat Hotshot's back, warm tears meandering down her face, feeling helpless, needing him to be happy again. "See?" she said. "It's all right."

"Lordamighty," Jubil said one more time. "The child is simpleminded. I wasn't noticing, but it's a clear thing now."

"Well he can learn not to be," Elizabeth said. "I can teach him things. Like how to eat with better manners. He eats like my Great Aunt Freida, the one that had to go to Milledgeville because she thought she was a lady-in-waiting to Queen Isabella of Spain and had to wear diapers and all."

Jubil was still watching Hotshot. "It's clear to me," she said again.

"Jubil?" Elizabeth said. "Why did you get mad at us?"

"'Cause I got a quick tongue, and that ain't right. Say for me a proverb about it."

"'He that is soon angry dealeth foolishly,'" Elizabeth recited.

"That's right," Jubil said. "And Jubil done gone off and acted a fool." She sighed. "But it's because I know things you don't know. And this is part of it: if you tell your folks what I say about Mr. Campbell, then I'm going to be let go."

"You mean they'll send you away?" Elizabeth said.

"That's a fact. Miss Pearl all the time looking for a reason."

"Why?"

"I don't know. I think maybe she eyeing Bonita, that one that works for Miss Deborah Maxwell up the street."

"No! I promise, then. I promise not to ever say anything about anything you say. I promise! You can't ever go."

"Lord, let me have that one dream."

"To go?"

"Yes, honey. Going to Texas one day and stay with my sister, help her look after Mama. But don't worry. It's going to be a spell."

"But you would really be happy?"

"Lord, yes. I ain't seen my people in over fifteen years."

"Then I want you to go. You should go. Sometime. Later."

"Thank you, honey." She laid her warm palm against Elizabeth's cheek. "Lord knows you got a pure heart."

"I seen a midget one time," Hotshot said.

Jubil laughed. "And you, boy, you got a pure heart, too. I was wrong to be 'soon angry.' See, I thought he was being fresh with me, acting like he don't know how to do. But come to find out he really don't, do you, boy?"

Hotshot grinned a gappy, jack o' lantern grin. He had settled down, was back to sipping his tea, a happy expression taking his hollow cheeks.

Jubil looked up at Elizabeth. "It's a shame he got off from his daddy. A child like this needs somebody in the world."

"He's got me," Elizabeth said.

Jubil sighed. "You go on and teach him manners and how to cipher and do the alphabet, if you can, but child, there's some things you ain't going to be able to get him to know, and that's a thing puts chills all up in me."

"Why?"

Jubil studied the boy. "You just look out for him best you can, honey. He's got him a hard row, and it might take a nasty turn if his mind ain't all the way with him." She shook her head, looking sad, resigned. "You do the best you can, you hear?"

"I will," Elizabeth said. "I promise."

Elizabeth and Hotshot walked over to Golden's Feed & Seed, across the street from her grandmother's house in the middle of town. They wandered up and down the aisles of fat croaker sacks dribbling corn kernels onto the floor, rough wood crates spilling straw packing, and a maze of tools for turning and nurturing the earth. They found their way to the back of the store, where hundreds of biddies chirped and stumbled across mesh-lined wooden shelves, caged by more wire across the front. The chirps of the little birds swelled into a whistling roar as the two children approached, and the noise did not die down until the humans, creatures associated with relief from hunger, retreated, taking the promise of food with them.

Elizabeth introduced Hotshot to Mr. Bennie Golden and Mr. Sam Dannie, who lounged at the cash counter as she told the story about how Hotshot was separated from his daddy. "Do this, Hotshot," and she bowed.

Hotshot replicated her gesture toward the men.

"Damned if she ain't got him trained," Dannie snickered. "Princess has a pet, don't she?"

"I'm teaching him all kinds of things," Elizabeth said. "But mainly manners. Hotshot, say 'Very nice to meet you, sir.'"

"Very nice to meet you, sir," Hotshot said.

The two men laughed. "Did you hear that?" Golden said. "Ain't that a nugget?"

Dannie slapped the counter, face reddening. "He's a goddamn little gentleman, ain't he?"

Hotshot laughed along with them, a strange, mimicking laugh, a laugh that, Elizabeth thought, sounded one part copycat, one part fear. Then, suddenly, Hotshot began clapping his hands, counting, "One, two, three, four," then breaking into a chanty tune, "Hambone, hambone, where you been?" Next he slapped his thighs in a rhythm, brushing his palms to his chest, tapping the rhythm from chest to thigh. "Been round the world and back again," and again he slapped out a rhythm to punctuate the spaces between words. He went through several verses, ending with, "Went to the jailhouse, fell on my knees," slap tappety-slap-tap, slap slap. "First thing I wanted was a pan of peas," slap tappety-slap-tap, slap slap. "The peas was good and the meat was fat," slap tappety-slap-tap, slap slap. "I stayed at the jailhouse just for that." And here he broke into the rhythm in earnest, hopping about in a kind of dance, crossing his arms over to beat the rhythm on his inner thighs, then both arms side to side, brushing each thigh two-handed.

The men were enthralled, along with Elizabeth, all watching, caught up in the boy's performance, laughing when he delivered a funny line, applauding when he did his hop-dance at the end.

After the big finish, Hotshot approached the counter with his hand held out, palm up. "Obliged," he said.

"What you want, boy?" Mr. Golden said.

"The folks at the train station gives me tips," Hotshot said.

Elizabeth reached for his arm. "No, Hotshot. My mama says it's not polite to ask for money."

"That's all right, little princess," Mr. Golden said, pushing a key on the swirly-patterned iron cash register, its drawer spitting open. "Here goes two cents, boy."

"Say, 'I appreciate your generosity,' Hotshot."

"I appreciate your generosity, Hotshot," Hotshot said.

The men hooted. "That is one well-brought-up nigger," Mr. Dannie said.

Elizabeth wanted to ask the men what was so funny about Hotshot having good manners, but she was anxious to show him the rest of the town. They ran back across the street to the courthouse, a brownish-red brick colossus, with two-story columns in front like giant sequoias and a silver-domed cap where the clock chimed each hour and half hour. The cavernous hallway, where two staircases curved down on either side from the courtroom above, echoed their laughter back at them as they raced to the sheriff's office at the left rear corner of the building. Elizabeth's daddy gave them sticks of candy, let them type on the Underwood typewriter awhile, then told them to run along, he had paperwork to do.

They wandered the square of the town, past Hooker's Mercantile; Mason's Drug Store, with its shiny soda fountain spigots framed by a picture window; the pool hall, where the best pimento cheese sandwiches in the county could be purchased for ten cents (only women and colored folks, who were not allowed in, had to buy theirs from two separate windows that opened onto the sidewalk); Cecil's Barber Shop, with its red and white pole undulating a constant, dizzying spin; and the South Georgia Bank building, a façade of slick black marble, shut down and silent. It was the silent bank building that had quieted the once-bustling town so that now, as Elizabeth and Hotshot roamed the sidewalks, they had the place pretty much to themselves. Most of the smaller shops and businesses had "Closed until Further Notice" signs in the windows, and the larger stores threatened, at regular intervals, to put up such signs. But Elizabeth's grandmother said things were looking up, that Roosevelt was taking care of things, no matter what anybody said about him.

"Is that 'hambone' dance hard to do?" Elizabeth asked.

"No'm," he said.

"How did you learn it?"

"My daddy taught me."

"Will you teach me?"

"Yes'm," he said. "And so on and so forth and dog-gone luck."

"I'll make up more words, okay? It'll be fun."

The courthouse clock struck four, vibrating its deep tone straight into her, as it always did. Elizabeth took Hotshot's arm. "Come on!" she yelled, heading toward the peanut-processing house, down by the railroad tracks. It had shut down for two years immediately following the Crash but had been back in limited operation, with half the original number of employees, for the past two. One of those employees was the Chinaman, and Elizabeth knew he would be walking home from work, right about now, to his whitewashed shotgun house perched by the tracks.

"What a Chinaman?" Hotshot asked.

"Well, it's a man from China," Elizabeth said. "Chen Ling is from China, but most people think his name is silly so they just call him 'the Chinaman.' I like his name, though. Chen Ling, Chen Ling, ring, sing, singsong. It sounds like an emerald green music note." She let herself hear the sound of his name, the tinkling of ice in one of her grandmother's crystal goblets, then continued, "He's really nice, and he has these treasures in his house, treasures all the way from China."

"Where China is?"

"All the way on the other side of the world," Elizabeth said. "We'll dig our way there one day. And when we get to China all the people will be walking around upside down. At least, that's what my grandmother says, but I think she's just funning with me. It just doesn't make sense when I try to picture it. "

Chen Ling was a slender man with gentle eyes drawn up at the outer corners, whose voice, in spite of its choppy, broken English, was bigger than his physical presence. "Elly-beth!" he shouted from the porch of his shotgun. "Where you been? Not visit Chen more two week."

"I had to bring Hotshot and show you to him. He's never seen a Chinaman."

Chen Ling laughed. "Chinaman like Niagara Fall number two. Tourist place, but here, South Georgia."

"Hotshot, say, 'It's a pure pleasure to meet you, sir.'"

The boy took a step back.

"Go ahead, Hotshot. It's okay. He's nice. Say, 'It's a pure pleasure to meet you, sir.'"

"It's a pure pleasure to meet you, sir."

"Pleasure all mine," Chen Ling said, holding out his hand.

"Shake his hand, Hotshot," Elizabeth instructed.

The boy stood rooted to the spot while Elizabeth elbowed him, saying, "Go on, do it."

"Hotshot. Good name. Elly-beth best name. Elly-beth bring pretty thoughts to little shack here. You like little shack, Hotshot?"

Hotshot only stared. "Law," he said. "Dog gone luck."

"Hotshot, you can't be shy around the Chinaman," Elizabeth said. "He's the nicest, most musical-named person in Sumner. Come on. Come on and show him the hambone dance you do, okay?"

Hotshot grinned, sliding into his role of performer without hesitation, as if it were a task he had been thoroughly trained to do, so that it was second nature for any shyness to disintegrate on demand. He proceeded to tap his foot—one, two, three, four. He hopped and slapped his thighs in rhythm to the verses he had performed at the Feed & Seed while Chen Ling cackled and clapped his hands in time. Then came the same big finish, after which the boy held his palm out for change.

Chen Ling reached out and shook his hand, leaving Hotshot with a puzzled look on his face.

"No, Chen Ling. He wants money," Elizabeth said. "I told him it's not nice to ask, but he says it was kind of like a job, to sing and dance at the train stations, and folks would give him nickels. Mr. Golden gave him two cents."

"Sorry. No money here, Hotshot," Chen Ling said.

"That's all right," Elizabeth said.

"Good words," the Chinaman said, "but no money. Sorry. Bill purse not fat, not thick," he said, holding his thumb and index finger barely apart to illustrate.

"And so forth," Hotshot said. "Dog-gone luck."

They went inside and looked at Chen Ling's photographs of Shanghai and city streets crowded with little two-wheeled carts hauled by men and other pictures of the beautiful dark-haired woman who was Chen Ling's mother. In one photograph she stood by an ornate gate and wore the beautiful shirt Elizabeth loved and coveted, the one Chen Ling kept in a special box. Her hair was swept up, her eyes cast down. In another picture she was standing with two other women, all of them dressed in ankle-length cheongsams, and she seemed about to laugh. Elizabeth always wondered about that verge of laughter, wondered what had just been said and whether it would be funny in English as well.

Elizabeth showed Hotshot a pair of chopsticks but could not convince him that folks really used such things to put food in their mouths. So Chen Ling demonstrated with some sweet potatoes left over in the icebox, and Hotshot was stunned with fascination. They looked at wood carvings and stone figurines of deep green: a creature like a bulldog with ferociously enlarged teeth, an ornate bowl, a round-bellied man in diapers that the Chinaman said was a warrior. One of Elizabeth's favorites was a figure carved from a kind of wood that felt light, not dense but almost hollow feeling. It was an old man leaning on a staff, looking out into the distance. He had a long mustache and a little beard, wore a round hat that was kind of pointy on top, and seemed tired but very determined, like he had a ways to go but would certainly get there. She ran her fingertips along grooves in the porous wood, stroking the craftsmanship, conjuring up the vast countryside, green and rolling, trying to see what the old man with the staff was seeing.

"That's a midget," Hotshot said, tapping at bamboo wind chimes, sending a deep clacking through the little house.

"No, it's not," said Elizabeth. "It's a traveler, like you. Like us."

"Like my daddy," Hotshot said.

"Yes. Like that," Elizabeth said, wishing she could find his daddy for him. She told Chen Ling the circumstances of Hotshot's arrival.

"Yes, yes," the Chinaman said. "Very sad. Hotshot, you come see Chen Ling whenever time, just like Elly-beth. Just like Roy Fitz."

"Where is Royce?" Elizabeth asked. She sometimes played with Royce Fitzhugh, Chen Ling's next-door neighbor, though her family could never know. Royce was older, sullen-eyed, something of a bully at school, but Elizabeth sensed he was bruised, on the inside, and went out of her way to be nice to him when their paths crossed.

Her mother threw a Gramophone record across the living room the first and only time Elizabeth mentioned Royce. The thick black disc went to jagged bits against the marble fireplace. "Why don't you play with decent children?" Miss Pearl shrieked. "Why do you have nothing to do with little girls? What is wrong with you?"

Elizabeth, struck mute at the aberrant outburst, could only watch as her father led Miss Pearl to the bedroom, saying he might have to call Dr. Walt to get her easy. "She refuses to join in," her mother continued to rant, from behind the closed bedroom door, "with decent children her age. She'd rather play with Fitzhugh trash. What is wrong with her?"

"Roy Fitz not home," Chen Ling said. "Go fish."

Elizabeth's thoughts switched gears rapidly. "Can we see the beautiful shirt?" she asked. "The one that will be mine one day?"

"Ah, yes, the beautiful shirt. Special thing Elly-Beth like." He walked over to a high shelf, took down a gold-edged, black lacquer box, and set it on the table. Then, with ceremony, he slowly opened the brass-hinged lid and brought out the beautiful shirt that had been nestled in the box, unfurling it with a flourish. It had belonged to his mother, he explained to Hotshot. She got it in Shanghai before stepping onto a big ship to seek her fortune in Los Angeles, California. It was black satiny silk, with tiny, detailed embroideries of exotic flowers—pale pink, light amber, a dusting of blue—scattered across its surface. Elizabeth brushed her fingertips across the roped buttonhole wrapped about a knob of black, then down to the floral patterns of slick thread, taking the impressions of the threads into her, trying to absorb the beauty of a thing brought halfway around the world.

"Elly-Beth like shirt. You have shirt one day. Chen write down on Will paper, 'I leave beautiful shirt Elly-Beth.'"

"I had a shirt one time," Hotshot said. He walked back over to the bamboo tubes and knocked their sound all around the room.

"But this is a forever shirt," Elizabeth said to no one, caressing the glittering jewel that was the fabric of Shanghai, far and forever away from the peanut fields of South Georgia.

When the time came to leave, Elizabeth peeked out the Chinaman's front window. Sometimes Royce's mama would be sitting on the front porch in a yellow housecoat, and Elizabeth was determined to avoid her, not so much because of what the Lacey family said—that Mona Anne Fitzhugh "did things" and was "up to no good"—but because the woman glared so, with the sun-yellow of the quilted cloth and with the tightness of her eyes. Royce's mama had eyes that pricked Elizabeth's joy, deflating it, almost threatening to expose—something, though she didn't know what. It made Elizabeth skittish and confused.

"You go now," Chen Ling said, as if he understood her hesitation. Then he smiled. "Make quick! Coast clear!"

Elizabeth giggled herself out the door, twirling down the steps, imagining herself in the beautiful shirt and a matching skirt that billowed out on musical notes of air.

Over the next few years she began to think of the embroidery of her self, of Elizabeth, how some people ran little patterns of silk threads, delicate and subtle, through her soul. Hotshot was like that. As she grew and changed, he became a wispy bit of embroidery in her life, a presence, willing to join her when she beckoned him, content to clean in and around the jailhouse, run errands for the prisoners, dig and build dirt mounds in Jubil's yard, or just sit on Jubil's porch, as though pretending he lived there. He sometimes did his hambone dance in town on Saturdays, when there were more people around, farmers mostly, who drove in from the county to spend what little money they had. They rarely had tips for him. He taught Elizabeth the rhythm, they practiced for a week, then showed Jubil, who tossed her deep laugh skyward, to the trees, where Elizabeth watched it rustle the uppermost leaves.

She was disappointed that Hotshot could not go to school with her, where she set about going through the motions of learning, hating the place immediately, even more by second grade. For a while she tried to be obedient, sit in her assigned seat in the assigned row, but it was miserable, sitting, sitting, not exploring. She read the notes her teacher sent home, full of concerned phrases: "such a sad child," "withdrawn and reluctant to engage in play with the others," and "heartbreaking lack of interest."

But she was not entertained by her classmates, never cared about socializing with them, was beyond them in intellect and imagination. They didn't speak her language, a language of possibility and changing purpose, full of images they could never see. They played the usual games in the usual ways. Elizabeth wanted to run beyond experience and feel the curve of humid air around her body as she moved, shout into the softness and hear the echo of her own thoughts. Her intentions of obedience dwindled by third grade and she began garnering reprimands—for daydreaming or for leaving her seat in the middle of a lesson to put her head out the window, just to smell the sweet olive, or for upsetting the inkwell or drawing silly pictures on the teacher's slate board or curling up in the cloakroom to take a nap. Now the notes sent home were written in a furious hand with fresh descriptors: "defiant and unruly," "fails to see the importance," and "certain she will give up on her studies."

"Elizabeth, you are going to be my undoing," her mother said in a flat voice, taking a long swallow of peach brandy, as if she, too, had surrendered some of her hopes for her only child.

"Try your best, Baby," her father said in his steady, laid-back voice. "I know how hard it is for you to be still."

"Go to your room," her grandmother said, her tone clipped, shoulders squared. "Don't come out until you can behave for your teacher."

Sometimes Elizabeth lay on her bed, frustrated, feeling like nothing more than never-good-enough, wishing she could sit still in a desk row like her classmates, promising herself to be better. But other times she simply shrugged and climbed through the open window to go play outside with Hotshot.

Her grandmother sought Jack Lacey's support, demanded that he punish his daughter for being so disrespectful as to make an escape from her room, but Elizabeth's father, when met with her dirty knees, scratched ankles, and mischievous eyes, could only shake his head and laugh.

Elizabeth's once-determined attempt at some kind of conformity unraveled in no time. She began to avoid school, playing hooky instead, coaxing Hotshot to Cane Creek, feeling free, in charge of herself, unrepentant when her grandmother tried to chastise her, smiling up at her, ultimately succeeding in stealing a smile back from the older woman. Yes, Elizabeth knew she was disappointing everyone, but she also knew how to turn the disappointment around, in an arena other than school, the arena of her own ability to delight. By fourth grade she had come to accept the fact that she would always disappoint, and teachers did no more than shake their heads in resignation. "The nut doesn't fall far from the tree," Elizabeth heard one of them whisper to another as they stood chatting on the playground one day, and, another time, "You can't breed it out of her mama's people, you know," but Elizabeth didn't care to wonder what it meant.

Meanwhile, Hotshot showed her how to do boy things, like make a fishing pole out of a sturdy branch, a length of twine, a small piece of tin, and a bent nail; and shoot craps like his daddy used to do; and construct a slow-burning campfire. She bought a pair of dice at the dime store in

Albany and they spent hours at Cane Creek, fishing to Elizabeth's own "hambone" lyrics and rolling the dice across the concrete slab beneath the bridge. He showed her how to blow on the dice for luck and call out, "Come on, lucky seven!"

She continued her own project to educate Hotshot in turn. Her grandmother called it a "valiant effort." But, even though he was willing to try to replicate the poems, Bible verses, and basic math facts Elizabeth wanted to teach him, he wasn't very good at remembering what he had been taught after only a bit of time passed. She had the most success with the hambone songs, and she thought it was because they fit the pattern embroidered into his thoughts by his daddy. And as little as that was, Hotshot did not seem to have room in his head for much more. Still, he was compliant as she put him through the paces, and he did learn some of the things she wished were taught at school, such as how to invent colors and paints by mixing up different kinds of mud, how to use that mud paint to turn an old cardboard box into a bejeweled treasure chest, or how to listen to the moon.

"Do you hear it?" she said, as they sat on the top step of Jubil's porch at early dark. "Do you hear that noise like the kitchen fan, only just barely, like it's way far away, just barely?"

"Yes'm," Hotshot said.

"Well that's how it always sounds this time of year. In the dead of winter, though, it sounds more like a sparrow chirping, but real quiet. And slow, too. A chirp every eight or nine seconds or so. Sometimes much longer, especially if there's a hard freeze. Isn't it strange and pretty?"

"Yes'm," Hotshot said.

"I love the moon." Elizabeth watched whispers of clouds wash over the glow. She rested her chin on her knees.

"I seen a full moon one time," Hotshot said.

"Sure you did. There's a full moon once a month, except when there's a blue moon," she answered.

He was quiet for a moment, then, "I seen a dead dog in the road one time."

Elizabeth put her hands over her ears. "Don't tell bad things to me."

"Azaleas are pretty," Hotshot said, offering a quick recovery.

If Hotshot was a muted thread in her tapestry, there were others making bold contrasts, digging into her spirit, contrasts such as going to school, or watching Jubil wring the neck of a chicken for her grandmother to cook for supper, or her mother's hidden self—the self she covered over with hair treatments or colognes spritzed from ornate, big-bulbed bottles on her dressing table. And then there was always Elizabeth's grandfather, aiming his pistol at his head, a mental still life in her mind. It terrified her every time he did it, but one of the worst times, when he was the most displeased with her, was when she and Hotshot accidentally hopped a freight train and ended up two hours away, in Bainbridge, Georgia.

She was a few months before turning nine the late afternoon she and Hotshot found their way into a freight car, its big metal door gaping open, the dim interior empty, sitting near the Sumner Depot. She had been questioning him that day, about his years hopping freights with his daddy, then insisted on walking over to the tracks so he could show her how they would sneak aboard the cars. The town was quiet, the day slipping toward sunset.

"We hiding in the bushes or down in the ditch when it pulling out of town," he said. "If it a big town we hide in the train yard if we can."

"What would happen when you hid in the ditch or the bushes?"

"Just come out from there and run 'longside the cars and hop on. Like this." He ran up beside the open car, grabbed onto a steel handle, and skip-hopped up with the agility of a hambone dance move, pulling with his upper body, throwing his legs up and into the car, rolling out of sight. Then he slid back to the opening and looked down at her. "Only my daddy get on first and help pull me up. Or some other riders might, too." He lay on his stomach, eye to eye with Elizabeth.

"Let me try," she said, backing up as Hotshot stood. She showed no fear, no hesitation, running up to the car, grasping at the handle, which she could not begin to reach.

He extended his arm, a reflex as she jumped, missing the handle, and helped her up the rest of the way. He had grown taller and stronger, approaching the neighborhood of eleven or twelve, and he easily lifted her into the car.

A fixture at the jailhouse and around town, Hotshot was only slightly more mature than he had been upon his arrival, given to easy upsets and disjointed thoughts. Aunt Frances said he was mentally retarded, according to her tenant, Miss Martha, who taught fifth grade, but he seemed all right to Elizabeth, seemed to enjoy playing with her, letting her teach him things, and doing the hambone dance.

He showed her how to crouch in the front corners to avoid the crewmen who sometimes checked for stowaways, sometimes putting them off the train but more often letting them be. Times were hard, after all. He showed her how to roll across the floor, not resist a fall in a train car that would be moving, and she practiced a few times, the two of them finally lying with their chins on their arms, facing out the doorway of the freight carrier.

They lay there for a while, Elizabeth getting bits of stories about Hotshot's traveling days. She thought it sounded exciting, setting out with no particular destination, just town to town, city to city, feeling a kinship with fellow travelers, helping one another get by. There would be kind folks in every town, folks like her grandmother, who never let a hobo leave her back door without something in his stomach. There would be warmth and stories to hear beside campfires along the way, long-burning campfires she would help build, and laughter riding the curls of ashes and sparks that wound their way up to the stars.

"I seen a man get his legs cut off one time," Hotshot said.

Elizabeth put her palms over her ears. "No!" she said. "I told you never tell me things like that! I can't see that in my head."

"Birds are nice," Hotshot said.

"The only bad things we can talk about are things not real. Like stories. Want me to tell you a story?"

Hotshot nodded yes, so Elizabeth told the story her aunt had told her, the story of Hamlet, the tragic hero, how he brought himself down, how he unwittingly sent his love, Ophelia, into madness.

"Why that man did that?" Hotshot asked.

"He didn't mean to."

"Why that girl got drowned?"

"She lost her mind."

"Where her mind went?"

Elizabeth knew she could not make him understand, wished she could, yet she did not fully understand herself. Why would love for a man have that kind of power over someone? Why did the power of it all go back and forth, from the man to the woman, and where was it supposed to land? The only thing that came to mind was a piece of strange music, one resonant chord that harmonized with another: "I remember." It was the chord she had struck when she spoke of President Roosevelt at the parade. It was a kind of recognition but not the kind for understanding. Not yet.

"Where that girl's mind went?" Hotshot asked again.

Elizabeth sighed, frustrated. "It doesn't matter. Don't think about it."

There was a taste of autumn on the breeze that wandered through the open door, and Elizabeth thought of a cardinal floating on that breeze, dipping and rising as if gliding over invisible hills in the air, a brilliant red ambassador from the earth to the sky. She was imagining white clouds blushing pink from the brush of the cardinal's wings when she heard a faraway clank of metal hitting metal.

"What was that?" Elizabeth asked, just as the boxcar lurched backward, pushing the two of them forward, Hotshot rolling into Elizabeth.

"Feel like a engine hitching up," Hotshot said.

"We should get off," she said, rolling slightly backward, into him, with the recoil of the last car.

"Yes'm."

"Or maybe we could jump off," she said, "when it's going real slow out of town."

"Yes'm. Dog-gone luck."

"Is it easy?"

"Easier'n getting on."

The car jolted again, backward, the two of them rolling with the force of it, both giggling now. Then came another jolt forward, and barely back again, as if it were a giant, sectioned snake undertaking a slow, mechanical slither, muscled body pulling this way, then that. A whistle sounded and the snake's undulation picked up by degrees. They watched the depot pass by, then the stores on the blocks facing the tracks. She looked up one alley and spied her own house in the length of a glance, its white wood and high-pitched green roof fronted by the large, open porch her grandmother wanted to enclose one day, when it wouldn't be show-offy. They passed a row of shotgun houses on the white side of the tracks, the Chinaman's among them, decked out in flower boxes and wind chimes and a straw-bottomed rocking chair. "Hello, Chen Ling," she whispered, "and farewell."

She watched the steeples of the Methodist and Baptist churches float past, in the background, let the push of wind cool her, let herself imagine she was on her way to Columbus or even Atlanta, where Aunt Frances and Miss Martha were going over Christmas holidays. Autumn smoke from trash barrels and limb fires whipped in through the door, but briefly, the train rushing past them in a gathering of rhythm and speed, a clack-clack-clack of wheel against rail that snatched her out of her fascination with passing scenery and into the moment.

"We're going too fast to jump now, huh?" she said.

"I done it before this fast. Hurt my leg and got skin't right smart, and so on and so forth and dog-gone luck."

Elizabeth laughed, not caring that they were riding fast away from Sumner. It would be easy enough to get off at the next stop and have somebody call her daddy. She laughed even louder, stood on uncertain legs, and ran staggering to the back of the car, squealing, "We're travelers! We're vagabonds!" until the shifting rhythm of motion sent her to the floor, and she remembered to roll, still feeling an exhilarating rush of liberation. She wanted it to last, wished they were heading out for the far coast of America.

She dropped to a sitting position and shrilled, "I am the edge of a star! I am on a journey to where the light skips across emerald green music notes!" She threw her head back and yelled louder, "Into the distance!" Then she collapsed onto her back, laughing uncontrollably.

Hotshot still sat near the open door, oblivious, staring out at fields just harvested, stripped of crops and waiting to be plowed anew. Elizabeth crawled to him on her hands and knees, a steadier way to move in the side-jerking boxcar. "Let's pretend we are going to the Pacific Ocean, okay?"

"Yes'm."

"We're going there as gleams from a star's light, to glitter the Pacific Ocean, okay?"

"Yes'm."

"I mean, I know we have to get off at the next town and call Daddy to come and get us, but for now we're going to the Pacific Ocean where the sand on the beach is brown and not white like down at Apalachicola, and it's—oh! Look at that!"

The opening to the car framed a sunset smeared behind sparse scatterings of longleaf pines, and the lingering light had just dimmed to that one perfect movement in a sunset Elizabeth had discovered when she was not yet five. There was a moment, an instant, just after day and just before night, when the rich tones of the sky deepened into a dense orange, burgundy red, and purple-black edged in gold, just before they would melt into one another, at once swallowed into the horizon. It was a moment she recognized as perfection, no sense of time, as if everything that ever was or would be was held in that beautiful, dissolving band across the far curve of the world. It was a moment she did not see very often, caught up as she was in whatever it was that held her attention elsewhere, and it was the only thing she had ever recognized as something like what God must be.

She glanced at Hotshot, who was engrossed in scraping the floor with a bent penny he had picked up on the street earlier in the day. She wanted to tell him, explain what she saw so that he would understand, but the sky had her now, had her transfixed. She slid down to lie on the floor of the emptied freight car, watching as strands of clouds were folded into the night, like her grandmother's whipped egg whites into chocolate.

*

"What did you do to her?"

"Sir?"

"Tell me what the goddamn hell you did to her!" Her grandfather's face was red, eyes narrowed.

"Granddaddy, we were on the car, and it started to move too fast. He didn't do anything." Elizabeth had seen her grandfather angry lots of times, but never anything like he looked now. He paced, spat at the dirt, ran his fingers over the brown leather holster.

The train had not stopped in the next town, or the next; did not stop, in fact, until the sky was well past nightfall and the two of them had been two hours asleep on the floor of the boxcar, the cessation of motion jarring them awake. The ticketmaster at the train station in Bainbridge had seemed nervous when he heard Elizabeth's tale, and in an instant he had a Decatur County sheriff's deputy at the station. The deputy talked on the wall phone at the depot, presumably to Elizabeth's daddy or grandfather, looking somber, though she couldn't understand why. Finally he loaded Hotshot in the backseat of his patrol car, Elizabeth in the front, and they were bound for Sumner.

"What did you do to her?" her grandfather demanded again.

"Daddy, I don't think there's anything to—" Jack said, as Hotshot began to whimper.

"The goddamn nigger took off with your little girl and I want to know what he did to her!" Camp yelled, then turned back to Hotshot, grabbing him by the arms, shaking him.

"Stop!" Elizabeth called out.

"Hush up, Elizabeth!" Camp snapped at her before shaking Hotshot even harder, then pushing him so that he stumbled backward before catching his balance. "What did you do? You answer me that, boy. What did you do to her?"

"I didn't, I didn't, I didn't," Hotshot moaned, dropping to a squatting position, then sitting, rocking back and forth. "I didn't, I didn't."

"Hotshot didn't do anything," Elizabeth protested.

"I knew this one was trouble back years ago," Camp said, pulling his revolver from its holster.

"Did he lay a hand on you, Baby?" Jack Lacey asked his daughter.

"No! He's never even pinched me. Why do you think he would hurt me?"

Jack ran his hand through his hair. "There are things you don't understand, Elizabeth, that's all. Now if you say he didn't touch you, then I
believe you." He turned to Camp. "I think we can just—"

"No, goddamn it, I want a straight answer from this lying nigger,"
Camp said, raising the pistol, resting the barrel against the side of Hotshot's head.

Elizabeth was confused by the whole progression of events: the
Decatur County deputy's refusal to talk to her on the ride back to Sumner;
her grandfather's ranting there in the backyard, banishing her mother and
grandmother to the inner regions of the big white house; her father's discomfort with the "things" she didn't understand; and now, her grandfather's gun against Hotshot's head.

The boy flinched and whimpered and sobbed. Elizabeth thought to
run and fetch Jubil, could see Jubil's eyes peering out at them from behind
the curtains of her shotgun house in the back yard. Elizabeth wanted to
run to her porch, tell her to come out and help Hotshot, make them all
understand. Camp pulled the trigger and Hotshot covered his ears with his
palms, repeating, "Didn't, didn't, didn't."

"You tell me right now what happened, or I'll blast your skull all the
way back to the railroad tracks, you hear? Now!"

"Take it easy, Daddy," Jack said in his ever-calm tone.

"'Take it easy' to hell," Camp said, mashing Hotshot's coarse black hair
against his skull with the mouth of the gun.

Hotshot could only exhale little moans.

Elizabeth wanted to tell Hotshot not to worry, that her granddaddy
was joking him, but something kept her seized up with fear, too. This felt
very different from all the other times. She did not understand the fuss
everybody was making, and at that moment she realized she was crying,
sobbing even, in soft little hiccups. She wanted her grandfather to stop
holding his pistol to Hotshot's head, laugh about how silly they were to
think they could jump off a fast-moving train without breaking their
necks. She wanted her daddy to say what a funny story it would be to tell
in a month or two. She wanted Jubil. And then Jubil *was* there beside her,

an arm around her shoulder, saying, "That boy ain't done nothing. It ain't in him."

"What the hell do you think you're doing, woman? You ain't got a bit of business out here." Camp pushed the barrel harder against Hotshot's head, while the boy whimpered like Mr. Golden's prize bird dog did when he got run over by a chicken truck that time.

"You go on back to the house now, Jubil," Jack said. "I believe you're right about the boy, so go on back in."

"Naw, Mr. Jack. I got to see to the boy."

"Goddammit to goddamn hell!" Camp thundered. "Every nigger on the place has gone crazy! I'll show you how I'm going to see to the boy. I'm going to put a goddamn bullet in his nappy head."

"No!" Elizabeth screamed, jerking forward, toward Hotshot, but her father caught her by the arm.

"It's all right, Baby Girl."

But Elizabeth was inconsolable, screaming "No!" over and over again.

Camp squeezed the trigger. Click. The hammer knocked out its familiar sound, no explosion, no blood, but Hotshot let out a wail like she had never heard, and the kitchen window rattled behind her. She turned to see her grandmother pounding with her knuckles against the glass as if to say, *Enough.*

"There's nothing to this, Daddy," Jack said. "I think we can be satisfied that Elizabeth is telling the truth and Hotshot would have told it too, after all this."

Campbell turned to face them, stared cold and long at Jubil then looked at Elizabeth and grinned. "Disappointed in you, little girl," he said, almost lightheartedly. "Reckon I'll say goodbye now." He aimed the gun at his own head, pulling the trigger, producing the small sound that always came out like an explosion, because that was what Elizabeth had always been afraid to hear. It was the sound that always sent her screaming to her daddy's lap, but this time, for the first time, ever, she did not scream. She even found herself wishing it would happen, that the gun would go off, and she would not even hide her face against Jack Lacey's thighs like the little girl she used to be.

But then the gun did go off, in a deafening burst of reports. Her granddaddy pointed it skyward and fired—one, two, three times. Elizabeth flinched with each explosion, felt her daddy pulling her next to his chest. Then Campbell Lacey looked down at Hotshot and said, "I don't fool around when it comes to mine. You best remember that." Then he turned and strode to the back door, slamming the screen, his boots pounding their way across the wood floor of the back hallway.

The next day Jubil was gone, "For good," Miss Pearl said. Elizabeth and Hotshot grieved—the boy for weeks that would turn into months and even years, in strange contrast to his lack of grief over his lost daddy.

"Why?" Elizabeth asked her mother.

"She never did know her place."

"She's always been here, though," Elizabeth said. "This *is* her place."

Her mother sighed one of her exasperated little gusts. "She never was truly loyal to this family. I could see it in her eyes."

"Did she at least go to Texas?"

"How would I know that?"

"I hope so," Elizabeth said, voice breaking, running for her room, for a feather pillow to cry into, hearing the murmured thud of *Now look what you've done, Elizabeth* pulsing through her ears. "I hope she at least went to Texas," she called back over her shoulder, catching her mother's baffled, head-shaking expression.

And in her mind, with the snap of a shutter, Elizabeth situated Jubil in a house in Texas with Jubil's long-missed mother and sister, a nice little white house with yellow trim and yellow window boxes that held blooms of every color imaginable. But Elizabeth felt more detached from her own family than ever before, filled with a deep sense of lurking betrayal and a kind of powerlessness. Up until now her force of will had been a thing she took for granted, skipping and running through life, believing she could eventually have things the way she wanted, turn any no into a yes. It might take years, but she had always felt she could turn anyone around—anyone she cared to spin. Yet, directly because of Elizabeth, Jubil had been sent away, and Hotshot had been accused of doing something that all of Elizabeth's wishing could not get anyone to name. She spent hour upon hour puzzling over it, wanting to figure it out. But then, that same autumn, her attention shifted and her focus crystallized when a very important man, Eugene Talmadge, came to town.

Elizabeth sat on the front porch and watched all morning as the crowd in town grew and grew, waiting to wave at Gene, to get a look at the man dubbed by the press as "the wild man from Sugar Hill." He was running for U.S. senator, but one would think it was more like president, judging by the scores of folks who migrated to Sumner that day from little farms and a scattering of communities across the region. They rolled into town all day: work-dented pickup trucks carrying extended families in the truck beds, a couple of flatbeds carrying entire church congregations, a steady stream of automobiles, including old Ford T models and a Pullman or two, and more than a few mule-drawn wagons. Most of the sun-weathered faces belonged to white farmers who cropped on someone else's land, paying rent with a chunk of the harvest. Others were merchant class from stores set at crossroads out in the county. Then there were the town folk, residents of Sumner, who wore nicer clothes and citified attitudes in the presence of the denizens of rural Blackshear County.

When the day grew hot, Elizabeth went inside to cool off beside the heavy black oscillating fan in the living room. Her grandmother was in the kitchen frying up a mess of chicken she would carry to the courthouse on a platter for Mr. Talmadge. Elizabeth, antsy with anticipation, decided to pass the time reading. She plopped onto the floor next to a long roll of a cushion that served as a foot prop near the divan and opened her book of Shakespeare.

Her mother went directly to the liquor cabinet and poured a glass of brandy. Next she went into her bedroom, coming out with the little leather case that held some of her beauty supplies. "If I don't lotion my hands and do my nails, people will think I've hired out as a washerwoman." On the end table beside her, she lined up her manicure tools with the care of a surgeon. Then she set out bottles containing several different colors of nail polish, a sure signal that she did not want to talk.

Elizabeth rolled onto her stomach, onto the pillow, letting it cushion her body, and turned to where she had left Romeo and Juliet, envious, caught up in Verona, wishing for the kind of intense passion they had. "Juliet is the sun," Romeo said, and he called her "bright angel," and Elizabeth longed for someone to say something as musical and romantic to her someday. She fell into the reading of Act II while her mother fiddled with her nails in Elizabeth's peripheral vision.

Elizabeth shifted, sliding her book to the floor near chin level, and wrapped her legs around the cushion, the place between her legs feeling the rough scratch of the upholstery, catching into a strange, pleasant feeling, one she had discovered before when she bathed. She had never pursued it, though, intimidated by the foreign feeling, not sure where it would lead her. But now she shifted again, deliberately, moved her pubic bone against the material. It felt nice. She moved again, thrusting her hips into it, and the feeling spilled outward, into a deeper sense of something too enjoyable to stop. She moved with a rhythm, a steady push against the grain of the big cushion between her legs. She could hear her mother opening the polish remover, fumbling around for tissue. But the sounds faded to background noise while her ear, the one resting on the pillow, could hear the regular, rhythmic rubs of her own body against the stuffed material. It was dreamlike and floaty, and she bore down a little more, pressing with the place where her thighs joined, aware of a growing kind of warmth, a promise implied. She moved faster. In a while, a sizzle of scents wafted up from the kitchen, and she could hear the scrape of her mother's nail file, still a faraway sound. Now she could feel the swirled patterns in the heavy cloth as she moved, an added texture, stirring into her, the promise building—to what, she had no idea, did not care. She heard the scrape of her mother's nail file, and she moved even faster against the cushion. At that moment, her mother cried out. The filing stopped, the metal clattering to the table top.

"My God, no! Elizabeth! Get up from there!"

Elizabeth rolled over, not wanting to release the pillow from between her knees. "Why?"

"Just get up from there! This minute!" her mother's eyes were full of panic, her tone urgent, as if Elizabeth was in danger.

"But why?"

"Get up from there now!" The command was more intense, severe, and strange than any her mother had ever issued.

Elizabeth stood. "What's the matter?"

At that moment her mother's face flushed pink and further, into a blaze of crimson.

"What is it?" Elizabeth asked again.

Her mother fumbled for words, then blurted, "It's just that you are so twisty and wiggly. You've got me all on edge. Now take your book out on the porch and read there. Or just watch the people again. Or go outside and play, for goodness sakes."

Elizabeth had always been twisty and wiggly, and her mother never reacted so violently to it. Why was she so upset now? Did it have something to do with that warm feeling Elizabeth was finding at the place between her legs? Why did that place make her mother, she wondered with a Shakespearean flourish, blush so bold?

She stepped back out onto the porch with her book, but felt distracted by the feeling her mother had interrupted, could not concentrate on *Romeo and Juliet* now, wished the day would rush on to the appointed time she was to go to the courthouse. In a while her grandmother brought tomato sandwiches out to her, and Elizabeth's mother joined them, still seeming uncomfortable, unable to look Elizabeth in the eye.

By now there were even more men with their womenfolk milling on the streets, men in overalls, farmers who often combined monthly visits to the Feed & Seed with a few steps across the street to her grandfather's front porch to talk crops, politics, fishing, or personal troubles with the law. It was plain, Elizabeth could tell, they thought a lot of Gene Talmadge. Some of them had come very far, burning gasoline they could hardly afford, just to see him.

"I do think he is a magnetic individual," Miss Lucille said. "I simply do not go along with the way he attacks Roosevelt."

"Goodness," Miss Pearl said, absently, flipping through a *Life* magazine, nibbling at her sandwich.

"Attacks him how?" Elizabeth asked.

Her grandmother took a long swallow of the iced tea she held. "Oh, it's over your head, Sweetness. Just a lot of demagoguery." She turned her drink up again. A thin sediment of sugar snowflaked the bottom of the glass and Elizabeth watched it slide into a thickness as syrupy-slow as the courthouse clock.

"What's demagoguery?" Elizabeth asked.

"Goodness," her mother said. "The questions you ask!"

"But what is it?" she insisted.

"Just think of it as the rantings of a demigod," her grandmother said.

"That's quite funny," her mother said, still flipping through the magazine, but Elizabeth did not get the humor.

The crowd was swelling even more, children running, barefoot and squealing, in and out of the groups of men and women. Finally Elizabeth was unable to bear the excitement leaking from the crowd and into her pores and had to be where the important men were. She bounded down the six cement steps, cut around to the side alley, across a narrow lot dense with shrubbery, and past the fish pool, where fat orange goldfish undulated their sheer, billowing tails at her. At the rear of the courthouse, her father was lining up the cars for the Talmadge motorcade. It was to meander through town, around the block of stores, the next block of churches, the funeral home, and across the highway to a stretch of Victorian homes where rye grass feathered its silk along glittering sidewalks. Then it was to roll on to Moultrie, where he was to deliver a speech at the baseball park. Elizabeth was to ride along with her daddy in the lead patrol escort.

"You're just in time, Baby Girl."

"Where is he?"

"In yonder." Jack nodded at the window of the sheriff's office. Inside, Elizabeth could see through open blinds, were some men. Beyond that, through the open door of the bathroom, she could see her grandfather, his foot propped up on the commode, talking to a big man with a white linen suit coat slung over his shoulder. Her granddaddy was smoking, and they were both talking very intently, hands moving, punctuating whatever important things they were saying.

Her grandfather waved another man over and took a bottle of amber liquid from him, offering it to the big man, who took a swallow. Then her grandfather took a swallow and said something, and all three men threw back their heads and laughed. Elizabeth wished she could be inside, be in on the joke, be a part of something different.

When folks were situated and the motorcade finally began its trek through town, Elizabeth saw even further into the power this man, this Eugene Talmadge, had. People waved and shouted, "We love you, Gene!" "Give 'em hell, Gene!" "Tear 'em up, Gene!" She could look out the rear window of her daddy's patrol car and see the man standing in the back of a pickup truck with raised, wood-slatted sides behind them, waving to the spectators, moving about once in a while to shout something, maybe a hello or a specific message, at an individual in the crowd, which would cause a burst of cheers and shouts to ripple outward from that individual's spot.

Talmadge's motorcade began with eleven cars: four Moultrie police cars brought up the rear, the two Sumner County sheriff's cars led and followed the pickup, then came several cars carrying mayors and county commissioners, local and regional politicians getting in on the action. But as the line of vehicles traveled, it grew; regular citizens joined in. As they rolled through the country outside Sumner, short lines of cars were parked along the roadside, and some of them hooked on to the end of the caravan. Folks at farmhouses waved, and men would scramble into more cars and pickups to follow the caravan on into Moultrie, some forty miles from Sumner. Elizabeth could look back at the little rises of hills behind them and see miles of cars strung out and out and out, like a banded coral snake, creeping along the two-lane highway, and the image coiled into a mental imprint.

The bleachers were overflowing at the high school baseball diamond in Moultrie, and folks steadily streamed in from the three-mile-long caravan. A large flatbed truck, festooned with red, white, and blue bunting and signs commanding, "Send Talmadge to Washington," and declaring,

"Talmadge for U.S. Senator," was parked on the ball field, directly in front of a crowd that broke into loud cheers as Gene Talmadge hopped, gracefully, like Hotshot hopping a freight car, from the pickup bed up onto the platform of the larger truck. Elizabeth wandered through the crowd, watching the eager faces, tasting the anticipation.

There were whistles and cheers and applause for the man in the linen trousers, a once crisp white cotton shirt now ringed beneath the arms with perspiration, and red suspenders. Elizabeth, leaning against the side of the bleachers, only then noticed that he was even bigger than he had at first appeared—tall, a commanding presence, just like her daddy, a graceful, easy presence.

"Friends, good afternoon," Talmadge began.

"Afternoon, Gene," someone shouted.

"Hidy, Gene," came from another.

"Mighty hot for the fall, ain't it?" Talmadge said to twitters of laughter. Elizabeth watched the faces of the people, all expectant, hanging on to the tall man's movements and words as he continued, "But I'm mighty hot myself, even without the weather."

"Tell it, Gene," a man said.

"Say it," another echoed.

"I'm hot around the collar. I'm downright disgusted. I'm sick and tired, friends. Are you?"

Applause and murmurs of "yes" and "uh-huh" rippled across the gathering.

The man on the flatbed paced a little one way, a little the other, then stopped, holding the audience suspended in silence for a few beats. "Friends, are you tired of New Dealers meddling with the honorable principles of the Democratic Party?"

Folks applauded.

"You bet we are, Gene!"

"Are you sick and tired of turning your money over to the government so the government can turn around and give it away?"

"Damn right!" came the responses filtering through the applause.

Elizabeth was enthralled by the crowd's reaction. It put her in mind of the times her family would be gone and Jubil would carry her to the colored church by Cane Creek, where the staid, scripted, responsive readings of the white Methodists were replaced by shouts of "Yes, Lord!" and "Hallelujah!" and "Amen!" She didn't understand exactly what Gene Talmadge was talking about, but she did recognize that he held the crowd just like Reverend Willis, the colored preacher, did.

Talmadge picked up the cadence of his words. "Should we hold on to our sacred form of government or abolish it? Should we continue to borrow and spend or settle down and settle up?" His voice rose with each question, as did the level of applause and cheers from the crowd. "Do we want to share the wealth through charity, by giving it to our Christian churches, or lose it through taxation? To be doled out by communists?"

"Share it!" someone called out.

Staying with the rhythm and increasing volume, Talmadge threw his arms out to his sides, palms up, and bellowed, "Shall we substitute sheer lunacy for the sanity of George Washington?"

"No!"

"Tell it to us, Gene,"

He lowered his voice a bit. "Friends, listen here." He paused, then, "Are we going to convert Democrats to ...*burro*-crats?"

There were hoots of laughter and more shouts. Elizabeth did not get the joke, but she was enthralled with the man's power to steer the crowd one way, then another, from serious to angry to funny and back again. She envied him, wanted that sort of power, a power that pulled every current in the crowd into whatever bends and eddies he selected. She was wanting that invulnerability and force of control when someone nudged her in the ribs.

"Hey."

She turned to look up at Royce Fitzhugh. "What are you doing here?"

"I can come here like anyone else," he said. She had not talked with him in a while, and they had long passed the "play" stage. Royce had grown taller, pimply cheeked, but his eyes were as sullen as ever.

"Didn't say you couldn't," she said. "Said why." She could tell he had a chaw in his mouth, knew he liked to do spit tricks to show off. She knew his reputation for fighting and bragging, how that reputation had grown with him, into his teens.

"I seen you riding in the parade," he said, "waving and showing out like some kind of a queen."

"Shut up, Royce," she said, slapping his arm.

"You think you're going to be a queen, don't you?"

Something in his voice, an implication, made her suspicious of his interior bruises, but she couldn't name it, so she only said, "I don't care to be a queen."

"Sure."

"Shh! I want to hear."

Talmadge had let the laughter die down. "You all know what I like to say."

"Tell us, Gene!"

"I like to say this: You got three friends in this life," Talmadge grinned.

The crowd broke into applause and cheers, the kind that gave Elizabeth the sense that they knew what was coming, embraced what was coming.

"This is the best part," Royce said.

"Shh!"

"Queenie," Royce whispered.

Elizabeth slapped his arm again.

"First, you got the Lord Almighty," the politician said, holding up one finger.

"Amen!"

Talmadge grinned wider and held up a second finger. "Then you got Sears and Roebuck," he said, rocking back on his heels as the crowd guffawed and cheered at that one, then he hooked his thumbs in the red suspenders. "And finally, friends, and this is important…"

"Say it, Gene!"

"You got Eugene Herman Talmadge!" The crowd again broke into wild applause and yells of affirmation. Royce guffawed. Talmadge pulled the suspenders out with his thumbs, then slid his thumbs free, letting the suspenders pop back to his chest, to more swelling applause and laughter. He began to pace again, slowly, and Elizabeth knew by now this was a signal that he was about to lead up to something significant. She was recognizing the rhythm of his dance with the crowd. He played them like a fisherman would play a largemouth bass, like she had seen her daddy do when she was four and he took her to Brewer's Pond. But more than that, this Gene Talmadge turned the fishing lines into the fine strings of a marionette. He pulled the strings, letting them criss and cross, and the masses bowed, lifted their arms in gestures of welcome, bent their hinged knees to do a little step with him, for him. They held on to and loved every word he gave them. They loved him, loved *him*, and that was exactly what Elizabeth wanted. Maybe Royce was right. Maybe she did want to be some kind of a queen.

"Yeah, you're a queen, all right," Royce said, as though reading her thoughts. Then he whispered, "Queen of the kiddies. But you got potential." He cut his eyes at her and leered.

Something in his expression snatched her attention from the speech making. He looked as if he had a secret about her, knew something beyond significant. "What are you talking about?"

"Some girls grow up faster than others. That's all." He glanced around at some of the adults nearby, who were absorbed by the oration, oblivious to the two of them.

"Grow up faster how?"

Royce leered again. "You'll see."

"You don't know everything. And you don't know anything about me." But her words were not ringing true to her. Maybe he really did know something. He was older, after all. And as little time as she had spent with him, ever, it was more than she socialized with anyone else, except her own family and Hotshot.

Talmadge stopped pacing, suddenly, creating an even thicker silence. He stood with his body a few degrees sideward, his left shoulder out, and turned his face to the carpet of people suspended by his gaze. A shock of dark hair hung down across his forehead and he ran his fingers through it, pushing it back, but it fell loose again as he spoke. "Friends, let me tell you what I want to do," he said, reaching down, slow, deliberate, turning up the end of his left sleeve with his right hand, folding the sleeve over, then over again while the crowd cheered with fresh fervor. It was something else they expected and loved, Elizabeth thought.

"Roll 'em up, Gene!"

"Show 'em, Gene!"

"Roll 'em on up!" Royce yelled.

"I'm just going to tell you what I want to do," Talmadge said, having turned to face them full-on, having rolled up both sleeves to just below the elbow. The wet spots curving from beneath his arms had gotten larger, and his starched white shirt was long wilted, his sleeveless undershirt showing through. "Friends," he said, intense and strong, "I want to go to Washington."

A huge, collective cheer gathered like the swelling of a Gulf wave down at Apalachicola, and Elizabeth let it lift her on the buoyant roll of words from his tongue.

Talmadge raised his voice, strong and loud. "I want to go to Washington and help our great state fight the communistic policies of the present administration."

Wild cheers washed over the ballpark. Women jumped up and down, men held up fists, and Gene Talmadge began to pace again, gathering a fresh wave of silence for what would certainly be another crescendo. He ran his fingers through his hair again, then turned to face the faces that adored him. Elizabeth could already feel currents, the gathering push of the ocean, felt herself treading water, making ready.

Royce leaned down, put his mouth to her ear. "You look way older than you are. Folks always said you acted too old for your age."

"So what?"

"So what is I know what you're up to."

"What's that?"

"I know your mama can't hardly make you go to school, that you do pretty much what you want to." He grinned. "And you not long shy of growing up."

"You don't make sense," she said, but something about his tone was intriguing.

He spat a stream of tobacco juice to the ground. "Yeah, I do. I do make sense, 'cause I know what it means when your mama can't make you do nothing."

"What does it mean?"

"Means you're off to the races. You're a automobile and your mama's a buggy."

Elizabeth was mystified, so she shushed him again.

"Shiny and fast," Royce said.

"Shh!"

"We've had hard times, friends," Talmadge was saying, now somber, reverent. "You all know it. We've had hard times since way back in '32 when the present administration went in. They wrote a platform. They promised certain things that they would do, then they violated those principles!"

"That's right!"

"Tell us!"

Elizabeth turned back to Royce, unable to contain herself. "What do you care what I do?" she asked, torn between the speech and the taunt.

Royce smiled, slow and knowing. "Like I said, I see the potential. I'm surprised you ain't seen it by now."

"Maybe I have," she said, stubborn, determined not to let him get whatever upper hand he was going for.

Royce spat again. "I bet you have. Can't nobody make you toe the line, can they?"

"I tried," she offered.

"Tried, hell. You too hell-bent to try."

She was going to argue, but was stopped by a shrill voice calling, "Royce!"

"Goddammit," he mumbled, turning to face the woman Elizabeth knew to be his mother. "What do you want?" he demanded.

"Don't you talk to me thataway, boy," the woman, Mona Anne, said.

People standing nearby were cutting their eyes at her, whispering to one another. She stood out for different, loud-voiced and mismatched, wearing bold pink lip color and a loose-necked, hip-clinging blue dress with red, open-toed heels. Her left hand clutched a cheap, beige-beaded handbag. Her dark hair was mussed and she ran her fingers through it. "We got to go, boy."

Royce sneered. "Speech ain't over."

"Don't matter," Mona Anne said. "I got a date." There were a few snickers that quickly died down as she glared at her audience, letting her mean-edged stare rest on Elizabeth. "*She* sure as hell ain't old enough for a date."

"Won't be long, though," Royce said, grinning at Elizabeth.

"You leave that little play-pretty alone and come on, boy." She turned on her heel, flared skirt flipping, and walked with haughty determination through the parting crowd.

Royce shrugged, then leaned down to Elizabeth's ear one more time and whispered, "I'll have something for you in a couple or three years, Little Girl." Then he, too, turned and zigzagged his way through the crowd, away from her.

Elizabeth squinted after him. What did that mean, "hell-bent"? Bent by hell? She felt unsettled by Mona Anne Fitzhugh's brief appearance, the vicious-feeling eyes that had rested on her, so she shifted her full attention to the man on the flatbed, reaching to settle back into the crowd's emotion.

Talmadge was going full bore by now, easily pulling her in again, his right arm punctuating the cadence of his words, blending into a build of passionate anger. "When our principles are violated, the party that's in are not Democrats. They are stealing a name," he said, lifting his right arm to the sky, "to defile it!"

More cheers filled Elizabeth's head in one big noise, as Talmadge began to shout. "So I want to go to Washington and take back the name they stole: Democrat!"

The noise grew larger.

"I want to go to Washington and take your money out of the collective fist of the New Dealers that stole it from you!"

A roar of a conch shell against Elizabeth's ears, one on either side.

"I want to go to Washington and tell the usurpers we've got good, decent Christian folks down here in the great state of Georgia."

"Damn right!" men yelled.

"Christian folks who know what it is to offer charity to their neighbors," he continued.

"Amen!"

"That's right!"

"We don't need the government picking our charities for us, do we?" he challenged.

"No!"

"Hell, no, Gene!"

Talmadge held out his arms, palms up. "Will you send me there, friends?"

"Yes!"

"If you don't, they'll take it as your endorsement of every one of their communistic schemes and make usurpers of us all!"

"We ain't fools, Gene!"

"That's right, friend," Talmadge said. "We ain't fools. Are we?"

"No!"

"Hell no!"

"We have a duty," he said, large and strong and unfinished, throwing out a last bit of bait for the big catch.

"Tell us, Gene!"

"Say it to us!"

"Yes!"

And now he used both arms to punctuate the rhythm of his words. "It is a duty of the men that love and respect the memory of Jefferson, Jackson, and that stalwart soldier George Washington, who gave us a grim warning when our country was just a baby, when democracy was just an infant."

"What was it, Gene?" an old man in overalls called out.

"George Washington, that stalwart soldier, stated that in times of emergency in this country, the usurpers will try to change our form of government."

"We ain't gonna let 'em!" the old man yelled.

"That's right, friend, we ain't gonna let 'em. Because George Washington, the father of our country, gave us this admonition: Whenever this is done,"—and here Talmadge lifted both arms, just like Reverend Willis, lifting his voice, too—"whenever this is done, rise up and smite them!"

Another surging, deafening roar took the crowd, took Elizabeth to the highest crest of the swell.

"It is a duty!" Talmadge shouted.

And the highest crest of the swell went higher.

"Yes!"

"It is a duty!"

And in her stomach, Elizabeth could feel the highest crest that had gone higher, felt it go still higher.

Talmadge, his arms flailing at the heavens, let loose one final roar. "It is a duty of the men that love and respect the memory of Jefferson, Jackson, and Washington to rise up and smite the usurpers down!"

The ensuing frenzy took Elizabeth into the bursting point, the break in the swell, senses humming with the energy of random experiences blended—the brush of her skirts at her knees as she undressed, the lay of the claw-foot iron bathtub against her back, the thick scent of dusting powder in her steam-dampened bathroom, the rough-swirled texture of the long foot-pillow in the living room—incidental tactile moments she crawled inside, felt from the inside out, within that instant. The sounds of the crowd were at once pin-prick sharp and fuzzy-bold; then muffled, as if her head were beneath a feather pillow; finally sparse and hollow and echoed, like a jewelry box waltz played through a drain pipe. That was when the explosion of foam and salt water pounded her, roiling deep layers of sand, snatching bits of shell up from the bottom, swirling them in millions of tiny maelstroms, until the wet lip of sand at the water's edge gave it back to the sea.

Elizabeth was so caught up in that moment, electric—a photographic moment of Talmadge calling out to God, it seemed—she did not realize he had gotten down from the flatbed, could not see him shaking hands, working the crowd, could only feel her daddy's hand on her arm, hear him say they had to go because the Moultrie police were to hand the politician off to another batch of lawmen out of Macon, and wouldn't *that* be some kind of a rally? Elizabeth could not imagine another, bigger speech to another, bigger crowd. She only knew that something in her felt changed, a shift in her advantage, with Royce, like some rank part of her conscience, reiterating it in her ear.

As she and her daddy drove back to Sumner, down a dusky highway where the thin traffic grew more sparse with every mile, Elizabeth thought of the man in the linen suit with the red suspenders, how he dipped and twirled and dangled his words until he manipulated out of his supporters the precise response he wanted, and she appreciated all over again the power of his words, whatever they meant. She watched the night reach up and pull the sunset away in scented colors, tasting the trickle of the moon's juices the way she did sometimes when it shone across her canopy bed at midnight. She was determined, finally, to find a kind of power someday. While it was true that no one seemed to know what to make of her, that she might indeed be bent by hell, she would turn it in another direction. Royce Fitzhugh didn't know for certain. He only gave hints, but he did say she had potential, just as Jubil had said long ago, that she would make things happen. And at that moment she knew she would be formidable, would hold tight to that one certainty, hell-bent as it might be, until it became the boldest pattern in the embroidery of herself.

I: ii

R oyce Fitzhugh was feeling pretty good for a change, knowing there
would be a way out soon, away from Sumner, Georgia, away from
his slut of a mother, and out into the world, a world that was lining
up for war, he hoped. The only sad thing about leaving was that he
wouldn't see Elizabeth Lacey, who was finally, at twelve, coming into her
own, in exactly the way he predicted to her at a political rally, a little over
two years earlier.

Royce had always been curious about Elizabeth, ever since the days
when she visited Chen Ling and the three of them would toss horseshoes
in the Chinaman's backyard or play dominoes on the porch. But now
Royce was seventeen years old, a frustrated pursuer of girls, still watching
Elizabeth, ever and always miles ahead of the other girls her own age, but
never more than now. What he saw in Elizabeth these days promised to
overtake even the girls *his* age, girls already three, four, five years older than
she, girls who criticized her while they vied for her attention, hoping some
of the mystique might rub off on them. These days, when Elizabeth visited
the Chinaman, Chen Ling blushed and looked down with increasing fre-
quency. These days, Royce felt a shift in the repartee—both spoken and
unspoken—between himself and Elizabeth. These days, boys in the upper
grades were mentioning her name, looking at Royce with a new respect,
keenly aware of his access to her. Royce knew what she promised to repre-
sent for the boys in town: the magnetic force in their tiny universe, the sun
at the center of their solar system, already exemplified by their willingness
to take up one, just one, of Lizzie's dares, win her delight when, the task

complete, she charged over to offer a hug, a kiss, or, for himself, Royce hoped, someday, that confection of a galaxy between her legs.

At only twelve years of age Elizabeth was getting noticed.

But Royce also knew that Elizabeth had something much more than extraordinary good looks, something not as obvious as overly developed curves and thick, wavy hair and sapphire blue eyes; but something subtle and stinging and sensual, some kind of musky certainty that promised to intimidate as it beckoned, overlaid with the ripening glaze of potential, just on the verge, poised there, on the sweet verge of something he sensed in the most primal way. Hell, she was just a kid, on paper; but he could always see that those blue eyes knew things, that she was watching far into some peripheral kind of anticipation and had the carnal capacity to wash over men with the pull of a rip current, carrying them out to sea on a sweet, rough-and-tumble tide. It was the precursor of swollen flesh and hidden renderings of sexuality, the burst of an egg through a Fallopian bloom, the sigh of a scent of that first heat, folds of skin pushed out, making ready, waiting for the lunar signal to set it all in motion.

"You've been bruised, on the inside, like me," Elizabeth said to him from time to time.

"Why do you think that?"

"I've seen it in your mama's eyes," she'd say, and her own eyes would fill with tears, but only for a second.

Bruised on the inside? It seemed to make her feel tender and kindly toward him, so he let her believe it was true. Hell, he would let her believe anything as long as it gave him an edge, a shot at being the one who would get close, who would conquer that sweet, rich part of her. If she wanted him to be bruised, by god, she could have him that way, though he was anything but bruised.

Royce had, in fact, calloused over so many times he was hard as stone by the time he was twelve. His daddy was long gone, had spent only five years as a fixture in Royce's life, a presence that reminded him daily how worthless and stupid he was, welting Royce's back with a razor strap or a buggy whip, wrenching his little arm in its socket in order to lay into his bare buttocks with one of his brogans, snatched in anger from beneath the sofa. Royce hated him, resented his mother's silence, her tacit approval of Lucas Fitzhugh's brand of discipline. The only days his daddy missed out on administering a beating were those welcome periods when he disappeared for weeks at a time, on a drinking and cheating tear, his mama said, seeming relieved that her husband was, at the moment, not a presence in her life, a relief that gave way to fear and fretting over money, which gave way to nights out, away from Royce, when she stayed out late, sometimes overnight. Royce had vague memories of playing in his crib in the dark, in the silence, having cried himself spent, and without anyone coming to see to him.

The Chinaman came, though, from next door, every so often, when he heard Royce screaming for a mama who was not there. On those nights Chen Ling would sit by his crib and tell stories half in English, half in Chinese, until Royce fell asleep. By the time he was three, Royce knew not to mention Chen Ling's presence in their home—she had gone next door one Sunday and railed at Ling for meddling, screaming and cussing so loud the law had to come—and by the time Royce was four, he began to notice that his mama had grocery money on those mornings after she had stayed out all night.

His daddy would finally come home, and there would be cursing accusations and arguments and his mother thrown into walls or slapped around or punched. "You need to sport a shiner for a while behind that shit," Lucas sometimes said. Then he proceeded to give her one while Royce looked on, at once both afraid for her and glad she was getting what she allowed Royce to get with brutal regularity.

One day when Royce was five years old, perhaps after weighing the solitary freedom Lucas's absences afforded her against the misery and cruelty he brought, his mama finally stood up for her son. His daddy had just cussed him and slid the belt out of his pants, whipping through the loops, a quick leather snake to accompany the venom of his words: "You goddamn idiot. Why you want to be such a goddamn idiot, boy?"

But on this day his mama stepped forward with a Colt .45, a gift from one of her man friends, leveled at Lucas Fitzhugh, a gesture that said, without hesitation, *Stop*. It was the first time Royce had ever seen that side of his mother, the reservoir of determination, the certainty that acted in this brief battle as the element of surprise.

Lucas let go of his arm as an expression of shock took his face. "Woman, have you gone around the bend?"

"You ain't going to do him that way," she said. "It will come to your fists by the time he's eight, and then what? Either you'll kill him, or he'll get growed up and kill you. Best for you to get on gone, right now, before I kill you instead."

Royce always thought it strange how quickly his daddy left, and how permanently, too. Royce never laid eyes on him again, and if his mama did, well, she never let on. His daddy didn't even pack up his clothes. Lucas Fitzhugh offered up no argument, no inclination to compromise, just a sneer of a snarl at Royce's mama, with the words, "He ain't none of mine noway."

The boy watched him walk away, the back of his neck wearing the V of dark hair that curled all the way down his back, beneath the work shirt, arms bowed out at his sides, fists balled up, itching for a fight. It was only a few months later that the implications of his daddy's last words began to sink in, when his ears picked up on the whispers of the decent folks of the town, how Mona Anne Fitzhugh was a two-dollar whore for sale down by the tracks, down near nigger town. And, even though Royce could not fully comprehend—not yet—what a "two-dollar whore" was, he could not help but notice that, once Lucas was gone for good, the men began to trickle in to the little shack, for drinks and laughter, until his mother's bedroom door swung shut and the bedsprings squawked out a rhythm picking up faster and faster. Sometimes the boy heard mumbled curses or loud moans, even shouts that startled him out of his slumber and into those provinces of the man-woman world he was only beginning to fathom, and much too early.

When he was six, seven, eight, he wandered out on the back porch when the bedsprings started screeching. He lay on the glider and waited for trains to roar past and drown out the sounds. Sometimes the Chinaman stepped out on his own porch, saw the boy lying there, and whispered, "Come here, Roy Fitz. Come play domino Chen." And they would steal into the Chinaman's little shotgun house and play rounds of dominoes until Royce was sleepy enough to go home and crawl into bed.

"You stay night if want," the Chinaman always said.

But Royce never stayed. He asked his mother, once, if he could stay overnight with the Chinaman, but she squashed the idea fast. "Hell no, you can't sleep over there with that slanty-eyed devil. He ain't like us," she said. "He's a foreigner. They got strange ways that you ain't liable to know what he might be up to. Worser than a nigger. Now go on and don't ask me about that Chinaman again."

So Royce continued, when he was eight, nine, to sleep on the glider some nights, play dominoes at the Chinaman's house other nights, and feel relief on the nights when his mama did not have company. It was the late nights that got him, though, when he heard a knock at the door around midnight, the swish of his mama's bare feet against linoleum, a hushed, murmured conversation ending with his mama's, "Okay. Come on in." Then muted words from the front room, the room next to his, followed by his mother's moans and the uneven squeak of the bedsprings, the sound that drove into him like a jackhammer, stirred in him the suspicion that his mama could not be okay, not with that racket going on, yet the human sounds he heard seemed to be expressions of pleasure. It did not make sense, and so finally, at ten, Royce slipped to her cracked bedroom door one late night, just past midnight, just as the mattress began to squawk. He put his face to the doorway's opening and let his eyes adjust to the dark, making out a man's bare backside, that bare backside moving toward and away from the bed. And then he realized it was his mama the man was moving onto, and her knees were drawn up and he heard her say, "That's good, Daddy. Do it like that. Show me." Then the man moved faster and Royce was afraid to stay there, afraid of what he would see next that he did not understand.

He tried, in his child's way, to get the Chinaman to explain it over dominoes one night.

"Ah, no," Chen said. He seemed embarrassed and just as awkward as Royce had felt in asking, the Chinaman's English breaking up even more from the awkwardness. "No say much. Maybe say too much. Mama no make fuck. Now you play domino."

By the time he was eleven, Royce had figured out what the man was doing to his mother, there on the bed with her knees drawn up, and he had figured out some of the other things she probably did with them, things he heard older boys bragging about. And it was around the same time that some of the boys at school began to taunt him once in a while on the playground, where they played baseball to the peripheral squeals of the smaller children, and thick ropes dangling tire swings groaned their deep-toned rhythms.

"Know where we can get a piece of tail, Fitzhugh?"

"A piece of tail for sale?"

"Who can pleasure many a man?" one rhyme went. "Go see Moaning Mona Anne."

Royce knew he was fated to be either a sissy or a scrapper, with no in-between. He chose to be a scrapper, to be Lucas Fitzhugh's son, whether or not he was claimed as a son, and beat the shit out of anybody who teased him, and then some, serving up preemptive beatings before the other boys had the chance to think. Sometimes he lost the fight, but most times he won, getting a meaner and meaner reputation that eventually silenced those inclined to say anything about Mona Anne—to his face, anyway.

So it was that, as Royce entered adolescence, his already muted love for his mother had grown tainted with disgust, and he spent more and more time away from the shack and the men and the woman who spread her legs to keep him in milk and eggs and cornmeal and shame. He never mentioned her to his friends in high school, and they were by then mature enough and kind enough not to mention her, either, even though there was the occasional rumor that some of the athletes were going to go visit Mona Anne this night or that one. The bitter taste of her name in its carnal contexts slid down his throat and deep into his gut, eating away any kind of respect or caring he might have been able to conjure up for her. Finally, in the months leading up to his seventeenth year, he began to see a way out.

The Germans were all over Europe, and folks claimed it wouldn't be long before Roosevelt went on and committed to helping out, running the Krauts back to Berlin, and Royce aimed to be signed up and in on that detail if it happened. He even began to hope for it, in spite of the fact that the popular sentiment in Blackshear County was that Roosevelt had no business even thinking about sending troops. Royce didn't care whose opinion was right; he only wanted to get the hell away from his whore of a mama, away from the stares of the church folks, and maybe even come back a hero in the process. He already had a career for himself in mind. He had taken to killing time around the sheriff's office, talking tough with the High Sheriff, sometimes running errands for him and Deputy Jack, cleaning up for a tip or two. Old Man Lacey seemed to like him, telling him more than a few times, "You got a hard edge to you, Royce, and I guess you come by it honest. You ought to get into law enforcement."

"Would you take me on?"

"You just a pup. I need me a full-growed feist. Get out in the world and get some experience. Then we'll take another look."

It was during his days as a hanger-on at the sheriff's office that he began to plot and attempt to worm his way into Elizabeth's heart in earnest. She was young, certainly, but it was not uncommon for girls of twelve, thirteen, fourteen, to be married, here in the rural part of the state. Maybe he could rescue her from her burgeoning reputation as a flirt—she was, after all, coming out of her social seclusion, and dramatically, to amuse herself with the antics of a few of the boys around town—and make a war bride of her, or at least make an engagement come about.

He knew it was a long shot, though, knew she had a flip attitude about having and keeping a boyfriend, pronounced it "a bore." Moreover, she did not even seem to care that there were social codes demanding adherence or that folks looked to judge the missteps of others on an hourly basis. The gossip about Mona Anne and his low-level social status always ate at him; Elizabeth cared not one whit about the talk she generated with her wild actions as well as her simple ones, such as strolling through town with Hotshot trailing after, like the day she confirmed her sexual confidence, just strolled right into the sheriff's office, where Royce sat alone doing some filing for Mr. Jack.

"Where's Josephine?" she asked, referring to one of a couple of courthouse cats that roamed in and out of the sheriff's office, the office of the judge of probate, the county clerk's office, animals that served as pets for those county employees who took the time to feed them. Long blonde braids hung down her back, brushing at her tiny waist.

"I don't know," he said, rolling his eyes as Hotshot followed her into the room. He couldn't for the life of him understand Elizabeth's willingness to put up with Hotshot's idiot ways.

"Oh, but I want to pet her," Elizabeth said.

"She's probably off somewhere getting knocked up again. I think she's about ready to be. Again. Why don't you send the nigger to find her?"

"Shut up, Royce," she said. "Hey," she said, sitting on the sill of the open window, turning sideward, propping her feet on the sill as well, "you think you'll ever get sent to go fight those Germans?"

It was an autumn afternoon. She wore a light green shirtwaist dress, patterned with cherries, apples, and grapes across thin cotton, thin enough for Royce to know the new secrets her body was keeping, the fresh, rounded rises at her chest, unencumbered by a second dressing of an undershirt or even, he suspected, step-ins; and the juncture of her thighs, the slope of those very thighs set off by the sun spilling its light through the open window. Hell, she was just twelve years old, but she did something to him.

"If I do, you're going to see some flat-out dead Germans," Royce said, thinking how that would sure as hell give him some experience in the world to put before Campbell Lacey.

"My grandmother says they're running crazy all over Europe."

"Well, that's a fact. Crazy as hell. Done took Poland, France, coming right at England."

"My daddy said I was crazy as a one-eyed dog." This came from Hotshot, who was standing at the bulletin board, staring at "Wanted" posters.

Royce could hardly abide Hotshot, with his stupid sayings and his gappy-toothed grin. He was close to Royce in age but acted like a little kid, had been a fixture at the jailhouse for years, had become a source of amusement for the townspeople who threw him change when he sang and danced on the street.

"You aren't crazy, Hotshot," Elizabeth said. "You're original."

"Why you got to carry him around everywhere you go?" Royce chewed on a toothpick he took from Jack Lacey's desk drawer.

"I don't 'carry' him anywhere. He's my shadow. That's what my daddy says."

Royce rolled his eyes again, not believing Mr. Jack condoned his daughter running all over creation with a nigger that was probably up to no good, putting on an act for the white folks. "Well, you ought to be careful. Do you even know what people think about it and what they say?"

"Why would I care?"

"Well, because of your reputation, I reckon."

"Who am I trying to impress? The people who think they are so good and then talk bad about other people? I don't care about any of what any-body says."

"Not even about what they say he done on that train that time?"

"Shh!"

Hotshot whirled around. "I didn't, I didn't, I didn't," he said.

Elizabeth got up and took Hotshot by the arm. "It's okay, now. Stop that." She led him to a chair by the door.

"He ain't going to get that gun. Is he? I didn't," Hotshot said, eyes large and fearful, looking for the weapon associated with that specific time and place and incident.

"No gun," Elizabeth said. "Don't worry, Hotshot."

"I can get you a gun," Royce grinned. "Does your shadow want a gun?"

"Shut up, Royce," she said, and he kind of liked the way she said it, so he did.

"I didn't, I didn't, I didn't," Hotshot whimpered.

"Wait here," she said, stepping out into the hallway, turning back to Royce. "Don't get him scared any more than he is," she said, "or I'll…"

"Or you'll what?"

"Just don't!"

"Yes, sir!" he said, saluting her, playing at being a soldier.

Royce glared at the boy sitting opposite him. Hotshot did not look up, only rubbed his palms back and forth across his thighs, staring down at the backs of his black hands.

Goddamn retard, Royce thought. One day he's going to do something crazy, hurt somebody, and then what? Those Laceys were loony as hell, letting a girl like Elizabeth—just now coming into a more inviting kind of womanhood than most, a rare kind, even—take up with a nigger who was bound to step over the line, would have to step over it, being grown, if he—and here was a thought that made the blood burn through Royce's veins: if he hadn't already.

When Elizabeth returned she was carrying Josephine, a gray and orange tabby with honey-colored eyes. "Here, Hotshot," she said, laying the cat in his lap.

Hotshot rubbed the cat's back. "Josephine's a crazy cat," he said. The animal mewed a guttural sound and writhed against Hotshot's palm.

"You really don't care what folks think about you?" Royce asked.

"No, I don't," Elizabeth said. "The Bible's full of warnings about gossip and judgment."

"Still and all, you ought to know folks don't think a girl your age should be roaming the streets with a grown nigger."

"He's not grown," Elizabeth said. "My Aunt Frances says he'll never be grown in his mind. And even if he was, I would still take up time with him, even more, because he would be more like a friend and not a shadow."

"A friend?"

"Yes."

"Well you better be goddamn glad he ain't grown in the head, then, 'cause you ain't got no business, at your age, taking up with a nigger friend."

"That's all you know," Elizabeth said, as Josephine mewed in agreement, wallowing against Hotshot's thighs.

"Yeah, I do know," he said. "You need yourself a big brother kind of feller, to look out for you." He grinned, letting his gaze glide down her body.

"I'll never need a boy to look out for me," Elizabeth said.

The cat mewed another deep-noted sound.

"Oh, yes, you will," Royce said. "Believe me. I know. You're turning into something that's going to need a lot of looking out for."

"Says who?"

"Says me. I hear things."

"Like what?"

"Like how you smoke cigarettes on the street."

"So?"

"I bet you already been into the brandy, just like your mama."

Elizabeth shrugged.

"Well, have you?" It was appealing, Royce thought, the picture of a liquored-up Elizabeth with her braids down, lying on top of him, loose hair hanging down across her face and into his.

She smiled. "Maybe."

Royce laughed. "I heard how you dared Bobby Dees to steal a pack of his daddy's Picayunes, how the preacher caught y'all smoking on the front steps of the church."

"I'll say it again." She flipped one braid back. "So?"

"And I heard you got Stew Weatherall to steal all the ladies' corsets from the Empire department store round the corner."

Elizabeth broke into laughter herself then. "We had the best time lacing them onto the pine trees by the picnic grounds!"

"Yeah, I heard old Stew got a whipping from his daddy behind that."

Elizabeth rolled her eyes. "I'm afraid so," she sighed with exaggerated drama.

"I don't reckon anybody whipped you?"

She laughed again, and the sound melted over him.

"You didn't get in no kind of trouble?"

"Well, my mama got drunk and my grandmamma fussed, but my daddy just had to laugh. It was a funny prank, that's all."

"What about your granddaddy?"

She bit her lip and her eyes shadowed over with a kind of angry sadness. "He did *his* usual prank with his pistol and—"

A sudden screech and the pop of a hiss came from the cat.

"Josephine, what?" Hotshot shouted.

The cat had leapt from his lap and lay writhing and growl-mewing on the floor. Then she rolled over, the front half of her body in a crouch, her hind end raised, twisting at her rib cage, making more feral sounds, long, drawn-out groans.

Hotshot stood, agitated. "What you doing, crazy cat?"

"It's all right," Elizabeth said, and Royce winced at the calming effect her words had on the solidly muscled, solidly black teenager. She got up and squatted down next to the cat, her dress sliding up over her knees. Royce wanted to be in front of her, getting a look up that thin dress.

"She's in heat again," Elizabeth said. "Remember the last batch of kittens, Hotshot? Remember I told you she had a litter once or twice a year, spring and fall?"

"She ain't hot," he said, kneeling, putting his hand on the cat's haunches. Josephine wriggled against his touch.

Royce stood, thinking how Elizabeth had not one whit of shame in her, to be squatting down watching a needing-to-be-fucked cat with a horny nigger.

"She wants a boy cat," Elizabeth said, pointing to a place beneath the cat's tail, where its fur made a deep black Y shape, "to put it in her."

"Like them dogs at Miss Martha and them's house," Hotshot said.

"Yes, like that. But cats have really vicious fights, the boys against the boys, and even the girl fights it. And when the boy cat finally gets on her, she makes all kinds of racket, like she is now."

Royce had maneuvered around to the chair in front of Elizabeth, who had dropped back on her rear, sitting with her knees drawn up now, ankles crossed, not caring, enthralled as she was with watching the cat, that her dress crept further up her thighs. Royce glanced at Hotshot, to see if he was looking up that dress, but the ungrown boy was only studying the cat's rolling, writhing motions along with Elizabeth.

"Poor thing," Elizabeth said. "She wants a boy cat really bad."

"Just what we need around here," Royce said. "Another mess of kittens for me to have to carry off and drown." He let his eyes take in the flesh of her thighs, already promising himself he would touch them one day.

"No! Don't talk about things like that! And don't you dare hurt her babies," Elizabeth said. "Ever." She scratched Josephine's head.

Royce did not tell her that it was her own grandfather who routinely gave him the order to execute the kittens no one cared to adopt from the courthouse grounds. Usually he carried them in a croaker sack to Cane Creek on the edge of town, weighted the sack down and chunked it under the bridge. Sometimes, though, he would wring their necks or pound their skulls with a heavy rock before throwing them in the water, but that was only if there weren't too many of them and he didn't need a sack to carry them all.

"Do you see how puffy it gets?" she said. "And sometimes the way they carry on is like they're really hurting."

As if in response, Josephine let howl an even longer cat moan, flipping to her back, twisting back and forth sideways against the floor. Royce let his eyes find the place, the white cotton of her step-ins, and stay there a while, wondering what she looked like, right—*there*, thinking it would maybe be smooth and pink and sweet, not like the overused, worn-out one that certainly resided between his mother's routinely pounded thighs. He conjured up the image of Elizabeth's flesh, where his gaze rested, shucking the undergarment from his vision, seeing it there, waiting for him. Then he noticed the silence in the room, save for the cat's fevered growls, and he glanced up. Elizabeth was watching him, a knowing smirk on her face.

Royce looked at Hotshot, but the boy was focused on the cat's contortions. "You ought not to go letting your skirt up," he said.

"Do you think I give a care if you look at my underdrawers?"

"Well, you should," he said. "Look at you. You ain't even trying to cover up."

"You're pretty stupid," she said, scratching Josephine's head. "You really think I care if you see."

"You know what the Bible says about modesty, don't you?"

"How do you know what it says?" she countered.

"Because the Primitive Baptists are all the time hauling me to Sunday school, trying to make me out a lost lamb."

"Are you a lost lamb?"

He liked the way she looked at him in that moment, all concern and tenderness, so he replied, "Maybe I am," before adding, "but hadn't you better cover up your drawers?"

She smiled. "Maybe you better read more Bible verses if you're so concerned about my drawers."

"What the hell more I got to learn from the Bible?" She still had not moved, and his eyes kept making fleeting returns to the white cotton underwear.

"Well, for one thing, the Bible says, 'Flee also youthful lusts.' That's Second Timothy." And she giggled as Royce's face went red. "Let's go, Hotshot. We'll go find Josephine a boyfriend. Pull me up."

Royce watched Hotshot take her hand and bring her to her feet, hating the boy's familiarity with her, the ease with which she cared for the jailhouse orphan. He sat for a long time after they left, watching goddamned Josephine carrying on like a cathouse whore, growling and gyrating. He thought of the untouched place between Elizabeth's legs. He hoped like hell it was soft as a hen's feather, pristine, that the whispers of speculation about Hotshot and the long-ago train ride were just rumors. Was that place she had just shown him really untouched, unlike the one used so regularly by Moaning Mona Anne? Elizabeth sure acted like she knew more than other girls her age. He stared at the cat, struck again by how Elizabeth had described Josephine's estrus with such utter unselfconsciousness, just as she refused to feel embarrassed to have him studying her underwear, imagining her flesh. Shit, she would probably describe the fine details of her own body with an equal absence of shame, a thought which teased excitement into him. He put his hand to his crotch. Maybe she would do that sometime, tell him what she saw when she looked at herself.

Josephine let out a piercing wail that droned into a groan and lifted her haunches again, curving her backbone downward, amber eyes pupil-dilated with a primal, wild look, and his mind took a turn. Maybe she would tell him what she really saw when she looked at that ungrown nigger. He imagined Elizabeth and Hotshot sitting side by side on the floor of a boxcar. They were watching a coupling of cats, to a quickening rattle of the rails and blows of a train whistle. Swallowed up by the motion and the rhythm, they were fascinated by the orgasmic tenor of it all, maybe even aroused by it. Maybe they had felt it before. Josephine rolled over again on the office floor, pawing her feet at the air, then over again, to raise the vulval offering high as she mewed, deep and long. He stood, leaned over her, reaching with both hands, getting both hands around her neck, squeezing tight and lifting fast. And just as fast, before the animal could get claw the first in him, Royce flip-flopped her body over with a circular swing of his arms, feeling the snap of the spine's crack from the cat's skull, Josephine limp and heavy in his grasp, dead weight hitting the floor. He walked into the bathroom and opened a cabinet beneath the sink. He found a croaker sack there and raked the lifeless feline into it, unapologetic, unsympathetic, and unaware of the lifelessness within himself.

He wasn't sorry for his mama, "Moaning Mona Anne," never for one second bought her story that she had to get money to support him, that there was no other way when times were so bad for everybody. He wasn't sorry for Hotshot. Lost from his daddy? It was probably more like his daddy lost him on purpose, saw through that retard act and knew he was a lunatic likely to do somebody in one day. And Josephine? He wasn't one bit sorry that goddamn cat was dead. Elizabeth would sure as hell never have to know and, if the sheriff ever figured out what he did, well, Old Man Lacey would probably thank him for solving the population problem. Royce smiled and reached down to grasp the rough weave of the fabric into a tight bunch, bringing it up off the deep brown hardwood floor, straightening his body and his sense of purpose. He slung the sack over his shoulder and headed for the bridge over Cane Creek.

*

Elizabeth lay on her bed, naked, staring up at the canopy, the breeze from a heavy black oscillating fan on the trunk at the foot of the bed brushing back and forth across her skin. She watched the bed linens flutter with the fan's movement and imagined she was in a royal tent at a lush oasis in the Sahara. It was thick with green leaves sheltering strange fruit she found and bit into, juices dancing down over her chin, and the brush was layered with the chirps and trills of unknown creatures, calling out to her. It was as if God had scooped up a bit of the rain forest and dropped it into the desert. The air was humid, aberrant, dripping moisture, so she closed her eyes and pictured herself wearing nothing but a flowing, loose-fitting white dress, tied at the tops of her shoulders, and thick bracelets, and the golden asp headdress of Cleopatra. Sand-stained breezes billowed the tent, and her dress brushed against her legs, caressed her thighs, her stomach.

Elizabeth sat up, unsure if she was ready for this, uncertain about whether she could follow through. After all, it was becoming clearer and clearer that not even a few others felt or heard or thought things the way she did, and there were days when the sounds and shapes in her head seemed to take a turn back on her, sending her into fits of sadness and fear.

"It's your time of the month in the making," her grandmother said. "That's what puts girls your age in such tender moods." But Elizabeth had listened to the other girls at school, knew their world did not overlap hers by much.

"Sure I know what you mean," her father said, not meaning it at all, wanting to reassure her, she knew.

"Oh, Elizabeth," Miss Pearl sighed. "Stop being so dramatic. It upsets the whole household. You mustn't do that."

"You've always been sensitive," Aunt Frances said. "Maybe it's something you can use to your advantage as you grow up." And she sounded the least convincing of all.

They made it all seem normally abnormal or, in the case of her mother, unacceptable, and all Elizabeth felt was more and more alienation from what little mooring she had. She continued to wander, as always, through the house late at night, in those hours when the house seemed empty and the only obvious sound was the ticking of the mantel clock above the fireplace. She still heard the other sounds, though, the ones no one else seemed to ever hear, and they emboldened her, the skitter of moth's wings against purple air, the hum of night clouds. She continued to approach, to touch, her grandfather's pistol; she even withdrew it from its holster and held it loose and easy in her palm, wishing she could fire it. But that was only for boys and men to do.

Yet she also knew males of all ages responded to her in a way that intrigued her. There were the boys at school, the ones who made fools of themselves to get her to notice—childish boys who made her tired with their lack of imagination, devoid of inquisitiveness, forever willing to do her bidding, she was learning. Then there were the older, upper-school boys who whistled at her now, who never whistled at other girls her age, who made her feel like something to be desired, something like a treasure. Finally there were the older men, men who watched her in a way new and different from the way they had when she was younger. "She's going to be a heartbreaker," they said to her daddy, standing in the courthouse hallway. "She's a real looker, Jack. Better keep an eye on that one." Even Brother Stryker at the Methodist Church sent her knowing glances, placed his palm at the small of her back when he congratulated her on another Bible bee win. "You're growing into quite a young lady," he said, pressing the heel of his hand into her spine. "If you ever have a need to talk things over, you just come and see me."

Once she had taken him up on his offer, just last month. She had gone to see him in his big office in the parsonage next door to the church. She sat across from him at his desk, could look over his shoulder and out the window, across the street to the high school gym. He wore dark trousers, a white, short-sleeved shirt, and a striped tie, his usual attire of a weekday. On Sunday there would be beautiful, flowing black robes and a big gold cross around his neck, a cross glinting fire.

They chatted a while, the preacher asking her the usual questions grownups typically recited, about school, about friends, about what she enjoyed doing.

"I want to be different," she said, finally. "I don't really want friends, but I do want to have an effect on people. But a good effect, not a bad one."

His eyes were piercing, seemed to look into her soul, and in a frightening way, as if he knew her secrets. "You do have an effect on people, Elizabeth, and I believe that will grow."

"It's not a sin?"

"I can't imagine that anything you would do would be a sin."

"What if I have a bad effect on people? What if I cause bad things to happen?"

Brother Stryker smiled. "God is the cause of all things. You cannot cause things to happen, good or bad. God has a plan. You can *be* good or bad, but you can't *cause* good or bad things to happen."

"But I have caused bad things to happen."

"No. It had to have been in God's plan to happen or else it wouldn't have happened."

"Then God plans for me to make misery," she said.

His gaze bore into her. "Is that right?"

"Yes. And harming others is the only sin there is."

"The only one?"

"Yes. I have decided the only sin ever, from beginning to now, is to do harm to others."

He smiled. "That would certainly be in line with the teachings of Christ. Although I'm certain there are many more sins."

"Do you think Jesus would like me?"

"He already loves you." Brother Stryker stood, walked around the desk, and took her hands, pulling her to her feet. "You are going to make all kinds of things happen. You are very dynamic."

She felt flattered and beyond special, and when Brother Stryker hugged her she thought little of it at first. He was always hugging on the ladies, slapping the men on the shoulder, being a "part of everyone's family," he said. But when he hugged her there in his office, he pressed his lips close to her ear and whispered, "You are just the sort of little lady Jesus

wants," and she felt a strange shift in his touch, in the way he left his lips
near her ear and breathed into it, four, five, six breaths, hugging her tight,
pushing against her with his hips, a strange pressure next to the pit of her
stomach, something like a threat.

"Come back and see me," he said as she left. But she had not, would
not, she decided. She was even thinking of staying away from church altogether, quitting the Bible bees, spending time figuring it all out for herself,
in the solitude of her bedroom.

She reached up and fidgeted with her long hair, tickling her cheek
with the ends of a waved tress, thinking about how Royce Fitzhugh had
stared at her step-ins as if he were hypnotized. She glanced at the clock on
her bedside table. One forty-five in the morning. She leaned over and felt
under the ruffled skirt of the little table, bringing out an ash tray, then a
small box of matches and a pack of Chesterfields. She wondered about the
brandy. She had played it coy with Royce about that, did not want to admit
that she had never tasted brandy. She wished she had told him about the
three mason jars of warm beer, her daddy's home brew, after a summertime fishing trip on the Flint River, left in the bottom of his boat, parked
on its trailer under the shed behind the garage. She and Hotshot shared it,
laughing and lightheaded with a sudsy, tipsy feeling. That was only a
couple of months ago, but it was a feeling she had revisited a few times, pil-
fering a cold home brew every now and again from the jars in the icebox.
Brandy would be even better, she decided, and not as easily missed, since
her mother drank so much of it. She lit the cigarette, then leaned back and
exhaled, deciding she would pilfer a bottle of peach brandy from the liquor
cabinet before she went to sleep. Just to see how it felt.

Scattered about the room, across the floor, were tumbles of clothing,
tried on, cast off, tried on again. She had spent the evening studying herself in the mirror in all kinds of dress and stages of undress and no dress,
sizing up the newness of her body, settling into the comfort of listening to,
and then knowing, the fresh secrets it was murmuring to her. Royce had
given her confirmation of the power her body held, the power Brother
Stryker's disturbing touch sent into full retreat, and she was determined to

understand the difference, even if she had to read the Holy Bible front-
wards and backwards to find the answer. All her life she had been told that
all explanations were in that one book, so surely the questions of a twelve-
year-old girl could be answered there.

Two Bibles, one a family Bible, with a worn black cover and gold let-
tering; the other a white one, a gift from some pastel Easter gone by, lay
open on the bed, particular passages starred, some underlined in blue ink,
notes to herself in the margins, some dated, some not, all serving as a kind
of diary. She had always made little notes in the smaller white Bible, but
only this fall began them in earnest, in the larger book, in the white spaces
around the scriptures. She thought it made a certain sense for her to have
a diary of short notes, since she would never be still long enough to fill in
whole pages at a time. She wanted some kind of record, ever certain that
she was going to do something that mattered with her life. After all, both
Jubil and Royce, and now Brother Stryker, had said she would. Jubil. It had
been over three years, but she still missed Jubil.

Elizabeth reached for the white Easter Bible, leaving the Sahara
behind, for now, and flipped through the pages with the glassy, gold-
sheened edges, to where she had underlined Proverbs 28:1: "The wicked
flee when no man pursueth, but the righteous are bold as a lion." In the
margin she had written, simply, "Jubil of the autumn," and some time later,
"Senator Talmadge?" Then she found the verse in Psalms she had marked:
"Weeping may endure for a night, but joy cometh in the morning." She
remembered memorizing that one when Jubil was sent away, how she tried
to teach it to Hotshot, how he could never repeat it to her satisfaction. On
that page she had printed: "November—But then another night comes.
After the morning of joy. Why?"

Proverbs was especially cluttered with stars and lines and notes. "All
the days of the afflicted are evil, but he that is of a merry heart hath a con-
tinual feast," read one verse, and in the white space she had written, "Hotshot afflicted—M. Martha says. FDR, too." A row of stars marked 3:13,
"Happy is the man that findeth wisdom, and the man that getteth understanding," and the notation: "Understanding is all I will ever want." A

"Ha!" in the margin was a response to 26:11, "As a dog returneth to his vomit, so a fool returneth to his folly." These were among the markings in the small white Bible of her childhood. But, by August of this year, she was rarely feeling like a child, and it seemed more adult-like to take her musings to the bigger Bible. She was too keenly aware of a change in the ether that spilled into a deeper transformation, one she could feel when the little brushes of tickling warmth came, deep in the back of her stomach. It happened with more and more regularity, especially when boys were around, and especially more when they were older, like Royce Fitzhugh. She was more cognizant than ever of her own burgeoning beauty and the attention it summoned, an attention full of a mysterious, promised pleasure. She wanted to understand it and know what was to come of her, what extraordinary mark she would make in life.

Her thirteenth birthday was only a little over a month away, in February. The Chinaman told her she was born in the year of the dragon, which meant she was honest, daring, and full of energy, which made her want to know even more. She tried to persuade her grandmother to take her to Sister Ruby, who read palms from a little house on the highway to Albany.

"The sign says Sister Ruby has the gift of the Third Eye," Elizabeth said. "She reads Tarot cards and holds séances and sees into the future."

"You'll make your own unique future," Miss Lucille said. "There's no need to have someone tell it to you from some zodiac formula or a bunch of cards that I am not so sure are not of the Devil. Don't worry. You will definitely make an impact in your future."

And since that prediction coincided with Brother Stryker's, and with Jubil's, and with Royce's, Elizabeth said, "So be it, then."

Elizabeth looked at some of the passages she had marked and noted in recent months. She was seeing more layers in the Bible now. It was more than a convenient resource book of easy-to-memorize sayings, taken out of context to recite in a competition or to insert in other contexts. There was another dimension to it, a vivid description here, a rich story there, a warning just beyond. What she took away from it depended upon her general frame of mind in the reading of it. She found that she could leave off bits of a verse and the words were colored in a new meaning, one just for her. She read about love and courage and power and boldness, searching out those descriptors that had attached themselves to her over the years.

The passages of lust, too, snared her interest. "The lips of a strange woman drop as an honeycomb, and her mouth is smoother than oil" leapt out from Proverbs. Beautiful words, she thought, passing over the words that followed: "But her end is bitter as wormwood, sharp as a two-edged sword." She wondered at the descriptor—"strange," giving it the only meaning she knew, one that certainly applied to herself, as she was, after all, as everyone said, "strange."

Once, on a night like this one, when she was making to finally explore what she knew would become the taste of her, she had marked the lines, "Stolen waters are sweet, and bread eaten in secret is pleasant." Tonight she revisited that verse, captivated by the image of the stolen waters, thinking of the pulse of her longing, the twinge of recognition in her thighs, as a watery current of lust, and she wanted to know it from the inside out. She reread several verses in Proverbs: "I have decked my bed with coverings of tapestry, with carved works, with fine linen of Egypt. I have perfumed my bed with myrrh, aloes, and cinnamon. Come, let us take our fill of love until the morning: let us solace ourselves with loves." The words coaxed a longing ache into her limbs, and other lush words tumbled into her head, words from Shakespeare, from *Othello*, from *Romeo and Juliet*, singing of the same kind of pleasure. The ache grew fuller, demanding the final exploration of her touch to its conclusion, when she would be certain to know what it held for her.

She lay back on the bed again, closing her eyes, returning to Egypt, to the touch of the desert air against her skin. She untied the fastenings at her shoulders and let the dress fall away so that the wind could have her, the south wind, warm and thick. She let it curl against the length of her body, finding tender rises and hollows. She arched her back, pushing into it, letting it cup her breasts, kiss down her stomach with its humid mouth, blow currents of nimble breezes along the inside of her right thigh, and up, and over. Then the breezes blended together and became a gusting wind, rising, falling, building up, dying back, pressing against her, pulling away. She turned her head from side to side, letting it taste her neck, her shoulders, licking heated blasts across her breasts, down her sides, until it found the place there, the place that drew Royce's gaze with so much force. That was where she wanted the wind to go, and she let it nudge her thighs further and further apart, until she felt herself lifting her hips to meet it, limbs tense, breaths short. It hesitated, a brief lull, but she coaxed it back, wanting it, urging it to roar past her ears and explore every ripple in the dunes, finding hidden, exotic underground pools that pushed cool spring water into virgin sand. And she felt the currents in the well of water, subtle, then stronger as the sand went shade after shade darker, heavy with a wet density, dropping into a bowl of sand now, where waters from all directions collected and deepened and filled, no longer slow and sluggish, but building in momentum, then another lull followed by a quickening rush, rising fast. And what was once a seething breeze was a gale now, with powerful blows sustained, and the pool wanted only to widen and swallow itself, bearing down on the bowl's walls of sand, saturated and crumbling, until one final surge brought down the last weakening bulk of the walls in a roiling thunder, a swelling crash, washing them down, down, and under, dissolving them into a liquid calm.

Elizabeth let the fan's rhythmic hum send its breath back and forth across her, feeling a kind of exhaustion she had never imagined, reveling in new-found completion. She had wanted to look through the Bible some more, put away her clothes, slip into the dining room and retrieve a bottle of peach brandy, but the time spent inside her thoughts, inside the newness of her body, had taken her to a place that begged to be savored for as long as it lasted. She felt the brush of the fan's breath, heard the pages of the Bibles, pages thin as skin or the wings of a moth, rustling and fluttering into the quiet. She reached for it and took up a pen, supine, turning her head to see the pages, thumbing the pages back to Proverbs, Chapter 7, scripting, "October 15 '41 and I am overwhelmed by a power—such a power." She laid her pen on the pages, catching a glimpse of a verse: "For she hath cast down many wounded : yea, many strong men have been slain by her." Elizabeth let her lids drop, brought her forearm up and laid it across her forehead, eyes closed, all intentions and questions taken away, spirited away, into a seductive kind of sleep.

It was less than a week later that Elizabeth stepped out of the claw-foot iron bathtub after a long soak to soothe the stomachache she had been feeling all day, a twist of an ache that left her shaky and sullen. She stood dripping on the white oval bath rug and put a dry towel, blue blooms of roses on a white background, to her chest, down her arms, up her legs, around her back, thinking she would go ask her grandmother for a cup of hot tea. She put the towel to the place between her legs and she could feel it then, a warm release, a bit of her, falling out of her. When she withdrew the towel from that place, she saw it, stained across a blue rose, and on the oval rug, a red circle set against the nap of white cotton. Then she wept, knowing her own touch had pulled the menstrual fluid from her, before God's intended time. She wept, not saying aloud how she wanted the blood to spill instead from a straight-razored jugular or a dagger driven into her heart with the force of a Juliet, that she wanted to make only good things happen, feared the others, those that took up residence in her mind with the most cruel clarity, wondering why God let her cause such things to happen.

Her mother fretted over her as if she were an invalid, helped her with the pins and the bulky homemade pad, brought her St. Joseph aspirin tablets and soup and crackers. But Miss Lucille pooh-poohed the drama, coming into Elizabeth's room, not with hot tea but warm bourbon diluted with water and lemon. "It's a curse," she said. "It's the curse of Eve and I won't pretend it isn't. But it's not an affliction. You don't need to let your mama convince you to take on like Camille. Just take it with a shot of whiskey and go on to the next day, that's all."

Elizabeth sat up in her bed late that night, sipping the warm bourbon and water, smoking Chesterfields, letting the heated tingle of the whiskey soothe her down to her toes. She read and reread the story of Eve and original sin, seeing the layers in that story, seeing the temptress as a usurper of

God in the mind of a man who desired her flesh so fiercely that she held every bit of his soul in the balance. A usurper of God—He who caused all to happen, good and bad. The phrase kept blaspheming its way through her head, captioning all the pictures residing there. A usurper of God. Was she willing to go that far? Could she pull the strings and make the hinged joints jump and quiver, grind the organ and make the monkey dance? Would she be a queen, after all, like the Queen of the Nile, moving armies across ancient dunes? The more the phrase circled, the more embedded it grew, taking root, inking its way into permanence beneath the photographs, until the notion became both sweet and noble, both frightening and daring. A usurper of God. She let it nestle beneath her crippled consciousness, embraced it, fell into its cadence. She could follow through. She could see herself taking it to its logical inevitability. *A usurper of God.* There could certainly be nothing more exquisite and forbidden and formidable, than that.

*

Eula Lura Sutton was five feet, eleven inches tall, with long feet and a thick frame, physically intimidating, sturdy, firm. She could not remember when she had ever felt dainty or feminine or especially fragile, like some girls pretended to be. She could not remember ever being the small one in the group, experiencing the phenomenon of relative diminutiveness. "That Eula Lura. She's a big girl," folks would say, with a kind of awe, as opposed to a tone of criticism. Folks admired her towering presence and her strength, the fact that she could work hard and work well. As a result, Eula Lura—with the exception of a brief second during adolescence when she felt herself to be some kind of an awkward giant next to the other girls, and once again, when she found herself falling in love for the first and only time—was always comfortable in her body and comfortable in her skin.

She married at fourteen, and her husband Ned told her she was beautiful, that he had always wanted a woman with plenty of territory to explore. Not a fat woman. Fat did not invite exploration because it was the same all over—same texture, same flesh-pounded appearance. But a big woman who was solid, well, that woman had swelling rises and bluffs, miles of flood plains and plateaus, and one deep, sweet sugar grove for a man to get lost in. And it was during their courtship, as he explored the sinew of her arms, her back, the plunge of her thighs into depth, that he gave her the nickname, "LittleBit." And it stuck as long as they were together.

She met Ned in '36 when he was just turned twenty, peddling coal up and down the streets of Cordele, Georgia, singing out, "Coal! Coal for the stove! Coal!" His voice was deep, resonating into the drab lives of folks beat down by the Depression. She had heard him often, knew he passed by the house at least twice a week, that Miss Clarice Pearson, the lady of the house, bought coal from him once or twice a month, depending on how much egg money there was, to heat the big house in the winter.

"You 'bout as pretty a thing as I ever saw." He had just pulled his wagon up by the front yard of the white folks' house where her mama, Pinky, tended two little babies. Eula Lura took care of the housework, most cooking, and light yard chores.

She blushed and dropped her eyes.

"What's the matter?" he said. "Ain't nobody never told you how pretty you are?"

She looked down, her eyes resting on her shoes, the size twelves that were so hard to find she sometimes had to wear cast-off men's shoes. She was immediately grateful she was not wearing men's shoes at this moment.

"Cat got your tongue?" he laughed.

She let her chin drop further. "No."

He leaned on the fence, ducking his head to find her face. "You sure you can talk? Look up here at me. Where is that damn tongue-thievin' cat?"

She lifted her eyes to meet his light brown ones, smiling eyes that told her he was gentle but spirited, the kind of boy she would like. "I can talk."

"How old are you?"

"Thirteen."

"Can't be. You're too much like a woman, too pretty," he said, looking full-on into her stare as if daring her to look away. His expression was unnerving in its familiarity, as if he knew her already, as if there were things he already understood about her that she did not begin to understand herself.

"I'll go and get Miss Clarice," she said, retreating, afraid to hope he was truly attracted to her. She was long-footed and plain and no good with words, never had been. She was certainly not pretty. He had to be fooling her.

"No! Stay here and talk with me!" he called out, but she had already wound around the side of the house, making for the back door, looking to hide. "I'll give you a chunk of coal! No charge!" he yelled, and she couldn't help smiling as the back door slapped shut.

She peered out the front window as Miss Clarice bartered with him, admiring the ease of his movements, the adult way he carried himself, even as he spoke with the white lady. It was a rare thing, she knew, and she wanted to learn more, much more, about him.

She took to listening for him as the days passed, straining to hear the sing-song "Coal! Coal for the stove! Coal!" and seeing to it that she was doing something in the front yard—pulling weeds or raking or heading out for the market for Miss Clarice—every time he came by. It was not long before she noticed he was coming by more and more often. He would roll his wagon up, act surprised to see her there, then say, "I been needing me a pretty girl, much like a woman, to talk to." And she began to believe he really did think she was pretty, so their conversations grew longer, and she found herself easing more and more into their exchanges.

He told her about how his grandmother was brought from Africa on the *Clothilde*, the last slave ship to hit America's shores at Mobile, Alabama; about how she married a free man named Leviticus Hubbard Sutton, who had been a Buffalo Soldier out West; how they settled in South Georgia, deep in the country, where the earth was rich. He told how his own father, Edward Hubbard Sutton, had enlisted during the Great War against Germany with Ned just a minute in his mother's womb, how his father spent the war years digging trenches and latrines before the mustard gas did him in. Ned's mother died of pneumonia when Ned was only eleven, and he had been fending for himself ever since.

Eula Lura did not know much about her own lineage, had never thought to ask her mother about it, and when she finally did ask, all her mother said was, "Them folks is dead. Ain't nothing to know." They were lost to her, she told Ned, just like her daddy.

"More like stolen property," Ned said, and though she didn't understand what he meant, it sounded bold, and she was intrigued by his independence, the pride he carried in himself.

She told him about how she and her sister Pruella had grown up working crops with their mama and daddy, traveling from farm to farm until her daddy finally found a patch of land to sharecrop, land owned by Miss Clarice's daddy, outside Cordele. But by then times were harder than ever. When the price of cotton went low, her daddy had to leave home to look for work. It fell to Pinky, Pruella, and Eula Lura to do the cropping.

She told him about how her daddy rode the train to Birmingham, Alabama, with two other men named Willie and Loper, men who passed through town with high talk of work to be had a state or two over. They rode on to Memphis, where, Willie told her mama later when he passed back through, Eula Lura's daddy broke off from the other two, said he might find more possibilities up North, in Baltimore or Philadelphia. That was the last anyone heard from him. Her mama always believed the two drifters did something to him, maybe something really bad, because she never trusted them, not one bit, and it wasn't at all like her husband to up and leave his children. Pinky believed maybe her husband had come to a murderous end, but she was powerless to do anything about it. They were having trouble harvesting the sugar cane, a woman and two girls with no man to do the heaviest work. That was when Miss Clarice took pity on them, helped Pruella get hired by a friend and put Pinky to work tending to her two little white babies.

"They some ugly-looking little things, ain't they?" Ned said.

"What is?"

"White babies."

She laughed. "Ned, you ain't right."

"No, listen. They got that real pink skin, kind of like a fish fillet gone bad or the hind end of a shoat. And just born you'll see them all wrinkled and pinched up in the face when they squall."

"Ned," she said, slapping the air, "you so bad!"

"When I find the right woman," he said, lifting one brow at her, "I'm going to give her pretty black babies with skin like the smoothest sugar-and-cream chocolate frosting you ever put in your mouth, and they'll be too happy to ever pinch up their faces and cry,"

"All babies cry."

"Well, they won't be ugly when they cry. And when they cry, it will be a song. You'll see."

It was just like him to talk about babies. Ned talked more than most boys about the future, about where he wanted to be inside of a decade, about his dream of moving north to Chicago, Illinois, opening some kind of business since he was good with figures and better with people. He always seemed to be including her in his plans. Beyond that, he paid her attention, gave her compliments. He kept insisting she was not simply pretty, now, but beautiful. "Like a diamond," he said. "You ever see a diamond?"

"Miss Clarice has a diamond ring her husband give her. And one of her lady friends named Mrs. Donley has three or four she wears all the time, big ones that—"

"That's right. White folks got all the diamonds. Got all the everything." And he didn't say it bitter and hopeless, like some boys did, but matter-of-fact, like he'd do something to change that reality.

"They're mighty pretty, though," she said. "Diamonds."

"You know how a diamond gets made?"

"Diamonds just be, that's all," she said.

He laughed his deep, husky laugh and it gave her chill bumps and butterflies. "What do you think, a cloud burst comes along and diamonds fall out the sky or something?"

"Well, no. I don't—I just—I never thought on it, I reckon."

"You should, though. Think on it. It's a hell of a story."

"Tell me then," she said, infected with his enthusiasm.

"First of all, diamonds come from Africa, and how they get made is, down deep in the ground, where it's hot as the Devil 'cause it's the Devil's territory, see, all this coal gets heated and compressed till it changes into something so hard it can't be busted up, hardly."

"So you make them out of coal?" she asked.

"Well, no. Not like the coal I push. The coal that makes diamonds has to get the heat and pressure that can only be had deep in the ground, and even then, they're rare. In the fields of coal, I mean."

"Huh?" Eula Lura was curious but confused, unable to conjure an image of such things going on beneath the surface of the earth. It sounded like the fires of hell, and she didn't think a beautiful jewel could come out of hell.

"It's like a pearl getting made inside an oyster," he continued. "Conditions got to be perfect and it takes a long, long time."

He had so much in his head it muddled her own. He had read so many books and she could barely even read, had never spent time in such a place as "school," like he had. Eula Lura had lived her childhood stooped over in cotton fields, or up and down rows of tall corn, or digging potatoes out of black dirt. But he never acted superior, always explained things to her, told her the things he knew, shared them with her.

They were married in February, just a few months after they met, wanting to avoid wasting any more time. They settled into a life together, and he saw to it that her people were taken care of, adopted her family as his. They went about doing what folks did to get a child, but Jesus did not see fit to grant them that blessing. On two different occasions, when she thought she must certainly be pregnant, the Lord snatched it from her, and her womb emptied itself as she sat on the toilet, doubled over with cramping, searing pains, sobbing and begging God not to take her child. Her mama came over and put her to bed both times, saying she had surely spilled the fruit. Pinky set a brick in the oven, got it through and though hot, then wrapped it in a thick towel and laid it on Eula Lura's stomach and said prayers over her.

If Ned was disappointed, he said nothing of it to her, and now it had been going on six years of a life together, working hard, making a slow progress through a bleak decade, childless. In the last year, though, Ned had taken keen interest in the talk of the country going to war. It was an unpopular notion, to be certain, but it was also a surefire way, he said, to better himself and to lay out a much better life for the two of them in the process.

"How you going to better yourself?" she asked him one early morning before sunup. "You already the best man I know."

He smiled. "Oh, you know. Get experience. Maybe see more of the world. Maybe get the respect a soldier is due. Maybe pull up stakes and move North."

He had talked to her about W. E. B. DuBois, about Booker T. Washington, about how important it was to become independent, economically liberated from the Southern system of sharecroppers and legal overseers. "I respect you," she said, wishing she could satisfy that particular need in him. She sat across from him at their little kitchen table inside the weathered shack where they lived, in spite of the fact that it leaned a bit to the side.

"I need more respect, though, from more people," he said, sipping a cup of strong coffee before taking his coal wagon out on the streets.

"You mean white people."

"I mean more people."

"You don't need to be thinking of going across the world to get shot at."

"You know where I come from, LittleBit."

"Just because your people was soldiers—"

"Warriors," he corrected.

"Don't mean you have to do the same thing."

"Ain't going to be the same thing at all."

"What do you mean?"

He sighed. "My daddy went to fight in the 'war to end all wars.' That's what they called it, and my daddy wanted to fight." His eyes narrowed. "But he did what all the colored soldiers did. Worked with a shovel."

"How will this war be different?"

"Well," Ned said, leaning back in his chair. "I'm reckoning FDR's going to make things a little better. Got Randolph kicking up sand. I'm reckoning

I might, just maybe, get to fight for me and my daddy both."

Eula Lura resisted the urge to question him too much about the things he said, the names he mentioned. She didn't want him to think she was stupid or that she did not listen, and she knew he had mentioned something about A. Phillip Randolph before. All she said was, "I sure wish I had all that book learning of yours in my head."

He held his hands out across the table and took hers. "This is what I'm telling you. This is the thing: we ain't going to be enslaved all through this life. And you'll read all the books you want to if you ain't afraid to learn."

And she deep down knew he was right. She had challenged him before about her family being enslaved at all, not really understanding how that could be. He had talked to her at length about books and quotes and ideas she found overwhelming. But she did trust him, of that she was certain. She was determined, too, that he should take hold of any piece of the dream he could latch onto. But at the same time she was afraid, had seen and heard too many stories of failure, of sabotage by white folks.

"I want to enlist now, today," he said, "but I'll give it some more thought if you'll give more thought to the future, too."

She nodded yes and watched him rise and walk out the front door and around the side of the house. In a while he reappeared, pushing his coal cart, full and heavy, shoulders bent, leaning into it, as he made his way out to the street.

She hoped against hope that he would stop his talk of joining up, going off from her, maybe getting himself hurt or killed. She consoled herself by telling herself a colored soldier would be assigned to something like cooking or cleaning up after an officer, something like that. She consoled herself by half-believing she could change his mind. And he did seem torn, at times, between the need to live a life here, with her, and the need to provide a better life *for* her, in the bargain claiming a bit of dignity to add to his own life, and hers. He did not run out and sign up, not that week or that month. Instead he talked and procrastinated, talked and procrastinated, and she became more and more confident that he would never leave her, never go charging off to some strange place with a strange language and folks shooting big guns at one another. So she remained quiet on the subject, content to believe that the tide had turned in her favor. What she did not know then was that the future would drop the war right into his lap, one early Sunday morning in the not too faraway month of December. That was when waves of Japanese bombers, pilots who were born and bred in a culture of warriors, all too willing to sacrifice themselves—with women and children and families left behind, people just like Eula Lura Sutton—would fly over blue Hawaiian waters and turn her world upside down.

The longer the Germans overran Europe, sparking debate within the United States about its potential role, the more tense the atmosphere inside the Lacey home became. Elizabeth's father and grandfather listened to the national radio news through October, November, and on, while they drank Early Times and ate boiled peanuts, the beans pilfered from the ice box and cooked in a tall pot of salty water. Campbell got more agitated with each report. "He's weak," he fumed. "He's a weak pantywaist if he doesn't stand up to the Brits and keep away from that mess. It ain't our fight."

"Is there ever going to be a war in Sumner?" Elizabeth asked. She lay on the floor, her head resting on the foot-cushion pillow, the family situated around the radio, something they typically did of a late afternoon, each family member fixed on some task: her mother—already having had her fill of the airwaves with *Pepper Young's Family* or *Ma Perkins*—reading a magazine or filing her nails, Miss Lucille sewing as she waited for a news bulletin, Campbell polishing his boots or cleaning one of the pistols he collected, her father reading the paper, smoking to the high drama of *Captain Midnight*, *Little Orphan Annie*, or an Ovaltine commercial.

"Is there ever going to be a war in Sumner?" Elizabeth asked.

A cloud of cigarette smoke writhed its way to the ceiling from her daddy's Camel. "No, Baby," Jack said. "It's on the other side of the ocean and it's going to stay there if Roosevelt doesn't get us all tangled up in it."

"Don't even think about it, Elizabeth," her mother said. "Run along and don't even think about such unpleasant things."

"But I want to listen to the radio."

"An 'unpleasant thing'? Is that what a war should be called?" Miss Lucille said from her perch on the mint-green Victorian divan.

Pearl's spine stiffened almost imperceptibly. "You know how Elizabeth takes things to heart. I don't want her to be upset. She'll upset the whole household."

"But she should be upset," Miss Lucille said. "War is an upsetting thing. The price to pay, the lives. But I think Roosevelt is right to be lending the airplanes and all. These are our friends, our allies."

"Good Lord, woman," Campbell thundered. "Do you think we ought to run all over the globe fighting for a bunch of sissies who can't do their own fighting?"

"I think Adolph Hitler is a frightening man who has designs on all of Europe. That is enough for me," she snapped.

Elizabeth had seen the newsreels at the picture show, seen the stern little man who shrieked his speeches to frenzied, cheering crowds, their voices swelling, unifying into a chant of homage to him, to his cause. It put her in mind of the Gene Talmadge speech she had heard years before, the building fervor, the response of the men massed at his feet. "He doesn't seem so scary," she said. "Just angry and good with words."

Jack put his cigarette out, exhaling a mushroom cloud to join the dying wisps above them. "He is a bad man, Baby," he said. "But like your granddaddy says, folks have to fight their own fight."

"But wouldn't you fight to help me if you could?" Elizabeth asked.

"Of course I would help you, Baby. But wars are different. A lot of blood to be spilled," her father said. "And—"

"Don't upset the child," Pearl interrupted.

"And they cost so much money that we'd run out of what little we have here," Jack continued.

"Because she'll take on and get me upset," Pearl went on.

"Oh, Jack," Miss Lucille said. "You know as well as I do that a war would be just the kind of boost the economy needs to pull folks out of this mess."

"Why are you all ignoring me?" Miss Pearl demanded. "I think we should talk about something else."

"Oh, I declare," Lucille sighed. "If a family cannot discuss the events of the day then I don't know what. And nobody is going to come marching up Isabella Street, Elizabeth, but when your friends need your help you should be there. Your granddaddy knows that from all the elections he's been through."

"Goddammit, woman!"

"Language, Camp."

"No, by God. The hell with 'language.' This is serious as hell and if that goddamn gimp of a leader doesn't have the steel to stand up to—"

Miss Lucille drew in a sharp breath, eyes wide and furious, an expression Elizabeth had never seen her wear.

"I need a taste of brandy, Jack," Miss Pearl said, too quickly.

"I'll get it," he said. "What about you, Mother?"

"It is one thing," Lucille said evenly, "to disagree with what one's president does. But it is low-down dirty pool to sink to insults and name-calling. And I won't have it. Not in this house."

Silence. Elizabeth watched them, all frozen in the moment, a standoff: her father half out of his chair, suspended in time in his quest for peach brandy; her mother holding a palm to her mouth, tense, alert; Miss Lucille's hardening fury at her husband's overt cruelty and determination to control her instincts; and Campbell's gaze back at her, sizing her up, reassessing, revising his vision of her. A snapshot of anger and fear. Elizabeth sensed that she was watching something significant, and in the space of seconds a subtle little current in the family tide had shifted. Her grandfather took a drink, ice cubes tickling the glass, a delicate clink. "Jack, you better get these ladies their brandies before there's a free-for-all," he said.

"Yes, sir."

And with that they all fell into their places on the stage, inhabiting their characters, her grandmother turning up the radio, her grandfather buffing the handle of a pistol, her mother flipping the grainy pages of a magazine. Elizabeth felt the prickle of the nap of fabric at her neck as she rested her head on the roll of cushioning. She watched the once-white ceiling, a whisper of beige now, from smoky evenings and time. She thought she heard someone laughing down the alley that ran alongside the house, just outside the windows. It was the kind of faraway laughter that barely brushed the trees outside, sending a gentle shiver through the leaves, and she wondered why her people could not just leave one another be.

The sounds of an argument woke her a couple of mornings later, before daylight. She could hear dishes rattling across the hall, in the kitchen, could smell the sausage cooking, hear the sizzle. But it was the words she homed in on, as lengthy, full-blown, high-volume arguments were rare, almost nonexistent, in the Lacey family.

"But this is the Saturday of the church bazaar, Camp," her grandmother was saying. "Elizabeth has to go to the church with us and help out." It was not an odd thing to say, but it was said so loudly.

"Dammit, I told you, woman, she can miss a church function one time!"

"It's all right Mama," Jack said, more quietly.

"You should be ashamed of yourself, Jackson Owens Lacey! To subject her to all of that on the eve of the Lord's day when she promised Reverend Stryker. Are you going to allow this, Pearl?"

Elizabeth's mother murmured something inaudible.

"Goddammit to hell," her grandfather shouted. "Nobody 'allows' anything in this house but me. And Jack stands in for me. Are you allowing it, Jack?"

"Yes, sir."

"The language! The Lord's name! This is all just because of the other night, isn't it?" her grandmother said. "It's because of what I said about Roosevelt."

"The hell with Roosevelt!" Camp yelled. "Get the goddamn breakfast on the table, woman!"

Silence for a few seconds, then a clatter of plates, a slamming of cabinet doors. In a moment, angry footsteps strode across the hall, her bedroom door was flung open, and her grandfather shouted, "Get up, girl! We got some bird shooting to do."

Elizabeth sat straight up in bed, eyes wide. "I can go?"

"Yes, by God, you can go. Now get dressed. Don't wear nothing fancy."

"Yes, sir!" She scrambled out of bed. This was it. She was being included in the men's world, invited without even asking. She didn't care why, didn't care that her grandmother disapproved, that she was being used as a pawn in a family squabble. She didn't mind the icy, silent breakfast with her family, the way her grandmother refused to pass things to her grandfather, the way her mother ran her fingers through her hair over and over, the way she always did when she was upset. All Elizabeth cared about was being included, being allowed to soak up every bit of the ritual, a thing she had wanted for so long she did not for a moment stop to think about the reality of it.

Her grandfather's farm was twelve miles north of town, had a little frame house on it where Styles Fetter lived, overseeing the planting of crops over 120 acres. They were to shoot on the east side of the property, where Styles had plowed over a harvested field a few weeks earlier. Every day since, he had baited the field with corn to draw the dove in to feed.

Hotshot, Jack, and Camp had loaded equipment and guns in the bed of a pickup where Elizabeth sat, looking at the morning sky, searching for birds, thinking of the sun as a big slice of cantaloupe dipped in raspberry sauce. The men dropped shells into the chambers of their shotguns, a thunking sound unfamiliar to her, as was their talk. They had brought Royce Fitzhugh along since he was becoming such a fixture in the sheriff's office. Besides, Camp said, Royce needed some decent influences in his life.

Every once in a while Elizabeth caught Royce passing her a glance, reaffirming her awareness that he was sweet on her, just like some of the other boys were. It filled her with a swell of confidence, this emotional consequence she was able to exact with nothing more than her presence.

"They're all over it this morning," Jack said, as a flurry of dove lifted from the field. "Hotshot is going to have a mess of birds to clean this evening." He raised his gun to check the sight.

"Floppy-head birds," Hotshot said. "Dog-gone luck and the creek don't rise."

"Do I get to shoot, Daddy?"

"Oh, no, Baby no. This thing would knock you on your caboose."

"Please?"

"Oh, let her shoot," Camp said.

"She can't shoot," Jack protested. "This thing is bad to kick."

"Them old mules be kicking sometime," Hotshot said, then, "I like to kick bottle caps."

"I'll let her shoot," Royce said, ignoring Hotshot. "She can lean back on me and the kick won't be bad."

Elizabeth rolled her eyes. Royce was trying to take charge, have her lean against him, and that was a thing she alone would decide and make happen. "I want to shoot with Daddy," she said, stern and full of force.

"I want to shoot with Daddy," Royce mocked good-naturedly.

Hotshot cackled. "My daddy said I was crazy."

Elizabeth slapped Royce's arm, wondering how long it would take to chip away at his full-of-himself, know-it-all look and dismantle his cockiness when it came to her.

"Why are you so set on shooting?" Royce asked, smirking.

"I just want to see how it feels, that's all," Elizabeth said.

"It feels loud and bruising, to a little girl," her father said.

"I'm not a little girl. I'll never be a little girl again. I'm a usurper and the edge of a star."

"Edge of a star," Hotshot echoed.

Her father chuckled. "You're a strange delight, Baby. That's for certain."

Royce winked at her.

"Come on," Elizabeth sing-songed. "Please?"

"Let her," Camp insisted. "Like Royce said, she can lean back against your chest. You can help her aim."

The Remington was much heavier than she expected. Her father showed her how to raise the barrel with her palm, how to move it, where to look to get the bird in her sights.

"My arm will give out," she said. "Help me hold it."

Her father helped her lift the gun, practicing a few times while her grandfather gave instructions. "Just pick one out and line him up, follow the sights here," he said, "and then, blam! Drop him out of the sky."

"Blam!" Hotshot said.

"Will it be loud?" she asked, knowing it would be, remembering her grandfather's pistol fired into the air, after it clicked against Hotshot's head.

"You get used to it," her grandfather said.

From the cover of the tree line, two, then four birds broke free, flapping and floating on the tepid November breeze. Elizabeth watched the way they dipped and rose past one another, leaving curled streaks of gray and dusty purple across the sky. They were beautiful, alive, artists of the atmosphere, sweeping their spirits across the canvas of clouds.

"Up!" her daddy said.

"Get him, get him!" came from Royce, raising his shotgun.

Elizabeth felt her arm lifted, and "Pull the trigger," he said, but she didn't really think she wanted to, not now, as it sank in, finally, what was expected. This thing that had been mysterious and desirable was no longer a thing she wanted to do, and she was many months past wanting to be a boy. This was a thing she wanted when she was a little girl, and she realized how it ran counter to the way she defined herself now, as a queen moving forces, strategizing victories for the good. She let the barrel drop, down from the birds, as her daddy put his finger over hers and squeezed, an ear-thudding explosion, and the recoil shoved her back into his chest. A second explosion came then, from her grandfather's shotgun, and through the ringing in her ears she heard him say, "You got him, Elizabeth! You got him!" and she saw the bird, zigzagging in a crazy, earth-bound motion.

"But I thought I missed," Elizabeth said.

"No, you got him good. You blew him right out of the sky," Camp said.

"Damn beginner's luck," Royce said.

"'Beginner's luck' nothing," Camp said. "She's got the Lacey eye. Now run pick him up."

"Where?" She felt disoriented, by the loudness of the gunshots, by the glee in her grandfather's voice, "You got him!" and because she was so certain she could not have possibly gotten him, was nowhere near him.

"He's over yonder," Royce said, pointing to the left, "about thirty yards out. Want me to go fetch it?"

"I'll send Hotshot after it," Jack said.

"Yes, sir," Hotshot said. "Doo-dah day."

"Hell, no," Camp said. "See, Baby, it's always been a rule—and a Lacey hunting rule is written in stone—that you got to pick up your own birds the first time out and not claim any you ain't shot." He turned to Jack. "Right, boy?"

Her father chuckled. "That's right. Run on, Elizabeth."

"Where?" she whispered, walking out into the plowed field, crushing dirt clods with the soles of her riding boots, thinking, *How could I have hit it? How could I have ever thought I wanted to do this?*

Then she saw it, a gray-feathered, blood-speckled creature making feeble little pulls with one of its wings, the other mangled at its side. It lay very still for a moment then thrashed against the ashy dirt clods.

Elizabeth dropped to her knees. "Come and help it! It's hurt!" She looked back over her shoulder and screamed. "Come help!"

Her father said something to Hotshot and the boy ran out to where she knelt, putting her fingers out, wanting to soothe the animal, but drawing her hand back whenever it jumped or quivered, horrified by the fact that they enjoyed killing such creatures and that she had hit one, too, or so her grandfather said.

"Come a thunder," Hotshot said.

"Help it!"

"Don't cry," Hotshot said, as she realized she was sobbing.

"Help it, Hotshot. Help it! Do something."

Hotshot reached down and, in one fluid motion, snatched the bird up by the head and flipped the body around, breaking its neck. "Floppy-head bird," he grinned.

"No!" Elizabeth screamed, flailing at him, pounding on his back, his upper arms, with her fists. Hotshot dropped the bird as the two of them fell into the furrows, at the same time she heard someone running toward them, felt arms pulling her away from Hotshot, heard Royce's voice saying,

"Take it easy, girl. Easy."

"Shut up!" Elizabeth said, sitting up in the dirt. She pointed to Hotshot, who had picked up the bird again. "Give it to me!"

"Damn, you're a scrapper," Royce said.

"You give it to me," Elizabeth cried, hiccupping.

"Give what?" Royce asked, kneeling, pulling her next to him, his arm around her shoulder, feeling like Brother Stryker's touch when he hugged her that time.

She wrenched away from Royce and toward Hotshot. "You give me my bird."

Hotshot sat up, giving her a dazed look, dropping the dove one more time, then, "I didn't, I didn't, I didn't."

"Yes, you did!" Elizabeth screamed.

"Damn sure did," Royce agreed.

"You killed it!" she screamed louder. "Why did you do that? Why?" She scooped the bird up in her palms, still crying, standing, leaving Hotshot mumbling, "I didn't," over and over again, Royce shaking his head. She walked toward the men and held the bird out like an offering.

"Good God Almighty," her grandfather said. "Has everybody lost their goddamn mind?"

"Hotshot killed it," Elizabeth sobbed.

Her father put his arm around her shoulders. "It was going to die, Baby. Hotshot just made it quicker. It was a kindness."

"Stop your crying," her grandfather said.

"I want to go home," she said, "and bury it."

"Lord God! Stop that crying," her grandfather said. "And now she's got the nigger crying." He jerked his head at Hotshot, who sat in the dirt, knees up, with his head buried in his arms.

A piece of Elizabeth wanted to go see about Hotshot, but he was just like the rest of them, had participated in it all, did so regularly. She looked down at the bird. "I want to go home."

"I tell you what," her grandfather yelled. "You always wanted to be a boy, always after your daddy and me to bring you along. Well you better be glad you ain't a boy, 'cause I'd damn sure be ashamed of the way you're carrying on right now."

"It's all right," Jack said. "She can go home. I'll take her and come right back."

"This is ridiculous."

"I want to go home. I hate this," Elizabeth sobbed. "I hate you," she said to her grandfather.

"Don't you talk to me like that!"

"I don't care." She cradled the bird next to her chest. "I don't care."

"That's enough, Baby Doll," her daddy said.

"You ain't going to let her—"

"Yes, sir, I am," her daddy said. "And I'm carrying her home."

Elizabeth climbed into the cab of the truck while Campbell followed her every move with a furious stare. Then he walked over to her open window. "I'll hit a few for you, then," he said, cold-eyed. He marched back over to the edge of the field, just as another flurry of birds scattered across the sky. Her grandfather arched the barrel of his shotgun across the horizon and fired, cackling as two doves plummeted to the dirt not far from where Hotshot sat, Royce standing beside him. Elizabeth did not see Royce draw back his foot, kicking into Hotshot with all his might, then again, while Hotshot covered his head and wailed until Campbell Lacey finally hollered to Royce, "That's enough, son. I think you've made your point."

"Don't be too hard on your granddaddy," her father said as they rode toward home. "He doesn't really know how to be tender."

Elizabeth still cradled the bird next to her. "It isn't right," she said. "It's my fault."

"That's a strange thing to say."

"Why? It *is* my fault."

"Oh, Baby Doll, you can't take it all to heart. It's part of life, that's all. You just shouldn't be up in it, that's all."

"It isn't right," she repeated.

"What will you do with your bird?"

"I'm going to bury it by the goldfish pond and say a prayer over it."

"Alright. You do that. But don't be hard on your granddaddy and don't speak to him with disrespect."

"Yes, sir," she said, thinking she would never feel the same toward her granddaddy, that no matter how she spoke to him or pretended to feel, she would never trust him again, had not, in fact, for quite a while. She thought of the way Campbell Lacey put his empty pistol to his head, so casual, so tickled to get a reaction from her. Well she would never give him that satisfaction again. Things were different now. *He that telleth lies shall not tarry in my sight,* she thought. Everybody else in her family might fear his sharp words, his presence, but she would never again let him know he could draw such feelings out of her.

She buried the dead creature as soon as they got home, its limp head flopping over, just as Hotshot described, the blood-speckled body with its mangled wing nestled in one of her mother's old doilies. She dug a hole in the black dirt with a gardening spade and, once the dove was interred, she sat by the goldfish pond a long time, smoking, an open Bible in her lap, poring over the pages, wondering why she had ever thought the pastimes of the men appealing. She had gotten it wrong, had confused the things they did together with the advantage they had. And at once she was more certain that she would have the ultimate advantage, now that she was coming to know the earthy pull of her own flesh.

She thought of how easily she had drawn Royce Fitzhugh's stare to her bare thighs, how Brother Stryker watched her from the pulpit on those Sundays she went through the motions of attending church with her family. She would test the waters, she decided, with lots of boys, get a true idea of how malleable they could be. She would test them, and then others. She would begin by getting Royce to drive her to a honky-tonk in Albany, show her places, dance with her, and find out how far he was willing to go to get another glance—just a glance—at her panties. She pressed her palm to the little mound of rich, moss-rooted soil and felt the push of the dove's corpse against the cool black dirt, while a photograph configured itself in her mind, a picture all wings and feathers and pellets and blood, shading over another fragment of her sense of safety.

*

The goddamn runty little bastards had done it, really fucking done it. What had at first been a deadening shock was now melting into hot, molten anger. The goddamn cowards had sneaked up on them while they were sleeping and blasted them the hell out of their bunks.

Royce folded back the front page of the *Albany Herald* to read the articles one more time, about the great plumes of smoke from the battleships, about the ocean's oil-slicked surface laced with flames, about the waves of planes diving, letting loose their cargo, obliterating much of the fleet, crippling even more. He read about the dead and the soon-to-be-dead, about the shock of the explosions and the flesh-eating flames that sprawled across a quiet, routine Sunday morning in the Pacific. "Sons of bitches," he muttered.

"Read me what it says." His mother lay on her bed in the front room, bedside table cluttered with beer bottles, a stiff-breaded, half-eaten peanut butter sandwich, and a heavy red glass ash tray overflowing with butts and peelings from the orange she was sucking on. Her dull brown hair was tangled and she wore an aging, quilted yellow robe. Royce sat across from her, on the brown sofa, its cushions mangled and stained with the spilled drinks of evenings past.

A train whistle sounded and the little house trembled as a freight pulled into town, coming to a squealing stop on the tracks outside. His mother slurped on a section of the orange, and the gas heater hissed red-and-blue-flamed heat into the drafty room while he read, his anger rising with each paragraph, his desire to be away from her intensifying with every slurp of her lips against orange pulp.

"I'm signing up first thing tomorrow," he said, finally.

"What do you mean?" She licked sticky fingers.

"I mean I'm planning to join up and go kick some Jap butts, that's what. I knew it would come to this."

"But there's no fight going on," she said, picking up one of the beer bottles, checking to see if there was any liquid left, then turning it up.

"Hell, ain't you heard what I just read? That don't sound like a fight to you?" He watched her pick some orange pulp from her eyetooth and flick the pulp to the floor beside the bed. "Trust me, there'll be a fight."

"That don't mean you got to go," she said, picking up another bottle.

"Sure it does," Royce said. Maybe, he thought, he should even thank the little yellow bastards for giving him a way out of his mother's third-rate, one-woman bordello.

"But you're just a baby," she whined.

The sound of her voice made his skin crawl. She whined like that to some of the men who dropped in. "Didn't you bring me no beer, Baby?" she would say, or, "Aw, where's my big kiss?" or, when they were leaving, "Is Daddy coming back to see me?"

Royce stood, tossing the newspaper on the gnarled sofa cushions. "I ain't a damn baby. And I'm signing up tomorrow to go pound some Japs."

"Well, I can't say as I blame you." She sat up a little taller. "And won't you be handsome in a uniform! I'll be so proud."

What do you know about pride, he thought, just as the sound of glass breaking next door caught their attention, and then a shout, "Get out here, Ling!"

Royce stood, slipped into his jacket, and stepped out on the front porch, into December's chill. A half dozen men stood in the front yard of the Chinaman's house, murmuring to one another. "Hidy, Royce," one of them said, and Royce recognized him as one named Earl, who stopped in to see his mother every once in a while.

Another man, Joe Taylor, said, "Reckon you can get your coward of a neighbor to come out here?"

Before Royce could answer, the Chinaman's door opened.

"That's right, get on out here!" someone yelled.

Chen looked uncertain, confused. "You want Chen Ling?" He walked to the top of the steps, where the men were grouped up.

"Naw, hell, we sure as hell don't."

The men chuckled, and Royce studied the Chinaman's dazed expression, thinking about the kindness he had offered Royce years earlier, the refuge he had taken on Chen Ling's porch, the late-night games of dominoes.

"Don't want your kind nowhere around here," Earl said.

Royce's mother joined him on the porch. "Y'all going to run him off, I hope?" she said.

"You got it, Mona," one of the men said.

"I don't know. I think we might just whup him good," Taylor said, climbing the steps and grabbing Chen's arm before he could retreat.

Chen's voice broke a little, his eyes now fearful. "You explain Chen."

"You explain Chen," someone mocked. "Little gook can't even talk right."

Royce had a fleeting urge to speak up for the Chinaman, tell them he was not all bad, that he wasn't in on the attack, being all the way in Georgia when it happened. Then he thought it was odd that Chen Ling had not entered his thoughts today, not until now.

Taylor shoved the Chinaman down the steps. The group moved back and let him tumble onto the dirt yard. He pulled himself into a sitting position and looked up with a beseeching kind of expression. "No hurt Chen. Chen good neighbor."

"Well, whup him if you have to," Royce's mother said. "But I've always wanted him gone from here. He gives me the creeps."

"Don't worry, Mona," Earl said. "We got that covered, too." He jerked his head toward the railroad tracks. "See that boxcar yonder?"

"Yeah," she said.

"Well, Joe's got friends with the railroad. Done worked out a free one-way ticket."

"Where to?" Royce asked.

"To a place called Someplace Else."

"No. Chen good neighbor. Elly-Beth, Hotshot come see. Roy Fitz."

"Good neighbor, my ass."

"Ain't you seen the newspapers today?"

The newspaper. The attack. The carnage. The implications. At once Royce knew what he had to do. He slipped back into the house, walked over to his mama's bedside table and opened the drawer. He could hear the conversation, just out front.

"Sure. Sure. Very bad news. Bad."

"You really think it's bad news, huh?"

"Very bad. Also sad. Very bad shame."

Royce picked up his mama's pistol, the Colt .45 she had used to chase Lucas Fitzhugh away. He flicked open the cylinder to make sure it had bullets in it, knowing it did, just in case some man got rough with her.

"It's a shame all right," Taylor said. "It's a shame we got savages like you in the world. And right here, up in and amongst us."

"No. No," Chen pleaded. "Chen good neighbor. Attack bad news. Bad shame."

Royce stepped back onto the porch, the pistol nestled in the pocket of his jacket, cool against his palm.

"Lying bastard. You really are proud of your people, ain't you?"

"People?"

"Yeah, your people. Fucking Japs."

"Oh, no!" Ling said, letting go of a laugh that was tense and relieved at the same time. "America citizen, America citizen." He slapped his chest with his palm.

"I don't give a shit how you slipped into the country," Taylor said.

"Born Los Angeles," Chen slapped his chest again. "America citizen."

"You think that gets the sorry Jap blood out of your veins?"

Chen laughed the tense laugh again. "No. Got wrong. Not Japanese. *Chinese. Chinese.*"

"Japanese, Chinese, what difference does it make? They all a bunch of slanty-eyed gooks."

"Hey, chink," Earl said. "Is it true a chink's pussy gaps sidewards?"

The men laughed.

"Chen good neighbor," the Chinaman said again, his voice trembling, breaking.

Taylor drew his arm up and came down hard on the side of the Chinaman's head in a backhand. "Shut your savage mouth!"

Royce gripped the handle of the pistol, slid it out of his pocket, and leveled it at the group. He imagined he was a lawman, bringing order to the mob. "Don't hurt him," he said, adopting the deep, authoritative voice he had practiced on solitary afternoons at the sheriff's office.

"The hell you say."

"What the—"

"Royce, put that away!" his mama said.

"Who does he think he is?"

"Hey, Mona, do something about your boy."

"Royce, put my gun up," his mother said again.

"Shut up," he said, one of the few times he had spoken such words to her, letting out a little of the venom stored up in him behind her years of betrayal.

"What did you say to me? You got no truck—"

"Shut up!" Royce yelled, teeth gritted.

She shrank back against the banister. The group of men was silent. Chen Ling's eyes begged him and thanked him at the same time.

Taylor waved him off. "Go on, Royce. You just a kid."

The men chuckled, but fell silent when Royce pulled back the hammer, a silence deepening with his next words.

"Yeah, I'm a kid all right. I'm a kid who's going to be a soldier come tomorrow."

Some of the men looked down at their feet. A couple of them cleared their throats.

Taylor squinted. "That is a fact." he said in a quiet, even reverent tone. "But—"

"That is a damn true fact," Royce said. "Any of you old geezers going to join up?"

"That ain't fair, Royce," Earl said. "You know we'd go with you if we could."

"Hell yeah!"

"That's right."

"But you ain't going, right?" Royce moved the aim of the barrel from man to man. "Am I right?"

Taylor sighed, deep, heavy. "What's your point?"

"The point is, y'all ain't going to hurt him," Royce said, and Chen sent him a slight nod, encouraging him, expressing gratitude with his eyes.

"How you figure that?" Taylor said.

"Easy. Three things. First, I got a gun. Second, I'm fixing to go do some for-real fighting, not beating up a skinny little chink and calling myself helping my country out."

"And what else?"

"What else is I figure on coming back in one piece and getting on as a deputy. It might make a good impression on Old Man Lacey if I take y'all in right now."

"Wait a damn—"

"But I'd just as soon forget it," Royce said. "Can we do that?"

The group of men exchanged glances. Chen Ling nodded at Royce, sending him an echo of a smile. Finally Taylor said, "Yeah, Royce. I reckon we can do that."

"Get up, Chen Ling," Royce said.

The Chinaman stood. "Thank you Roy Fitz." He nodded at the men, who were turning to leave. "Thank you. All good neighbor. All good."

"Wait a minute," Royce said.

Taylor turned around. "Yeah?"

"I didn't mean I don't want him gone."

Chen looked puzzled all over again. "Roy Fitz?"

Royce sent him a cold, unforgiving stare.

"Say what, Royce?" Earl asked.

"I said I want him gone. This town don't need no murdering gooks in it. And it's the least I can do for my poor old mama."

"No problem," Earl said.

"No! Roy Fitz!"

Now Royce leveled the gun at the Chinaman. "You shut up, god-dammit! You shut up and I'll let you leave without getting the shit beat out of you, you understand?"

Chen let out a shocked whisper. "Roy Fitz?"

"I'm doing you a favor," Royce insisted.

"No. No." Chen Ling's broken English dissolved into sobs, then, "Roy

Fitz good neighbor. This only home. No."

"If you don't shut your goddamn mouth I'm going to let them have you, you hear? Don't you get it? I'm going to let you out of this here, you son of a slit-eyed bitch. You understand?"

The Chinaman nodded, taking little breaths that got tangled up in an occasional sob.

"So we going to use that free ticket after all, huh?" one of the men asked.

"Yeah," Royce said, looking at the eyes of the Chinaman, eyes just as slanty and nasty as any pilot in the Japanese Imperial Air Force, hating him, thinking it wouldn't be soon enough when he finally got to slit a goddamn Jap from chin to nuts and gut him like a catfish.

"Hear that, chink? You going on a nice one-way trip."

Chen dropped his head, put his palm to his chest one last time. "America citizen," he whispered.

"All aboard," Taylor said.

"Just let him get some food and a blanket and put his murdering ass on the freight car."

"Then we're going to forget this. No bad feelings?" Taylor said.

"We're going to forget the whole thing," Royce said, staring at Chen's drooped shoulder, the shock of black hair on the bowed head.

"Thank you, Sweetie," his mama said, as a couple of the men led Chen into his house to gather up the items he would be allowed.

Royce did not answer. He simply lowered the gun and handed it off to her.

Taylor spoke to the men remaining outside. "I hear there's a lot of chinky knick knacks up in that house. Don't seem right to leave that stuff intact."

"Yeah, but we might ought to move on before any for-real laws come around," one of the men said.

"Hey, I seen Hotshot round by the bus station a while ago. Let's get him to do it."

"The dumb-ass nigger."

"Yeah!"

"That fool won't think nothing about smashing up a house. All we got to do is convince him it's fun."

"Piece of cake."

Royce looked at his mama. She had de-cocked the gun and put it in the pocket of her robe, and the weight of it tugged down on the material, pulling it a little ways open, exposing most of her right breast. He started to tell her to have at least a little bit of shame, but figured it wasn't worth the fuss she would raise. He wished he was already on an island in the Pacific, gutting the bastards right and left, away from her moans and her men and her fetid scent. He glanced down at that bare breast shrouded in the faded yellow, quilted robe, pretty much all she ever wore anymore. She had just now gathered the attention of a couple of the men with that bit of flesh, and she stared in a specific way at Joe Taylor, sending him an invitation with her eyes and a little grin. Taylor grinned back.

Royce went on inside to the smell of the gas heat and stale cigarette smoke. His mother followed in a minute and crawled back into the bed with the squeaky springs, curling up beneath the quilts. "I'm going to take a little nap," she said, as if he might actually be interested to know that. He picked up the newspaper and began rereading the articles yet again. Soon he heard the Chinaman's front door slam, heard the men's boots scuffing in the dirt of the yard, then the gravel near the tracks. In a few moments he could hear the heavy, rattling sound of a freight car door sliding open, along with some garbled shouts. Then the door slid shut. By the time he finished reading the front page of the *Herald*, the train had pulled out of town, and the only accompaniment to the gas heater's hiss was the droning rhythm of his mother's snores.

He reckoned he would hear a racket in a while, when Hotshot began trashing the abandoned house next door, if the men indeed found him as they planned. There would be furniture overturned, plates and glasses shattered, and urine on the walls, he bet, but for now the only sound was Moaning Mona Anne, breathing, sleeping, doing something most folks took care of at night. She groaned in her sleep and rolled over, sending a forgotten section of orange tumbling across the unswept linoleum. Royce folded the newspaper back, and over, to page two, lay back on the lumpy cushions, and continued reading.

*

Elizabeth's Aunt Frances told her about the Chinaman the following day, as they sat on the side porch of the big Victorian house on Isabella Street, and Elizabeth dissolved into sobs. She put her head in her aunt's lap, cheeks wet against khaki slacks, remembering the kind eyes and big voice of Chen Ling, how he sang out her name, not nearly as musical as his.

She had awakened that morning to find the house swelling with the somber mood brought by prior news of the attack, the reality of it sinking in, and it was a mood she hoped would finally put her family at peace. After all, her father said, a declaration of war was the only reasonable thing to be done, so the entire family tide had turned in Miss Lucille's favor.

"War?" Elizabeth breathed, a sense of exhilaration rising in her, then a twinge of guilt at such dread-filled excitement.

"There is nothing else to do now. It's clear," her father said.

"Pearl Harbor is such a beautiful name for a place," Elizabeth said, turning her emotions to a different picture from war altogether. She repeated, "Pearl Harbor. Pearl Harbor." She let herself imagine sparkly white sand and beige, beauty-in-the-rough pearls strung into strands by mermaids and sea captains. She thought of how delicate and pale her own mother, Pearl-like-the-Harbor, was, just like the treasured bead.

"It's not so beautiful a place right now," her father said, and her mind's eye tried to see something not beautiful. She put her palms over her face.

"Don't fret everybody, Elizabeth," her mother said.

Elizabeth dropped her hands. "I won't. It's just hard to keep from thinking about it."

"Then shush about it," her mother said.

"I can't do that, either. Tell me more, Daddy."

Her mother sighed and picked up a crossword puzzle book.

Her father explained how the Japanese had bombed the ships, how they had slipped up on the fleet as most of the sailors were just waking up, how it was an outright murderous dare, an evil taunt, from a barbaric enemy with no honor whatsoever. "Remember that, Elizabeth. If ever a man takes on a fight, he should have the honor to fight fair. Anything else is the mark of a coward."

"Goddamn a mongrel race, just like the darkies and the Jews," her grandfather said. "Some breeds of folks ought to be eliminated altogether, I say."

"None of that!" her grandmother snapped. "None of that kind of talk. You promised!"

Elizabeth's mother laid down the puzzle she had been pretending to study and rubbed her forehead. "Now look what you've done, Elizabeth, with your questions. My head is splitting and you've made everybody touchy. Why don't you go outside and play?"

Elizabeth draped her body over the pillow on the floor, rolling it back and forth.

"Mongrels," her grandfather said under his breath as his wife swept out of the room. Then he stewed and huffed before leaving for work, while her grandmother began making grocery lists and menu plans for the coming week—to take her mind off the tension, Elizabeth decided. She rolled onto her back and held the long pillow next to her, embracing it. Then she began tossing and twirling it, a foot or so up, catching it into another embrace.

"Elizabeth!" her mother said. "Stop wiggling. Do something calming."

Elizabeth decided to try to read for a while. She was working her way through a dictionary-sized volume titled *The Complete Works of William Shakespeare*, rereading those she already knew, discovering those she did not. She took an obsessive interest in the tragedies these days, loved the way a particular plot would be woven through the cadences and intricacies of the meter. Now she could see Macbeth on the bloody field of battle, strategizing, being checkmated by the double-dealing lovers of power who would do him in along with themselves. She wondered if the soon-to-be war against the Japanese would have as many twists and ironies as a Shakespearean tragedy, knowing right away that it would.

Go outside and play, her mother had said, as if Elizabeth were still five years old and full of impotence cut by self-loathing. *Look what you've done.*

Go out and play. The refrain of her mother's words spun its thin threads around her spirit like the silky strands of a spider's web; Elizabeth had knocked that cobweb away over and over again until it made her too tired to bother anymore. She closed her book, deciding not to let the family's mood infect her or inhibit the strange feeling of excitement at the thought of living in a country at war.

Hotshot was sitting on the porch of Jubil's long-abandoned house, wearing one of Jack Lacey's handed-down corduroy jackets, sitting with a sad, head-dropped attitude of waiting, as if he still expected Jubil to come walking up at any moment. Even though he was a grown-bodied, whiskered-lipped young man past sixteen, he spent his days, when he was not doing chores, playing as if he were still very young. On this day there were a toy drum and a small American flag on the steps near his feet. When he heard Elizabeth approaching, he looked up and grinned big. "Look yonder," he said, pointing to his treasures.

"Where'd you get them?"

"Lady at the mercantile give it."

"She actually gave it to you? Old stingy Onnie Mae White?"

"On account of the 'tack."

"Pearl Harbor?" He seemed sad, Elizabeth thought, unusual for him. But she didn't believe he understood the magnitude of the previous day's events.

"I reckon. The 'tack in the train yard."

"No, it was ships," Elizabeth corrected. "Why are you sad?"

"What ships?"

"Never mind. Tell me more about why she gave it to you."

"One reason why is 'cause I was sad."

Elizabeth sighed. Finally. Now she might get the full story. "About the attack?"

"Yes'm."

"But there was another reason?" Hotshot could be patience-draining, when words had to be pulled from him, when sense had to be put together like a puzzle.

"Yes'm. She said I can march round the town."

"Why?"

"She say, call up folks' spirits."

Elizabeth decided to give up searching for the reason for his sadness and instead steer the conversation in a more cheerful direction. "Oh, like a call to arms."

"I reckon."

It came to her in an instant, a way to give Hotshot a lift. She thought of flags and frenzy and FDR headed for Warm Springs. "Like a parade!"

"Yes'm."

"Oh, Hotshot, wouldn't a parade be perfect?"

"Yes'm."

"Let's do that. Let's go all over the town. You bang the drum and I'll hold the flag."

"Yes'm."

The two of them marched up and down the streets, and people smiled at them, waved from passing cars, and a few even gave Hotshot a nickel for being such a good citizen. They marched through the courthouse, around the post office, in and out of stores, and along the railroad tracks. Then Elizabeth decided they should take their parade even further, to the neighborhoods, starting with Isabella Street and her Aunt Frances.

When they rounded the side of the house that faced a forest of azalea bushes, what Aunt Frances called the "private" side of the house, Elizabeth could see Aunt Frances and Miss Martha on the side porch. They sat close together on the soft-cushioned glider, sipping Coca-Colas. Miss Martha had her legs tucked beneath her, her hand on Aunt Frances's shoulder, and she was speaking softly to her and smiling. When Elizabeth and Hotshot approached the steps, she could see Miss Martha shift and turn away from her aunt, but that was how it was with them. Miss Martha often excused herself and went up to her room, the room she rented from Aunt Frances; yet Elizabeth knew, too, that they shared a room, at least sometimes, because once, when she dropped by with a bouquet of gardenias from Miss Lucille, she found signs of it. She entered through the never-locked side door and bounded up the steps to her aunt's room. The house was quiet, empty. Her aunt's sheets were all in a tumble and both sides of the bed had been slept in. There were iced tea glasses on both end tables and Miss Martha's school satchel was at the foot of the bed, along with her blue-ruffled robe. Beyond that, the room held an intense, secretive feeling. It was intriguing—that was the flavor Elizabeth always tasted when she was around them, forever coming upon the edge of a moment missed, knowing there was that hidden aspect of the relationship the two women kept only for themselves.

Jaffe and Mary Margaret, Aunt Frances's Boston terriers, skittered yapping out onto the porch from their permanent lounging spots on the living room divan, and Hotshot shrieked with delight. When Elizabeth had first started bringing him around her aunt's house, years ago, he had been terrified of the dogs and would dip his head and hide behind Elizabeth's tiny frame. But Elizabeth taught him to be gentle with the dogs, to talk to them in a calm, slow voice, showed him how Jaffe liked to be rubbed on the stomach, how both dogs would run and fetch a knotted-up ball of old wool stockings. Soon Hotshot loved nothing better than watching the dogs chase the ragged ball across the back yard, nipping and growling at one another over which would get possession of it, which would have the honor of returning it to whoever had the patience to pitch it again.

"Here you are, Hotshot," Aunt Frances said, handing him a newer version of the stocking ball, holding the door open for the dogs, who now wagged their little nubbed tails, panted their excitement, and pawed at the boy to come and play.

"Dogs!" he yelled, dropping the toy drum to the grass. "Snappy jaws!" And he ran out onto the lawn.

Elizabeth sat on the glider next to her aunt, pushing with her feet until it went back and forth far enough to satisfy her. It made squenching, squeaking sounds that blended with the droning hum of the ceiling fan. "I'm so exasperated with Hotshot," she said.

"What is it, Waterbug?"

"He doesn't understand me. He hasn't for a long time. I can't talk to him. He doesn't explain things to me, either."

"You know how hard it is for him to understand," Aunt Frances said, "and express himself, too."

"I know. But I've talked to him so much. You'd think it would sink in sooner or later."

Aunt Frances sighed. "You know, I can't help thinking you've missed out by never having girlfriends over the years. Just Hotshot."

"I haven't missed out on anything," Elizabeth said. "Except not being understood."

"But I thought you had Hotshot for that."

Now it was Elizabeth who sighed. "I guess so. Hotshot and everybody else. I believe I've outgrown him. It's sad."

"You haven't outgrown me, Waterbug. And I do try to understand."

"Do you think you will ever understand me?"

"I'll try. But wouldn't you like some girlfriends to talk to as well? Tell your secrets to?"

"I have you to tell my secrets to. Anyway, they make me ill, all of them. They act so insipid. And they don't have any sense of the moment."

"What do you mean?"

"You know what I mean, Aunt Frances. How to keep from letting moments pass—moments that have the potential to be felt and heard and held. The ones that might turn into one of the photographs in my head, you know?"

"Not exactly," Aunt Frances said.

"Only I can't choose the photographs. I try, all the time. But they choose me."

"Why is that, do you think?"

"Because there was nothing there—nothing good, anyway. I think the pictures are painting me, for good or not."

Aunt Frances was looking at her the way she always did, betraying no emotion, no condemnation, no befuddlement. Her questions were always simple and to the point. "Don't you think you can decide who you are? Can't you paint yourself?"

"Well, yes. Some. And I already have, sort of. But the bad pictures will never go away."

"What have you sort of decided to paint?"

Elizabeth smiled. "Mainly I've decided to be bold, bold, bold. And honest."

"When did you decide that?"

Elizabeth loved the way her Aunt Frances talked with her, never reacting in the extreme, like Miss Pearl, but never under-reacting, like her father. "I've been deciding it for a while. Don't you think it's a good plan?"

"It is well and good to be bold," Aunt Frances said. "And especially good to be honest. Just try not to be reckless."

Elizabeth let that advice pass and asked, "Do you think Mama and Daddy understand each other?"

"I imagine so, in their way."

"I don't think they do. They are never together. She sleeps alone at night and he is at work all day."

Aunt Frances reached over and patted her knee. "Waterbug, that's not a thing for you to worry about."

"I just want to know if they have—or ever had—a great love. I don't think they do, not now. Why do you think that is?"

Her aunt leaned back in the glider. "Oh, I think it amounts to a sort of distance. And the distance was always there. Pearl has never been all that affectionate with him. She has a hard time, for some reason. But I do believe he loves her."

"I gave up on her understanding me a long time ago."

"That is probably very wise of you," Aunt Frances laughed.

"And I used to really like spending time with Hotshot. I felt like he understood me."

"And you were right. He did understand a lot of what you talked about when you were younger. But you know his situation. It's just as you said. You've grown way past him, that's all."

"I love him," Elizabeth said.

"I know. And do be sweet to him right in through now, Waterbug."

"Why now?"

"You know. About all the trouble yesterday."

"What trouble?"

"Good Lord, your granddaddy didn't tell you about Chen Ling? Everybody in town knows."

That was when Elizabeth buried her face in her aunt's lap and listened, tears staining a picture through her thoughts, while Aunt Frances told her the story. About how the sheriff was called when a passerby saw Hotshot carrying armfuls of Chen Ling's possessions, handing out trinkets to folks out for an evening walk. How her granddaddy wanted to lock him up but Jack told him there had to be more to it. How Hotshot cried and carried on and said a bunch of men gave him a quarter to go over there and tear up the place, that the Chinaman would laugh and think it was a good joke. How Hotshot didn't know any names, just said it was a bunch of men, men who were laughing real loud. How Mona Fitzhugh allowed she heard voices, thought she heard somebody say to put the gook on the train, but she wasn't too sure. No, Royce had not been there, she said.

Elizabeth was stunned. Not Hotshot. He liked the Chinaman, visited him often, played with the wind chimes every time the two of them stopped by.

The boy ran panting to the steps where he collapsed in a sitting position, the squatty little dogs jumping on him, licking his arms.

"Why did you do it?" Elizabeth screamed at him.

"Elizabeth!" Aunt Frances breathed.

The boy jumped. "Come a thunder?"

"Why did you take Chen Ling's treasures?"

Hotshot shook his head, fast and exaggerated. "I didn't. Nope. No'm." Then he muttered, "Crazy as a one-eyed dog."

"They sent him away. How could they send Chen Ling away?" She buried her head in her aunt's lap again.

Aunt Frances patted her and said, "Hotshot, run around front and get my mail, won't you?"

"Yes'm." He stood and the dogs trotted in circles around him. "Crazy dogs," he said. "One-eyed dogs."

Aunt Frances waited until he walked around the shrubbery to speak. "You have to be easy with Hotshot. I explained that. He is retarded. Martha said he had to have been manipulated somehow, and he is very easy to manipulate. He's not even in any trouble with your daddy, just like I said. Jack knows there were instigators involved."

"How does he know?"

"Your daddy said Hotshot wouldn't have acted that way on his own, and he's right, of course."

Elizabeth lifted her head from her aunt's lap. "But why would anyone make Chen Ling go away? And make Hotshot steal things? Who did it?"

"I don't know who it was," Aunt Frances said. "All I heard was a bunch of men went storming over to his house because of the news about Pearl Harbor."

"But why Chen Ling? He isn't even Japanese."

"People so full of hate are nothing but pure ignorance," her aunt said. "Chen Ling could have been Mexican or, hell, Hawaiian even, and they would have done the same thing."

"Did they hurt him?"

"They didn't beat him, if that's what you mean, according to what Mona Fitzhugh heard. Just shoved him around and told him they'd kill him if he didn't get out of town."

"So they did hurt him." Elizabeth felt her stomach go into dips, imagining how frightened and wounded inside the kind man must have been.

"Of course they did. It had to hurt him to have to leave his home and all of his possessions. A lifetime of memories." She sighed and sipped her Coca-Cola.

"I have to go over there," Elizabeth said.

"Oh, Sweetie, no. I'm sure it's a mess. And what if those men come back?"

"I don't have to go by myself. You could take me there."

"I don't know. It's—"

Elizabeth put her hands over her ears. "No. You don't understand. I have to go there. I have to go there and say goodbye."

*

The signs said "No Trespassing" and "By Order of the Blackshear County Sheriff," and there was the biggest padlock Elizabeth had ever seen on the door. Hotshot hung back from the porch, mumbling, shaking his head, but Elizabeth and her aunt peered in through the front window.

"Good Lord," Aunt Frances breathed.

Furniture was overturned, sofa cushions scattered, and sections of newspaper sprawled out the headlines: "Japan Attacks U.S. Pearl Harbor" and "FDR to Address Nation." The precious trinkets and wood carvings were strewn across the floor. Elizabeth pressed her palm against the glass pane, next to one that was shattered, its sharp, ragged edges framing the destruction inside.

A door slammed. "I reckon y'all ain't got no business here," a woman's voice said.

Elizabeth turned to the sound, which came from the house next door. Royce's mother slouched against the banister, holding a cigarette, wearing a bathrobe, open and loose. Her dark hair was tangled and one of her front teeth was missing where it had not been missing a few years earlier, when Elizabeth saw her at the Talmadge rally. The thing that struck Elizabeth was Mona Anne's eyes, chocolate brown and soulless, with a stare that seemed to look into nothing and care about less than that.

"The sheriff tacked up them signs last evening after that nigger yonder tore the place up." She jerked her head to indicate Hotshot.

Hotshot looked down at his feet and continued to mumble.

"It's all right," Aunt Frances said. "I'm Sheriff Lacey's daughter. We just came by to look."

"Camp Lacey's daughter, huh?" the woman said, taking a drag on the cigarette. "Well your money ain't no good here. I only take men."

Elizabeth felt her aunt's mood shift, heard her say, "We don't have any need to talk to you at all. Come on, Elizabeth."

But Elizabeth was not budging, wanted to know more. "Do you remember me? I used to come visit Chen Ling."

"Sure I remember you. I remember you bringing that half-wit nigger over time to time. I never thought you had no business over there. It just encouraged that foreigner to stay, that's all."

"Now you stop fussing at this child," Aunt Frances said.

"I know all you fine folks," Mona Anne went on, "and the airs you put on when everybody knows—"

"Get in the car, both of you," Aunt Frances snapped.

Hotshot scrambled into the rear of the coupe, but Elizabeth stared at the woman on the porch, putting together bits and pieces of things she heard the boys at school say, about a lady by the tracks who took money for letting men do things with her, things Elizabeth read about at the library. She thought of her own family's talk, and the way folks stared at Mona Anne at the Talmadge rally years ago, and what the biblical tales of "strange" women might really mean. "Are you a whore?" she asked, calm and matter-of-fact.

"What kind of a smart-mouthed little brat says a thing like that?"

"Oh, Lord," Hotshot said from the back seat. "It's the Judgment."

"Elizabeth! What are you doing? That's not any way to—"

"Bold, Aunt Frances. Remember? It's a vow. And honest."

"I always had you pegged for a brat," Mona Anne continued. "Flouncing up them steps and going right on in that chinky-eyed thing's house like it was tea time at the Ladies' Club."

"Let's go, Elizabeth," Aunt Frances said.

But Elizabeth persisted, taking the boldness Chen Ling said was hers. "Are you the one? The lady by the tracks who takes money and does things with men?"

"What if I am?"

"It's just that I never knew a whore. And I didn't realize the one whore in town was Royce's mama."

"At least he's got a mama that ain't loony," Mona Anne retorted.

Aunt Frances took her by the arm, but Elizabeth pulled away. "Who did this to Chen Ling?" she said. "What did he ever do to anybody?"

The woman pushed back her hair in a haughty gesture and grinned. "I done been asked all that by the laws. I ain't about to let no snot-nosed little brat ask me nothing."

"Do not talk to this child that way," Aunt Frances said.

"I'm not a child," Elizabeth said.

The woman on the porch snorted. "A spoiled-rotten little brat. I seen you over at the Chinaman's, making over him like he's something special. Making over my Royce like he's the sheik of the world."

"Chen Ling *was* special," Elizabeth said. "He is. He has a musical name and says my name like music. Anyone who didn't like him is lost."

The woman looked at her as if she were speaking Chinese all of a sudden, then she wrinkled her brow and said. "Well, me personally, I'm glad he's gone. He give me the heebie-jeebies."

"Mona!" a man's voice came from inside her house.

"What, Sugar Doll?"

"Get your hiney in here. I got to get on home."

"We have to go now, Elizabeth." Aunt Frances said. "You shouldn't be around this."

"I don't care," Elizabeth said, catching Mona's eye.

The woman gave her a withering, hate-filled look and said, "You are a wicked little brat that talks crazy. I bet you create a mess wherever you are," and she turned to go inside.

"Don't pay attention to her," Aunt Frances said, loud enough for Mona to hear. "She's a pitiful, dried-up seed hull of a woman who knows she only has one thing to offer, and not a very good thing at that."

Mona responded by turning and making kissy-lips at Frances, whose face reddened. "Pitiful," Aunt Frances repeated as Mona Anne slammed her screen door.

"Her house is dead," Elizabeth said, wondering how Royce had stood living there. Then she turned back to Chen Ling's front window. "But Chen Ling's house won't ever die. Ever. I want to take one more look."

Aunt Frances squeezed her shoulder. "I'll be in the car."

Elizabeth pressed her nose against the window and squinted again. Nothing had changed. Chen Ling was still gone. The rooms of his tiny home still looked as though they had been tumped over. He was still somewhere else, not here, where he belonged, where he would wave and sing out her name in three tones of pure goodness. She squinted harder into the dimness. The hanging picture of Shanghai was crooked, glass cracked in a spread web; the wood carvings and black lacquer box were no longer on the book shelves; and the floor was still littered with the Chinaman's knickknacks, brought to America by his mother, from far on the other side of the world, where people walked upside down.

That night Elizabeth lay on her bed, staring up at the dome of the canopy, wondering where Chen Ling was. Maybe he had found a nice little house not far from Sumner, another little by-the-tracks house he could fix up with new treasures he might find by the side of the road. Maybe he had run into Hotshot's daddy and they were riding the rails together, cooking over an open fire—a long-burning one—and laughing about the hambone dance. Maybe he was thinking about her, right this minute, and saying hello through the night's network of clouds. Maybe, if she tried really hard, she could will the moon's light to curl around him and keep him safe, so that the thin strands of silk in the beautiful Shanghai shirt did not cut and sting and blister across her renegade heart.

By Christmas of '42 young men were leaving Sumner in droves, going off to fight the Germans, the Italians, the Japanese. And in Albany, just a few miles up the road, in the clubs near Turner Field, Frances knew there was a steady stream of airmen, supply units, and mechanics making its way to the taverns and dance halls her niece—wild, rebellious, growing more so by the minute—loved to frequent these days.

It had started back in the summer, activity and exhilaration building with the swell in the ranks. That was when Elizabeth sought out those particular clubs, to feel the exhilaration, the turning of the wheels, the vibrant urgency, she told her aunt. Transportation was no problem. Elizabeth would simply bat her lashes and line up a ride with anyone—any male—who had enough gas ration to drive her over to Albany of a weekend.

The club owners near the airfield did not really care that she was underage. All she did was dance, at first, barefoot and beautiful. The Air Force boys loved her—gave her engraved charms for the jingly bracelets she wore—and the club owners wanted the Air Force boys to be happy, spend their cash freely. Lots of other teenage girls, albeit older, were in and out of the clubs, but Elizabeth seemed far ahead of them in awareness, especially when she was outside the margins of social expectations. And she loved breaking the rules.

It was not long before rumors floated around Sumner about Elizabeth being seen late into the night, at this club or that, drinking a bottle of beer, smoking a Chesterfield, beckoning servicemen to dance with her, even slipping her hand beneath their uniform blouses, pulling out their neck-

ties, and leading them onto the floor. Frances was not surprised at the stories, had seen something similar coming for years, even without the playground of a war effort. More than a few folks found Elizabeth's sensuality
unsettling, even though plenty of young soldiers had even younger girlfriends wearing engagement rings back home. Frances thought it was
probably more the attitude with which her niece conducted herself than
the specific things she supposedly did that had old ladies in an uproar. Still,
she felt compelled to check, to question, to see that Elizabeth was not
falling in over her head.

"Jack," she said to her brother, "You can't agree with her going off with
these—grown men who drive her to the bars and let her drink and carry
on."

"These 'grown men' are our friends and neighbors. And she's not 'carrying on,'" Jack would say, cementing his refusal to open his eyes. "She's
dancing with boys not much older than she is. She's on board with the war
effort. She's a one-gal U.S.O."

"Heavens," Miss Pearl would say, repeating Elizabeth's lies like a ven-
triloquist's dummy. "She rides over with her girlfriends from school, the
ones who are older and can drive." Then she would put her attention on
curling her hair or rubbing face cream on her wan cheeks.

But Frances knew there were no girlfriends, and the boys Elizabeth
flagged down for rides were hardly friends. They were chauffeurs, willing
servants, anxious to catch and hold a whiff of Elizabeth's scent in the cabs
of their trucks, and Elizabeth knew exactly how to manipulate each one.
Yes, it was a different dynamic than most girls her age had with boys. Most
girls had crushes and pined for steady boyfriends and played it coy. But not
Elizabeth. Elizabeth was fulfilling her vow to be bold, bold, bold.

"You are her grandmother," Frances said to her own mother, Lucille.
"It isn't like you not to step in and take charge of her. You did when she was
little."

Her mother sighed. "I *tried* to when she was little, remember? Elizabeth has always been a go-ahead child. She always went ahead and did
what she wanted. Always. Besides," Lucille said, as though she was trying to

convince herself, "I believe she's just out dancing, like she says."

Frances did not bother to approach her father with her concerns. Campbell had no sway whatsoever with Elizabeth, not any more. Once upon a time, Elizabeth had been a lot fearful, and later a bit fearful of Camp; but their piece of the family dynamic had shifted miles along that fault line, because of the dove-hunting incident, Frances's mother said. It was as if Elizabeth had simply made up her mind to pointedly ignore her grandfather's commandments, sometimes throwing out a good-natured "You don't mean that, Granddaddy, so I won't take that," or a vague Bible verse: "The froward tongue shall be cut out," or "Deliver me from the hand of strange children," or a hodgepodge of several verses. Elizabeth was not even frightened of the pistol that used to send her screaming to her daddy whenever Camp pointed it at his own head. But Frances was shocked the day Elizabeth pranked her grandfather by slipping the gun out of the holster as it hung on the hat tree. Her niece had sneaked off and unloaded it, then replaced it in the holster, Frances later found out.

"Watch this," Elizabeth whispered to Frances, who was over that evening for dinner. They sat in the living room waiting for the rest of the family to return from a shopping trip to Albany.

"Granddaddy, I'm disappointed in you," Elizabeth said, walking over to the holster.

"What for?" he said, before what she was doing sank in.

She snatched the gun from the holster and held it to her head. "I'm going to have to say goodbye," she said, shaking her head, slow and sad. "'Yea, though I walk through the valley of the sha—'"

"Good Lord!" Frances shrieked, and Camp leapt to his feet in a panic.

"Put that down!" he yelled. "Now! Put it down!"

But Elizabeth ran into the dining room, eluding him, pulling the trigger, click, then squealing with laughter as he realized the joke.

"You are not to touch that gun, ever," he said. "If your mother or your grandmother had seen that, you would have given them a heart attack."

"That's true, Elizabeth. That might have pushed your mother over the edge," Frances said.

"What edge?" Elizabeth asked, still laughing, pointing the gun at the ceiling, pulling the trigger.

"And where did you learn how to unload a pistol?"

"I think his name was, um, Ralph? Or Roger? It was an 'R' name. He took me out to the creek bank and let me shoot his gun."

Campbell reached for the weapon, but she aimed and clicked at the ceiling one last time.

Frances could not help smiling, even though she had been terrified moments earlier. Elizabeth had a nice sense of justice, it seemed, with a bit of the biblical "eye for an eye" thrown in.

Campbell snatched the gun from Elizabeth's grasp. "I forbid it," he said. "I forbid you to touch this gun."

But Elizabeth went on laughing. "Oh, Granddaddy," she said, "you don't mean that."

Frances savored that sense of justice, relished seeing her father get a bit of comeuppance from his granddaughter, even though this would not deter him from continuing the prank, relentlessly, in spite of the fact that it would never again—save one mind-numbing instance more than a decade later—get a reaction from her, other than, "You don't mean that, Granddaddy." And Frances shared her thoughts with Elizabeth.

"Granddaddy's only getting what he deserves," Elizabeth said of her table-turning prank with Campbell's gun. "Didn't he ever pull mean pranks on you?"

"One after another," Frances told her, reaching back to retrieve stifled memories, painful ones. "He would hold up Indigo, my pet rabbit, by the ears and say he was going to wring her neck and we were going to eat rabbit stew for dinner."

"Oh, but how awful. I can't hear about that. I can't," Elizabeth said, then, "only it's strange. It feels like something I have to know. Don't I?"

"No, Waterbug. You don't have to. But if you have a curiosity I will answer what I can."

"Tell me more, then."

"All right."

"All of it, honest?"

"Yes. Honest." She flipped through her mental memory book. "Sometimes he turned out the lights in the privy and held the door closed while I was in there—trying to cure my fear of the dark, is what he told Mama."

"And you were terrified."

"Of course. The dark. The unknown. It was torture."

"And did he do things like that to Daddy?"

"Both of us. All the time. He'd jump out at us in the middle of the night. He'd swerve the automobile from side to side when we were riding in the T Model. If we whimpered he'd tell us to 'toughen up, by damn. You have to be hardened to fear in this life.'"

Elizabeth asked one of her standard questions. "Do you think he and Miss Lucille have a great love between them? Do you?"

"You know, I've wondered that very same thing, especially when I was younger, right when I was finding love for the first time myself. I even asked her about it."

"How did you put it to her?"

"I just came right out and asked her what she saw in him."

"And?"

"She said he was a good provider."

"But that sounds so practical."

"True. And she said it in a very sort of sad tone, so I asked her if she loved him."

"What did she say?"

"She said the strangest thing. She said, 'Sometimes our choices in love are limited, and sometimes we make choices at weak moments.' And she said more, about how women, or rather, ladies, especially, have to live with their choices." Frances knew well the distinction between women and ladies. Ladies did not raise their voices, or voice their opinions too strongly, or show too much strength, or smoke on the street. Ladies lived by a different code, a stiffer one, one she herself certainly had no inclination to follow, even though she managed to keep up a certain appearance; and she was momentarily thankful that Elizabeth was not as restricted by such a code.

"Do you think she ever felt passion for him?"

"Goodness! What do you know about passion?" Frances asked, thinking of Martha's freckled skin, the way her fingers clung to Frances's hand like it was a lifeline.

"I know that passion is the only thing," Elizabeth said. "Do you think Miss Lucille ever knew that?"

"Of course she did. In fact, she said she let passion lead her where she never should have gone."

Elizabeth's eyes widened. "Do you know what she meant by that?"

"I think it had to do with the fact that she went against her family because she had to have Campbell Lacey. Her people cut her off and they've never laid eyes on me or Jack or you, for that matter."

Elizabeth shook her head. "How can a family turn on one of their own?"

"There are some crazy folks running through your lineage. What about Pearl's mother, taking her life for the same reason my mother's people turned on her?"

Elizabeth shuddered. "Lye," she whispered.

"But yes," Frances went on, "I'd call it pretty damn passionate of Mama to follow her heart, even if she let her people down." At once the question ran through her mind: Would Frances's family, too, turn on her if they knew about Martha?

"I wonder if she regretted it."

"Sure she did. At least, she said a few times that she shouldn't have defied her folks, that it was a high price to pay. But she's always said she's grateful for what she has, that she wouldn't take all the tea in China for me. Of course, Jack, too. But she said to me, 'You, precious girl, you were a child of passion.'"

What Frances did not say was that her mother seemed to be trying to tell her something without putting it into ordinary words, guarding a vulnerable part of her past. And how intriguing it was, a phrase of allure, an enigma, even. Was Frances really a child of passion? And what did that mean for her? Could she live a fully passionate life with her passion hidden away? And as for her mother, Lucille's predicament had been grave, indeed. A young woman—no, a young *lady*—who came up pregnant out of wedlock at the turn of the century would have been a pariah, had few options indeed, and even though her mother was living out her sentence, Frances was relieved to know her mother had experienced the intensity of love, at least once. Frances was evidence of that. Frances was a child of passion, supposedly. Yet she could not hold a candle to Elizabeth, who was steeped in it.

By the spring of '43 Elizabeth's passion was at an all-time high, and Frances was determined to always be available as a confidante, wrestled with herself to keep from lecturing, beating her head against the brick wall that was Elizabeth's intention to define herself.

"What do you do with them?" Frances asked.

"Careful." Elizabeth wore her impish look and fingered some of the silver charms on her bracelets—a cross, an engraved disc, a cluster of music notes. "You know I will tell the truth."

"What do you do with them?" Frances braced herself for the answer.

Elizabeth giggled. "What do you do with Martha?"

It always took Frances aback, those kinds of questions, the ones Elizabeth never hesitated to throw at her, questions Frances always glossed over or guided in another direction. How was it that Elizabeth knew? Did she sense it? With a gut feeling and no real evidence? No wonder Martha felt so horribly vulnerable to a world that would surely hate her, in spite of the scores of schoolchildren who loved her and learned from her. "I need to know, Waterbug. What do you do with them? It's important."

Elizabeth sighed. "All right." She held her wrists up and twisted them, rattling the charms, then, in a small voice, "I keep the bad pictures in the background. I don't have to see the broken feathers and the blood."

Frances put her hand over Elizabeth's. "How do you do that, Waterbug?"

"Well," Elizabeth shook her wrists again, with summoned gaiety. "I laugh. And I play. And I dance and dance and dance. I want to dance with every soldier in every branch of the service."

Frances couldn't help laughing. "That's quite a goal. But I was asking something else, really."

"And what would that be?" Elizabeth raised her left eyebrow.

"What I really need to know is—I mean, not what do you do with them, but what do you *do* with them?

Elizabeth giggled. "Oh," she said in a long, drawn-out, conspiratorial whisper. "You want to know if I let them touch me."

Frances's instinct was to shy away, retreat behind her mother's code, but she managed to maintain her resolve. "Yes," she said. "And if you let them do other things."

Elizabeth seemed to be having great fun, making big eyes, toying with her. "Like have sexual relations?" Elizabeth said, then leaned forward to whisper, "Do I let them put it in?"

"Elizabeth!"

Her niece laughed and slumped back into the sofa cushions, powder blue and navy plaid skirt draped out at her sides. "Well that's what you're asking, aren't you? You want to know if I let them put it in."

It was so very like Elizabeth to get to the heart of things, and to make it seem so inconsequential, the "putting in" of the thing. But Frances blundered on, "I—well—yes, that is what I want to know."

"Have you ever thought about how desperately most men want to do that one thing?" Elizabeth shook her head, amazement taking her face.

"Not really," Frances said, blushing deep.

"Well, they do."

Frances steeled herself again, for what she didn't know. "And you have let them?"

Elizabeth did not miss a beat. "Only a very few times, and just barely, because that would give them the upper hand, somehow. This way I keep the victory. And I only do any of that with soldiers, because they are so afraid. And especially, especially, *only* when I want to."

"What?" Even though Frances could not help feeling a little dismayed by Elizabeth's blasé attitude, Frances felt something else, there, on the heels of that dismay. Another feeling came blistering into her consciousness: envy.

"Some of them are so young, but even the older ones are innocent and afraid, in a way—in the way of the war, I mean. I can't even start to imagine it. I really hate to think of them being maybe shipped out. And getting wounded, or worse," Elizabeth said. "They are so sweet. And I make them laugh. Isn't it silly to think it would matter to anyone how far I let them put it in?"

"You don't think it matters?" Frances asked, and somewhere inside her she tried to think of how wonderful it would be, not to care.

"Of course not."

"It would matter to your mother," Frances offered, weak of argument, running out of steam fast.

"I know it would, but you won't tell, will you? I mean, it will only upset her, and I'm going to do what I want anyway. It is decided, and that is that." Elizabeth rattled her charms again, for emphasis.

Frances knew that no, of course she would never betray her niece's confidence. But she made one last, hollow appeal. "Your family just wants to protect you, Elizabeth. You know that."

"And they do, sort of. Protect me, I mean. But they don't understand me. And you don't either, do you?"

Frances was not sure how to answer.

"'Happy is the man that findeth wisdom and the man that getteth understanding.'"

Frances was at a loss, searching Elizabeth's eyes with her own.

"That's it," Elizabeth said.

"That's what?"

"That's what the best people do when I ask them if they understand something I say. Sometimes they say yes and I can always tell it's a lie, and sometimes they say no and that's when I know they wouldn't even try. I think I prefer silence. It's more honest."

"I try to understand, Waterbug. I always have tried."

"Oh!" Elizabeth shouted, then she threw her arms around Frances's neck and hugged her. "I know you do. More than anyone else."

"Always be honest with me, all right?"

Elizabeth smiled. "Sure. And bold."

"And you know I won't tell anyone."

"Well, except for Miss Martha," Elizabeth said. "You can tell her."

Frances let yet another reference to Martha go by without comment. Instead, she said, "Tell me what you experience when you go out to those places."

Elizabeth shifted on the sofa, pulling her feet underneath her. "It starts with the atmosphere. It's always smoky and the music is so loud you have to speak up to be heard. Everything is magnified. The bartenders are friendly, and they call out to the soldiers and say funny things." She squinted her eyes, blue slits of concentration, then opened them, opening up her thoughts. "That's when the smoke starts to curl around in loops that seem like they keep time with the music. And I want to move like that, do a fox-trot or a Lindy-Hop." She let a different expression have her face, one of wonder, as if she was saying all this out loud for the very first time, seeing it in a different way as she spoke. "So the bartenders usually give me free beer, even though they aren't supposed to, but nobody cares. The soldiers buy it for me, too, but they won't let me get drunk. They accept me. They like everything I do, and even that is magnified. That's when my inside feels like the smoke, and I want to curl around it all, too. Does that make sense?"

Frances found herself, again, feeling envious of Elizabeth's enthusiasm, wanting to be as passionate, wishing she and Martha could simply not care how anyone looked at them, could go out together and have a beer with the soldiers. And she put part of her envy, but only part of it, into words. "I would love it if I could go out and see you dance. I'll bet you are beautiful."

"Oh, but it is all beautiful. The entire picture." And Elizabeth spoke with a fresh exhilaration about how the colors on the dance floor, the blurs of other patrons, blended into music when she joined hands with a partner, their clasped hands bobbing to the rhythm of the swing, or laid her cheek against the starched uniform of a boy far away from home and a little sad, or told an older officer on a barstool to kiss the beer suds off her lips. And she was the conductor, directing the music, pointing the notes in the right direction, breaking colors apart, blending them together. She would beckon and one would follow, and everyone wanted to dance with her.

Frances was caught up in the contagious spirit of her niece for a few moments before practicality reared its responsible head. "You know, don't you, that there are those who would take advantage of you."

"No, they won't. See? You don't understand. I can feel that they won't. I think a lot of them don't really know what to make of me, so they do protect me." She hugged a sofa pillow, a pattern of tiny roses and ivy, to her chest.

Frances believed her. Surely none of them knew what to make of Elizabeth's oddities, her raw honesty, the way she saw how particles of pictures held together, things that alienated her from most people. She and Martha often wondered how stable Elizabeth was, given her tendency to make odd and broken connections and transitions, to take the misfortunes of others so personally it often colored her mood for a very long time. And it was true that the more strange one was, the more the instinct to either protect or ignore seemed to kick in from the larger group in any society. Still she felt compelled to warn, "Please be careful, Elizabeth."

"What are you so afraid of?" Elizabeth challenged

"I'm afraid you might be mistreated. That you are being mistreated."

"Mistreated how?"

Frances hesitated, then, "Being used for—you know—carnal amusement."

Elizabeth threw up her arms in a gesture of frustration, bracelets tinkling like ice chips in a china cup. "How can somebody use me if I only do what I want to do? Don't you see? I decide everything. I make everything happen."

Frances felt herself surrendering. "Anyway, Elizabeth, aside from that, bars can be rough places late at night."

"Oh, I know that, but like I said, the boys are really sweet. I mean, I've seen some fights get started and all that. Sometimes there's a raid. That's as close as I ever get to any danger."

"But that is a danger, true?"

"Not really. Because the funniest thing happens. Whenever something bad gets started, somebody always takes me outside. One of the guys from Turner will say, 'Let's bail on out, Angel,' and lead me out the front door or duck me out the back. Don't you see? No one will hurt me. They all protect me."

"But you've never thought of any of them as a real boyfriend?"

Elizabeth laughed, threw out her arms again, then brought them in to hug her shoulders. "How incredibly bland that would be!"

"You've never been in love?" Frances pressed.

"Of course. All the time. I'm in love with them all."

"My God, Elizabeth, do you ever see bad in anyone?"

"I see people who see bad in me sometimes, but I try not to let it turn me away from them. Like that lady, Mona, next door to the Chinaman. Royce's mama. She sees bad in me, but she is empty." Elizabeth's eyes showed fear, then, "She lives in a house of death and she is as empty as that."

"Who else sees bad in you?"

A giggle from Elizabeth, and her mood had shifted.

"Oh, Mama does, all the time. Everybody else in the family does sometimes, except maybe Daddy. And you, of course."

How fragile that has made you, Frances thought. *It is the other side of the boldness.* But she only asked, "Does it hurt when they don't understand? When they see bad in you?"

"No," Elizabeth said. "Well, yes, it used to. But now I just ignore what they say. I just ignore them as people for a while."

"How?"

"I just go into my room and think about words, read the Bible or Shakespeare—you know," she giggled, "because it is *Elizabethan*—or look at magazines until it's time to face them again."

"It really doesn't hurt you?"

"Not really. Not anymore." But there was a tremor in her tone.

"Really?"

"Really. They can't control me ever, not ever. No one can." And the tremor was shrouded in defiance. "No one ever will."

"And you can always ignore them?" Frances persisted.

"I try," she said, and now her eyes filled. Out of nowhere there were tears. "I try really, really hard, but sometimes I'm afraid."

"Afraid?"

"That they truly are lost. That they are killing themselves." And the tears spilled down her face. "Lost."

If Frances did not completely understand Elizabeth, she did realize that any concerns about Elizabeth's emotional stability were both correct and futile at the same time. Her niece was barreling ahead, into whatever enthused her at any given moment, on a tear, pure and simple. And if she was ever briefly caught up in her family's sphere of control, she had a way of turning it back on them. Such was the case of the spring formal at the county high school gymnasium.

Pearl stayed after Elizabeth for months to attend the annual formal dance, let her daddy buy her a beautiful gown, let her grandmother put her hair up and dress it with flowers, see how truly lovely she could be. There were spats over dinner, and Frances was there to witness the most recent one.

"You could be so gorgeous, Elizabeth," Pearl said, spooning mashed potatoes onto her plate.

"I thought I already was."

"Of course you are, Sugar. But I mean in a really fixed-up way."

"I don't like to fix up the way you do."

"Then Miss Lucille and I will do it for you. Isn't that right, Miss Lucille?"

"Oh, it would be grand fun," Frances's mother agreed.

"I want everyone to appreciate how lovely you are."

"But I don't care about that. I want to be different. Strangely different."

"You can be different and lovely at the same time," Pearl insisted.

The exchange ground on and on until Campbell Lacey snapped, "That's enough fashion talk. There's a war on."

The matter was finally settled via compromise and bribery. Pearl somehow persuaded Jack to get his hands on one of the sporty vehicles impounded by the sheriff's office and to dangle it beneath the nose of her daughter, who wanted nothing more than to have a car at her own disposal. There happened to be a blue Ford coupe, a convertible, whose owner would be locked away in the penitentiary for at least a dozen years. Jack Lacey would teach her to drive it. And, since the dance was just around the corner, not far from the house, she could drive herself there and back. Elizabeth was delighted to accept the bribe, but only if she could wear her mother's wedding dress to the dance. Since the dress was a ballerina length, ivory-colored lace gown that could pass as something one might, conceivably, wear to a high school dance, the deal was sealed.

Frances had dinner at the Lacey home that evening, just so she could watch the transformation, and Jack already had the moving picture camera ready, itching to add to the next canister in the "Elizabeth" series. Lucille and Pearl had set Elizabeth's hair, then styled it in waved upsweeps, anchoring it with pearl combs. They painted her nails, applied her makeup, and helped her step into the silk-covered pumps from Rosenberg's in Albany. Lucille had sewn a beige slip of thin satin for Elizabeth to wear beneath the gown, giving the antique lace a quiet backdrop, and Pearl loaned her a beaded gold handbag. Frances had to admit that Elizabeth did look like a movie star. She was that kind of beautiful. But it was also jarring, how unlike herself Elizabeth appeared, and Frances thought it was more than a little sad.

Elizabeth was not sad, though, not in the least. She had a car her granddaddy had filled up from his own gasoline pump out back, from the county ration. She also had a very smug look on her face, Frances thought, which could not bode well for Miss Pearl's designs on reinventing her daughter, waving the fairy godmother wand over her wild hellion and turning her into a proper young lady.

"It would be nice if you had a young man to drive you," Pearl said.

"It would not. Besides, I have a late date after the dance."

"Oh, really?" Pearl was obviously curious. Elizabeth had never used the word "date" to describe her meetings with men. "Who is it with? Will he be at the dance?"

Elizabeth giggled. "They'll be dancing, but at the Teddy Bear."

"They?"

"Just some soldiers."

"Well you are not to even think of driving that car to Albany," Pearl said. "Around the corner is quite far enough at your age."

Elizabeth smiled. "It's all right. I'll have them pick me up at the school."

"I don't like that phrasing," Pearl said.

"I'm sure they're fine young men," Jack said, settling into his chair. "Aren't they, Baby?"

"Yes," Elizabeth said. "Bravo Squad. I am afraid they are in love with me."

"They'd be crazy not to be in love with you," Jack said. "I've never seen you looking so beautiful. You ought to be a pinup girl. Betty Grable ain't got nothing on you."

Elizabeth twirled over to where her father sat and kissed him on the forehead. "Thank you, Daddy," and she was off to her first high school dance.

Being a longtime faculty member at the Blackshear County Elementary School, Martha helped chaperone the dances at the high school and came home to Frances with the tale that would go around town the next day about Elizabeth. It was a tale about how Elizabeth—having parked the newly acquired automobile, the one she was too young to bring onto the campus, across the street at the Methodist Church—smuggled a flask of whiskey into the dance, carried it nestled in her gold beaded bag, shared it with some of the boys who, having slipped away from their dates, were sworn to a secrecy that was bound to disintegrate, given the nature of high school boys. After a few nips Elizabeth announced that she wanted to dance by shaking her hips to the music, then kicked off her shoes and took her hair down, slinging it around, "because that is how free I love to feel," she told the boys, many of whom packed up around her like hounds sniffing out a heat. She took them one by one to the dance floor, then to the back corner of the gym, where more whiskey was sipped, where her

eyes took on their feral glaze and she began toying with the boys more bla-
tantly, like a cat batting at a trapped insect.

"You want to kiss me, don't you? Maybe I'll let you later," she told several of them, who passed it on.

"Have you ever touched a girl, down there? Maybe I'll let you, later,"
she told some of them, who raced to tell friends of their good fortune.

"With all the rationing and no elastic for panties and all, do you know
Mama has to buy me underwear that buttons?" she told a few of them, "I'd
just as soon not wear any as wear panties with buttons. I'm a good mind
to take them off right now," and that information, too, made its way
around the gymnasium.

She danced each Lindy with more and more intensity, each slow-step
with more and more raw sultriness, pressing against the boys in ways nice
girls never did. More and more of them begged her to dance, but quickly
caught on to the fact that Elizabeth would not allow them to select her. She
selected them, if they were lucky. She might be surrounded by five or six
suitors, then, catching the eye of one across the floor, even one with a girl
on his arm, she would point and beckon to him, crook her finger the way
she sometimes did in the nightclubs. None of them refused.

She took Freddie Jackson underneath the bleachers, pulled up her
dress and unbuttoned her panties, letting them fall in a puddle around her
feet. She stepped out of them and smiled. She would hand them over to
him on the condition that they be placed upon the desk of Mr. Silas, the
principal, who had told her in more than a few "conferences" that she was
earning a salacious reputation and no academic success because of her
dismal attendance record. "He seems so concerned," Elizabeth told
Freddie, "but he always stares at me like he's seeing me in my underwear.
This way he'll finally get a good look at it." She laughed herself breathless,
slapping Freddie's shoulder, wrapping her arms around his neck and
kissing his cheek and ear. He promised to pull the prank. He had nothing
to lose, he would tell the principal later. After all, he had gotten a flashing
glimpse, as did a small band of lookouts turned voyeurs, of a bare-bot-
tomed Elizabeth Lacey as her panties slid down the pale flesh of her thighs.

The girls wearing corsages, holding their dates' arms with stern determination to keep them put, watched her from the moment of her entrance with shock-widened eyes, with exaggerated whispers into one another's ears, their only mode of impotent attack, Elizabeth oblivious to their disapproval. And the high school girls watched it unfold or listened to juicy tidbits about anything they missed, the performance of this peer of theirs who had never shown one whit of interest in the boys or the football games or the dances that had gone before, who was the long-standing subject of rumors nice girls were scandalized to repeat. They watched it unfold with building indignation at the ease with which she swept into their world and turned it inside out. They watched their boyfriends and dates watching it. A few of the girls even crumbled into tears when the loves of their lives participated in a dance or walked to the back corner of the gym with Elizabeth. And they finally decided to report her, even if it meant more fights with boyfriends for being snitches. After all, she had liquor and that was against the rules. Never mind that half the boys at the dance had flasks in the side pockets of their dark suits. Boys did that sort of thing all the time. Elizabeth was a girl, and she was no kind of lady. Glenda Fortner, the most popular girl in school, who was also Peanut Queen of Blackshear County, was drafted to go to Mr. Silas and inform him of Elizabeth's flouting of the rules.

So it was that Martha heard the tale and now recounted it as she changed into her nightgown. "Of course she'll be suspended for a while," Martha said.

"She'll enjoy that. How did she take it?" Frances was already in bed, had been dozing, but now lit a half-smoked cigarette.

"She didn't. By the time Mr. Silas had us looking for her, somebody apparently had warned her. She was gone. The window in the boys' washroom was open. I imagine she had plenty of help, but no one is owning up to that."

"The boys' washroom. Smart girl."

"Yes. And of course there are rumors about all kinds of things happening in there." Martha blushed.

"Like what?"

"Oh, nothing I would want to repeat. Besides, I'm sure none of the really disturbing things are true, not after what she has confided in you. It's just a bunch of boys seeing an opportunity for false glory."

"You're right," Frances said, exhaling smoke, thinking of her niece dancing through the musical smoke of the Teddy Bear Club. "Elizabeth has no interest in those boys. She just wanted to have fun while she was forced to be there."

Martha sighed, "I really am afraid she is not well. Mentally, I mean."

"That's a thought that sets Pearl's teeth on edge."

"I imagine so." She crawled into bed beside Frances.

Frances stubbed out her cigarette, put her arm around Martha and drew her close. "Thank you for being so concerned about Elizabeth."

Martha nuzzled against Frances's shoulder, yawned, then remarked, "I have never, in my life, seen anyone so unconcerned about what people think. It's incredible."

"And enviable, don't you think?"

"Yes," Martha said in a sad, trembling voice. "Quite enviable."

Frances thought about Elizabeth again, how she really *had* looked like a pinup girl, just as Jack said. And the servicemen were loving her right about now, she figured, maneuvering her all around the dance floor, ivory lace and all. She pulled the sheet up around her waist and gazed into the dimness of the bedroom. The coming week would have the switchboard buzzing with fresh gossip after the spring formal shenanigans. And Frances would hear it all, about how the Laceys did not have the spine it took to manage that wild girl of theirs, how Elizabeth had brought her corruption to the innocence of Blackshear County High School, how Elizabeth was bound to find herself in trouble by one of those pilots she was so crazy to run with.

Frances would also hear that Jack's little pinup girl did not make it to the Teddy Bear, that the flyboys did not get a look at Elizabeth made into someone else. By the time Elizabeth arrived at the Teddy Bear, having driven herself all the way there and in a frenzy of exuberance, Frances would hear, her feet were bare and dirty, her hair was down and tangled, and the lace dress had been cast off in favor of a beige satin slip that revealed every curve of her young body.

*

So far, after more than two miserable years, Royce Fitzhugh figured the only good things about the U.S. Army were the breakfasts and the uniforms. At breakfast they had everything, anything they wanted: pancakes, eggs, sausage—hell, even steak. After a lifetime of his mama's greasy, overcooked government pork, he felt he had landed in a high-class restaurant. As for the uniform, it erased a chunk of the shame of living in a shack by the railroad tracks, in his mama's house. The uniform garnered him respect, admiration, favors, and preferential treatment when he was among the civilians of Columbus, Georgia, where he was stationed, had been forever, it seemed.

He arrived at Fort Benning directly after basic training at Fort Dix, New Jersey. He was attached to the 101st Air-Land Supply Company, worked at the loading bay, one of sixty soldiers whose job it was to sort crates, push hand trucks, and use up muscle lifting boxes onto bigger trucks that would drive to other bases or to airfields where they would be loaded onto aircraft and flown to ports where they would be lifted onto ships or put into other planes to find their way to the men who were seeing the sureenough *real* action. He hated the goddamn army. The U.S. Army was a sorry outfit that had not one speck of an idea how to put him to good use, and, because of that, he sometimes dwelled on what he wasn't. He wasn't Audie Murphy. He wasn't going on top-secret missions into the guts of enemy territory, slaying the bad guy, throwing himself between his buddies and certain death, collecting commendations and medals and stripes. Hell, no. He was nothing more than a worker bee, in a hive of thousands, going through the repetitive motions of what, in civilian life, would be a nothing job, pitching boxes into the butt holes of canvas-clad cargo trucks.

But the uniform worked, in spite of the lousy, no-hero-making job. The uniform gave him a free pass into the lives of families who wanted nothing more than to make a fuss over a G.I., wanted to bring him home from church, feed him, introduce him to their daughters and the friends of their daughters, tell him how grateful they were for what he was sacrificing. The uniform gave him entrée; it leveled some of the barriers of class that had always left him an outsider, and he enjoyed that notion, the idea that he was good enough to eat Sunday dinner with them.

The uniform got him laid, too. Not by the nice girls with the clean hair and manicured lawns, the ones whose folks were always having him to Sunday dinner. But the women in the bars, late Saturday night, the loud, party girls wearing plunging necklines or skin-tight sweaters, the ones he drank with and danced with when he had a weekend pass—those were the ones who seemed to consider it their patriotic duty to spread their legs for the boys. The uniform did pay off, and in gold coins, in that regard.

Sometimes he went further, to the prostitutes in Phenix City with his buddies, Slim and Bob-o, where they would size up the goods, turn up the intensity, and be as crude as they wanted to be, because even with the party girls at the bar, a measure of decorum was expected. With the bar girls, you had to buy drinks, make conversation, act like you gave a shit about something besides getting into their panties. With prostitutes, the uniform and the niceties came off immediately. With prostitutes, you could be nothing but bottom-line instinct. Royce usually gave the woman, whatever one he had paid for, a hard, angry fucking, muttering curses in her ear, calling her a cunt piece of ass or a son of a bitch. Sometimes, when they were low on cash, he shared a whore with Slim, who liked to watch and jerk off, but Bob-o was strictly an on-his-own kind of a guy.

When he arrived at Fort Benning, the first thing the new guys were filled in on was where to get pussy, and Phenix City, the same place General George Patton had once threatened to flatten with tanks for preying on the soldiers, was indeed a soldier's dream. Even though it was off limits, most of the guys managed to find their way across the Chattahoochee River to a city full of gambling joints, nightclubs, easy women, and, most important, pussy for sale. His unit arrived horny as the Devil, fresh off of six weeks of basic, where there was nothing like a female within miles, only drills and degradation, and a lot of looking at a bunch of boys being whipped into men. They ate together, showered together, and shit together, an interdependent mass of testosterone, hairy butts, and flatulence. But at the end of it, they all had a pocket full of cash and a horny itch to get scratched, so the first weekend pass he and his buddies got was nothing but a rip-roar, forty-eight hours of nonstop drinking and bought blow jobs.

It was after that first binge, with a head-splitting hangover and a stomach sour with nausea, that Royce hit upon a way to weasel out of work from time to time, and all it took was a visit with the medic. Royce held his palm to his back, turning at the waist and grimacing.

"Yeah," he said, "I think I wrenched it good, throwing them crates last week. Thought it would be better by now but I think I might have tore a muscle or throwed my back out. Can you give me something?"

And the medic, a sleepy-looking second lieutenant named Meyers, smirked, handed him some pills, and put his signature on a form, giving Royce permission to rest in his bunk that day.

It was a tactic Royce exploited every once in a while—not too often, not so often as to arouse suspicion, he thought, just every few weeks or so. He was four months in when Meyers began to question his sincerity. "You might want to try sucking it up today," Meyers said.

"Hell, I'm hurting."

"Yeah?"

"Hell, yeah. My back's done seized up on me."

Meyers shook his head and wrote his signature on the form again so that Royce could take it easy.

After six months in and several trips to Meyers, the medic said, "You seem to hurt a lot, don't you?"

"It's hell having a bum back."

"And you're planning on fighting some Germans."

"That's a fact." Royce had told everyone who would listen, including Meyers, about how he wasn't going home without licking some Japs or Krauts, that he had to have a medal to win this wild girl, to become a deputy sheriff.

"If you can't work on base with a sore back, how are you going to do in combat?"

"I'll do well enough to get that damn medal that ought to be mine."

Meyers smirked and signed the form again, but the very next time Royce went to him complaining about his back, Meyers said, "That's it. I think you've run out of passes."

"Shit, man, come on." There was a letter he'd been putting off writing, and he wanted to get it mailed off to Elizabeth today.

"Can't do it."

"Look here," Royce said, pulling out his wallet. "You a Jew, right? You love the hell out of some cash, right?"

Meyers stared at him with his sleepy eyes.

"Come on, here's a five."

Meyers' stare went squinty.

"Six? Hell, seven. It's cash, right?"

Meyers was silent for a few more moments, then, "Okay. Sure. I'll take your money."

"Good enough."

So a new pattern emerged, that after an especially vicious weekend or whenever he wanted to take some time to write a letter to Elizabeth, he would go see Meyers, bearing a little cash. "Man, oh man, I'm sure glad you a Jew-boy," he would say, peeling off another five and collecting his signed form.

The money spent was well worth it. He would nurse his hangover with lazy mornings in his bunk or write long letters to Elizabeth, letters that boasted of his indispensability to the unit, the company, how he was sure to advance, get some stripes, especially when he finally got to go fight some Krauts. He would also tell her he missed her, that she was pretty and fun and just the kind of girl he would like to go out with. She wrote him back from time to time, not letters, but disjointed phrases and images in black ink, smudged in places; and she might include a hair ribbon, or a stick of gum finessed from a soldier, or a pressed flower. Sometimes she even left kiss marks with her painted lips on the outside, "S.W.A.K." printed along the seal. Those were the best ones.

He wished he could see her, go to his home town for a visit and see how the uniform worked on her, see if she might open her legs for a G.I., or at least let him get a feel of it. But leave was almost nonexistent. Whenever he mentioned it to Sergeant Madison, a big, burly bricklayer from Wichita, he would be met with laughter and, "Haven't you heard there's a war on? Nobody's getting too far from here." Yeah, Royce would think, I'm doing my bit for the big goddamn war they ain't letting me fight in, and he would sulk around the barracks for a day or two. Then, in October of '43, out of nowhere, he was granted a four-day leave, Thursday through Sunday, a jackpot of a leave, to take the Hummingbird from Columbus to Sumner, Georgia, to attend his mama's funeral.

Campbell Lacey contacted the U.S.O., which contacted Sergeant Madison, who gave him the news. It was a freak accident and Sheriff Lacey didn't think there was any foul play involved. She probably was intoxicated when she wandered onto the tracks in the hours before dawn. If the train had been scheduled to stop in Sumner it never would have happened. But there was no scheduled stop, just an engine pulling fifty-six freight and tanker cars, barreling through the night-foggy town at fifty miles per hour. The conductor said how he seemed to see her one second and hit the next, didn't see her pushed, didn't see anybody else at all, didn't even see her react, as if she never even knew what hit her. And that was that.

Royce squelched any semblance of an inclination to grieve and simply dreaded the funeral, dreaded sitting and listening to folks talk about what a good Christian soul Mona Anne was, how kind, what a good friend, and everybody knowing she was a money-taking whore who drank herself into the path of a train. He even debated it, whether to bother with the fresh shame her burial would retrieve. But there was one thing that brought him around to the decision to appear. Elizabeth Lacey would see him in the uniform. Everybody would, but especially Elizabeth would.

"I keep hearing they're going to ship us out any time now," Royce lied. He was visiting with Camp Lacey, who welcomed him into the sheriff's office with a bear hug and a drink of confiscated shinny. "I keep hearing we're fixing to see plenty of action."

"Goddammit, boy, that's what we need you to do. See some action.

Time for a big damn turnaround in that fight."

"My sergeant tells me I'm a natural born soldier, how it's going to be a waste if I don't get my chance to trade bullets with somebody."

"Don't you worry, boy," Camp said. "You got a job waiting for you when you get home, and you might find yourself trading bullets with some criminals." And he slapped Royce's shoulder and they had another drink of moonshine.

"How's Elizabeth?"

"Wild as hell," Camp said, but did not elaborate.

"Is she at home?"

"No. She said to tell you she'd try to get up with you, that she doesn't go to funerals because they're too sad. I told her, 'Little Girl, what's a funeral going to be besides sad?' and all she said back was, 'I'm not a little girl.'"

No kidding, Royce thought. She hadn't been a little girl in a long, long, time, and he was antsy to see what kind of a woman she was turning into. But first he had to get through a ceremony of folks eulogizing and making over his mama before they pitched her in the ground and covered her casket with rich dirt, like a black velvet blanket, then walked away for good.

Royce was glad to be at least a little liquored up when he got to the funeral home. It was the only way he could stand to be around the no-'count relatives he barely knew, relatives who lived along tucked-away, backwoodsy dirt roads woven deep in the country, all semi-strangers from his mother's side of the family. His Aunt Freddie, who had an extra nostril that always made him think of her face as a bowling ball, wailed and carried on so much the preacher, a Brother Lex from out in the county, could hardly make himself heard.

Brother Lex wore a dark suit, thick-heeled black lace-up shoes, a string tie, and a white shirt that had some kind of amber stain on the pocket. He read long, rambling Scripture verses about glorifying the Lord, lines of judgment etched in his weathered face. His eyes were different hues, the left a more pale, bleached-out version of his dark brown right eye.

"Ain't you tore up?" Aunt Freddie squalled to Royce. "You don't have to be strong. Let it out."

"Let Royce be," Freddie's sister-in-law, Royce's Aunt Trudy said. "He'll grieve in his own way. Ain't that right, Brother Lex?"

"The Lord will speak to him and guide him," Brother Lex said, seeming irritated to have had his Bible reading interrupted. Something in his tone was familiar to Royce, so he studied the preacher's slicked-over hair and his odd, mismatched eyes. "Now let's proceed with the service."

Royce wished Brother Lex would not read the Bible on and on, but that was exactly what he did, talking about how Mona Anne was going to walk with Jesus in Heaven until her family came home to her. Royce wondered if this man of the cloth had ever preached a sermon on lust and the evils of fornication and perverse sex acts. And if he had, how could he stand there and say Mona Anne Fitzhugh would ever walk with Jesus?

Royce's sorry Uncle Shorty sat to his left holding a small sack of boiled peanuts, said he had to have something if he couldn't chew his tobacco; his wife, Trudy, told him way ahead of time that he weren't going to chaw on no tobacco at Mona Anne's service. So Uncle Shorty ate boiled peanuts all the way through the eulogy, cracking the shells with his teeth before he sucked the peas and juice into his mouth and dropped the hulls in his coat pocket. Every once in a while he held a palm full of peanuts out to Royce, who nudged him away.

The preacher went on about what a good woman Royce's mama was. "I'll tell you what Mona Anne Fitzhugh gave folks, brothers and sisters," he said. "She gave them joy."

No shit, Royce thought, she sure as hell gave them joy. To everybody but me, I reckon. Still, he was feeling glad that Bother Lex was through reading from the Bible, with all its "thou shalts" and "whosoevers" and "verily, verilys," when the preacher dove right back in, his voice rising as he spoke.

"Psalm 89 says, 'Blessed is the people that know the joyful sound: they shall walk, O Lord, in the light of thy countenance,' and Mona Anne brought the joyful sound to people from all walks of life. Many a troubled soul called on her, and did she turn them away? Did she fail to take them to her breast and comfort them?" Another pause, then, with gusto and volume, "No! She did not! Hallelujah! She brought the joyful sound to those of misery! The sound of giving!"

"Amen!" some responded.

Aunt Freddie sobbed her three nostrils into a folded square of a handkerchief. "My only sister," she blubbered. "Oh, Royce." She wrestled her way into his arms. "Bless your poor heart, burying your mama, and you on the way to war. Let it out. Let it on out."

"Leave him be!" Aunt Trudy hissed.

"Come on, boy, take a goober," Uncle Shorty said. "Don't let them women worry you."

Brother Lex waited for Shorty to stop sucking on his peanut hull, then yelled, "And the Holy Bible says, 'God loveth a cheerful giver.'" He punctuated each word with a thrust of his arms. "Hallelujah!"

Aunt Freddie was hiccupping loud sobs now, snouting a preponderance of three-nostriled snot into her handkerchief at regular intervals.

Royce could not help smirking at the preacher's words, at the image of his mama holding a bottle of beer and a cigarette, her faded yellow robe draped open, telling the man on the porch she'd be done finished with the man in her bed in a while, to just set on the steps there until she was done finished sharing her abundance.

Uncle Shorty slurped the juice out of another brown shell. Aunt Trudy reached across Freddie and patted Royce's wrist. He ignored her.

"Mona Anne leaves behind an only child, a son. And I know she took pride in this child of hers, put his needs in front of her own, for all his days," Brother Lex said. His eyes found Royce's, and there was the familiarity again, subtle and strange, the left eye a shade different from the right. "Young man, you are a fortunate fellow. You can live your life knowing your mama was cared for and relied upon for the joy she brought, and for her kindness, that she gave so much to others in this life. She drew them into the bosom of her home and ministered to them." His left eye bore into Royce with the color of the film over it, the beige of its iris at odds with that of the dark brown right eye, and at once Royce realized what the familiarity was. He had seen those eyes, noticed the discrepancy of color, before. He had seen them in his mother's bed early one morning years ago, when he was eight years old. "Run on, boy," the man in the bed had told him in an impatient, curt tone. Royce sneered at the preacher and shook his head to let him know that *yes, I do remember you. I remember you in my mama's bed. And you're just one more hypocrite in the body of Christ.*

Afterwards, Royce suffered through the mingling, wanting to tell everybody to hurry up, to get gone, to "run on," that the show was over, time to go home. "Let it out," Aunt Freddie kept sobbing, clutching at him. He flinched at the hugs and clucks of sympathy, knowing there was nothing in him that needed to be let out, and it was just fine that Moaning Mona's presence would not be hanging over him when he returned from the war. At graveside, he wondered aloud to his Uncle Jimmy about settling up with the undertaker, but was told that an anonymous band of folks had paid for the funeral, bought a simple pine casket, a plot at the cemetery, and were even going to have a headstone done up. Some of Mona Anne's people had been buried in nice caskets, but she'd be the first one in the family to have a real, granite headstone, ever.

"I speck it were some of them clienteles of hers," Jimmy said.

Damn right it was, Royce thought. It had to be some of her customers, because nobody in his sorry family had any money to speak of. And wasn't that fucking noble of them, whoever they were. A group of guys grieving over a lost piece of tail. They were probably having a drink somewhere right now, in her memory, recalling all the ways they fucked her, singing the praises of her blow jobs. It would probably take them at least a day or two to find a replacement for her, a new place to put their peckers, a new woman who didn't give a shit about her kid. Yeah, they were probably having their own little memorial service. They had to be. They sure as hell hadn't shown up here. The only man who paid for his mama's pussy that made it to her funeral was the goddamn preacher.

*

He had three more days to, as he told Sergeant Madison, "take care of the estate" and "get all the papers and possessions in order." But there was no estate. He didn't even go to the little shack by the railroad tracks, opting instead to stay at Mattie Freeman's boarding house on Isabella Street, on the fancy side of town. He would show them. He would let them know he had arrived. From now on he was good enough to stay on their end of Sumner, Georgia.

On Friday and Saturday, Royce made a point of swaggering around town, but was careful to appear somewhat bereaved, talking to enthralled listeners about how he was just before going to where he was really needed, to Europe, he suspected, and even if he knew he couldn't say for sure, because of "loose lips" and all that. He was a fawned-over object of admiration in his crisp uniform, but he did not happen upon Elizabeth, and it was her admiration he wanted most. He thought about stopping by her house, then reconsidered, thinking how it might seem out of the way. He did stop by the courthouse again to see Camp Lacey, who asked if Royce planned to do anything with Mona's shack.

"Just put a sign and a big padlock on it, like you done the Chinaman's place," Royce said, and, in a while, "Is Elizabeth around?"

"Hell, no. That thing is too busy running the roads to stay around Sumner for long."

The mayor heard he was in town and invited him to his home, to the biggest house on Isabella Street, threw an impromptu lawn party, with invitations spreading by word of mouth. Royce spent that Saturday afternoon standing around drinking lemonade, eating finger food passed around by three colored women in starched white aprons over black uniforms, and looking for Elizabeth, hoping she would show up.

Elizabeth never did show up, but plenty more food did. Ladies up and down the block brought fried chicken and potato salad and more fried chicken, laughing about the servicemen getting the beef ration for the rest of the country. They made a fuss over how handsome he looked in his uniform, how proud they were of him, and here, have another piece of chicken. Hell, they couldn't shove enough food at him. He was a goddamn hero just wearing that uniform. Girls who had never noticed him in school competed with each other for his attention. And the younger girls, the ones still in high school, told him all the latest gossip, told him how afraid they were for him, told him they would write him all the time when he went overseas.

But he was not all that interested in them. They would not do for him what the easy women in the Albany clubs would, now that he had the suit. The real focus of his interest was the meat of their gossip, about how wild Elizabeth Lacey had gotten, how she hardly ever came to class, didn't care about her reputation, and how it was known that she "did things" with the soldiers at the clubs in Albany.

What things? he wanted to ask, but knew better, so he manipulated the talk into a discovery of the names of Elizabeth's favorite haunts, clubs popular with the guys from Turner Field—Jimmy's Tavern, the Teddy Bear, Forrestine's—before he turned his attention to talking to some of the boys about the specific "things" Elizabeth Lacey did.

"I heard she don't wear no underdrawers," Stuart Law said.

"Just some of the time," Rob Somebody corrected.

"I heard it was all the time," another said.

"No," Rob said. "It's only on the nights she's really wild. I got a big brother that's danced with her."

Everyone in the group had a slice of a tale to add to the larger story of Elizabeth's doings. They stood in the shade, smoking cigarettes, far enough away from the mingling guests to be as specific as Royce needed them to be.

"I heard she gave a pilot her slip to carry on his P-51 for when he gets to fly missions over France."

"Sometimes she don't wear no slip, neither."

"Jerry Maloney said he heard she gave hand jobs out behind Forrestine's."

"Jerry Maloney lies all the damn time."

"I heard that after the spring formal she stripped down to nothing but a slip you could see all the way through and went to the Teddy Bear Club. And didn't have a stitch of nothing on underneath."

"That one is true," Rob said, "but that was only one time."

"My brother knows a base mechanic that she let touch it for fourteen seconds. Made him count out loud."

Somebody let out a long whistle.

"Man, oh man," another boy said, echoing the thoughts in Royce's head.

"You can't tell me she don't give it away."

"She don't," Rob said.

"Seems like somebody would take it then," Royce said.

"Naw, my brother said word gets around pretty damn quick to the new guys that don't know her. How the pilots took to calling her "Angel" when she first started coming around. How she's kind of like the base mascot."

"Yeah?" Royce said. "And that's enough?"

"Well, they get told about how she's Camp Lacey's granddaughter, too. And how she's the best-looking girl in Blackshear County, how if you lay a hand on her you'll have the whole Airborne Division on your ass before you get the shit kicked out of you by some laws."

"Come on, there's more to it than that," Stuart said.

"Like what?"

"Think on it a minute. Wouldn't none of us take advantage of her, would we?"

"I see what you m—"

"It's her. She's—I don't know. She's—"

"Different," someone finished.

"Crazy as hell is the fact of it," said another.

"Lots crazier since that dance at the school, what I hear."

"That's right," Stuart continued. "Makes it go a whole different way, don't it? Wouldn't none of us do a goddamned thing to hurt her. She ain't like any old cheap, whorin'-around—" he glanced at Royce, then dropped his eyes into an uncomfortable silence.

A couple of the boys cleared their throats. Royce felt more eyes on him.

"Yeah, well, like I say," Stuart mumbled, awkward sounding, "wouldn't do to disrespect a nice girl that's… " his voice trailed off.

Royce felt his neck growing hot with the embarrassment. Of course they had been with her, these high school football studs. Hell, it was a fucking tradition by now, an initiation into the club, that first visit to

Moaning Mona Anne. Even from the grave she altered how people saw him, even with the uniform. "Let me get back over here," he said, pointing to the folks on the back porch, talking and laughing near fancy wrought iron tables. "Good to see y'all."

"Yeah, you too," several of the boys said.

Royce turned and walked toward the big white home, its street-facing side fronted with four huge columns, its interior full of Oriental rugs, crystal vases, and expensive Scotch whisky. He hated it and wanted it all at the same time. If the uniform wasn't enough then he would damn sure get some medals pinned to it. He had to, if he was ever to get a piece of the power he craved.

"Royce!" one of the boys called from behind him.

Royce turned. "Yeah."

"We're sorry about your mama," Stuart said, and he seemed to mean it. "Really. We're awful sorry."

Royce wanted to tell them not to feel sorry for him, he wouldn't miss the bitch one damn bit, quit caring about her centuries ago, but all he did was nod his head, turn, and rejoin the folks at the mayor's party in his honor.

*

He found her at the Teddy Bear that night, couldn't get to the juke joint fast enough after he left the party. When he saw her, leaning on the end of the bar, talking to a young man in the uniform of the British R.A.F., the music seemed to be playing only for her. She twirled strands of hair around her finger and swayed with the gentle rhythm of "Sentimental Journey." She wore a full, cream-colored skirt, all chiffony looking, with an aviator's uniform blouse and no shoes. He wondered about the underwear.

When she saw him she yelled, "Royce! Catch me!" and ran full speed toward him, leapt into his arms, giggling, wrapping her legs around his waist, pelviture pressed against his stomach, nuzzling her nose and lips into his neck.

Soldiers whistled. Some applauded or called out, "Angel Girl!" and "Fly, Angel Girl, fly!" It seemed to Royce to be some kind of routine, but done reverently, more like a sacred ritual.

They sat in the back corner booth, away from the dance floor, and Royce attempted to carry on a conversation while she fidgeted. She was more jumpy than she used to be, seemed tight and tense, different, and Royce asked her why.

"No-no-no," she said, startled. "I only know things, more notions to know that I don't want to know." She forced a giggle. "You know?"

She sat across from him, knees up against the table, soles on the bench. The chiffon-looking skirt was mashed down between her legs and he wondered again about the underwear. He tried to make more small talk, but she was not about to be still for that.

"I feel like I'm sitting in my living room with my family," she said. "If you don't entertain me I'm going to go elsewhere."

"What would entertain you?"

"Tell me about some of your adventures."

"Well, I haven't seen any action yet. I will, though."

"What about other adventures?"

"Like what?"

"Like with women. Still looking up little girls' dresses?"

"Wouldn't mind taking another look up yours."

"So you still think of me as a little girl?"

He looked at the play of her eyes, the way her smile was full of implications, then down her neck, soft and pale, and down to the full breasts hidden beneath some lucky guy's uniform shirt. Damn the tits, she could pass for twenty-one on the attitude alone. "I don't think anybody sees you as a little girl, Elizabeth. And I think your adventures would be a sight more interesting than mine."

"Maybe."

"Is it true you let a guy touch it for fourteen seconds?"

"No," she said, sliding her right leg down, until her foot was on the floor. She leaned forward. "That is such a lie."

"So you—"

"It was for forty-eight seconds, and he had to count 'one Mississippi, two Mississippi,' out loud the whole time, you know? Oh, and he couldn't move his hand one bit the whole time or I would make him stop. He made it to fourteen before he moved."

Royce squirmed on the inside. "How did you have him touching it that he only lasted fourteen seconds?"

"I sat next to him on the hood of a Buick at Forrestine's," she said, lifting her foot to press against his kneecap before she rested it on the bench, against his outer thigh. "I sat to his right." She slid the sole of her foot over his thigh. "And I laid back and told him to put his hand at the very inside top of my left thigh so that his pinky finger was just sort of... nestled at its outer edges, you know?"

He didn't know, not really. How could anyone know who had not touched such a place as Elizabeth's singular, unique place? He managed to say, "Yeah, so what happened?"

"Well, he only made it to fourteen, I told you, because he moved it." She worked her foot further over his thigh toward his crotch. "He had his pinky finger right at the outer edge, so that he just could feel the part that's, you know, sort of... misty." She pushed her foot onto the rise of his zipper, threw him the knowing little smirk, then cupped her hands around her mouth. "Steely!" she yelled. "Steely Dan!"

"What the h—"

"Ten-hut!" someone in the club called out, then another.

A few young recruits, fresh out of basic, leapt off their bar stools, stood straight and tall, saluting a phantom officer.

"Ten-hut!" several other airmen yelled out, followed by more shouts of the same, and "Steely!"

The young recruits slowly dropped their salutes and traded confused glances.

And it spread through the crowd and grew into a group shout: "Ten-hut!"

Then there were more whistles and applause, then a dying down into the former rhythms of the bar.

"What the hell was that?" Royce asked.

"Just a game we play," Elizabeth said. "If I know I've given a guy one of those, you know, steelies, and I actually check to see, maybe just by leaning against it or brushing by it—if I give myself proof, then I have to yell 'Steely Dan,' and any guy who's ever had one because of me has to yell it back or holler 'ten-hut.' Isn't it delicious?"

Royce shook his head. The girl was off in territory that would, just like the boys at the lawn party had said, make any other girl a whore. He couldn't quite figure it, though. "You're crazy," was all he could say.

Strains of Glenn Miller curled around her. "Everything's crazy. Come dance with me," she said, sliding out of the booth. "But after that I have to go. I promised this guy Jay I would dance with his whole squad, one fast and one slow, with each of them."

"But we didn't spend much time—"

"Time is so unimportant. What if we had spent an hour talking about nothing? We didn't."

"Come on, Elizabeth, what about me?"

"Let's dance," she insisted. "You're wasting the notes." She twirled toward the dance floor, her skirt pinwheeling around her knees and up. "If you don't come on, I'll get someone else," she called out.

She came up to his shoulders, and when he placed his palm against the small of her back, then over to the side, he could feel the uppermost curves of her hips. He took her hand and she stepped closer in than he would have taken her, at first. And she moved against him with the gentle brass, the way the party girls in Phenix City could never do, with the promise of something he would think about the next day, as the Hummingbird roared up the tracks, back to his no-hero-making duty with the U.S. Army.

He continued to throw crates, dance the Continental with "talk to me" girls, and visit whores with Slim and Bob-o, the routine grinding on like a bad tune on an old Victrola. He made several more trips to Meyers, who had taken to shaking his head and smirking even more whenever he saw Royce coming. He would listen to Royce complain about the senseless work he had to do and how he wouldn't have signed up in the first place if he was going to be used like a nigger. "I can't show my face at home if I don't get in the fight," Royce said. "It'll be bad enough to have to go home without no medal, but not to ever fight at all? Shit."

Meyers squinted at him. "It's damned important that you get over there, huh? I mean, I know you have a girl waiting, but it seems like more than that to me."

Royce felt his neck get hot at the memory of his mama's funeral but recovered with, "It's just that my little gal would be mighty damned impressed by some jewelry. She might even give me some pussy."

"Hmm," Meyers said. "Well, she wouldn't be impressed if you gave her the clap. And it's all over Sin City, over there across the Chattahoochee where you guys sneak off to."

"I ain't going to give her the clap, and she ain't the only one that's going to be impressed."

"How's that?"

"When I get home after I get to be a hero, I'm going to be the goddamn king of the town."

"And you need to see combat to get what you want."

"Yeah. And what I want is a decent job that pays," Royce said. "See, I didn't have no rich daddy like you did. And I ain't some money-grubbing Jew-boy that's rolling in dough 'cause he takes bribes off of poor Georgia crackers."

"Speaking of that, fork it over," Meyers said, giving him a significant look along with the signed form Royce needed.

Meyers. He was a strange son of a bitch, Royce decided, thinking what a pain in the ass it was to be mixed up in one army with guys from all over, with guys like Meyers who didn't even believe in God, he reckoned, being a Jew and all. What was worse than the Jews, though, were the colored soldiers, strutting around in the same uniform Royce wore, thinking they were big shit, thanks to FDR. Their barracks were separate from the white soldiers, though, so Royce did not have to look at their cocky nigger faces too much, but he seethed at the fact that some of those black bastards wore stripes, that the army had given them rank over him.

Sergeant Madison told him how the army had shipped out a couple of nigger companies, that they had even seen some action. And if that wasn't bad enough, Madison had even heard tell that the French women and the Eye-talians made over them just like they did the white soldiers. "We might have to break a few monkey skulls open if their heads get too big," Madison said, fueling Royce's eating-away resentment, turning it into a cancerous anger, which would throb large into rage if he thought about it very long. He took to getting into scraps at some of the bars, wanted to hurt somebody, he didn't care who, wished it was a nigger, wished he'd been around for the lynching of that nigger soldier back in '41 he'd heard about. At any rate, he took on anybody he could goad into a fight. Usually Slim and Bob-o managed to break it up, but Royce could feel it building and building in him, thought he would sure enough do some hurt if he ever got the opportunity.

Then, in the spring of '44, the pulse of the entire base quickened and its pace picked up, like a trotting horse spurred to a canter, on the verge of a full-out gallop. He began hearing speculation, whispered, fevered with secrecy, that something big was coming up, big as all get out. Not long after the first swell of rumors rippling across the base, his company got the word they would be shipping out in two days. No one would say where.

"I bet it's Italy," Bob-o said. "I hope it is. I always wanted to see the Leaning Tower of Eiffel."

"The what?" Royce said.

"The goddamn Leaning Tower of Eiffel," Bob-o repeated.

Royce rolled his eyes. "Numb nuts."

"You damn fool, that's in France," Slim said. "And it don't lean."

"And France is where the women are so free with it they give it to niggers," Royce said, "so I think that's where we want to be going."

"Two days," Bob-o said. "Damm-a-mighty."

"Good thing," Slim said. "The way Royce's been wanting to wale on everybody and his brother, he'd have got us a date with the MP before too much longer."

Royce waited along with the others, to load up, collect more guesses about where they might be headed, feel a slow build of adrenaline as they met their destination and Royce met his destiny. By God, he was going to do it. He knew he would do it. He could taste her lips and feel the swell of his chest as he walked through Sumner, a decorated hero. Then, just as quickly as the excitement built, the bottom dropped out of it.

"Naw, son, you're not going nowhere." Sergeant Madison stood in front of him with a clipboard. He jerked his head at the rest of the soldiers in his barracks. "Jenkins, Bryant, grab your gear, get on out, and load up!"

Royce felt like he'd been punched in the stomach. "What the hell, Sarge?"

"Sorry, but Uncle Sam's going to get what he needs out of you around here."

"What the goddamn hell, Sarge? There ain't no reason I shouldn't go with the rest of the company. I got to go."

"Sorry, son, this right here says you aren't going nowhere."

"What the fuck is it?"

"Doc's been going through the files, flagging any boys might not have all the salt they need. You know, been hurt, not as fit as they'll need to be over yonder."

"I'm fine. I ain't broke nothing. Ain't even had a damn cold."

"'Chronic back problem,'" Sergeant Madison read. "'Administered medication eighteen times and release from work detail forty-four times over a twenty-six-month period. Recommend stateside.' That's what it says here." He held out the clipboard, pointing to the form that bore Second Lieutenant Leon Meyers's signature.

"You let me talk to him," Royce said.

"There's no time for that. We ship out now."

"You let me at the slimy Jew motherfucker!"

"He's already shipped."

"Goddammit!" Royce punched his fist into the clipboard. "This is bullshit!"

"Private!"

"The conniving little Jew took my money!" Royce yelled.

But Sergeant Madison's voice was louder. "Private Fitzhugh!"

Royce stood straight. "Sir!"

"Report to Sergeant Johns, 27th Supply Company!"

"But, Sarge." Royce's voice sounded plaintive, defeated.

"Now, soldier!" Sergeant Madison boomed.

"Yes, sir!" Royce reached for his dufflebag as Madison exited the barracks. He could hear the whine of the convoy trucks' engines, one by one, as the motors turned over. He followed Madison out of the barracks and stood at the entrance. The sergeant walked over to the large flatbed covered with a tent of green canvas and threw his foot up onto the bar, extending his hand. Tony Allegri, a scrawny Italian kid from Syracuse, New York, reached down and helped him onto the truck. In that instant, Royce hated Tony Allegri. He hated them all, every one of the soldiers leaving him here in Fort fucking Benning while they rolled to the airfield. He hated Sergeant Madison for leaving him behind, giving him over to another company, the rejects, the scrubs who would be forever stuck stateside. He even hated Slim and Bob-o, could see Slim's high-cheekboned profile a little ways in the truck, wanted to work him over for getting him drunk all those nights out, making him sick, causing him to have to lay out of work detail. But most of all he hated Leon Meyers, the goddamn Christ-hating, money-stealing, slimy little rat of a Jew who set him up, fucking set the whole thing up, stealing more than Royce's money. Leon Meyers had stolen Royce's one and only shot at the medal, and, along with it, Elizabeth Lacey's potential adoration.

*

Eula Lura Sutton sat at a picnic table out back of Sweetie Pie's Café in Cordele, smoking a Picayune, "The taste of New Orleans." It was a habit she had picked up when she began working in the café's kitchen, soon after Ned joined up with the army. It was a decent job, much better than cleaning some white lady's house like her mother did, now that the white lady's children were old enough to take care of themselves. Besides, Eula Lura loved to cook, had always found a kind of self-expression in the way she combined ingredients: an extra dollop of bacon grease in the greens, a secret splash of pepper vinegar in the mashed potatoes, a bit of sugar in the cucumber juice. But now she was an artist, she had discovered, and her work was appreciated, a fact that gave her a new dimension of pride to add to that which she carried for her husband.

Sweetie Pie's Café had grown more popular since Eula Lura started cooking there—huge pots of turnip greens swimming as they boiled in a liquor of water and bacon drippings and chunks of ham fat; skillets sizzling fried chicken, juices sealed in a sumptuous gold crust; ovens warming the sweetest cornbread, the most perfectly textured hoecake imaginable; blackberry cobbler, bursts of purple confectioned in flaking, sugared pastry. The multilayered scents of Eula Lura's cooking infused the street outside and its surrounding spaces with the beckoning lure of epicurean delectability, and, though she was rarely credited, she found a certain satisfaction in drawing in the customers.

Jolene Tolbert, who also cooked with her in the kitchen, sat across from her at the picnic table. At twenty-three Jolene was a washed-out-looking, small-boned white lady, originally from the coalfields near Jenkin-Jones, West Virginia. She had come up hard, she said, one of the middle children in a family of fifteen. When she was working in the kitchen, she was quiet in an intense, focused way, but during their off time she would become more loose and talkative, telling all kinds of deep, dark secrets, like about how her daddy and an uncle had molested her from the time she was eight, how she latched onto a man as soon as she was old enough, how the only reason she was still married to Victor Tolbert was that she had nowhere else to go. He was her ticket out of coal country, she said. She didn't love him, not even a little. He was not very kind to her, but he could provide her with a right smart more than she had grown up with. From what Eula Lura had heard of Victor Tolbert, he sounded like a mean man, and she knew she would not like him. Jolene had shown up to work more than a few times with a bruised neck, a sore arm, a shiner or two, and that was enough for Eula Lura.

Jolene wouldn't let Eula Lura call her "Miss Jolene," saying she wasn't no refined lady and wasn't going to pretend to be one. Jolene claimed she had more in common with Eula Lura than any of the white ladies she had worked for, and when they sat smoking cigarettes at the picnic table out back, Eula Lura felt strangely like a friend to her. It was odd to be on such terms with a white lady, but Eula Lura never voiced such a thought.

Besides, the fact that Jolene confided in her took down some of the barriers, but nowhere near all of them, and she reckoned it just was not meant to be, not a true and deep friendship. Still, there was a certain level of comfort in it, so she, in turn, confided snippets to Jolene, told her about Ned and his dream of moving North, about how he thought she was beautiful, about how she wished for a baby that never came. Jolene also wished for a baby, wished even harder that it would not have to be Victor's child, longed for another man to take on that role. And, on this day, babies were the topic of conversation yet again.

Jolene leaned forward, elbows on the table, tone dropped and conspiratorial. "I think I might be—you know, preggie."

Eula Lura pushed back the urge to envy this woman who, even with all her potential choices, had so little, compared to herself. "Is that a fact?"

"I think so." The corners of Jolene's mouth turned up, the kind of smile Eula Lura had seen before, a smile simmering in secrets.

"Why you got that wily grin on your face?"

"Because I think—I hope it ain't Victor's."

"Oh, Lord." Eula Lura had seen the other man come into the café a handful of times. She would peer out into the big room full of tables and booths, where Jolene could go and sit during a break, but Eula Lura could not, since coloreds were not served there. They could only order food around back and have it passed to them through the screen door, their almost furtive, apologetic faces nodding a thank-you.

From what she had seen of the other man, through the window where the waitresses' orders were placed, he seemed like a gentleman. He and Jolene would sit at a booth and sip coffee. He seemed kind and attentive, always stood when she got up to take care of something in the kitchen, stood when she came back. He was a good twenty years older than Jolene, but Eula Lura thought that might account for how much he seemed to appreciate the young woman who wanted to break away from the man who wore her down.

Eula Lura knew, too, that the other man, like Jolene, was married. It was a hard pill to swallow, that this lady, who was something of a friend to her, would be capable of not only disregarding her own thin vows but also of interfering with the vows of another couple. She could not imagine thinking to run around on Ned, would not allow herself to think of him doing such a thing, far off and lonely as he was. It was a daily exercise, not to judge, not to cast stones.

"Victor'll kill me if he ever finds out." Jolene stubbed out her cigarette in a seashell that doubled as an ashtray.

"You going to tell that man—that other one—what you thinking?" Eula Lura asked.

"If it's so, I'll tell him," she said. "And what he'll do, knowing him, is think of some way to take care of the young 'un without nobody letting on nothing to nobody else."

"Lord, Lord." Eula Lura couldn't help thinking how wrong it was to let such a lie become a part of a life, but again she resolved not to judge too harshly. After all, Jolene had come from hard times and, for all she knew, so had this older gentleman. Folks always had their reasons. She put her hand in the pocket of her apron, let it caress the folded envelope, the latest word from her husband. She leaned back, wondering if the appropriate length of time had passed for her to change the subject.

"You got a letter for me, ain't you?" Jolene said, changing the subject for her.

Eula Lura smiled and pulled the envelope, stamped with Italian postage and Army clearance, from her apron pocket. "It come yesterday evening." She was thankful to have Jolene to read to her from Ned's letters, since she herself could not make out all the words. And, even though she stumbled over long words and strange words, Jolene enjoyed the letters, said how they made her picture things that were far away, across the ocean. *Ned always was good with words*, Eula Lura thought.

There had been a lull in the letters, at first coming from Fort McClellan, Alabama, all full of descriptions of men and boys from all over the country, colored men in the 92nd Infantry Division who had signed on with the war effort, hoping there would be a difference in the way they were treated when the fighting was over. And if they were killed, the lot of those left behind would improve, and it would have been a death well worth dying. The lull came in the spring of '44, and, in the days following the invasion of Normandy, the stories Jolene read out of the *Albany Herald* told the tale of why there was such a lull. Eula Lura had agonized with the silence, up all night worrying about whether he was there, preoccupied at work, while Jolene assured her they would never send colored soldiers to fight in Europe. Jolene had been proven wrong, though, when the first letter arrived, months after D-Day, all the way from Italy, where Ned's tank unit had been sent. Then, as victory became more and more apparent, a flurry of letters, and now this one.

Jolene unfolded the envelope and slipped the paper out. "This is a long one. Front and back," she said, and began to read. "'My Sweet LittleBit.'" She stopped and smiled. "I think that's such a romantic nickname. I never had me a nickname. I think we should all call you that."

"Nobody but my family does that. And Ned."

"You're so lucky to have a man like Ned." She turned her attention back to the letter, her reading slow and deliberate. "'I miss you all the time these days, but that is nothing new, is it? Ever since the beginning of the fight all I could think of was let's whip them and get it over with so I can be home with that woman of mine. Whenever Sergeant Lewis brags on his woman I say I've got one to put her in the shade. I've got one with miles of skin and places to see to. Sarge's wife is five feet three and weighs not even a hundred pounds. I'd be afraid to touch a woman like that. She might break. I tell him I've got a tough, sturdy woman who can take all kinds of love with not a bit held back out of the fear of her little bones snapping. I got a LittleBit of a big bunch of love, huh?

"'I wish you could see this place. Tuscany is beautiful, in spite of the mess. Yesterday we rolled into a town called Massa. And such a crowd came to greet us I really did feel like the conquering hero. The people are so friendly. It's like they don't see color. The only hell we ever catch for that is from the white soldiers, the American ones. Ain't that a twist?

"'Anyway, the countryside is beautiful, with rolling hills and little villages and cafés. I met a café owner named Giovanni. He's also a wood carver. A real craftsman. He's working on a staff for me, carving it with all kinds of designs and American flags. It'll be a real treasure I can pass on to my own son.'"

Eula Lura's heart dipped. It was rare that Ned mentioned children, but he had done so in more than a few of his letters. She wondered if it was because he was in such danger, if he worried about dying, wanted to live on through another generation's heartbeat. She wondered if he would stay true to her when he got home, or if he would go elsewhere to make a baby, and she was at once ashamed for doubting him.

Jolene seemed to read her mind. "Don't worry. You'll be swole up with a young 'un when you least expect it. You just wait till he gets home, honey. He's going to be on you like white on rice."

They both giggled, then Eula Lura nodded at the creased paper. "Is there more?"

"Oh, there sure is." Jolene resumed her reading, turning the page over to read the back, sharing Ned's news of wine and victory, then, "'I'll think of you tonight, LittleBit. And I'll think of kissing you and loving all over you. And you know what else? I'll think about how much this old C-Rationed gut could use some of your sweet potato pie. That's another thing I get to brag about. I got me a woman who can cook up some love *and* cook up some food.

"'I miss you. I love you. Your Ned.'" Now Jolene's eyes were the ones full of envy. "You're so lucky," she said again.

Eula Lura wanted to ask her more about the older gentleman who was so attentive when he came in the café. Was he a man she would be lucky to have? And if that was true, then why was he running around on his wife? But she was too accustomed to not asking white folks personal questions and felt she had already questioned Jolene enough for one day. It was a part of the code of conduct embedded in her reflexes, so all she said was, "He's a good man. That's a fact."

Jolene sighed, "I guess I'll see how good a man I got. It's a gamble I took when I let him get me preggie."

Eula Lura, glanced up, startled, and could not help asking, in spite of her reservations, "What the hell you up to?"

"You ain't figured it out?" Jolene asked.

"Reckon not. You *let* him get you in the family way?"

"That's what I done."

"Why?" Eula Lura asked, and again, "What the hell you up to?"

Jolene did not bat an eye and dove right in. "I got to take this chance. I never had nobody that was a gentleman. And he has plenty of money. If there's even the littlest chance that he'll leave his wife I got to take it."

"And what if he don't?"

Jolene laid her palms on the table and stared at the backs of her hands. "Like I said, it's a gamble and chances are he won't leave her."

"But maybe?"

"Probably not even that, but there's always a 'maybe' ain't there?"

"How big of a 'maybe' you thinking?"

"Well, he ain't never said he loved me, so I reckon it's a itty-bitty one. But he's an honorable man. I mean, he tells me he cares for me, and that he loves his wife, but she ain't well. He says they ain't had relations—that's what he calls it, 'relations'—in over three years, and, I'm telling you, that man likes it."

Eula Lura smiled and thought of how Ned used to pull her over to his side of the bed, where she would find him so aroused, so ready he could not possibly be slow.

"The thing is, he's an honorable man, like I say. I think there's a real good chance he'll take care of me some kind of way," Jolene said.

"You mean pay you money?"

"That's what I'm hoping."

Eula Lura did not say how cheap she thought it was, to use the conception of a baby, especially when she herself could not conceive, as a chance to coax money from a rich man. "You reckon Victor won't know?"

"If I get me a big chunk of money, Victor won't know 'cause I'll be long gone."

That's one thing you done said makes sense, Eula Lura thought, saying, "How long you been planning this out?"

"Pretty much the whole time. That first day he came in here, and I sat down to let him tell me how good the meat loaf was, I knew he was a gentleman. And I dropped my eyes down and let him know in those kinds of ways that I was interested and then I told him to come back whenever he could on a Wednesday 'cause Wednesday is meat loaf day."

Eula Lura shook her head, not understanding such manipulation.

Jolene went on, "And it got to where he was coming around every once in a while, always on a Wednesday, and I was all the time giving him signals, telling him stories and making him laugh, and he got to talking about his wife and I knew right then he wasn't satisfied. You know, you can tell pretty quick if a man's not satisfied."

"That's the truth." And Eula Lura did believe that. Men on the make were always easy to spot, even respectable ones. It was in the way they carried themselves, the search of an eye, the edge of a smile.

"And I kind of made up some stuff about Victor, about how I was real devoted to him and all, but that he had problems of a intimate kind," Jolene continued. "And the short of it is we been meeting on a back road near the Flint River, up near Americus, most Tuesdays."

Eula Lura wondered how Jolene explained to Victor what she did on her days off, but decided not to ask. They chatted on, about men and love and hard lives, until it was time to make ready for the supper crowd. She put the letter back in her pocket, pressing her palm to it. She would take it back out tonight, as she lay in bed. She would look at the words and piece it together herself, remembering some of the sentences and phrases Jolene had read aloud, in her halting, coal-country-bred way. And she would dream of Ned, peaceful dreams that always followed the reassurance of a letter. She would embrace the night, finding him in her slumber.

Three weeks later she and Jolene were once again sitting at the picnic table, smoking, but this day found Jolene hard-faced and angry.

"I reckon I ain't going to be working here much longer," she spat out.

"Ain't?"

"No, I ain't. I had me a talk with my Blackshear County feller, and he's got a whole different set of plans than I ever thought about."

Eula Lura was intrigued. "What kind of plans?"

Jolene shook her head, smirking. "Going to give Victor Tolbert a job."

"That's good ain't it?"

"It ain't good up next to a chunk of cash for me to run off on."

Eula Lura tapped her ashes against the seashell, hesitated, then, "So he ain't giving you any money?"

"No. Well, he'll give this job to Victor and support the baby. Wants me to be off my feet, take it easy. Damn, if I'd known he was this damn honorable I'd have thought twice, you know?"

"What about his wife?"

"She won't never know. He said he wants to keep the young 'un near enough, but not to outright claim it. Hell, he says he'll send it to boarding school as soon as it's old enough. Nothing but the best, he says."

Eula Lura was mystified by Jolene's reaction. It seemed she had a golden life for her baby dropped into her lap, yet she wasn't satisfied. "You going to let him? Send the young 'un off?"

Jolene sighed. "It's a condition."

"Of what?"

"Of getting Victor set up with a steady job for as long as he wants it. And he'll be paid extra, off to the side, 'cause a jailer don't make all that much."

The two were silent for a moment, Eula Lura wondering how a mama could let her baby be sent off, even if it was to a fancy school.

Jolene sighed. "Blackshear County Jail. I might as well be in jail my ownself."

"Ain't there another way?" Eula Lura asked.

"None that I can see. Maybe someday."

"That man. The one that's giving the job. Will you be—spending time with him?"

Jolene rested her chin in her hands and smirked. "That's another condition. We can't be carrying on, not none. I've done lost all the way around. But we'll have something of a life. Till I figure another way, anyway."

They went through the next three months chopping and shredding and boiling and baking, and chatting at the picnic table but saying little of the coming change. Jolene claimed her stomach was beginning to protrude and her breasts were swollen but it was really too early to tell, Eula Lura thought. Still, she was through and through jealous. Whenever Jolene smelled nutmeg it made her nauseous, but Eula Lura even envied her the sickness of pregnancy. And then one day the West Virginia mountain girl was gone, to take up residence in Sumner, Georgia, and Eula Lura was struck by how lonely it was then, how much a friend Jolene had been to her after all.

She continued to receive letters from Ned, full of plans and thick with descriptions of that faraway front. She took the letters to Poythra Jennett, an elderly neighbor who was full of herself because of her education and because she sang solo in the Arabi Zion Church choir. Poythra was snooty and chaste and unmarried, and could never do Ned's letters justice, Eula Lura decided. Like some dogs had a taste for blood, Jolene had a taste for desire, and it had always shone through in the way she read Ned's letters, no matter how haltingly or easily sidetracked. Poythra read them cold, with a twinge of virginal disdain.

Finally Eula Lura took to deciphering the letters herself, what little she could, rather than enduring Poythra's withered renditions. She kept them in a cedar box by her bed, sequenced by the postmark dates on the envelopes. And often on the nights when she could not sleep, she would take a fistful of letters from the box and spread them on the sheet beside her, laying her palm against the paper envelopes, feeling through to the words with her fingertips, pulling the essence of him from the scratch of the deep blue ink.

I: v

The bars near Turner Field pulsed with a new rhythm, celebratory, expectant, vigilant in the months following the D-Day invasion, and Elizabeth successfully avoided school most of the time, then all the time, as the Allies took back Europe a piece at a time. Her father kept a map on the wall of his office, tracking the movement of the Allies with map pins, and each month the map reconfigured, some lines advancing, occasionally falling, but growing into country after country. By the following winter the pins were making their way into Poland, taking back what Hitler had snatched.

There were casualties, plenty of them, among the boys Elizabeth had shepherded through Albany en route to war. But after hearing about Hank Fenton early on, from some of his buddies, and being devastated at the thought of having him in her arms, swaying with the music, safe, laughing, nineteen years old and certain he could whip the Krauts with one hand tied behind his back, Elizabeth begged them not to tell her any more names of dead soldiers she had ever danced with or known for even a quarter note.

When she heard about Hank Fenton, she retreated to her bedroom, hidden from the world for three weeks, unable to think any thoughts that were not morbid. She kept seeing his body, ripped and mangled by a German hand grenade, his eyes frozen wide from that last instant of recognition. She wished she could dance with him again, unmake the events, and her thoughts oozed into the other dance, the one at the high school. She saw herself, lying on the grass where she was pushed down beside the car, where she remained for a time, after he got off her and left, her eyes cast up to the stars, tears warming the skin around her ears. She willed herself to get up, get away, a ragged soreness between her legs, a feeling of revulsion prodding her to get out of it, take it off, and her fingers clutched at the lace wedding dress. She pulled at the delicate fabric, leaned over, clutched at the hem, taking the garment over her head and wadding it up before she threw it in the floor of the blue coupe. That was the image eating into all the other images that swirled together like a mix of spilled paints: the gun at her grandfather's head, the bloodied dove, the burned flesh of Hank Fenton's corpse, the shame and betrayal that must have been reflected on Chen Ling's face. She felt filthy and evil and strange, and wanted nothing more than to disappear, burrow back into nonexistence, let the pain keep her forever.

But her grandmother left her trays of food, her father looked in on her with eyes too sad to see who she really was, and Aunt Frances stopped by every afternoon to say the soldiers at the bars surely missed her, that the family counted on her, that there were things to be done and boys to make laugh. And she gradually let her spirits lift, "came to" as her mother said, and wrapped herself into her bold persona, determined to have fun, to move. The airmen had, indeed, missed her, so her request—that she not be told any more names of boys killed—was honored and strictly enforced. "Don't muddy up Angel's day," they would say to anyone threatening sadness.

A few times she passed the jail yard and saw Hotshot marching around, an air rifle on his shoulder, pretending to be a G.I. He was fully developed, grown into physical manhood, but had never become a different, more grown-up-acting version of himself. She waved to him as he went through his drills, saluting, saying "left, right, left" as he marched. He grinned at her and sang, "I'm in the Army now!" then "You want to go fish?" As much as she missed him, though, she never went fishing with him, the emotional distance between them too great. She did not even tell him she had quit going to school.

"Maybe in a year or so you'll go back and finish high school," her mother said. They were in her mother's bedroom, cleaning out a closet, Elizabeth scavenging some of the cast-off items of clothing.

"What for?" Elizabeth wore a purple and yellow striped top that tied around the back of her neck and a full skirt of baby blue satin, feeling like spring.

"I always hoped you might attend Judson, like your grandmother and Aunt Frances."

"But what for?" Elizabeth demanded again. She picked up a wide-brimmed hat of lacquered yellow straw, strands of lilac netting across the top, then dangling down through slits in the sides of the crown.

"It's just nice for a young lady to be educated. And Judson is such a lovely girls' school." Her mother held out a pink taffeta dress and cocked her head to the side before tossing it to the reject mound of clothes.

"I'd be climbing the walls inside a half hour, being around a bunch of prissy girls, watching them do their hair and write in their diaries and paint fake seams down the backs of their legs." She placed the hat on her head, strands of lilac netting fluttering down to her waist.

"But you'd have boys nearby, those cadets at Marion."

"Boys. Military school cadets. They'd seem like babies after all the men I've been with." She preened before the oak-framed mirror above her mother's vanity.

Pearl flinched. "Don't say 'been with.' It sounds so—coarse."

"I'd rather be coarse than prissy any day," Elizabeth said, wishing her mother would see, finally, that she was not going to change. "Prissy is cruelty and judgment. Coarse is honest and humble."

"No. Coarse is trash like that Jolene woman next door at the jail. I swanee I don't know where your daddy found those people."

"She doesn't seem that bad. She's about to pop, though."

Pearl flinched again. "Let's not discuss things like childbirth, please."

"But I imagine I will have a baby someday," Elizabeth said, wondering at the feeling, unable to think of anything like a mate, which she did not desire. "Babies are pure. They are renewed souls."

Her mother sighed. "I just do not understand you sometimes." She rubbed her forehead.

"I know." Elizabeth watched her own eyes in the mirror, how easy it was to see when pain dropped a veil across them. But no one ever seemed to notice, especially not her mother.

"Now look what you've done, Elizabeth. You've given me a splitting headache." She continued to rub her forehead and repeated, "Absolutely splitting."

"Go lie down, Mama, before you have a stroke trying to understand me." She didn't let her mother see the tears she could feel welling up in her eyes, only felt the familiar urge to run, a need for flight grabbing onto her, the need to get out of that house where she sometimes felt so alone. She wanted to go have some fun, play with the men over in Albany, listen to the French and British pilots who trained there, let their rich, European accents press faraway places against her flesh.

She walked over to the courthouse and climbed the fire escape to the balcony on the second floor, waiting for the clock to chime, thinking she might see Frank Stallings or Nick Temple or any of her regular chauffeurs drive past. She still wore the wide-brimmed hat and tugged at the lilac netting to tie a bow beneath her chin. She thought of Boomer, the old colored man whose job it used to be to wind the clock once a month or so, how she had slipped up to the tower with him when she was small, up the narrow steps to the room that housed groaning gears eating each other into circles and clicks and creaks of time. She had covered her ears and squealed when the clapper drew back to strike the huge dome of the bell. The sound had been bigger than she ever imagined, consuming her, shaking her insides, vibrating her to the core of her soul. Ever since, she climbed up to the balcony from time to time, just to be closer to the tower, waiting for the wash of time's explosions to wave over her. Now Hotshot had taken over the task of winding the clock, had been trained by Boomer's son, who was moving North. She thought maybe she would go up into the clock tower with Hotshot sometime—the next time she thought about it, maybe.

She sat in one of the half dozen white ladder-back rockers scattered across the green-painted wood floor, placing the sole of one foot on the railing, throwing the other leg over the arm of the chair, stuffing her full skirt between her legs. She still felt sad, did not like it one bit. She watched people down below, passing by along the sidewalk, tuned in to how they navigated, feeling their wake. Some of them moved with an ambling uncertainty, others with a rushed predictability, all with the sameness of one another, the absence of whim or irreverence. Why was it that she could feel the ripples others sent out, know them, or at least aspects of them, have the ability to fathom how far they might go to know her; yet she still, with truly honest folks, got only silence when she tried to make herself understood?

Then a different kind of movement caught her eye, the confident clip of an imaginative man, medium-built, wearing a seersucker suit striped the baby blue of her own skirt, something Elizabeth took for a good sign. The man carried a suitcase made of what looked like a kind of metal, and his wingtip shoes hit the sidewalk with a sound altogether apart from the others, a sound that sang out a unique story, of places seen, of bold experiences. He had a swarthy complexion and the blackest hair she had ever seen on a white man, putting the Mediterranean in her head.

When she yelled, "Hey! You!" down from the balcony, he turned and looked up at her. He was attractive, but not handsome until his lips parted into a smile, revealing the straightest, whitest teeth she had ever seen, book-ended by deep dimples.

"What's in your case?" she yelled.

He did not hesitate for a moment, just strode right over to the fire escape and clambered up the iron steps, sending vibrations along the railing where she rested her foot. When he stepped onto the balcony she could see the depth of experience in his eyes, and a rush of anticipation went through her at the idea of having someone, an attractive stranger, to play with for a few hours.

"Unusual getup," he said, nodding at the skirt. "Playing dress-up?"

"I'm not a child. But maybe I *am* playing dress-up."

"How old are you?"

"You tell me first," she said, smiling up at him.

"I'll be twenty-eight this June."

"Why aren't you in the war?"

"They wouldn't take me," he said. "Flat feet, all that stuff. But you're changing the subject. How old *are* you?"

"I'm nineteen," she lied, and it felt odd and unfamiliar. She was not sure why she bothered to lie now, when she only lied to her family anymore. Maybe it was because she sensed this might be someone to whom it would matter that she was sixteen, sensed further this might be someone who could matter to her.

"But you're still playing dress-up? That's interesting." And he gave her a look that reiterated his interest.

"I just like unusual things," she said, stretching, feeling the way his eyes followed her movements.

He set his case down and dragged another rocking chair up next to hers. "Why so?"

"Well, lots of reasons in general."

"What in particular? About the getup, I mean."

She fingered the satin skirt, making a tiny swishing sound, a light blue tone, and she saw the speckled eggs of a robin. "First of all," she said, "I like it because I can find full skirts at rummage sales, and it's not the popular style, not like all the other girls."

"That's a fact," he said, taking a bit of the fabric of the skirt between thumb and forefinger and rubbing for a second.

"And it feels nice when it brushes my skin." She liked that he wanted to touch her skirt, wondered if he would want to touch her elsewhere as well.

"How does it feel against your skin?"

"Cold and sweet. Like dewberries out of the icebox."

He smiled and his dimples drew themselves, and her, in even more. "I like the color. I'd like to paint that color."

"You a house painter?"

He laughed. "No. A canvas painter. An artist. This sales job is my bill-paying occupation."

An artist. A painter of pictures and emotions. Elizabeth was instantly taken with the idea of a man at an easel, inventing scenes, putting the shades of color into form.

"Of course, it's not a permanent job. Sort of a test job for the company, Landry and Sons, to see if there'll be a market to build on after the war. But when I make my cash I'm long gone."

"To where?"

"The Tropics. The islands. Maybe Hawaii. Paint the days away."

Elizabeth wondered what kinds of pictures he dabbed and stroked onto canvas squares, wondered if she would like the Tropics, at once knowing she would.

"What about you?" he asked. "What's your ambition?"

"Well, it has to do with this skirt."

"That so?"

"Yes. And besides the color, do you know what else is nice about this skirt?"

"What? Just the color is enough."

"No, there's more. It floats all around me when I dance, kind of like it's the bell and I'm the clapper."

"I don't get it."

Elizabeth laughed. "Silk and cotton twirl. But not satin. It's heavier even though it looks so delicate, like porcelain. But I like the way it floats around me when I dance."

"So you like to dance?"

"I love to dance. I'd rather do that than just about anything else in the world. Will you take me dancing?"

"I just might do that."

"And will you show me your paintings? And what's in your case?"

He chuckled. "Oh, I don't know if you're ready for what I have in there."

"You're selling something, is what you said. Do you travel all over?"

"All over the Southeast," he said. "I just added this little town to my route."

"And how long will you be here?"

"Just tonight. I've already worked the area for a few days, so I'll get back through here in another six to eight months. When the war's over and gasoline is easier to be had, I'll be through even more often than that. Until I make enough cash to move on."

Elizabeth felt a wash of disappointment. Only one night? But he would want to come back, of course. He would be anxious to come back, if he was anything like the rest of them. Then a tremor of uncertainty. After all, he wasn't like the others at all, wasn't headed for battle, wasn't desperate for fun. "Will you visit me on every trip through?" she asked, willing her thoughts to warm to the idea of a man coming from all over to see her, visiting her like a Canterbury pilgrim, as if she were a shrine.

He leaned back in the rocking chair. "I guess I'll have to see if there's anything to you that's worth revisiting, won't I?"

"I guess you will," she said, then, "Do you ever paint portraits?"

"Sometimes. They bring in a little dough."

"Oh! I want you to do my portrait. My daddy will pay."

"A little daddy's girl, huh?"

She blushed, an unusual thing for her, an odd feeling. "No, not a little girl. But my daddy would pay you, especially if you did a good job."

"Now how could I fail to do a good job with you as my subject?"

Elizabeth dropped her chin, feeling the hot flush take her cheeks again.

"She's shy."

"No, I'm not." Elizabeth looked up at him from beneath the brim of the hat, tasting a tinge of danger in the ether between them. "So aren't you going to show me what's in your case?"

"Take a ride with me and I'll show you." More deep dimples. He stood and extended his dark hand down to her, and she met it with her small pale one.

They drove through the country, twenty-odd miles to a dirt road near the hydroelectric dam on the Flint River. She knew a place, she said, where a side road ended at the bank of Lake Blackshear. He had a white chenille bedspread in the trunk of the car and he spread it across the grass at the edge of the water. It was an April day, clear with the promise of Easter, all green and damp.

"What about the case?" she asked, taking a sip from the pint of gin she had found in the car.

"Sure you want to see?" he asked.

"Of course."

"Sure thing, then. I'll be right back."

She watched reflections of clouds boil across the lake's surface, wondering over the strange fascination she felt, wanting to know him better. At the same time her stomach felt fluttery and nervous, and she pictured a skittish colt dancing sideways in a field of sunflowers before it bolted, mashing fallen yellow petals into the dirt with its hooves.

"Brushes," he said, dropping to his knees, startling her, flipping the case over, thumbing silver buttons to slap loose the stainless steel rectangles holding it shut.

"Brushes?" A breeze patted her face and the straw brim of the hat trembled.

"That's right." He opened the case to reveal all shapes and sizes and kinds of brushes, for scrubbing floors, cleaning pots, freshening toilet bowls, shining shoes, washing baby bottles, whisking away fuzz from a suit coat—and yes, even for painting on canvas.

She plopped down on the white chenille, skirt spread around her like a satin pillow, and began to plunder. "What does this one do?" and "What about that one?" On the cusp of Easter she felt like Christmas, felt like discovery.

He explained all their functions, laughing at her curiosity, telling her she had a beautiful voice, beautiful hair. "And speaking of that," he said, and pulled a smaller box out of the case. Inside the box were a dozen hairbrushes, different shapes and sizes, some with wooden handles and horsehair bristles, others more elegant, with mother-of-pearl wrapped around silver or grooved patterns of black on the flat side of a gold brush. But her favorite was a brass-handled one with an oval backing of sterling silver edged in brass rosebuds.

"Good choice," he said, taking it from her. "It's actually not part of the inventory. It belonged to an elderly lady who buys from me regularly. I admired it so she gave it to me, said she never used it, always intended to have her initials engraved on the back, but never got around to it."

"It's so unusual," Elizabeth said, the sound of his voice catching her, the cadence and pronunciation clearly from somewhere else.

"Touch the bristles," he said, tickling his fingers over them. "They're softer than most."

She hesitated, then ran her fingertips over the concentrated bunches of horsehair, thinking they felt like something akin to chicken feathers but not as soft. Just different and strange and nice. Like him. Then came another rush of trepidation.

As if he sensed her apprehension, he took her hand and ran the brush across her palm. "See how delicate, how soft?"

She nodded, hypnotized by the circles he tickled into the palm of her hand with the hairbrush, feeling a warm tightness in her chest. He trailed it up the inside of her arm, lightly, and little goose bumps rose up across her flesh. He moved it in a long, slow trail down the inside of her arm, lingering over the tender crease of her elbow. She closed her eyes and turned her face to the sky, fear now overtaken by pleasure.

Again she sensed him sensing her, as he laid the brush down and touched her skin with his fingers now, but barely, up and down her arm, over and under it, and she kept her eyes closed, imagining she was in the royal tent she went to so often in her head, a tent now alongside the Nile, with an Egyptian pharaoh, a powerful man, the most powerful man who had ever wanted her. He took his fingers up over her shoulder now, along her neck, tugging at the tail of the lilac netting, releasing the bow she had tied earlier. His movements were so slow and graceful, so unlike the quick fumblings of soldiers, drunk and sloppy, ready to follow her orders as if she were a drill sergeant or the Queen of the Nile. This man's hands were choreographing within her something the other boys and men could not orchestrate, a response, and she wanted him to keep touching her, just like that, taking it on its slow waltz to other places, exploring those places she already knew so well.

She lazed open her eyes and found him staring at her.

"You're beautiful," he said. "What's your name?"

"Elizabeth," she said.

He stroked her bottom lip with a brush of his thumb. "I'm Edward Marcus Frye. You can call me Eddie," he said. He took the hat from her head and combed his fingers through blonde waves.

Some of the fear caught up with her again. It felt too good. "Do you want to touch it?"

"Touch what?" His fingers seemed to savor their way through her hair, tangling themselves in the lushness of it.

"It," she said, an attempt to pull some control from her bar-game experiences. She knew she would let him touch it, for more than a little while. But as she retrieved all the talk she had heard in eavesdropped conversations over the years, talk among the teenage girls she despised, she decided she would not let him put it in, not at all, not until she at least discovered what this was. Surely it was not what she suspected it was.

"What do you want me to do?"

It was a question she had never heard, never been in a position to hear; she had never been in a place of wanting, not in relation to an in-the-flesh man, and she did not know how to answer. She would not in a million years tell him she wanted him to touch her that way, everywhere. She knew she would let him, but she would never tell him she wanted him to. He was to do the wanting. Her thoughts were muddling, the parameters of her impressions shifting, her unreal reality being tested.

"Kiss me," she said. There. An order. She would take back control.

He smiled, still roaming his fingers through her hair, making circles with his palm against her scalp. "No, I don't think I will," he said. "Not yet."

It was the first time a man had ever told her no. She started to bless him out, dress him down, get him to take her home, but his touch had her caught up in the idea of so much potential, a man who would never go off and be killed, but would take her to a faraway place and put pretty pictures all around her. "Then I won't kiss you later unless you take me dancing," she said, flip and detached.

He laughed, picked up the brush again, and ran it through her hair, slow as syrup, and again, bristles raking a delicious tickle against her bare shoulders and back each time he got to the ends of the blonde waves, and again, her skin now anticipating the tickle of the brush, her whole body straining to feel what her shoulders and back knew.

"I never had a man to brush my hair," she said, closing her eyes again. "Not even my daddy."

"What kind of men have you been seeing," he said, "who would be so stupid they wouldn't want to be covered up by this?" He laid down the brush then, and, straddling the full lap of her slick satin skirt, he took the fingers of both hands through the depths of blonde, pulling her to him, holding his mouth to hers, not touching, just breaths, just seconds, before he kissed her back against the blanket, the two of them rolling baby blue satin and seersucker across a white chenille bedspread littered with hairbrushes. She could feel him pressed against her, even through the muffling folds of her skirt. He kissed her neck and her back and her arms, kissed the rises of her chest for an aching eternity, sending warm breaths but nothing more beneath her top, the one that could be untied as easily as the hat had been. But he did not reach beneath any of her clothes as she wished he would, and he left her wishing for more while the sun dropped and he said it was time to go.

"Where?"

"You said you wouldn't kiss me unless I took you dancing."

"But I did kiss you."

"That's right. And I guess I'd better pay up."

And he did take her dancing that night, not to a honky-tonk, but to a fancy supper club in Albany, where they were told to sit on the balcony because Elizabeth had no shoes on and didn't fit with the dress requirements of the place. But Eddie didn't care. He bought champagne and ordered shrimp cocktail, and she dipped the pink meat in melted butter that slid spices across her tongue. Strains of Glenn Miller and Artie Shaw meandered from a phonograph attended by a colored man in a white jacket, while the patrons inside clustered on the dance floor. The music was easy to move to, especially with Eddie, who had the kind of confidence it took to truly lead Elizabeth on their own private dance floor, something she had only experienced occasionally with the soldiers she enthralled, in little glimpses of moments. She fell into Eddie's movements right away, a perfect fit, the press of her hips against his, thinking of him pressing against her skirt as they lay on the bank of Lake Blackshear. It was as if everything was good, as if she could forgive anyone anything—her grandfather, her mother, anyone who had hurt her, ever. It attached itself to her, this feeling she suspected was love, and she could not see herself ever wanting to shake free of it.

When he took her home she felt the disappointment of being left behind, knowing it would be a long time before she would see him again. She had not had enough of the brush of his fingertips, of his mouth pressed against hers. So after he kissed her one last time there, on the screened-in back porch of her grandparents' house, she heard herself say the words she never expected to utter, not ever. She leaned into him, arms around his neck, pressing the full length of her body against his, looked up at him. "I want to see you again. Will you come back, like you said you would?"

"Sure I will. Do you think I'm crazy?"

And as she lay on the canopy bed, letting it take her back to the Nile and the breezes and the wanting, she knew she was changed forever, that she had found something to hold and keep. She would continue to go out and laugh with her U.S. Air Force playmates, enjoy the thrill of being the orchestrator of games and rituals and codes of honor. She would take a second with this one, a minute with that one, a whole dance with another one, a game of touch on the hood of a car with a lucky one, each one a fleeting, in-the-moment sort of person in her life. But where Eddie Frye was concerned she wanted permanence, something truly lasting. She had to see him again. And as the hot coin of the Egyptian sun and the cool push of the river and its winds took her to crumbling sands and the deepening undulations of tidewaters, as she took herself over the erotic edge of her imagination, where the forces of nature were always there to make love to her, where not a human face had ever joined her until today, it was Eddie Frye who was in her head, and she knew he would be there always.

*

Eula Lura had dreams about Ned all the time. Some were warm and sensual, when he came to her other consciousness, kissing his way into her sleep. She would feel the mattress on his side of the bed dip and hear the scrape of the springs as he settled against her back. Then his lips would be exploring her back and the flesh between her shoulder blades, his mouth moving in a quickening, fevered path. It had been so long. She would press her hips into him and he would moan, rolling her onto her belly, knees at her sides, and enter her. Eula Lura would wake flushed and empty, with an ache of desire deep in her stomach.

Then there were the nightmares. There was Ned in the guts of his armed vehicle, screaming the agony of flames searing at his flesh. There was Ned on the march, his image suddenly obliterated by exploding mortar fire. There was Ned's Sherman tank, ordnances loaded into the tube of its big gun, swarmed over by Germans, who fed hand grenades into its gaping mouth. She had seen him die every way imaginable, in the dreams that woke her when she cried out in her sleep, eyes wide, skin damp with perspiration, and she would howl out to God, "No! Don't take my Ned!"

And then there were the other kinds of nightmares, the ones just as unthinkable and heartbreaking as his death would be. They were the nightmares that began as beautiful pictures of the Italy he described, a sunny village in the region of Tuscany, where Ned meandered down narrow streets, mobbed by little children who shrieked with delight when he handed them sticks of Juicy Fruit. There were the tones of a mandolin and the sun-slatted undersides of stands of grapevines, leaves draping and curling to the ground. And then there was a woman, waving to him from a table in the shade. She was a beautiful woman, big-breasted, dark-haired, with skin a warm brown from the sun and from her Mediterranean heritage, but white nonetheless. Ned would walk over to the table, sit across from her, take her hands in his, pressing his lips against her skin. And he would laugh and suck on her fingers when she dipped them in the wine and ran them across his lips. He would laugh and laugh, probably thinking how silly he was to have ever spent time with a big-boned plain-looking thing like the raggedy, no-reading wife waiting for him back home. These were the times Eula Lura would wake with her face in her pillow, sobbing in frustrated little gasps, saying, not to God but to the beautiful Italian woman, "No. Don't take my Ned."

She did not write him about her bad dreams, knew he did not need the weight of that on his mind. She did not write him much at all, since all she could do was print out some basic words in an embarrassing, childish scrawl of choppy little sentences: "How are you? I am well. I miss you. I love you. Be well." She used to dictate letters for Jolene to write down, but Jolene was long gone and besides, Eula Lura had been too self-conscious to speak her deepest feelings aloud, how she missed the way he kissed her, that she would love him forever, that he was the best man in the world for her, that she wanted to feel him against her, inside her. So she had only let Jolene write down newsy little retellings of Eula Lura's day-to-day doings, wishing she knew how to read and write better.

She heard from Jolene, finally, in March of '45, in a letter addressed to Sweetie Pie's Café. She sat out back at the picnic table, reading it, thinking how nice it was of Jolene to write in short, easy sentences she would be able to decipher.

"'Dear Eula Lura,'" it began. "'How are you? I am fine. I had my baby. A boy. Victor is proud but he is mean to me. The real daddy is proud, too. But I am sad. I am lonely. I hate it here. It is like my own jail, like I said. The man's wife is snooty. She doesn't speak to me. The man speaks to me sometimes, when he comes to see the boy, and I named him Jay, kind of like a 'J' standing for 'Jack.' But that man does not kiss me. Nothing. I wish I had a good man. I will try to write again. Sincerely, Jolene.'"

Eula Lura saved the letter, the only one she had ever received in her entire life, aside from Ned's letters, and she hoped Jolene would write more of them. A letter was a wave of excitement, a validation, a recognition of

one's existence. It was a cluster of words that traveled miles to find one particular person, and that person was Eula Lura Sutton. She put the letter in
her top bureau drawer, leaving room for others, though they never came.

She visited her mama and sister Pruella on Sunday evenings and they
asked after Ned. She read what she could of the newspaper, mostly headlines, so she could join in on the war talk with folks who drifted into and
out of her life. She worked, day in and day out, just like everyone else who
had a steady job. She went about her routine of walking to the café every
day, save Thursday, when it was closed. She fried fish and shucked corn and
ran the kernels across a grater so the juices could make a cream that she
sugared and salted. She filled pie crusts with thick-jellied cherries and cinnamon apples and whipped chocolate. She brewed tea and coffee and wondered where Ned was today and what Jolene was doing right that moment.
And when April came, she grieved along with everyone else, with the rest
of the country. She saw the headlines and felt the sorrow, felt it even a bit
keener than most folks in Cordele, white folks anyway. President Roosevelt
had held out a semblance of promise, a hint of possibility, however muted
and far from her world in rural Georgia, and now President Roosevelt was
dead. The hugeness of that death infected her hopes, heightened her vigilance. More and more she heard the words wrapping around the thoughts
in her head: Please come home, Ned. Please come home to me. It was time.
It was long past time.

*

If not for the circumstances, Frances thought, she might have been
more vigilant about this Eddie Frye character. If her head had been clear
she might have appreciated the implications, been more inclined to ana-
lyze Elizabeth's insistence on romanticizing him. Frances had always
known that Elizabeth was not likely to fall in love in the usual way, with the
usual man, had always worried at how her niece could let a single quality
override all evidence to the contrary about a person, at times giving the
attributes of a saint to a solid ne'er-do-well, like that Royce Fitzhugh. And
now she was doing the same thing with Eddie.

Yes, the circumstances had thrown Frances quite off guard: an early

morning in April, predawn; she and Martha in bed together, as usual, stirring into the coming sunrise, into one another, as they often did in the dim
mornings, the quiet, secret time of day. They were oblivious to the sound
of the unlocked door opening, the whisper of bare feet padding up the
back stairs, and nothing sank in until the bedroom door swung open.
Martha bolted upright and screamed into her palm, remembering, even in
that instant, not to call attention to herself, not to let the neighbors hear. If
it had been an escaped killer from the county jail, she would have covered
her mouth so as not to alert the neighbors that they were in bed together.

Frances rolled over to see Elizabeth standing in the dimness. "Oh,
Jesus!"

"I didn't mean to interrupt," Elizabeth said as the two women covered
themselves, "but I had to come and tell you what's happened. You won't
believe it!"

"Is someone sick?" Frances asked through stunned disbelief, her face
hot with humiliation. She glanced at Martha, who she could tell was struggling not to dissolve into tears.

Elizabeth seemed oblivious to their discomfort. She walked over and
plopped down on the foot of the bed, falling back, throwing out her arms.
"It is delicious and amazing!" She closed her eyes. "I finally know, and I
never even desired to know."

"What in the world?"

"I am in love. I have met the man who is to marry me."

Frances's shock quickly turned to indignation. It was not even a family
emergency, and the child had burst in on their privacy, their secrecy. "How
dare you?" she yelled. "How dare you barge into our—my home with—"

Martha touched her arm. "Shhh! Someone will hear." Her eyes were
panicked, pleading. "I don't want—the neighbors—" She buried her face
in her palms and began to sob in determined silence.

Elizabeth sat up. "Why is everyone so upset?"

"You had no right walking into our—my bedroom like that." Frances's
voice was icy.

"Don't be mad at me, Aunt Frances. Please. I always just walk into your house. Everybody does."

"Not at this hour. Not into my bedroom."

"Don't be mad. And why is Miss Martha crying?"

This sent Martha into a fresh wave of tears.

"Why? Because you were together?"

Frances stared with fresh disbelief. "Of course it is, Elizabeth."

"But I don't care about that."

"My God." Martha sat up, the bed sheet at her chin, and reached for a handkerchief on the bedside table.

Elizabeth's face was earnest, disarming. "I mean, I think I understand that kind of love now. The way Eddie Frye touched me yesterday. It was exquisite!"

In that instant it dawned on Frances that she was, indeed, contending with a family emergency—one named Elizabeth. This was the child—the young woman she had worried about, listened to for hours, hoping to get a handle on where she might be headed. Elizabeth was the family emergency no one in the Lacey family wanted to consider. And she seemed to be careening into yet another of her fantasies.

Martha wiggled over to the edge of the bed, sitting with her feet on the floor, a portion of the sheet still wrapped around her. "I need for you to turn away, Elizabeth." Her tone was hollow, defeated.

"Elizabeth," Frances said, "you must never mention a word about this—ever."

"God, please," Martha whispered.

"People can be cruel, Elizabeth," Frances said.

"I know," Elizabeth said. "Like they were with Chen Ling."

"Exactly. And Martha would be ruined if this got out. People would be cruel to her. And to me."

"Don't worry," Elizabeth said. "I don't carry tales. 'Surely the serpent will bite without enchantment; and a babbler is no better.'"

"Turn your head away then, so Martha can get dressed."

Elizabeth put her hands over her eyes and continued, "I think it would be curious to touch a woman, or have a woman touch me, but I don't think it could be any more delicious than the way Eddie Frye touched me yesterday."

"Who in hell is Eddie Frye?"

Frances watched as Martha stood and walked to the bathroom door, where she turned and gave Frances the look that said, *Please, please make this all right.* She closed the door as Elizabeth recounted her story to Frances, who tried to be attentive, tried to listen to every detail. At first she attempted to convince herself that Elizabeth was finally showing signs of having a relatively normal perspective—after all, being in love was a very natural thing—but she sensed something more threatening. Too, she found herself feeling almost happy for herself, a sort of new ease with herself, now that she had formed honesty into words, about her and Martha. Perhaps if she had not been so disarmed and full of mixed emotions she might have seen the writing on the wall more clearly. Perhaps in a way she was just as desperate to see Elizabeth as a "normal" young lady as the rest of the family was. Yes, she might actually be guilty of that.

It was eight days later when call after call jammed the switchboard at the little telephone office in Sumner where Frances worked as operator, and she knew the news would take a toll on Elizabeth. Her niece always responded to tragedies in a large way, and President Roosevelt's passing was a major tragedy. Even smaller-scale tragedies, like the death of Hank Fenton, a young man her niece had known only long enough to dance with a few times, sent her into a self-imposed seclusion. She had stayed in her room for days, crying, she told Frances later, or trying on odd outfits, or listening to the phonograph and dancing, or poring over the Bible, searching for a verse to explain away the pain.

But aside from the fact that this loss was so significant, so full of implications, Elizabeth had always felt a connection with FDR, a long-standing one. "He smiled and waved at me when I was three years old," she liked to tell people. "He looked right into my eyes and smiled, and I knew he was a good, kind man."

So Frances knew it was going to be difficult for Elizabeth, knew she could trust in the fact that Elizabeth would be particularly devastated by

this death. She also knew that in times of upset in her life, Elizabeth sometimes tended to ramble on about seemingly unimportant, disconnected
facts—"loose associations," the psychiatric textbooks called it—sometimes
saying a little too much. Other times she blurted out what was in her mind,
no matter how inappropriate. In light of that, Frances asked herself, could
she trust Elizabeth to keep the secret of her relationship with Martha?
Could she trust Elizabeth to keep quiet about what her niece had seen, just
eight days ago, in Frances's bedroom? Of course, her niece had not been
shocked or dismayed at what she saw. Elizabeth, after all, merely accepted
anything that wasn't sad or threatening, accepted most things, then, as an
interesting part of life.

"But acceptance isn't the same thing as discretion," Martha reminded
her. "And that man she's so in love with is nowhere to be seen."

True enough, Frances thought. Eddie Frye was apparently not one to
come rushing to be by his girl's side in times of trouble, even if he did think
of Elizabeth as "his girl," which Frances had to doubt.

"He'll come to me," Elizabeth said, repeatedly, after brief phone conversations with the man she had convinced herself was to marry her.

"Don't put all your hopes on this one fellow," Frances said. "You
hardly know him."

"I do know him. All I have to do is keep my spirits up and he'll be here
just as soon as he can be." And she would stay out later and later with her
barroom diversions, come home at dawn, and sleep until three or four in
the afternoon, then start again, grabbing for the fun of what became more
and more like false gaiety, more and more desperate as the weeks wore on.

And so it became a fervent prayer of Frances's that Elizabeth's hidden
sadness would not wear her down, break her down the way Pearl had been
broken down in the past. But her prayer had an ulterior motive, that Elizabeth's tenuous hold on the rituals that kept her lucid would not falter, that
her unpredictability would not spill over into Frances's life and damage the
one thing she had come to count on and love: Martha, the woman whose
love was returned remained forever and always poised on the border of
polite society—vigilant, waiting, braced for condemnation.

I: vi

At first the image of the man in the parade came back at her so fast she thought a piece of her own spirit had been knocked down, tangling her thoughts and emotions into a swirl of enmeshed colors that threatened to stay in the way of her senses, the true and exuberant ones. So Elizabeth decided to dance it all into oblivion, refuse to let any kind of dark imaginings take her. After all, she had to wait for Eddie. Eddie would come and see her before long and everything would be all right.

Her family tiptoed around her, and she knew they expected her to fall apart. She did not tell them, though, about her secret weapon. Only Aunt Frances and Miss Martha knew about Eddie, and she liked the fact that she had a secret love armed with soft-bristled brushes to protect her from all the bad images in the world. So she played on, watching for his arrival, counting on it.

She spent hours on end at the Teddy Bear Club, sometimes an entire day, and into the night. She drank herself numb some nights, drank herself sick others. "Easy, Angel," one or another of the soldiers would say. "Don't get yourself zonked tonight." But more often than not she would, and there was always someone there to hold her up, or to dance with her until she was all danced out, or to steady her if she threw up in the parking lot, or to see her home safely. And all the time she waited for Eddie, wondering why he did not call more often, why he did not talk longer when he did call; making up reasons and excuses while she laughed and swayed in smoky lounges and night clubs. Then came more news from Europe, news that pushed her into the dim middle of that clogged jumble in the center of her head.

An old college friend of Aunt Frances's, a Jewish lady named Mary Lou something, mailed a New York newspaper to Lucille. It was the fattest newspaper Elizabeth had ever seen, and she could not comprehend the bigness of a city with a newspaper that thick and full of places to go. But it was the pictures that stunned Elizabeth, the gray-hued photographs in that fat newspaper, and later in the Georgia newspapers and the *Life* magazine at the sheriff's office. In spite of the fact that she had always avoided unpleasant things, tried to pretend that pain and misfortune did not really visit good and decent people, she could not turn away from these photographs. Furthermore, her shock and disbelief were so overpowering she felt compelled to read the news stories, on automatic, none of it quite sinking in at first, but playing havoc with her later, when the reality set in.

The Nazi surrender was only weeks, maybe days away. Everyone knew it, and what the American soldiers were discovering as they marched across Europe—the trickle of evidence confirming gathering fears—and on into Poland and Germany, was nothing less than the purest evil Elizabeth could have ever imagined. Generals Patton and Eisenhower toured a place called Buchenwald, but there were other places like it, she read, places that butchered children and moved old women through the cogs and wheels of death factories. Thousands upon thousands, maybe more, had been herded into the bowels of that hellish place and places like it, never to emerge. They had looked into the eyes of Lucifer and found not an ounce of pity, and Elizabeth could not comprehend, let alone digest, that hard blade-edge of darkness.

At first she attempted to make sense of it through her family, bringing out the pictures, imploring them to attach some kind of explanation to the unthinkable. But their efforts were too measured and altogether impotent.

"It's a horrible thing," her grandmother said. "It's impossible to imagine the cruelty. Don't let yourself dwell on it, though."

And, when Elizabeth persisted, Lucille said, in resignation, defeated, "I don't know what to tell you," shaking her head, "I just don't."

Her grandfather seemed immune to any semblance of sadness, maintaining that war was war, that things like this were not unheard of. "It's not something that hasn't happened before, one bunch trying to eradicate another."

"And that is where hate for any race can lead," her grandmother said, giving him a meaningful look.

"Mongrel races," her grandfather stormed, "are a stain on the human condition."

Lucille stiffened, then snatched up her tatting and slammed out of the room.

Elizabeth approached her mother, knowing she would be met with some kind of apathy, hoping she would not.

"I don't understand why your grandmother allowed you to look at those ghoulish photographs," Pearl said. "Now you'll be fretting over something that can never, ever happen to you."

Elizabeth was distraught, agitated. "But this proves it could happen to anyone. *Anyone.* There are dead babies."

"Hush, Elizabeth. You'll upset me with talk about dead babies. And it could not happen to anyone. It couldn't happen to you. Even if you lived over there, it wouldn't have happened to you."

"Why not?"

"Because you are a Christian, and they did not kill any Christians."

When she tried to get an answer out of her father, he attempted to appease her with logic. "Think of it as a coin. Heads is good and tails is evil. Think of the odds. Fifty-fifty. So even with all this, when you think of all the people in the world, good has won out and beaten the odds." Then, to her silence, he added, "Don't you see?"

She took the *Life* magazine from the sheriff's office and kept it in her room, poring over the pictures of mounds of bodies, not recognizable at first as bodies, just piles of skeletal debris, arms, legs tangled where they had been thrown, like so much trash or scrap lumber. Then, a closer look, at the mouths gaped open, the eyes staring a powerless death, the naked, defiled bodies of the women, the gray-bearded old men, the children nestled in among the mangled limbs like stolen doll babies.

Elizabeth cried and could not be consoled. She curled up on her bed and wept, arms wrapped around her stomach, then up, over her head. Her mother and grandmother tried to comfort her, but she wrenched away from the touch they offered, would not let their words assuage her despair over it all.

"Miss Lucille, I wish you had not let her see those pictures," her mother said yet again.

"They aren't pictures that could have been hidden" was the curt reply. "And it is history. It is not a thing to be ignored."

Her mother sighed. "I supposed it will have to run its course." Then, to Elizabeth, in a loud tone, "You simply cannot take on the ills of the world. That is for Jesus to do."

"But Brother Stryker said Jesus had already done that," Elizabeth sobbed.

"And He did," her grandmother said.

"But Jews don't believe in Jesus, Elizabeth," her mother said, as if that could be any kind of justification.

"And Brother Stryker is a liar!" Elizabeth screamed. "I always knew he was a liar!" And it was screamed over and over and over until Dr. Nelson was called to come over and see to her. He gave her an injection that sent her consciousness cascading into a hole in the dirt, into a tunnel, where all the roots webbed with danglings of dirt became serpents, and the faces of gargoyles thrust themselves out at her. And there was Brother Stryker, pushing her into the grass by the blue coupe, telling her she asked for it, had been asking for it a long time, pushing at her mother's wedding dress, pushing the mouth of the serpent into her. He had his hand over her lips as he thrust his hips against her, repeating over and over, "You made me do this. It's your fault. You are the cause of my weakness and that is why you can never speak of this," until his words were inaudible, disintegrating into groans and shuddering breaths. And all the while the music drifted over from the high school gymnasium, where she had flirted with the silly young boys who could never understand her, would never be allowed to touch the place between her legs, shrouded in the lacy wedding gown now stained with grass and black soil, and fouled with the semen of a man of God.

Elizabeth had more injections over the following days, to keep her easy, the doctor said. She stayed in that hollowed-out tunnel for weeks beyond that, stealing into the dining room to carry a bottle of gin or whiskey back to her bedroom, covering her horror in a bath of alcohol. As weeks turned into months in the summer of '45, more images of death after the German surrender and, with the blinding blast of an A-bomb, the burned bodies of Hiroshima's babies seared their photographs onto her retina as well.

On those few days when her head was relatively clear, while the days of August dwindled into the close of the war, she begged her mother to find Eddie, bring him to her. She was met with confused grimaces until Aunt Frances happened by and explained just who Eddie Frye was. From far away she heard the sounds of her mother's delight at the fact that there was a real, live boyfriend. Then her father's eyes were above her and he was saying, "Don't worry, Elizabeth, Baby. I'll find your boyfriend for you," and she slept easier for a few days.

And then, finally, Eddie did come to her. She saw his face clear and handsome by her bed. He was speaking to her, through the haze of medication and booze. "You got to get yourself together, Little Girl," she heard him say, "if you want to paint the town red with me, okay?" Then the sound of his voice fuzzed into a scratchy, electronic hum, like the radio did sometimes when the station wasn't tuned in right. But Eddie had come. And he would be back. He was going to take her out to paint the town, was going to paint her into all kinds of lovely scenes. It was only then that a shaft of light pierced the tunnel, light dim and swimming with dust and floating ash, a vague hint at what was to come but an illumination nonetheless. It was then, with the emergence of this shift in the shading of her thoughts, that Elizabeth felt a turn in her spirit and her sanity; and she began to claw at the walls closing in, looking to punch holes in the littered landscape of her mind and dig her way to the one true love of her life.

*

The months crawled by after V-J Day, when car horns blasted, church bells tolled, and sirens celebrated what to Royce Fitzhugh was the bitter close of the war. He spent most of his time now doing a whole hell of a lot of unloading, but when his hitch was finally up, the trip back to Sumner was something sweet. It was sweet revenge when Royce and the other hometown boys came back, with the R.O.T.C. color guard and the Blackshear County High School marching band leading a parade, each of the returning heroes riding on the back of a never-ridden-on convertible, borrowed from Mighty Motors car lot in Albany. Folks cheered and whistled and waved American flags, and Royce did, indeed, feel like a hero.

It was common knowledge that his company had been sent overseas, so Royce never challenged anyone's assumption that he was there, too. "Where'd your unit land?" someone might ask, or, "Were you at Omaha?" And Royce squinted his eyes and looked off into nothing for a moment, then said, "I seen some things that could make any sane person go off of their nut. If you don't mind, I'd rather not talk about it just yet." His response was met with understanding nods and pats on the shoulder and another level of respect. Nobody ever had to know he spent the war slinging crates as long as he just played it quiet and proud.

But he could not play it quiet and proud with Elizabeth. She was not one to accept a dodge, let it go, or beat around anybody's bush. When he tried his standard line on her, she challenged him immediately.

"I don't want to hear about the bad stuff," she said. "Leave out anything bloody and give me the gist of it."

"It's not a thing you'd have the stomach for."

"I told you I don't want the bad details. Just the good details."

They were sitting in the sheriff's office, where Elizabeth had taken to passing some of her time since he got back and slipped into a deputy's uniform. The uniform gave him a new kind of presence, a commanding one, with the citizens who had once either shunned him or patronized him. He wore a heavy steel badge over his left shirt pocket and, because folks knew him as a veteran of the war, he came to think of the badge as a kind of medal, carried himself as if it were a Medal of Honor.

"There ain't no good details in a war," he said.

"Sure there are. What about the countries you saw? What about the people you saved? Didn't they celebrate you?" She walked over to his desk, cleared away some papers, and sat on the top of it, directly in front of him, pink skirt bunched between her legs, feet swinging, stirring at the air beside his knees. "Tell me all about that kind of stuff."

He leaned back in his chair, the leather holster at his side creaking with the movement. He liked the hell out of the way that holster creaked. He also liked the way she was all of a sudden willing to sit near him to hear about his exploits, albeit without the blood.

"Well sure they celebrated me—us," Royce said, then, in an attempt to keep it noble and vague, "but I didn't do it to be celebrated. I did it because the sergeant said to and because it was the right thing to do."

"Did what?" She wiggled a little and shifted forward, still swinging her bare feet.

"Went to war. War things." Royce wondered about her feet. As much as she went without shoes they ought to be rough and calloused, but they sure did look the opposite, dainty, soft, red polish chipped and fading. Yet Elizabeth herself seemed more calloused, determined to hold in, still her old rebellious self but with something like muted panic thrown into the mix.

"And where did you go first?" she insisted. "What country? Was it strange and beautiful? Aside from the bullets, I mean."

He saw that it was going to be futile to keep her questions at bay, and he tried to give her just enough to satisfy her so that he could move on with laying the groundwork for his dedicated seduction of her. "We landed in France," he said. "At Utah."

"That was one of the big battles," she said. "My daddy showed it to me on the map he kept."

"It was hellacious," he lied.

She stretched her feet out toward his chair. "Move closer. I can't reach."

Using his feet, he rolled the chair closer to the desk.

"Tell me more," she said, resting her soles on either side of him on the arms of the chair.

"Well, like I say, it was hellacious," he said. "But I won't go into that part." This was not bad at all, sitting between Elizabeth Lacey's open thighs, regaling her with bullshit.

"Did you save anyone?"

"Just this one guy. Slim, we called him. He got a load of shrapnel in his chest and—"

"He got wounded," Elizabeth corrected.

"Sorry," Royce said, wishing he could stroke her feet, find out it they were as soft as they looked.

"Go on."

"Well, Slim got wounded, and the medic was sixty yards over, and there was shells pounding all around, so I had to tote him—Slim—across my back and keep dodging the shells and the bullets falling like a steady rain."

"And you made it? I mean, I know *you* made it, but you saved Slim?"

"Yeah."

"That is so honorable. It's loyal. It's the kind of loyalty I wish for," she said. "It's the kind of loyalty I already have the recipe for."

"It wasn't nothing," he said wondering just what recipe she was talking about.

"You want to touch me, don't you?" It was out of the blue, in her usual way.

"I thought you had done had enough of that."

"Of what?"

"All them touching games."

"Why?"

"Because you got a boyfriend now. Or so I hear."

"Who says?"

"Everybody. They say you got some slick salesman type that nobody ever sees."

"He is an artist. A creator of scenes."

"Hey, is that the recipe you was talking about?"

She sighed. "Yes, it is true. I am in love. But I only see him every two months or so because he has to go all over. And for the first five months I only saw him twice. He calls me, though, every week."

"What about all the games with the other boys?"

"Oh, that." She moved her feet, to rest one on each of Royce's thighs.

He took a chance. He put his hands on the tops of her feet.

"I didn't say you could do that," she said. "I was explaining something."

"Sorry," he said withdrawing his touch.

"Thank you," she said with an exaggerated prudishness. "As I was saying before being so rudely interrupted, I am in love. I intend for Eddie Frye to marry me. But in the meantime I am conducting my life as usual."

"Meaning?"

"Meaning—and you can rub my feet now—I can't do without the fun. I won't do without it. I have to go out and play. I am a nocturnal creature, do you know that?"

Royce ran his hands over the tops of her feet, and they were as soft as he had expected. "But you plan on marrying a man you only saw twice in the first five months? Damn, girl."

"You don't understand. Those first two times I saw him were remarkable."

"How's that?"

"Okay, the first time, we sat on a blanket by Lake Blackshear and he touched me everywhere that wasn't covered with clothes and—" Elizabeth closed her eyes and moaned from a place down deep in her throat, squirming on the desk.

"That good, huh?" He didn't understand females, how a thing like that would make them moan when all he wanted to do right now was get her out of those clothes. She brought to mind that damned courthouse cat in heat, the one he had secretly killed for her honor a few years back, and that made him want Elizabeth even more.

She sighed, opened her eyes wide, running her hands up her waist, over her breasts, down her shoulders, quick and shuddery, shaking her head, throwing her long hair out and across her face. Then she looked at him. "Yes, it was that good," she said, glancing down at his crotch. "Good enough to give you a—" she cupped her hands and yelled, "Steely!"

"Why don't you put your foot on it like you did in Albany that time?"

"Because I don't want to now. Anyway, I'm telling you about Eddie."

Royce didn't want to hear about Eddie, but did want to continue touching her. He rubbed her ankles and around behind her heels. There was a small square of gauze bandaged onto her right heel with adhesive tape. He wondered if she had a blister and how she might have gotten it. "What about Eddie?"

"The second time I saw him was a few months later. That was a year ago last August. My daddy asked him to come see about me because I couldn't get out of the bed. I was too sad to even think. It was awful."

Royce remembered hearing, when he first got back to town, how Elizabeth had suffered some kind of breakdown. He remembered thinking how strange that was for a girl in her teens before he also remembered how much of her mind was so much older than that, not to mention the broth of the family bloodlines. The rumor, one that Royce had not believed before now, was that she stayed in her room, refused to wear clothes, refused to eat, said she wanted to die if Eddie did not come see her. And as she related the Second Coming of Eddie Frye, most of the stories he had heard were confirmed.

"Damn, girl, what got you so off in the head?"

She stiffened, like a stalked animal sensing danger. "The pictures," she whispered. "Of the camps." Her eyes were wide, full of fear.

"Oh," he said, wondering at her fierce reaction. "That was bad, all right." He tried to wear a mask of sensitivity.

"More than bad." Her voice was low, urgent. "It was demonic, sounds like demagogue." Then she giggled, tight and tense. "Or a demigod. You see?"

He nodded, even though he did not see at all.

"No, you don't." She looked down at her skirt, then up at him again. "Did you see any of that? No, don't tell me, don't. Don't."

"I ain't going to say nothing bad, Elizabeth. You tell me, though. Tell me what this Eddie Frye did for you."

"He saved me."

"How so?"

"He shone a light through the shaft. He lets me at least be a little yellow bird, like a canary, released in the mine."

"Girl, you talking way past me."

"He showed me permanence, that he would come back. I could fly through the shadows and the air wouldn't kill me. And he promised that once I was more like myself he would come back and take me dancing. He said we'd paint the town red. And he did take me dancing. And he does take me dancing, when he comes to see me."

Royce looked into her eyes, blue and inviting. "Well?" he said.

"Well what?"

"You going to let him do it?

She smiled and pushed on his knees with her feet. "Do what?"

"You know."

"Put it in?"

"Yeah. That."

"No," she said. "I can't. And it's so strange. He makes me want him to so bad, but he never says he wants to. It's like he's waiting for me to ask him to. Like he wants to make me ask him to."

"But you can't. Why?"

"It's just a thing I can—sense, you know? That if I ask him to do that, then he might not find me as interesting—I don't know—as exotic as he finds me now. So—not until we're married."

"Hell, Elizabeth, it ain't like you're a virgin or something, now is it?"

A look like confusion slipped across the blue eyes. "As a canary I am."

He let the odd remark pass. "Tell me why you so crazy about this guy Eddie."

"Because Eddie Frye is different."

"How?"

"I told you. He's an artist."

"Sounds kind of sissified to me," Royce sneered, thinking, *artist? More like a con artist is what.*

"That's all you know," She said. "He creates pictures from—nothing."

"Is that right?"

"Yes, that's right. And more. He holds back. He knows things and he doesn't spoil it. So he has to spend enough time with me to want me more and more, don't you see? Then he'll realize he wants to be with me always."

She damn sure was hard to follow, so he only said, "And then you'll give up the bars and the playing with fellers?"

Elizabeth cocked her head to the side and looked thoughtful. "I believe so," she said.

"Forever?" Royce asked. "For good and forever?" He lifted hid brows.

"That's going to be a damn sight, isn't it?" And she laughed a loud, giggly trill and crawled onto his lap with her legs splayed open, hugging him tight, laughing more, grinding against his khaki uniform, breathing into his neck. He put his arms around her, pulling her closer, and at that moment she sprang up, quick as a cat.

"I'll be going now," she said. "But I'll be back sooner or later, okay?"

He stared at her, but she only lifted her hand and wiggled her fingers in a little wave. "Sooner or later," she repeated, and twirled out the door and down the hall.

Royce squirmed in the chair. Goddamn her, he thought, standing and removing his holster, laying it on the chair. He walked over to a rickety door that had never hung right, always scraped against the floor until, over the years, it rubbed an arched groove into the wood. He entered the little bathroom and pulled the string hanging down from a bare bulb. Goddamn Elizabeth Lacey for messing with him, teasing him into a state. If she were any other woman he would have either spat on her for a cunt whore, like his mama, or gone ahead and stuck it to her, to teach her not to put it in a man's face unless she planned to give it over.

But Elizabeth was, as everybody agreed, different. She had a vulnerable craziness that made her legendary in this part of the state, and by now, Royce figured, the legend had been carried to the four corners of the world by the United States Air Force, not to mention the Brits and the Frogs— stories about a beautiful, insane girl down in South Georgia, a wild girl who made you count when you touched it, moved all over you until you moved back against her before she jumped off, who liked to feel your arousal and then, most times, to leave you with it, like she had left it with Royce now.

He closed the door, stepped over to the sink and unzipped his pants. Goddamn her, he thought, vowing again that he would have her, play the whole thing out until he got to be one of the lucky ones, maybe even got her to love him the way she thought she loved Eddie. Eddie Frye. There was a character he knew to be a weasel. But Royce was glad he had not told her the rest of what he had heard about Eddie Frye. That her father had paid for Eddie's initial train ticket down from Knoxville and, folks speculated, had probably been paying for subsequent trips and additional "expenses" if it meant keeping Elizabeth happy and relatively sane. That she had herself a bought boyfriend until she got tired of him or the money dried up. It was useful information, but it was not even near time to use it. He would wait until he was close to getting the prize before he risked alienating her with that information.

He thought about the feel of her there on his lap, with only three thin barriers of clothing between their touch, how she had left a damp spot on the outside of his uniform. He fumbled around now and found it, there on the khaki uniform trousers. He kissed his finger and put it to the place she had left, knowing he would have her, swearing it to himself one more time. Then he pressed his palm to the soap dispenser and reached down, closing his eyes, imagining that there were no barriers now.

*

Jolene had been right. Now that Ned was home he could not get enough of her. They made love at dawn, in the evenings, in the middle of the night when Ned woke up, and Eula Lura thought she was so full of him she would surely be in a family way in no time. They spent entire weekends making more love, some frenzied and some gentle, then lazing in bed, holding each other, sometimes talking about their plans. He wanted to save up his money, put his benefits and as much of his paycheck as possible into a savings account. Even if they had to eat sardine sandwiches they would accumulate enough money to move North. He could maybe get more education up there. Or start up a little business of some kind. He had a good head for business, he said. Then, with a raised eyebrow and a grin, "Maybe the restaurant business?" and she would blush and slap his shoulder.

There was a little house they could rent cheap in the agricultural depot crossroads of Warwick, a town surrounded by cotton, peanuts, soybeans, and corn, situated in the rural triangle between Albany, Ashburn, and Americus. The house was rickety, and the backyard was bordered by the railroad tracks, but it would do for them, for now. There were a few cracks in the rough wood boards, but Ned covered them with tar paper and whitewashed the exterior. He helped her plant a patch of marigolds and zinnias that she could see when she looked out the window of the tiny kitchen, where they spent so many hours together, having quiet talks over their predawn breakfasts and, on special days, their twilight suppers. Ned would laugh about how he would sure enough hold his head up high in Chicago, and smile about how rich they were in love, how living like paupers for a few years would be worth the investment they had already made in their caring for one another, and Eula Lura was ashamed that she had ever questioned his commitment to her, had ever dreamed of the Italian woman.

He bought a used pickup truck to get him to work every morning. The two of them would drive into Cordele, where he would drop her off around back at Sweetie Pie's Café. Then he would go about two miles further to Logan's Septic Service, where he had found a steady job. When he got off at five o'clock he would come back to the café, sitting out back where Miss Delia had finally put a tin roof over the picnic table, a place for colored folks to sit and wait for their orders to go. Under no circumstances, though, could anyone but Ned and the kitchen help eat there. She didn't want folks to see a bunch of nigras grouped up behind her place of business.

Eula Lura would fix Ned a plate, and he would eat supper and read his newspaper behind the café until the crowd cleared out enough for her to clean up the kitchen and go home, usually around seven o'clock. Finally, after the twelve-mile ride back to Warwick, they would bathe and fall into bed, exhausted, glad for that exhaustion, which brought them, inch by inch, closer to a new life.

"Did you know that in Italy we could walk right in the front door of any restaurant or hotel and nobody would bat an eye?"

"Do say." Eula Lura nestled her head against his shoulder as they lay on the iron bed.

"Sure could. Me and my buddies went to bars and cafés in those villages all the time. Didn't nobody, except a few white soldiers, ever say nothing."

She ran her fingers across the smooth scar on his left side, where a piece of shrapnel had ripped into his flesh. She had heard his stories many times, but always loved to watch the enjoyment on his face in the retelling. "Tell me about a place you went."

"Damn, there was so many of them." He thought a minute. "There was a little bar in this village near Massa, and the owner practically hauled a bunch of us in there off the street. Spoke a little English. Said he was proud to have American G.I.'s in his place. Wanted his customers to see us in there."

"Do say. That the man give you the staff he carved on?"

"That's right. Giovanni. And wouldn't let us pay for the drinks. And then he even got out some really old bottle of wine he'd been saving for a special occasion."

She propped up on her elbow. "Some of that fancy wine like in the movies?"

"I reckon. Only you know I ain't no wine connoisseur." He dabbed at his mouth with the corner of the bed sheet, pinky finger extended, pretending to be snooty.

She slapped at his hand, laughing. Then she stared at the ceiling, marveling at the image he had described. "That is a thing, all right," she said, trying to see herself sitting at the table with them. She would be wearing a fancy dress and ear bobs. She would sip her wine with her pinky finger extended, too, like a real, sure-enough lady.

She never tired of hearing about the faraway places Ned had seen. It was a part of the cadence of their life together, that she would lie with her head on his chest, hearing him breathe, listening to the rhythm of his heartbeat. "Tell me again about the boat coming into New York harbor," she often said.

"Mmmm," he breathed. "Now that was a spectacle. It was right at dark and the skyline all lit up, that big old Lady Liberty blazing light. I'm telling you, I don't think I ever saw a prettier sight. Except for this one here," and he swept her cheek with his fingertips.

"You a lie," she laughed as he pulled her up and kissed her, telling her she was the most beautiful thing in the big wide world.

"Tell me again about Harlem," she said.

"Like daylight!" he exclaimed. "Daylight out there on the streets, with all the signs blazing and the fine folks walking by, all decked out, women dripping in jewelry. And the music? Man, ain't nothing like it. Damn. The Cotton Club. You ain't never seen so many fancy colored folks in one place. And the shops, the businesses. It's a colored man's world, I mean to tell you. One of these days, when we get rolling in Chicago, I'm going to buy you some diamond earrings and carry you over to New York City, and you and me are going to step on out in some of them nightclubs."

She loved the way his eyes came alive when he talked about their future plans, when he acted so proud of her. It made her believe she really was desirable, even beautiful, and that he really did want to hang diamonds around her neck, from her earlobes.

There was nothing she believed in as fiercely as she believed in Ned, not even Jesus. She knew as certainly as Ned did that their hard work would pay off, that the fish he brought home from the river every so often, the fish he caught for sustenance rather than sport, would someday be filet mignon. Christmases and Easters came and went, still with no pregnancy, and the savings grew. And all the while, the dream became more and more of a thing to count on, a life to live that would be full of the dignity that came from self-denial and a sense of purpose. And the days of hard work went by like a flurry of November leaves. And another Christmas. And a summer. And an autumn harvest or two. And finally, one midnight at the end of a passing month of May, with no warning to the calm cadence of their lives, time came to a halt, when the dream went brittle and real as the thread of a frozen pulse, shattering into slivers that would dig at her heart forever.

Frances enjoyed the prosperity that came with the close of the war and the years climbing toward a new decade. She invested in some property in Apalachicola with Martha, and longed for the day when the two of them could leave Blackshear County behind. For a relatively young woman, she thought she looked forward to retirement much too much, though in truth it was a yearning for time alone with Martha and a place that might be a trifle more relaxed than this Bible-belted peanut country, with its penchant for suffocating those judged ungodly. And it took so little to be judged that she could not help admiring her niece for putting it directly in their faces, however insane it was becoming. Elizabeth, after all, was the only thing that held her in Sumner, and Frances needed to see it through. Frances might even be willing to look for work in Florida and move on, once Elizabeth was grown and gone—if, in fact, Elizabeth would ever be grown and gone.

Unfortunately for her niece, the exuberance of the war years fizzled into day-to-day routine. The activity around Turner Field died down, and the bars were filled with civilians, with bad boys from out in the county who didn't give a damn about Elizabeth's mythological status with the U.S. Air Force, the British Royal Air Force, and the Republican soldiers of France. Elizabeth still went to the clubs, still danced with the men, even though the soldiers had thinned out, leaving only those whose time was not up at Turner. And, while she was still "Angel" to the airmen, some of the hard-tails from out in the county saw her not as a mascot but as more of a maniac. "Crazy Lizzie" was one of the nicknames Frances heard some afternoons, sipping coffee at her switchboard, eavesdropping, and when Frances tried to envision what might lie ahead for her niece she could not see past tomorrow.

The self-destruction, it seemed, was a permanent inhabitant now in Elizabeth's demeanor, followed her into her eighteenth, then her nineteenth year, and beyond. There were tales about her drinking herself into blackness, once even passing out in a booth at the Teddy Bear Club, where that half-wit Dwayne Jeffries threatened to lift her skirt with a pool cue so he and his Neanderthal friends could help themselves to some free stuff, now that she was no longer a little girl. Frances shuddered to think what might have happened if not for the protective presence of a few airmen.

By the time her niece was eighteen, Frances regretted ever humoring Elizabeth where Eddie Frye was concerned. He was an opportunist, a con, a lowlife son of a bitch looking for easy cash. He was taking advantage of the entire situation, of Elizabeth's fragile reality, Jack Lacey's need to look out for her, and the entire family's concern.

When Eddie Frye breezed through town on his brush route, Elizabeth was courted, wined, dined, and treated to passionate afternoons by the lake at "our spot," as Elizabeth called it. She was filled with promises about how, as soon as he had enough money saved up, or as soon as he got a better job, or as soon as his ship came in, he would come for her and they would live happily ever after. He boasted about selling some of his paintings, but never brought any artwork to show Elizabeth, never painted her portrait, always put her off until Frances began to wonder if he had any kind of talent at all, other than the ability to read and take advantage of other folks' weaknesses. Jack Lacey compensated him for his time, the time he would normally be selling brushes, but Frances's brother apparently thought of it as money well spent, since Elizabeth got a fix that had her temporarily elated, back to her old self, almost.

When Eddie pulled out of town, Elizabeth, still full of the steep lift he delivered, rushed through two or three months of gaiety, running hither and yon, to nightclubs and creek bank parties and adventures. She dared the county boys to do ridiculous things and emasculated them if they let her down. She got drunk, created some kind of disturbance, and her daddy would get a call in the middle of the night from a sympathetic police officer or sheriff's deputy, whereupon Jack went and collected her, never letting on to Miss Pearl the full extent of what had happened.

"She's young and vivacious," Miss Pearl would say, checking her lipstick in her compact mirror.

"She's always been her own person, you know," Lucille would comment. "Independent. Bullheaded. It's her nature, that's all."

Campbell Lacey still tried taunting Elizabeth with his gun from time to time, and Elizabeth still laughed at him, which never failed to set him off on one of his rants. "She's ripping and tearing all over the county," he often yelled, slinging ice into his favorite whiskey glass. "She's the hub of the goddamn huckly-buck, by damn."

Frances's brother admitted to her, privately, that yes, he was concerned, but in the next breath he downplayed any suggestions Frances made that Elizabeth see a psychiatrist. "I see crazy folks all the time in my line of work," Jack said. "Elizabeth's not crazy. She's just high-spirited and sensitive, takes things too much to heart. She'll be all right as long as I'm around to look out for her."

"You won't be around forever."

"Such a prophet of doom," Jack replied.

Frances did not want to be a prophet of doom, but something about that initial breakdown had Elizabeth infected with a kind of muted despair. Martha thought it had to do with her awareness of man's capacity for cruelty, that the images of the Holocaust had damaged Elizabeth's capacity to see the delightful in everything, but Frances thought there was more to it. Elizabeth seemed to be carrying a deep wound of some kind, inside herself, a wound to her vulnerable self, and the years following the close of the war found that wound festering and opening and threatening to poison every aspect of Elizabeth's life.

It was Martha who suggested they drive Elizabeth up to Warm Springs, to tour the museum that was open to the public in October of '48. The Little White House, it was called, where Roosevelt had vacationed, where he had died.

Elizabeth was thrilled to be taking a road trip. She chattered away the whole drive up to the little community near Columbus, and Frances took advantage of the opportunity to question her about some of the rumors she was hearing at the switchboard, to get some help sorting truth from fiction, and she knew Elizabeth would tell her the truth, as always. Whatever dark corridors were forming in her mind, Elizabeth was still as honest as ever with those she trusted.

"Is it true you dared Marvin Dewberry to do a backflip off the roof of the Acorn Club and that's how he broke his ankle?"

"Yes," Elizabeth giggled, tossing her hair with the breeze from the cracked window.

"And did you dare Joe McGaha to jump off the Flint River Bridge in Albany and that got him arrested?"

"Yes, but that policeman was not reasonable at all. I told him I'd show him something if he'd let it go, and he gave me the meanest look."

At some points, though, the truth was much worse that the rumor itself.

"Is it true you took off your panties at the Texaco gas station and let Simp Welles wear them on his head?"

Elizabeth shrugged. "He was supposed to give them to the attendant instead of cash, but he decided he'd just rather wear them himself."

"How did he pay for the gas, then?"

Elizabeth shrugged again, as if she had left any concern for herself behind long ago. "I let the attendant put his hand on my left bosom and count to five."

"Right there in front of God and everybody?"

"Yes. Oh, but he was just the sweetest little shy guy. You should have seen him. He looked like he was going to wet himself." Elizabeth lifted her hair from her neck, leaned her head back and closed her eyes.

Frances traded a glance with Martha, who drove in silence, taking it all in. "Is it true you went with some airmen to a colored nightclub?"

"I rode with them to the Big Bam but they wouldn't let me go in. Only Randy went in."

"Randy who?"

"I don't know. Randy Somebody."

"Why was he the only one to go in?"

"To find somebody named Carmel."

"What for?"

"To get some reefer."

Martha made a little gasping sound.

"Oh my Lord, Elizabeth, you didn't take any of it, did you?" It was a mind-numbing, sickening thought, that Elizabeth might become a dope fiend.

"You don't 'take' it, Aunt Frances. You smoke it."

"And did you?"

"Of course I did. I was curious to see how it felt."

Another gasp from Martha.

"My God, Elizabeth. This is beyond going over the line. You'll end up in an opium den."

"Oh, Aunt Frances, don't be silly. I don't think there are any opium dens in Albany."

Frances knew nothing she could say would ever matter, so she lapsed into silence and let Elizabeth ramble on the rest of the way there.

When they walked through the museum and looked into the roped-off rooms, Elizabeth was not chatty at all, was instead quiet and solemn. She looked at each room in depth, and Frances thought she must be memorizing every detail, the rich-toned antiques, the deep weave of the rugs. But it was the portrait that drew a vocal response from her niece. "Oh! Look at that! Look at that!" A canvas of Roosevelt's head and shoulders was set on an easel, where the artist had been working on it. His face wore a sensitively dignified expression, and the shoulders were straight and proud. But the colors on the canvas dripped into blankness, where the artist had stopped, with Roosevelt's death. "I can feel that," Elizabeth said, fast, intense, and tearful. "That emptiness in the picture. It's me. An unfinished painting. It's me." She grew more and more agitated, breaking into fitful sobs, mumbling something about Amnon's sister and how she had to give up her colors and put ashes on her head. Finally Elizabeth covered her face. "I can't think of it. I can't look at it."

She and Martha hurried her into the car before she got completely beside herself. Elizabeth lay on her side on the back seat, arms wrapped around her shoulders as if trying to comfort herself, but drawing her knees up into a fetal position, moaning and crying, sometimes calling Eddie's name. In the space of an hour she had gone from giddy to solemn to guttural, from exhilarated to exhausted, leaving those who loved her helplessly puzzled in her uneven wake.

As she approached her twenties, Elizabeth cycled and recycled, with a ferocious humor, a crashing depression, a shot to the vein of Eddie Frye, then the frenzied partying that ultimately went dark and desperate again, downward spiraling back into cryptic, spiritual sayings and self-loathing, always circling back to the story of Amnon. Frances dusted off her Bible and re-read that story, of Absalom's revenge against his brother, and it filled her with questions, about what it might mean to Elizabeth. She watched for an opportunity to question her niece, but the girl was too unstable, unpredictable, vulnerable, and Frances feared what would happen if she pressed hard for information, even on Elizabeth's giddy days. Frances began to hold back even more, measure her words, and move in response to her niece's frame of mind. Just as it had the rest of the family, silent vigilance had taken Frances captive.

*

The day LittleBit's life, the dream she shared with her husband, came to a halt was so much a typical, cookie-cutter kind of day that she failed to pay attention to more than a few of the little details she would grasp at so desperately in the subsequent weeks, months, and years that would not let even her revenge give her peace. She would comb back over that day again and again, reaching for a way to prevent what happened, to turn events in a different direction, to do anything, in any instant, at any cost, to keep him safely wound up in her present, in their future of unfulfilled possibilities.

They had made love before they got up that morning, in the temporary cool of a deceptive South Georgia day in summer. Over breakfast she laughed at how Ned imitated Jim Leavett, showing her how the white man shoved his arm into septic swamps without a moment's hesitation, never minding the stench of fermented excrement; how Leavett would sling the foul sludge off his arm, wipe his palm on his khakis, and with that same hand rake back the thin hair from his forehead, leaving his hair damp and greased with sewage; how, just a few hours later, that same hand, never washed, would tear into the sardine sandwich his wife had packed him for lunch.

"Lord, he's a nasty thing," LittleBit said, crunching on a bit of bacon.

"I won't have to put up with it much longer, Baby," Ned said. "Just a couple more months, I figure. We'll be set up in Chicago by Christmas, for certain."

He kissed the top of her head as she finished her coffee, the way he did every morning as he went off to work. Sweetie Pie's Café had changed hands a year earlier, so LittleBit spent her days at home, doing ironing for the white ladies who brought her straw laundry baskets of their husbands' fine shirts, shirts good enough for Ned to wear, she thought. She watched him walk out the door. He carried a brown paper sack holding the meat loaf sandwich she had made as she prepared breakfast that morning. The white bread was thick with mayonnaise, just the way he liked it, and she wrapped the sandwich in wax paper to keep it moist until he broke for a meal.

She spent the day while he was at work imagining their little apartment in the big city, inventing neighbors who would bring them pies and hams to welcome them to the building, wondering if they would see her as a dumb country nigger, grateful that Ned was engaging and funny, with a way of winning folks over, grateful that he was so smart, insisting that they live below their means so they would be able to save money for as nice a place as they could imagine.

Since she didn't have any shirts to iron that day, she decided to clean out drawers and cull unnecessary items, just to have everything all lined up for the impending move. She inspected clothing for tears to be mended, sorted mementos into categories: his, hers, theirs. She fingered the fancy necklace and ear bobs he had sent her from Italy, the bracelets and lacy handkerchiefs from France, the silk scarf with a map of Long Island on it, and the tiny replica of the Statue of Liberty from his brief stay in New York. When they lived in Chicago there would be elegant nightclubs with combos playing smooth jazz, and she and Ned would go dancing and she would finally be able to wear the beautiful things he had given her over the years.

She opened a small box and lifted the Purple Heart he had been awarded, for catching the shrapnel in his side, and remembered how she had cried when he told her about the wound, the first night he was home, when he lay naked beside her. She told him he should have written her about it. No, he said, she would worry too much. But he did want her to have his medal, the one Sergeant Lewis pinned on him in the hospital. She held it up to catch the sun's light, wished she could wear it like a brooch, but that would be disrespectful. This was a symbol of Ned the warrior, from a long line of warriors, brave and determined.

She washed out her undergarments: three slips, a bra, and four pair of panties; then hung them out on the backyard line to dry. She swept the porches at the front and rear of the little house before she got a bound bundle of long sticks from beside the steps and set about raking the dirt yard into curling swirls of grooves, even and repeated in the gray grains of ground that had never been planted with grass. She would miss the pretty patterns in the soil when they lived in Chicago, but she would have much more to do than rake dirt, only to have it rained on and wind blown and tracked through. In Chicago she would arrange pictures on the walls and knickknacks on a tiered stand. She would sew pillow cushions out of green and blue velvet, add gold tasseled fringe, and place them on a sofa with curved legs, like the one she had seen in a store window in Albany. Their little apartment would be the envy of the building.

She put on supper at the usual time, warming the pole beans she had shelled and cooked a few days before. She rinsed off some pork chops, seasoned the meat, and blanketed it in a coating of flour while a mound of lard melted in the black skillet. Cooking for Ned was so different from cooking at Sweetie Pie's Café, hidden in the back with two other colored cooks, eating leftovers in the hot kitchen in between the lunch and supper crowds. At the café, she was just another appliance, detached, never knew who was eating what or how they liked it. But when she cooked for Ned it was an act of love, part of the tempo of their dance, sometimes an offering of comfort in exchange for approval, sometimes a bid for affection, sometimes a seduction. She wasn't all that good with words, so she spoke to him through the melting juices of a fried chicken breast or the custard-like base for her creamed corn, watching his eyes for signs of pleasure, listening for his moans of satisfaction.

"Mmmm, Baby," he said that evening. "You sure do know how to put a goddamn scald on a piece of meat." He cut into the golden crust of the pork. "We ought to open us up a restaurant up there in the big city, show them how the down-home folks eat."

LittleBit laughed. It was another part of the dream, to own such a business together, to have folks clustered in the doorway, just to get a whiff of LittleBit's mustard-glazed ham, Brunswick stew, and sweet potato pies.

"You going fishing with Odell tonight?" she asked.

"No. I think I'll go by myself, go to my secret spot."

"You ever going to show me that place before we go North?" she asked.

He leaned back in his chair. "I reckon I will, LittleBit. But not tonight. I'm going late tonight, do some thinking."

LittleBit began to clear the table, smiling at his habit of fishing at midnight every few months, so he could clear his head, he said, and get his mind right, count what was important more than really needing to count fish. Those were the times he would go to his own little spot up a branch off the Flint River instead of going off with Odell, his best friend, with whom he fished most weekends whether the fishing was good or not.

She stopped to squeeze his shoulder, remembering the starchy feel of his army shirt, the way he held his head even higher when he joined up. She remembered him handsome and straight in his uniform, wished she had been able to afford to get a picture made.

"Got bait?" she asked, knowing he did, but it was a part of their routine that she should ask, thereby allowing him to point out his pride in a thing done with success.

"Sure do. Right out yonder in the worm bed. Fixing to dig them on up." He stood and stretched. After he dug the worms he would go nap for a few hours, then he would get up and collect his poles and a few other things to throw in the beat-up truck. She would be asleep by then, having crawled into the bed next to him when she finished her house chores, but he would come and kiss her on the head, she knew, because he always did that one thing before leaving her. Finally he would drive out to a parking lot and boat launch near the hydroelectric dam on the Flint River, park the truck, then hike the half mile through the woods until he found his honey hole on Scratchy Branch.

LittleBit set about washing the dishes she had laid in the big sink. "I'll fix up that leftover hoecake for you to carry with you," she said.

She watched him through the window above the sink, watched him spade up the rich dirt he had nurtured into a crop of fat, tan-colored and gray earthworms. He loaded a mason jar with worms and dirt, then disappeared around the side of the house to get two cane poles, she knew, and make sure they were rigged to his satisfaction. In a while the screened door at the front of the house slammed and his footfalls went into the bathroom and, in another while, into the bedroom, where the groan of the mattress springs told her he was lying down.

She swept the kitchen, dried and put away the dishes, and poured herself a glass of buttermilk to help her get to sleep. Then she sat at the metal table and sipped the thick, sour-sweet liquid, thinking about how she would miss her mother and sister when she and Ned moved to the city, but at the same time she was sure she could convince them to follow her up there. She would tell them about the clubs and the nice people and the way colored folks were done right instead of being shut out of places, told where not to go, what not to touch, how not to be. Ned would be seen in Chicago, would cease to be invisible and become respected, a veteran of the war, a veteran of the South.

She rinsed out the glass and splashed cool water on her face, her neck, washing the day's sticky sweat away, rinsing off grit. Then she remembered the hoecake and wrapped two pieces in some wrinkled foil that had been used and reused, residing on a shelf with the other reused and washed pieces of foil; staples like cornmeal, flour, and lard; and canned goods. She set the silver package on the table and went back to the shelf, thinking to add a can of sardines to the snack of the hoecake.

After her shower she slipped into her nightgown and crawled into bed with him, soothed and cooled by the hum and breeze from the steel oscillating fan sweeping its rush of air back and forth and back across their bodies. The dimness of twilight had eased into darkness, and she could feel the evening taking her. She curved her body up next to his bare back, breathed in the scent of him, that man scent of hard-spent sweat. She listened to the cadence of his breathing, felt the rise and fall of his rib cage, relaxed into the familiar, the predictable, the essence of their comfort, one with the other, and she felt herself falling into a peaceful place, where her eyelids dropped shut and her consciousness went into hibernation.

Some time later, on the outside edge of her sleep, she felt the mattress sink, then rise to the sound of the springs, after which she slept deeply again, for what seemed like hours but it wasn't, because he was back again. No, not gone yet, because she felt his lips on the top of her head and he only did that when he was leaving, and she wanted to say something. What? I love you? Don't forget the hoecake? Lie on top of me and make love to me? Something. But sleep would not let her mouth form the words or her throat send any sound up to connect with her diminishing will to speak. So she gave herself over to it, let the possibility of rippling dreams have her, did not offer the words hovering at the edge of her awareness.

If only. If only she had given him her words. If only she had asked him not to do something he wanted to do, asked him to stay, a thing she had never done in their life together. If only this one time had been the first time for that, for asking him not to do a thing he wanted to do. But it wasn't. Instead, she let her fuzzy, peripheral impression of his presence drop into darkness, let him blend into the night apart from her, and in doing that, she allowed him to walk into an eternity, away from her.

*

This night, Elizabeth decided, would be the night of consummation, when she would ask Eddie Frye to make love to her. She had convinced herself slowly, in a gradual turn, over months and months of their piece-meal courtship, that it was the only way she might be able to hold him. Too, she thought it was possible that he was only waiting for her to ask so that he would know she trusted him. What had seemed like a silent kind of combat was really a test of trust, and when that matter was settled for him, marriage was sure to follow. It did taste something like defeat, but she was willing to give up her pride and her rules and her sense of safety for that one chance. Four years was a long time to be dedicated to a man, but she had been so sure that Eddie Frye would be swallowed up by desire that she had devoted those years to that unfruitful quest. She kept a log in the back of the Holy Bible, dates and hours spent, a list of days and weeks and weekends Eddie had given her. Altogether she had spent eighty-eight days and six hours with him over the past four years. That was enough time, she decided, for him to ask for marriage, or, at the very least, to beg her to part her legs for him. She had held on as long as she could, and she clung to her theory of trust as she wove her reasoning through the desperate justifica-tions in her head.

No, he had not come around to play through her original scenario, not at all; had, in fact, turned it all around on her. Instead of entreating her to let him go further, he held back, weakened her with his words, tempted her with the confidence of his touch, for the longest time keeping his hand over her clothes, until she finally, in a writhing moment of weakness, lifted her blouse and whispered, "Touch me, Eddie." And he did, for a moment, then drew his fingers back so that she had to take him by the wrist and press his palm to her breast. Elizabeth shushed her doubts and let it begin in earnest, cascading her into a fall, into the purest lust she had ever expe-rienced. Just as insistently as she had asked him to touch her up here, she then pulled his hand down there, against her flesh, and he continued to oblige. He grinned a kind of victory each time, putting his fingers to her thighs until she could not get her breath, and sounds she had never heard were pushed from her throat. Before long she asked if she could touch him, and he let her, lying back to enjoy and have it reciprocated, in full. But still, he did not attempt a consummation.

It was she who did all the asking, the pushing, and each time she became the bird in the coal mine, flapping madly down another tunnel, then flying back, safe and flushed and surprised. Finally, once she convinced herself it was his way of earning her trust, she resolved to ask him to make love to her, let him experience what they all—all the others—wanted. Then he would see how perfect a union theirs could be, how satisfying, how full of faith.

She told Aunt Frances about her decision on the way to Albany that Friday, on a shopping excursion for Miss Martha's forty-fifth birthday present. Miss Martha was a collector of antique plates and any kind of glass figurine of a fish or a mermaid. Elizabeth and Aunt Frances were in the habit of making occasional drives to Albany or Macon to visit junk shops and any rummage sales advertised in the newspaper. On such forays they found all kinds of treasures for Miss Martha: a pair of pink, salmon-shaped salt and pepper shakers, "Niagara Falls" written across the glass fish scales on their sides; a green ceramic bass, tail curled, amber-eyed; a figurine of a mermaid, lazing on her side, long hair blanketing her porcelain breasts. Elizabeth came to think of the rivers and lakes as being full of little crystal fish, and the oceans sparkling with delicate glass dolphins ridden by languid mermaids, nothing like the strange and threatening sea creatures in the Bible, the ones Daniel of Babylon saw in his symbolic dreams.

Aunt Frances was smoking a Chesterfield, her favorite tortoise-shell cigarette holder clicking against her teeth every so often. They sat in one of the bright red booths at Crowe's Drug Store, eating sundaes, talking about Eddie Frye. Elizabeth sipped on a soda, watching the music notes slide around the store from a radio in the back, behind a high counter where the pharmacist worked. "Tonight I will ask him," Elizabeth said, "to love me completely."

Aunt Frances leaned forward in the booth, set her chin on one palm, and sighed. "I have learned that I have no sway over you, Elizabeth. But I think I've made it clear how I feel about that man."

Elizabeth hugged her shoulders. "I love him. He's the only man I've ever loved. Really loved."

Aunt Frances hesitated, then, "Doesn't it strike you that he's the only man you've ever wanted that you could not get to do your bidding?"

"No. I love him."

"Maybe you are making him up in your head, like you do so many things."

"No. Don't you see? He makes me afraid, then he shows me I'm safe. I wish you would like him."

"Oh, Waterbug, I wish you could see him more accurately. In your mind it seems he can do no wrong. I don't want to see you disappointed."

Of course her aunt did not understand. "'O thou of little faith.'"

"All right, all right. I'm no fool," Aunt Frances said. "As I say, I won't lift my voice in vain."

It was a day hot with white sunshine, and the sidewalks sent heat bouncing up the sides of the brick and stone buildings. They found little side streets where the stores were cluttered with used items and racks of cast-off clothing. Elizabeth loved to plunder these alleys and found more for her wardrobe here than in Rosenberg's Department Store, where her mother liked to shop.

Elizabeth flipped through the racks of resale items, scavenging through the press of hanging clothes, until, "Oh!" Her eye caught the blood red stitch of a pattern embroidered onto deep blue silk, the kind of blue one rarely saw, fit for a high priest, a blue so deep into sapphire it was almost indigo, and the red threads seemed to vibrate with brilliance. Elizabeth's fingertips brushed the slick fabric. It felt like the cool of the afternoon grass. She took it down from its hanger and held it up before her. "The dragon," she breathed.

"What?" Aunt Frances was a few feet away, studying some chipped, mismatched china, searching for a treasure for Martha. "My, that is a beautiful kimono, Elizabeth." She walked over and lifted the hem, inspecting for rips. "And it's in perfect condition. You know, I'll bet someone got rid of that because of the war, even though it's not from—"

"The Chinaman," Elizabeth whispered, her eyes spilling tears. "The beautiful shirt."

"What shirt?"

"The beautiful shirt he was going to leave me in his Will. His mother's shirt. The most exquisite embroidery you have ever seen." She wiped at the wet streaks on her face.

"You know what, Waterbug? Maybe it's still there, in his house."

"Could it be?" The thought had never occurred to her, but now she latched onto it.

"After all, it's been boarded up all this time. All those old shacks are going to ruin, condemned."

"Yes," Elizabeth said, wondering, why not? Why not go over there, just go in and look for the shirt? Would that be wrong, a violation? "I haven't thought about him in so long. I feel bad for not thinking about him."

Aunt Frances put an arm around her shoulder. "I'll bet he found a lovely place to live, with nice people and—"

"The Chinaman told me I was a dragon, you know, because of my birthday." And another tear wiggled down her cheek.

"Goodness. That's nothing to cry about, is it?"

"I just haven't thought about him in so long. Years. I haven't been very loyal to his memory."

"You sound as if he died. He went—he was run off, that's all. I'm sure he found a very happy life somewhere, like I say."

"I should have at least thought about him," Elizabeth said. But then she giggled. "This is perfect for me. Absolutely perfect. Don't you think? The dragon?"

Aunt Frances nodded. "Yes. The dragon."

"Energetic, honest, and bold," Elizabeth said. Then she turned her attention to helping Aunt Frances find her birthday gift, mostly because she could not wait to get home and try on the kimono.

She took one of the longest baths of her life that evening, adding hot water and bubbling salts every fifteen minutes or so, until her skin was pink and soft, toe pads and fingertips wilted. She got out and rubbed scented lotion all over, from her shoulders to the soles of her feet, and spritzed cologne on her chest and thighs. Finally she stood before her bedroom mirror, the kimono cool against her warm skin. She put on her charm bracelets and thin silver bangles, then untied the deep blue silk sash and let the kimono slip from her shoulders, whispering a swish down her back, slipping past her calves to the floor. This was how she wanted Eddie to see her, and she decided she would wear the beautiful kimono and nothing else, have him take her to Lake Blackshear where her daddy had a small motorboat tied up at the Smoak Bridge Marina, and insist that they find a hidden-away creek and go skinny-dipping.

She heard the front doorbell ring at eight-thirty, knew she had time to brush her hair and paint her nails, because Eddie always spent at least the better part of an hour with her daddy, over at the sheriff's office, talking about she didn't know what all. She thought it was wonderful that her daddy liked and approved of Eddie, regardless of what her Aunt Frances said. Her mother liked Eddie too, she thought, because Eddie always kissed Pearl's hand and told her how beautiful she was and how it was no wonder her daughter was such a knockout, what with such good breeding and all. Her grandparents usually disappeared into their bedroom when Eddie was around, her grandmother especially reluctant to spend much time with him, though she didn't know why until Aunt Frances tried to explain it. "She sees something familiar in him that brings back a regretful memory, I think," Aunt Frances said. "He reminds her of a man in her own past who disappointed her."

"Disappointed how?"

"Oh, by not being what she thought he was."

"Eddie will never do that," Elizabeth said.

"I hope not, Waterbug," Aunt Frances said, but she didn't sound like she meant it.

When Elizabeth swept into the living room in the silk robe, Eddie whistled, and said, "You and your getups. Always a surprise."

She laughed and snatched a straw hat from a peg by the door, tying its long yellow ribbon beneath her chin.

Her mother sat in her usual spot on the divan, looking flattered and smug after Eddie's smooth compliments. "What do you have on underneath that thing, Elizabeth?"

"Nothing," Elizabeth laughed. "Not a stitch."

"Surely you are joking," her mother said.

"Of course she is," Eddie said. "Don't you worry, Miss Pearl, your daughter will be treated like the lady who bore her," and he kissed her hand.

Pearl smiled, sleepy-eyed with alcohol and attention, and took a dainty sip of brandy. "Have a wonderful time."

Eddie laughed them out the door, and, once on the other side, he kissed Elizabeth long on the lips and said, "Oh, I think we'll have more than a wonderful time. You really have on nothing under that?"

"Not a stitch."

"Don't you want to go dancing?"

Elizabeth pressed against him, lips on his neck, tasting the saltiness of his skin. "No," she said. "I've come up with something better."

It was a thirty-minute drive to the lake, a long body of water stretching from Warwick to Americus, sparsely dotted with fishing-camp houses. The Smoak Bridge Marina was deserted, a few boat lights out on the water. Eddie put a blanket, a bottle of whiskey, and a small flask in the boat, then helped Elizabeth in and shoved them off. It was a cloudy evening, but the moon hung huge and orange-red. Elizabeth watched it as the boat slapped its way across the water. A strange moon, a color she did not often see in the night sky. It seemed like an angry moon, and she shivered with the thought of it, glad that strands of clouds muted its glow. She looked for a diversion, made a request of Eddie, who insisted that no, he would not open the motor up all the way.

Normally she would have called him a coward and taken over as captain, aiming the small bow carelessly into the dark, full throttle. But this night would be slow and calm and monumental, no matter what color was suspended in the sky, she decided, as they made their way toward the dam and power plant, to where she knew a creek emptied its cold current into the Flint River. She sipped from the flask of moonshine Eddie had brought, moonshine her father had given him, over at the sheriff's office.

Her daddy only kept the best moonshine, tested and pronounced fit for human consumption, and it heated her all the way down to her toes.

"It's called Scratchy Branch," she said as they passed the dam. She pointed to some trees jutting up from the black water. "That's the landmark."

Eddie maneuvered the boat to a place where the woods parted to let the creek's waters flow through the cover, then meandered it upstream and just around the first bend, to a sandbar that stood out against the night, white and illuminated by the sky's subtle glow.

They tied up to a tree and Eddie spread a blanket on the shore opposite the sandbar. They sat on the blanket passing the flask to one another, smoking, talking quietly, Elizabeth feeling warmer and slower with the grain alcohol.

"You love me, don't you?" she asked, emboldened by the liquor and by the nearness of her plans fulfilled.

"You know I do, Sweet Cakes." Eddie held out a match to light her cigarette. "All the time." He said it in his grinning way.

"All the time?" she asked, invoking him to repeat it, his oft-used response to her, and she listened hard at the tone.

He obliged. "All the time," and this time it sounded more serious and believable.

"You must have girls chasing after you all the time. One in every port, all that." Her feet were halfway off the blanket and she dug her toes into the sand. With the movements of the tiny grains she felt a shifting foundation, as if something subtle were waiting to trip her up, turn her thoughts another way.

"Sure I do."

"And what do you tell them?" Elizabeth had asked him all the questions before, knew she would get the answers that satisfied her before, then came that niggling little doubt again, and she told herself in her head, *Stop it.*

He chuckled and lit another cigarette. "I tell them I gotta be true to my South Georgia gal."

"You are true, aren't you?"

"Sure I am."

"All the time?" she asked, needing to hear those words.

"All the time," he said, dimples winking at her.

"Will you ever be through traveling all the time?" She knew the answer to that one, too.

Eddie laughed. "I told you, Little Girl. I got to travel to get set for the Tropics."

"And when you are set?"

"Coming straight home to you."

Elizabeth took another sip from the flask, the charms on her bracelet catching the dim reflection of the moon's light. She thought she heard a lunar whisper, a malevolent one, and inhaled, catching the faint scent of strawberries, but berries too long sitting, just before turning bad.

Elizabeth decided to test the waters a little. "My Aunt Frances doesn't trust you."

"Why not?" He flicked some ashes toward the creek.

"She thinks you're too slick and you're up to no good."

"And you believe that? Come on, Little Girl, you know you got Eddie Frye for life."

He had never said "for life" before, never put it exactly that way, and Elizabeth took that as a sign of certain success. She put her hand on his thigh, just above the kneecap, and squeezed. "Aunt Frances says different," she said, but only as something like an afterthought.

Eddie threw his half-smoked cigarette into the creek. It hissed as it hit the water. "That old maid?" His tone was exasperated. "Goddamn. You know what she needs, don't you?"

"What?"

"She needs something a man can give her."

"Something like what?"

"Like something you're wanting, I'm thinking."

Elizabeth was confused. The moonshine was going to her head fast now. "What does she need?"

He threw his head back and laughed. "Come on, Elizabeth. You know.

She needs some of the main attraction in a fellow's trousers. Let her get some hard loving, then she'd understand."

"No, she doesn't need a man," Elizabeth said, thinking of her aunt and Miss Martha, and what she had seen them doing one early morning, the morning after her first time spent with Eddie. "All she needs is M—" Elizabeth caught herself. Had she really been about to tell Eddie the secret she promised to never give away? The secret that made Miss Martha cry out of so much fear of discovery?

She looked over at Eddie, who was in mid-swallow, the flask turned up. Then he sucked in a long breath through his teeth and passed the flask back to her. "That's some strong stuff." He leaned back on his palms and seemed to be oblivious to her nearly revealed secret.

She told herself this was even more evidence of the naturalness of their romance, that they must be soul mates, that she wanted to tell him all about the photographs in her head, about everything, including Aunt Frances, and she wished she *would* tell him, right now. He wouldn't do anything to make Miss Martha afraid. He was safe and trustworthy. But something held her back. She looked up at the sky and thought that yes, the moon *was* angry, with her, for her odd doubts and wavering spirit. She turned up the flask again, taking the last sip, making another grasp at conviction, getting her fingers around it.

Eddie opened the pint of whiskey and offered that to her. After the hot, harsh moonshine, regular whiskey tasted like tea.

"Better be careful," he teased.

She leaned and bumped against him with her shoulder. "I can drink you silly. You are an amateur."

Eddie sent a laugh into the summer air. "Is that a challenge?"

"No." She tossed her cigarette into the creek and stood, giggling as she stumbled a bit, untying the kimono, letting it slide down her body, just as she had in her room. "This is."

Eddie exhaled a long whistle. "You've got it all, Little Girl. And what exactly is the challenge?"

"I'm a grown woman," she said, a little disappointed that he did not

react as so many had before, when offered just a glance, all exuberance and
gratitude, if not senseless groveling.

He smiled and shifted his weight in the sand. "But what's the challenge?"

"Swim with me," she said. "Then bring me back here," she indicated
the blanket, "and make love to me."

"Sure thing." Again the understatement. Elizabeth felt another trickle
of disappointment, so she reached down and took another deep swallow
of bourbon. He was standing and taking off his clothes. They had never
been completely naked with each other, and she studied his body, tall, lean,
and olive-skinned. The dimness created dark places across his form, and
she could not see the place beneath his stomach until he turned sideways
to study the creek. She could see it then, an aroused, pronounced shape
jutting its silhouette against the liquid backdrop, and she thought it was
beautiful. She had touched it many times, felt the satisfaction of his
response, the way he groaned when the warm thickness melted over her
white fingers, but she had never seen it in this context, and her body sig-
naled its own response. But before she could go to him, abandoning the
swim, he caught her eye, caught her looking at it. He grinned and rushed
at her, and they splashed into the cold creek water, gasping with the shock
of it, ducking under to even out the feeling, swimming to the sandbar,
where a drop-off created a natural pool. They swam and laughed, and she
put her arms around his neck and kissed him. The length of his body
brushed against hers, sending the current in a different caress, off course,
and she could feel all of him in the water's rearrangement. She wrapped
her legs around his waist and closed her eyes, resisting the impulse to bear
down, to have him there, in the creek.

"Better watch out, Little Girl," he said into her neck, brushing it with
his tongue.

"Or what?"

"Or we'll get distracted and drown."

An image wafted through her head, of the two of them, joined, her
legs tight around him, spiraling down, beneath the water's surface, to

underground rivers and to the ocean, past blown-glass starfish and ceramic seahorses. Sea nymphs and mermaids lolled in the currents and stared, mesmerized, their long hair billowing in the weightless depth. And, as though infected with the passion of the couple they saw joined there, the mermaids put their arms out to lock hands, pulling close, dreamy-eyed, kissing salty lips, emerald tails twisting, bare breasts sliding against each other.

Elizabeth felt the press of her own breasts against his chest, and she could not wait another minute. "Come with me," she whispered, taking his hand, pulling him around to where the water was shallower. She stood, stumbling, feeling beyond tipsy, walking across the sandy bottom littered with flat rocks, worn flat by the continuous movement of the creek. She stepped onto the blanket and turned, heart thudding fast, blood burning through the delicate sheaths of her veins. He was standing in the shallow current, watching her. "Make love to me," she said. "Slow."

"Sure thing, Little Girl." He waded over to the water's edge and grinned. Then he reached for his pants and began fumbling in the pockets, taking out keys, coins, the small pistol he carried everywhere.

"Now," she said, sitting on the blanket, then repeated, "Slow."

He removed his wallet and rifled through it, whispering curses.

"What are you doing?" Elizabeth asked, some of the urgency of her desire threatening to fade.

"Gotta get a rubber. Hold on." He continued to dig in the wallet

She was horrified, had never even seen one of those things, knew what they were for, but knew also that it was a barrier to the truth of a real touch, a real closeness between two people. "No," she said, angry, insistent. "No rubber. That's nasty. How could you—"

He stopped. "But what if—"

"No rubber," she said.

"Okay, okay," he half-grumbled, refilling the pockets with all that resided there.

She did not like the tone of his voice, did not like being dismissed, but the urgency was growing again, pulling her deeper into it. It was no longer a question of resolve; it was a choice diminishing with every thud of the pulse in her ears, faster. She took another sip of bourbon, looking for calm, looking up at him, staring into him. He dropped to his knee and she lay back, shoulder blades pressing into the cool give of the sandbar beneath the blanket, and he began to kiss her, and any remnants of disappointment or uncertainty dissolved. She pressed her hips into his, mashed her palms into his shoulder blades, trying to pull him close, closer, unable to get close enough. She wished she could turn into warmed wax and their flesh could melt into one another's, their mouths melded in the deepest kiss possible. They rolled over and back and over on the blanket, breaths hard and quick, Elizabeth gasping with a clutching eagerness she had never let herself feel with any man, only Eddie, and only in glimpses until now. Then he was on top of her, eyes above her, and even in the dark she could see his open eyes, pupils dilated, large and black and every bit as full of wanting as hers must be. "Now, Eddie," she whispered. "Now."

She lifted her left knee, sliding the sole of her foot across the blanket, feeling the roll of grains of sand under the material, until her knee pointed to the sky, aiming at the moon's clouded face. She arched her back, straining, letting the curve of her body meet the push of his, the press of his belly against hers. Then it was there, the smooth, taut flesh of it nudging against the meeting of her thighs, the place she had let some visit—not like this, and only in timed increments—the place she used for games and bets and dares. And now she was begging, having taken him up on a silent dare, full of implications. Her body was begging and embracing and opening and pulling, and, as their bodies connected, she felt the perfect moment in the sunset, knew the fullness of her love for him. She would give herself over to him, *was* giving herself over.

He moaned, a deep, real sound. Now he would know. Now he would know how much she loved him, and he would never settle for anything less than this. He moved slowly, filling her with him, setting a rhythm that grew quicker by degree, and she wanted to swallow him, *be* him, to get inside the snapshot forming in her mind. Now he'll know, she kept telling herself, over and over, faster and faster, to the cadence of his breathing.

Now he knows, now he knows. But in spite of all she was telling herself, in spite of the isolated corridor she was exploring in her heart, something strange and threatening was growing in her, a knowledge she did not want to take in.

She pushed harder against him, lifting her gaze to the black-clouded sky, to the bands of black taking the moon from deep orange to red, to foreboding and malicious. She pushed harder, and he rolled over and she was sitting upright, taking him deep inside her, and Eddie was moving with such abandon as she had never seen in him. She could feel the turn he was making, directly into his life with her, careening into her life. It was then she heard the faraway cadence of the moon, like a clattering of lunar reeds. It was then she felt the hard turn in her own spirit, the wreckage he might inspire, and, though it felt like the close of another war, it was not a victory; it was a surrender, the white flag of sanity planted in the sand, staking territory, on a midnight bend in the current.

NIGHT FISHING

The big man, Ned Sutton, pushed at brambles bathed in humidity, sometimes knocking at webs of weeds and tangled briars with an intricately carved cypress staff, making his way to where the banks of the Flint River dipped into the woods. He ducked under a low limb, a shelter for a bowl-shaped dirt wallow, probably made by a nesting doe. He slid his hand over the top of the staff, which knobbed its perfect fit into his palm. His fingers could read the letters raised there, around the top of the staff, where Giovanni had carved "92nd." He ran his grip down the side of the walking stick, feeling the starred-and-striped grooves of a small American flag under which the words "Liberatore" and "Redentare" were nestled.

Ned used the stick to stir back some briars and brush. A good bit of the trail had gone under fresh growth in the space of only a couple of weeks, the warm rain of dog days soaking life into the dankness of rotting twigs. But he knew the way, even without a light, the moon's dark glowing the forest in a subtle illumination his eyes settled into with the ease of a nocturnal forager.

He carried two cane poles and, in a haversack slung over his shoulder, a tin of sardines, a couple of slabs of hoecake wrapped in crinkled foil, a Nehi, a bottle opener, a small paper sack holding sparse tackle—bobbers, weights, hooks, and line—a stringer, and a mason jar, lid punched with holes, full of black dirt and snail-gray earthworms, all knotted and slickly wrapping and sliding curled into, across, and around one another.

The night was electric with the crisp singing of crickets, chirping tree frogs, the deep bass of bullfrogs in the distance. An owl called into the din of sound, a lonely, purring, four-noted noise blending with the buzz of vibrating life. He pulled at vines winding over fallen oak limbs as his fine, heavy work boots, handed down from his boss, snapped sticks into the soil.

He had gone about a quarter of a mile when he began to hear the faint wash of the river's currents spilling around rooted tree trunks, a liquid whisper filtering through foliage. The trail would soon widen to finally fall open onto the high bank above his favorite fishing spot, the one he frequented regularly of a summer evening, the one where a pristine sandbar settled a ways back from the mouth of Scratchy Branch, where the catfish nestled in deep pools and silvery bream swam in water that window-glassed the rippling sand of the bottom, their fins stroking at gentle currents in the shallows.

It was the best spot on a river he had fished for twenty-six years, since he was three years old, trailing behind his uncle on long hikes through the woods in search of that magical place where the fish never failed to bite. He had discovered it not long after he was married, and told no one, could not tell his uncle, who had died when Ned was only a boy. He had only last spring told his wife of nine years, the wife who would fill a deep skillet with lard and heat it over a gas flame until the lard skated, skidded, turned clear, popped, and gurgled. Then she would lay the headless bream across the surface of the liquid grease, which would kick up a burbling fizz of wet heat, bubbles swallowing and rolling the fish until they went all golden and crusted as the sizzle died down. She would lay the fried fish out on brown paper sacks to drink up the grease. The next morning she would pour off the fish grease into a special molasses tin and wipe the remaining skim of oil out of the skillet with a dishtowel. Then she would rub a slick new shine of lard across the black iron surface.

The two of them would break off the fish tails to eat like bacon and have smiling conversation over their supper. They would talk about his job at Mr. Ches Logan's septic tank business in Cordele, how it paid good enough, would even pay off, when they had enough money saved up to finally move North, to Chicago. They would laugh about the fact that, on that good-enough paying job, he had to ride along as helper to Jim Leavett, a loudmouthed ex-G.I. who called himself a "turd wrestler" and a "shit shaker" and hardly ever washed his hands. Ned and his wife would talk about bad weather making up, and what the crops might look like in a few weeks, and how her sister's new baby was doing after that bout with the croup. In a while she would scrape back her chair and begin collecting the dishes. She would stand at the high sink, barefooted, her back to him, and he would watch the way her hips moved as she washed the plates and glasses. He would think about how, in a little while, he would lie between her open legs and make love to her, how her fingers would tighten around his upper arms, how she would breathe sharp, gaspy breaths into his neck and shoulder.

The sound of the water's motion came louder now, as the man stepped through the last pine-needled barrier and onto the lip of a bluff that watched down on the shore and sandbar. The moon's dim face sent hollows of dimpled shadows across the narrow creek, about thirty feet across, widening until it opened into the Flint, the part of the river turned lake, drawling its sluggish, dammed-up current along banks of oak and sweet gum. He looked up at points of stars, pale and veiled with murky clouds, taking in the spiraling presence of some kind of all-moving force, just what he didn't know. He made to rearrange his gear and take the red clay trail down to the water's edge.

It was then, as he turned to the sandbar hanging back from the mouth of the branch, that he caught a movement in the corner of his vision, and a sound like the jingling of keys, only octaves higher, more delicate. He squinted toward the white sand wrapped on all sides by wet reflections of the sky, then back to the shore below him, and made out a form, a rolling, moving form, the delicate tinkling sound rolling with it, then two forms blending into one, then apart, together, apart in a rhythm he recognized without allowing that recognition to take shape in his consciousness. It was out of place here on the river, in the dead of a night alive with summer, at midnight.

He could make out the sprawl of the woman's blonde hair against the square of a blanket, the reach of her arms around the man's back, the jingling flash of the bracelets on her arms, the puddles of clothing at their side. The lunar haze gave the woman's pale flesh a luminous sheen, ghost-like, otherworldly. But the reality of what he was seeing edged into his perception, accompanied by a swell of ingrained fear. He needed to be away from this, and quickly, yet the shock of what he saw rooted him at the top of the red clay trail.

The man on the sandbar was murmuring something, movements quickening, and they were rolling over again, and she was upright, palms against his shoulders, lifting, dropping, lifting, the stark white of her breasts catching the full moon's woods-filtered light and she cried out then, the man beneath her uttering a gruff, growling sound that startled Ned, finally, into motion. He turned, knocking the two cane poles into a sapling, sending them clattering to the ground, and the carpet of sounds in the forest took a breath of silence.

The woman screamed, her face finding his above her, on the bluff.

"What the hell?" The man on the blanket looked up to where her gaze had landed, and, shoving her aside, began snatching at some of the clothing. "What the hell are you doing?"

"Hey, I know him!" The woman said, laughing, her initial fear gone, speaking as if he were some long-lost friend. She stood, stumbling, ignoring her own clothing. "I know you! You're Thello. Hey!"

"You aren't going to know him for long 'cause he's about to be one dead nigger," the man said, stepping into his trousers.

"Oh, pooh. Nobody's going to be dead," she said, pushing back her hair, bracelets tinkling ominous recollections into Ned's mind. "It's just Thello. Hey! Come down here!"

"Goddammit, Elizabeth," the man on the sandbar said. "Don't just stand there. Put on your clothes."

"I apologize," Ned said, finally finding words. "I didn't know anybody was here."

The man, shirtless and sneering, approached him, stumbling up the bank, up the red clay trail. "You're a lying bastard."

"This is silly, silly, silly," the woman said, in a strange sing-song way, as she put on something like a robe.

"How could I know anybody was here?" Ned asked, the next layer of reality sinking in, a feeling of dread settling over him.

The man stepped up to where Ned stood. "You know because you been standing there watching the whole time," he said, glaring a challenge.

"No." Ned shook his head and kept his voice steady. "I was on my way fishing, that's all. And I can be on my way away from here, just as easy."

"You son of a bitch," the man mumbled, reaching into his pocket.

But Ned did not wait to see a weapon produced. With the reflex of his army training, he came across the man's jaw with a clenched fist, sending him tumbling down the dirt embankment, knowing at once what it meant and that he had no say in any of it anymore, had not, indeed, from the moment the man first spied him.

The woman let out a little cry, then an exasperated sigh. "Y'all don't do this."

"He's a dead bastard is what I know," the man said, struggling to his feet.

"Don't be silly," the woman laughed.

It was then that Ned was aware of his body moving, running, dropping the carved staff, too disoriented by fear and anger to follow the trail he had cleared just moments ago, instead stumbling through vines that pricked and scratched and tore at his arms, falling, rising, stumbling further. The fear was that he had, in one ridiculous moment, foiled all the plans kept on hold for years, plans just before coming to fruition. The anger was that the imperative of that fear existed in the first place. The anger was that, once upon a time, he had rolled a Sherman tank over ground held by an enemy of the United States, had taken that ground back and been welcomed into Massa with cheers and flowers thrown by the citizens. He was wounded, was decorated, was by no means a coward, yet here, back on the soil of his homeland, he had no choice but to run. It was the imperative of that ingrained, necessary fear, the fear of a much older, much more insidious enemy.

He could hear her calling after him: "Thello, wait! It's okay! Thello!"

He heard something else, too, the man's voice, the warning shot of a pistol, then the thrashing of brush at his back, shouts for him to *Stop, god-*

dammit. But he would not be still and wait; his only chance was to get away, hide, find a hollowed out nook in the woods and wait them out or make his way to his truck, race home, gather up his wife and money, and strike out for Chicago this night, tonight. The urgency of his pace increased with every second of recognition. *I know him,* the woman had laughed. *I know him.*

He let the knots and flashes of thoughts find her face, putting it in full light in his head, framed in the recollection taking shape there, held there since last summer, but as some kind of surreal shadow. It had played out in the back hallway of a beer joint in Albany, Georgia, the Teddy Bear Club. It was well over a year ago that he and Jim Leavett were there to work on a backed-up sink in the men's room. Jim was outside running a snake in a sewer line when the woman approached him. He had just leaned over to pick up his shirt, having shed it in the June heat, when she stepped out of the restroom and looked him up and down, gave him a wicked grin. It was there, in the back hallway of the Teddy Bear Club, while patrons laughed and danced to Tommy Dorsey recordings in the adjoining room, that her soft fingertips traced slow paths in the sweat of his chest, sliding over rises of muscle, gathering more salty wetness from his flesh. She wore a full skirt, a fancy, flowing one, light burgundy; and a man's shirt, loose and open to the third button down, showing a thin slip underneath. There were bracelets, too, dangling silver and gold objects and coins, tinkling with every turn of her hand. Her eyes were insistent, her voice edged with the kind of intensity that told on the fragmentation of her mind. "No. Don't you dare put that shirt on. You look nice. What's your name?"

He opened his mouth to speak, but she spoke first. "No. Don't say. I'm going to call you Thello. Do you know that play?"

"Ma'am?"

"That play, silly. That play. *Othello.* Do you know it?"

"Yes, ma'am. But not very well."

"Sure you do," she said with such conviction that, for a moment, he believed her. "O-Thello. Shakespeare. It was a tragedy, the Moor and Desdemona. Such a love to have for a woman. Wasn't it?"

She pressed her palm against his shoulder, the back of her hand scented and pale next to the deep brown of his own skin. Then she rolled her hand over, took it whispering down his chest again, rolled it back over to the palm, movements laced with the sound of the bracelet, fingers meeting the rippling hardness of his stomach, massaging sweat into skin. He knew she was not right in the head, but she was pretty; he knew she was putting him in danger, but he was powerless to do anything about it; he was devoted to his wife, yet he could feel his body responding to her touch, to her lush, confident lack of inhibition. He prayed that no one would see them there. She rolled her hand back over, dropping it so that her knuckles, then fingernails, brushed the crotch of his khaki work pants, just for an instant, but long enough for her to know and to smile some kind of crazy confidence at him. Finally, she put her index finger to his bare stomach, let her finger slide a series of little loops in trickling sweat, then brought her finger up to her mouth, her eyes never losing his. She parted her lips and met her finger with her lips, red nail lingering against those matching red lips, lingering more at her lower lip. Just before she turned to go back to the barroom she said, "Come dance with me when you finish, Thello. We'll put this place on the map."

The full recognition of that brief minute or two in his life unleashed a fresh reservoir of adrenaline now, seeded by the terror. It was a convergence of coincidence and material history that pushed him on. He ran harder, then he slowed, letting loose the haversack that was a hindrance now, letting it drop to the roots and limbs tangling his feet. Then he ran on, more fiercely than he had ever run in his life, running for his life. Crickets, frogs, the buzz of noise in his head crackled with every footfall, and he defied the cadence of the creatures as they sang to him that it was too late now, too late now, too late now. He kept moving, full of muffled determination, full of the surging swell of anger that had taken him, back there on the bluff. And the canvas of his mind sketched flickering pictures dancing like cold flames—images of the compost heap at the back of his yard, butted up next to the train tracks, where he had spaded up writhing strings of worms in the afternoon shade, just hours ago; of the back of his uncle's hand as he folded a curling worm into a hook, stabbing it onto the hook once, twice, three times—on a creek bank now aged, eroded, changed forever; and, finally, of his wife asleep in the iron bed where they often talked and argued and loved, in rich moments slipping by. She was wearing her thin cotton nightgown, the summertime gown scattered with fading rosebuds, the bedroom window open to suffocating summer air and the fluttering wings of moths and palmetto bugs, the cast-iron skillet sitting slick and empty on the gas stove in their threadbare little kitchen.

BOOK TWO
KANSAS LACEY
Summer 1962

At the age of twelve, Kansas Lacey was sure she would never be as pretty or as smart as her best friend Roxy Tolbert. She would more certainly never be as pretty as her mother had been, with soft, gardenia-pale skin, eyes the sapphire color of peacock feathers, and full pink lips. She would never have breasts and hips, the facial structure of a woman, or a menstrual period. Roxy had these things now, and when she wasn't attending to them she was engaging in her commitment to educate Kansas well about every aspect of burgeoning womanhood. Roxy had drawn pictures she copied from medical books at the public library, where she lived when she was not with Kansas or being punished. There were dozens of pictures she had drawn of naked women with elongated nipples and scribbles of pubic hair. There were diagrams of ovaries and Fallopian tubes and all things vaginal for Kansas's edification. Roxy did not draw men in full form, but did draw disembodied penises of all shapes and sizes, and in varied stages of rigidity. Kansas kept the drawings hidden under the corner of her bedroom carpet, to be brought out and puzzled over whenever she had another question for her friend or whenever she was good and alone.

Kansas puzzled over all kinds of things. She was particularly fascinated by the bigness and variety of places in the world, wondered if people on the other side of the globe felt as insignificant as she did, or if they wondered about her as well. She collected *National Geographic* magazines, enthralled with the periodical dedicated to displaying a planet so full of exotic folks, full of places so unlike South Georgia. The world held islands ringed in turquoise water, and mountains haloed by clouds. There were slabs of ice floes, and glaciers, bobbing like gargantuan chunks of jagged cork near the poles, far from the heated streams of the Southern summer. There were temples and stone ruins and ancient cities jammed with hordes of humans, shoulder to shoulder in currents on the streets. And everywhere, all over the world, were children with mothers and fathers who guided them, protected them, and gave them the security of knowing what was and what is. Kansas was certain of this as she studied the pictures of the girl in Thailand, the boy in Poland, the baby in India.

Kansas also wondered if she would never find the security of knowing about her own parents. Her family kept that information tucked beneath polite conversations, coded by euphemisms and hidden like the eggs under a setting hen. The hushed whispers at her mother's funeral let her know, even at the age of five, that this was no ordinary death, a fact that was confirmed when, in Kansas's seventh year, LittleBit, the cook, let it slip that Elizabeth Lacey had taken her own life. LittleBit had been reprimanded by Kansas's grandmother, and, if Kansas had not known better, she would have been worried that LittleBit would be fired. She did not worry, though, because, there was something else she knew, had learned through her practiced observation. Kansas knew her grandfather owed LittleBit some kind of awkward loyalty, as he often took up for her, whenever his wife criticized or complained about her.

Such were the sorts of impressions gathered by a child who was nurtured by impressions alone, as opposed to honest explanations. Kansas learned when a tone of voice indicated a swept-away secret, or a lift of an eyebrow sent out caution signals, or a polite reprimand symbolized volumes of untold reality. At the age of eleven, she began recording all the hints, codes, and dodges in a secret diary. She kept it in a Buster Brown shoebox on top of a locked cedar chest—the unopened property of her great-grandfather—that rested against the foot of her bed. She watched the pattern of family deception crawl across the pages whenever she added to the list. Then she continued her project, studying them, sending test questions out into the familial ether, receiving vague non-answers while she collected flakes of honesty from maids and cooks and the live-in workers at the jail next door, every tidbit making her even more determined in her quest.

But then, in Kansas Lacey's twelfth summer, a rush of odd circumstances fell out of the sky and brought her within touching distance of her mother's last days: her granddaddy bought a vacation home on the Flint River, a huge redwood home with a boathouse and a doorway to the past; she learned some of Roxy's most disturbing, most seductive secrets; Martin Luther King, Jr. returned to make even more trouble just up the road in Albany, this time causing havoc at her granddaddy's jail; and the moon began to tug at menstrual tides deep within her. Those were a few of the instances and days that blended and bled into one another over the course of Kansas's thirteenth summer, making it the summer that defined her, brought into clarity the jumble of kaleidoscopic glass bits she always felt herself to be, let the fragile glass bits of her personality fall into a pattern rich and unique.

The singular incident that got it all started was when Roxy's twin brother Leo carelessly took up a sharp hatchet, chopped off their four-year-old brother Coy's thumb, and threw it up on the sloping tin roof of the jailhouse. Over the sweltering days that followed, Kansas, Leo, and Roxy watched the tiny appendage go from orange to blue-green to black against hot silver, swirling small currents and sprinklings of decaying scents down to the scrubby backyard of the Blackshear County Jail. It was on a Thursday. It was 1962.

Leo, Roxy, and Coy were three of jailer Victor Tolbert's four children, had always lived where steel bars kept social misfits on the edge of their world, but still a presence, day after day. Kansas's grandfather, Jack Lacey, brought the Tolberts to the Blackshear County Jail years earlier, her nursemaid Pinky said, because he felt obligated to look after them. Kansas wondered about the reason for the obligation, but also accepted her grandfather as the "looking out for" type. If he shot a mess of dove or caught a string of fish, he always took the booty to Miss Lovie Macon or Fred Forbes, or anyone else who might not have anything to cook for supper that night. Once, when Kansas was riding in the patrol car with him on a Saturday evening, his headlights caught a dead possum in the road.

"I'd better check on that," he said, stopping the car. "Miss Lovie Macon is crazy about possum." And he backed the car up the highway, got out, and pronounced the road kill to be fresh enough to eat because it was still a bit warm. They rode back to town and across the railroad tracks, Kansas's grandfather holding the possum by the tail out the driver's-side window, right up to Miss Lovie's door, the eighty-year-old colored woman cackling with delight, her grayed-over, cataracted eyes studying the fine animal she would boil up tender, she said, "and get that wild taste gone."

It was even written in Kansas's diary of family clues that her grandfather was a "looking out for" kind of man. Other phrases Kansas had written to describe him were, "calm in a fight," "fair with money," "serious," "watches the news a lot," and "sad and lonesome-seeming at times." But "looks out for folks" was at the top of the list. And the fact that he had brought in Victor Tolbert to run the jail next door, which shared a clothes-lined side yard and back play yard with the Laceys' house, benefited Kansas by providing her with companions. Kansas grew up with Roxy, had someone to play with on a regular basis, even though her grandmother disapproved of the Tolberts. It made downtown Sumner, with its stores and thoroughfares barren of family households, more like a real neighborhood, with at least a few children running the streets and yards together.

The oldest Tolbert child was a boy, Jay, a shadow at the edge of his family's life, off at this boarding school or that since he was eight years old. Now seventeen, he had been at Marion Military Institute for the past four years. On those rare occasions when he visited, he was aloof, an awkward thread connecting him to the rest of the Tolberts, and Kansas never knew what to make of it. Her granddaddy took up time with him, though, carrying him on weekend hunting and fishing trips, and was even working on, via his political connections, getting him an appointment to West Point.

The youngest Tolbert child, Coy, was pale, blue-veined, and solemn, a quiet soul unperturbed by the voices of his parents, particularly his daddy's, a voice that berated and ridiculed, it seemed to Kansas, just to pass the time. Coy's only playmate was Hotshot, the simpleminded colored man who kept up the jailhouse, kept the courthouse clock wound up, and ran errands for the sheriff's office, with Coy at his heels.

Roxy's twin brother Leo was pudgy, "pork-fed with a butt full of lead," her grandfather would laugh, and redheaded with freckles all over; Roxy was more angular, rust-haired and speckle-flecked as well, but pretty to Leo's plain. Her body had just this winter erupted in swells of femininity now ripening and drawing looks from the boys at school and in town, and Kansas could not help wishing that her own breasts would lift and fill out and require the kind of bra Roxy wore instead of the flat triangles of lace-edged nylon Kansas's great-grandmother bought for her at the Empire department store around the corner or at Rosenberg's in Albany.

Roxy and her two remaining brothers lived in the house attached to the front of the jail, a dungeonesque, Victorian structure with steep, brick stairs and dark, barred windows glaring down at the backyards and alleys where they played. Victor Tolbert spent his days visiting a cold-edged humor on the inmates he kept, and Kansas was forever nervous when she found herself in his presence. He was never mean to her, but she didn't like him for the way he berated his children, and she didn't like the way he looked at her, his eyes narrowed as if he were seeing inside her thoughts. He had a hollow-cheeked face, a receding hairline, and a twitching jaw that foreshadowed wounding words. Sometimes he turned his hard taunts toward his wife, Jolene, a thin, red-haired woman who spent her days doing laundry and cleaning out things—closets, cabinets, toy boxes, anything. She rarely spoke to Kansas, always looked startled, and moved with her shoulders hunched over, as if her own spirit was broken across her back. Whenever Tolbert decided to throw his temper at Jolene, when stabbing words or the muffled pounding of a fist to a wall drifted from the open windows of the front rooms, the Tolbert children scurried like mice to Kansas's yard, the twins to create games and stay out of their daddy's way, and Coy to find a quiet piece of shade in which to repetitively carve in the dirt with a sharp stick, or pull grass to make little green mounds, or just to pick something— his latest scab, the flesh of his neck, his nose—while Hotshot sat next to him, a silent, hulking form, digging along with him.

On the far side of the jailhouse was the office of the *Sumner Local*, serving the small town with church notes, wedding pieces, and farm news. On the near side of the jailhouse was Kansas's grandparents' and great-grandmother's house, where Kansas had lived all her life, the first five years in the choppy wake of her mother's presence, the last seven in the deepening repercussions of her mother's death. She had vague memories, reinforced by photographs and home movies, of a mother who was blonde, beautiful, and moment-to-moment unpredictable. She remembered pieces of quarrels, her mother at odds with the rest of the family, but all the time getting her way. Kansas had recollections of sitting next to her on the hard, third-row pew of the First Methodist Church, her mother's legs crossed, ankle swinging fast and agitated throughout Brother Stryker's entire sermon; of long afternoons spent in the big kitchen, just Kansas, her mama, and the cook, Eula Lura—her mama and the cook sharing jokes and secrets and waves of unbridled laughter; of a blue convertible and squealing rides down dirt roads to hidden places her mother wanted to show her or to meet up with friends and make a party in the middle of nowhere, on a creek bank, at night; of sipping Royal Crown Colas on a bar stool in Albany while her mother danced with a string of laughing men, one by one waiting, some of them in uniform, men she collected like the charms that jangled on her silver bracelets; and of bare feet with red toenails, a cinched waist, flowing skirts in sherbet hues, and big straw hats to protect her face from the sun. Kansas could also remember being all the time cautious with her mother, never knowing what would set her off, send her into her fits of frustration or exhilaration or despair. She could remember being intimidated by and forever avoiding her now-deceased great-grandfather, Campbell, who was tall and gruff; and she continued to feel similarly about her grandmother, Miss Pearl, who grew more stiff-spined and aloof each day. She took refuge in the consistent warmth, however silent, of her grandfather, Jack Lacey, and great-grandmother, whom Kansas, at two, dubbed "Grandemona," replacing the much more formal "Miss Lucille" the family had once used.

She replaced another name, too. On an evening when her mother was laughing in the kitchen with Eula Lura, her mother referred to the cook as "LittleBit," and explained that Eula Lura's husband used to call her by that nickname because she was such a big woman; whereupon Kansas, the giver of nicknames, insisted the family begin calling her that as well. But the Eula Lura who had laughed with Kansas's mother was now the silent, emotionless LittleBit who had few words to say to Kansas. She had not seemed pleased when Kansas began calling her by her old nickname, and she rarely ever smiled.

These were the adults who populated Kansas's family. And she had learned not to ask any of them, save her great-aunt Frances and Pinky, too many questions about her mother. Kansas's daddy was yet another mystery she knew was not to be solved by her immediate family. Where Kansas perceived discomfort at the mention of her mother, she confronted downright hostility when she asked about her father. So over the years she learned to direct most of the big questions to LittleBit's mama, Pinky, the colored woman who had looked after her from birth and gave her an emotional and spiritual sense of some kind of potential, some kind of future resolution. Pinky did not dodge questions with the squirming avoidance so characteristic of Kansas's blood kin. If Pinky was unwilling to share a truth she simply said, "That ain't yet for your mind to know." But now Pinky was sick with the cancer, her voice weakening yet more forthcoming, more inclined to a final unburdening, Kansas sensed.

The Lacey home stood crisp and white, jalousied windows of an enclosed porch across its face, looking out over the main street of town. Across the side alley, the courthouse loomed like the Acropolis, its huge domed clock chiming out the increments of childhood in surreal crescendos of hours and half-hours building to sultry noons and coarse midnights. Kansas was aware of the prominence of the Lacey family in the workings of Sumner, Georgia; her great-grandfather, Campbell Lacey, had been county sheriff for more than a quarter century before he died of a heart attack when Kansas was small; and his son, Jack, for years a deputy, had held that office ever since. Jack's old-maid sister, Frances, lived with another spinster named Miss Martha in a big, white-columned house a couple of blocks over from the telephone office, which sat behind the courthouse. Kansas and Roxy spent summer mornings in the ladies' parlor eating pastries and giggling over the goings-on of the town. Kansas learned through Aunt Frances and Miss Martha that her grandmother, Miss Pearl, had once upon a time been an active club woman, a church leader, a regular hostess at social gatherings, but now she rarely left the house, instead sitting all day in her floral rocking chair in the living room, looking at the TV. Her emotions were shut off and sometimes the door to her bedroom, too, remained closed for days on end, and Kansas's grandfather slept in the guest bedroom, down the back hall near the kitchen.

The day of the thumb chopping, Kansas spent the morning helping Grandemona and LittleBit make dinner for her grandfather and the prisoners. Her grandfather was another whose name was rewritten at Kansas's insistence. When Kansas was orphaned at five, she desperately insisted on calling her grandfather "Daddy." After all, the one she called "Mama" was suddenly an echo in her world, and her little arms locked onto the big man who wore khaki pants, starched white shirts with elegant silk ties, and a holstered pistol at his side.

"It's 'Grandfather,'" Miss Pearl corrected her.

"'Daddy Jack,'" Kansas volleyed, stubborn and needing to finally have the presence of such a thing as a daddy in her life.

"'Grandfather,'" came the return.

"'Daddy,'" Kansas repeated, until the bastardized moniker finally stuck, becoming ingrained in the fabric of the familial landscape.

Daddy walked over from his office at the courthouse every day with the twelve o'clock chimes to have dinner with Kansas, Grandemona, and Miss Pearl, the dining room table set with silver and starched linen in his honor, and dotted with dishes of barefoot LittleBit's ham-juiced, fatback cooking and syrupy sweet tea. After dinner, the ritual moved to the living room, where Daddy knocked back a shot of Evan Williams, then savored a second shot, slowly, inhaling a Camel as he watched the midday news on the Albany TV station. After a fifteen-minute nap, he walked back over to the sheriff's office, leaving his wife to her soap operas: *As the World Turns, The Secret Storm, The Edge of Night,* followed by the blaring din of game shows and glass after glass of peach brandy.

Kansas stirred the amber liquid in the yellow ceramic pitcher, the wooden spoon clacking at ice cubes. "Our prisoners sure do eat good, don't they? Mr. Hooker over at the hardware store says they ought to get bread and water is all." She dipped her little finger into the liquid and sucked a sugary drop from the improvised teat.

Grandemona's deft white hands carved at a tomato, unwinding its skin into one languid serpentine strand. "Anybody can wind up in a jail," she said. "Imagine if it was one of your people. Cane Hooker is just a mean old man."

"I can never get the skins off in one piece," Kansas said, watching the red-orange tomato strip coil snakelike on the white metal tabletop as Grandemona slid the tiny paring knife between skin and meaty pulp. The old woman twirled the fruit between thumb and palm as she peeled, mucus-pouched seeds sliding across her thumbnail. "You will with practice."

Kansas walked over to the sink and looked out across the backyard to where coal-black Pruella sat on the porch of Pinky's shotgun house, fanning herself with a cardboard funeral parlor fan. Both LittleBit and her sister Pruella lived in the Quarter across the railroad tracks, but their mother, Pinky, had been living in the Lacey's back yard for a dozen years. Before Pinky was nursemaid to Kansas, she had cared for Kansas's mother Elizabeth when what Grandemona called "the dark sickness" took over Elizabeth's mind. Now Pinky lay dying of cancer, so her daughters took turns staying with her. Kansas sneaked and visited her, too, even though Miss Pearl did not want her entering colored folks' houses. Not anymore. Not since the trouble started up the road in Albany.

Kansas's kinship with Pinky grew out of penetrating black nights in the aftermath of her mother's death, when Miss Pearl moaned and cried out to Jesus for her daughter to come back to her, wandered through the house at all hours, drunk and inconsolable, calling Elizabeth's name over and over. Those were the hours when Kansas crept from the big house, away from the starch-scented sheets of the canopy bed her mother shared

with her on special nights—times her mother seemed so like a playmate—
to Pinky's spring-squeaking iron bed, nestling against the old woman's
flannel gown in a curled, soothing sleep. When the sun came up, Pinky
wrapped her in her arms in the warm bed and they talked about all kinds
of things.

"You ingrown, child. Ingrown like a toenail, into me," Pinky always
laughed, "because I tended your mama, all through her hard times, put my
soul into her when she in them dark fits. Then her soul go into you. We got
ourselves joined up at the spirit. And it's the spirit that gives us life. Your
grandmamma Miss Pearl always be a cold woman, even when she be putting on the dog at them teas and such. Now she cold and lifeless, too, since
her baby be dead. You come to Pinky when you want the truth. Pinky
might can't tell it all just yet, but Pinky can't lie, neither."

And Kansas did seek Pinky's truth over the years, instinctively in small
samplings, feeling the fuzz of danger that came along with the razor-thin
revelations. The implicit understanding between Kansas and Pinky was
that their shared truth was not to be undressed before the family, mired as
her folks were in ritual and propriety. Kansas understood, somehow, that
Pinky was taking risks for her, and a bond of trust grew exponentially
between them.

"Why do you reckon Mama killed herself?" Kansas asked when she was
nine. She and Pinky were sitting at the metal table in Pinky's tiny kitchen,
no wall separating it from the rest of the miniature house. Butterbeans
thumped into aluminum pots as they splayed the green sheaths, zipping
thumbnails through thin, moist membranes. Pinky gave her a matter-of-
fact version of the vague explanation her family sometimes shrouded in
terms like "dark sickness" or "nervous condition."

"She took a fit is all," Pinky said. "She were always one or the other.
High up in the trees or low down on the floor. She put that gun to her head
when she down on the floor."

It was the first Kansas knew of her mother's method of suicide, and
even at age nine, she had lived with veiled talk long enough to know that
even though Pinky seemed to have only mentioned the gun in passing, she

had really done it deliberately. "But why?" Kansas asked again.

"There's lots of reasons why, I reckon. But can't nobody know what's in another person's mind, especially not one that's bound for Milledgeville."

"What's Milledgeville?"

"It's where they put the folks that's feeble-minded. Or mongoloid and such as that."

"Like Hotshot?" Kansas at once thought of the colored man who lived in the jailhouse, the man who acted like a child, danced on the street corner for tips, played tag with her and the Tolbert children when they were small, who even now spent most afternoons rolling little plastic trucks across the dirt with Coy.

"Oh, Hotshot's feeble-brained, that's true. But he ain't a danger. And he ain't crazy. Them folks at Milledgeville is flat crazy."

Kansas was startled by the word, "crazy." Her mother was unpredictable and felt her feelings in the biggest ways possible, and the polite descriptions circulated among the family were nothing like what she was now hearing from Pinky. "Was my mama crazy?"

Pinky did not hesitate. "Yes, child."

"But nobody put her in Milledgeville."

"No. It was talked of, though, after—" Pinky stopped with the kind of deliberate abruptness Kansas knew was intended to allow that there was more to find out, but it was simply not time.

"Why didn't they put her in Milledgeville?"

Pinky opened another sheath of green and the bloated embryonic shapes hit the pot. "It don't work like that, Baby. Don't hardly nobody get sent off but poor folks or colored folks or pitiful folks. Your mama had plenty of money and somebody to look out for her. And your Daddy Jack was collecting papers behind his wife's back telling about all kinds of fancy insane asylums that wasn't like at Milledgeville."

Kansas digested this new information for a few minutes before she asked, "What's it like at Milledgeville?"

Pinky chuckled. "You don't think old Pinky done been in that place, do you?" She shook the aluminum pot and studied her progress in filling it.

They fell silent for a while before Kansas remembered her original question. "Will you tell me why you think Mama killed herself?"

"I reckon there'll come a day when I say what I truly think about it all. But for now all I can tell you is Miss Elizabeth just couldn't stand what all come behind her dealings with your daddy."

"Tell that part of the story," Kansas urged, biting on a raw butter bean, sending a waxy taste to the back of her tongue. This was another bit of truth Kansas had already heard from Pinky, but she loved hearing it told, bringing to life an image of her daddy.

"Yes, Lord. Your mama thought that man Eddie Frye was about the handsomest, wonderfullest thing on the world. He give you that tan complexion of yours and that thick dark hair. He were a traveling salesman she met out on the streets of town one day. From Topeka, Kansas, your daddy was."

"Like my name," the girl said. "I wish I had a really pretty name."

"That's exactly like your name, and it's a pretty enough name. And you can't tell your granddaddy this, but your mama sneaked that name right past him."

"Sneaked it?" Kansas's ears had tingled with familiar curiosity. This was another new bit of fact mentioned in Pinky's passing way.

"Yes, Lord. Your sneakin'-around mama went and sneaked you a name." Pinky fumbled through the butterbeans to find those still sheathed and hiding on the bottom of the pot, lying low beneath fallen kin.

"Sneaked how?"

"Well, when your mama told that Eddie Frye she were with child, he cut and run. He weren't a damn bit of good, just like I knew. He left some hurt folks in Blackshear County, hurt to the bone. Your daddy had all the deputy sheriffs and state police from here to Dothan chasing him down. They got him this side of the Chattahoochee. They must have worked him over real good, too, cause that handsome face of his was sure enough swole up when they brung him back. Took him to the courthouse with a cocked shotgun to his head. Had him say 'I do' and then run him straight back out of town again when he went to asking for money just for doing the right thing by your mama." She took the pot of beans to the rust-stained sink, poured them into a colander, and began rinsing them.

"But what about the name?" Kansas reminded her.

"Oh. Miss Elizabeth's daddy say the courthouse wedding made you legitimate—not a bastard child—but the sorry name of Eddie Frye weren't good enough for his grandchild, specially when it come to light that man already had him a wife in Southern Pines, North Carolina. That's why you took the Lacey name, on account of the 'nullment. Then, when you was birthed and your mama said, 'I think I'm going to call her Kansas,' Your daddy went on and on about what a pretty name it was, on account of his great-grandmama was named Missouri and he liked the idea of girls named for states. I don't reckon he knew where that man was from and don't still to this day."

And Kansas wrapped herself within the folds of that one sharp secret, still wishing for a pretty-girl name like Constance or Marilyn or Elizabeth, but comforted by the thought of a secretly sneaked name. She grew vigilant in watching her features in mirrors over the next four years, watching for the developing imprint of her no-good daddy—the olive skin, brown eyes, and ink-black hair that lived in her mother's last thoughts, when she put the silver barrel of a gun against the thick blonde waves Kansas remembered as a beautiful tumbling of hair around her mother's shoulders.

Kansas vaulted herself to the countertop where she sat by the eight-eyed, double-ovened gas stove watching LittleBit stir cornmeal and water in a thick mixing bowl. LittleBit's hands were large, as were her bare feet, and she stood nearly six feet tall. She worked the wooden spoon through a mixture that turned gummy before blending together in a smooth, speckled batter. Kansas liked the fact that she had resurrected Eula Lura's nickname, but she never could figure why LittleBit was so aloof to her, so remote. Roxy thought LittleBit was mysterious, that maybe she even practiced voodoo over there in colored town, but Kansas just thought she was very, very private with herself. Still, it stung that someone so important in her mother Elizabeth's life would be so uncaring toward Elizabeth's daughter. It was a thing she should ask Pinky about sometime, she told herself.

"Did you know," Kansas said, "that you would have an awful time stirring and Grandemona peeling if y'all didn't have opposable thumbs? I read it in a *National Geographic* magazine."

"You a reading somebody," LittleBit said in her flat, unimpressed way.

"It's true," Kansas went on. "When the monkeys and all sprouted a thumb, it got to where they could peel food like bananas and open nuts and all kinds of other things. And just look at us humans. When the apes turned to cave men and our brains got big, we could do all sorts of stuff, like art, because of our thumbs."

"You saying we come from apes?" LittleBit asked sharply. "'Cause that's evil talk." She poured the cornmeal mixture into a flat, iron skillet over a gas flame. Then she placed a large kitchen match between her teeth to suck up the stinging fumes of the white onion her knife pierced.

Kansas wiggled and curled the fingers of both hands into each other, then apart, then close to the eyes of LittleBit, who swatted them away. "Look how beautiful they are," Kansas insisted. She cupped them together in a gesture of prayer. "The Methodist preacher says God's hand hath wrought the Creation. Well, I say the human hand hath wrought even more. Like the cathedral at Aachen. I saw it in *National Geographic*, too. Those Germans are some building folks."

"You go on, now," LittleBit turned the cornmeal pie in the skillet. "Done wrought a mess," she muttered.

"Kansas, stop talking in riddles and don't contradict grownups, especially not preachers," Grandemona ordered.

"Yes'm." Kansas again looked out the window. Pruella had gone back inside the shack. The courthouse clock struck eleven-thirty with one reverberating tone.

"Yonder comes Hotshot," Grandemona said as LittleBit placed triangles of hoecake into the tins he would carry over to the jail on large, stacking trays. Today there were nine tins of snap beans, fried chicken, and

mashed potatoes. The squeal and smack of the screen door and the jangling of steel keys up the hall to the kitchen announced a tall, muscular
man the color of a seared andiron. He cackled his high laugh and lifted the
tray. "Them folks is hungry," and he held the stack in his awkward way that
made it seem he would drop the trays at any moment, but he never did. It
was second nature to him, after so many years, second nature like the
rhythmic hambone dance he liked to perform.

"I'm going with him," Kansas announced, following the man in the
white pants, a black stripe running up the outside of each leg, the prison
suit Hotshot liked to wear, just because. Then she thought to add, "Don't
tell Miss Pearl."

As Kansas passed through puberty, Miss Pearl was less inclined to
allow her to roam the jailhouse as she had in childhood. And since her
grandmother judged the Tolberts to be pure trash, Kansas was forbidden
to enter the front house where the Tolberts lived, ever. Miss Pearl sometimes did not even want Kansas playing in the jailhouse yard. It had been
a lifelong battle, years dedicated to the Tolbert debate, an argument her
grandfather thought well beside the point at this late date. Still, her grandmother would push the issue.

"That Roxy is too old for you," Miss Pearl usually sniffed.

"But we're the same age," Kansas replied.

"Well, she is—coarse," Miss Pearl always said, of late adding, "She is
too developed and it is unseemly."

Kansas blushed at the reference to her friend's blossoming form, then
pleaded some more until her grandmother invariably relented, saying,
"Oh, all right, then. But only because they are the only little white children
nearby."

"You be back by noon," Grandemona called after her, as she trailed
after Hotshot down the back hallway.

"Eeeee, Law," Hotshot cackled. "Bringing the tins, bringing the tins."

As a child Kansas followed Hotshot around as he did his chores, often
getting him sidetracked into a game or asking him questions about her
mother. Hotshot usually answered by telling stories that didn't make a

whole lot of sense when she was six and seven, but which she now thought
might offer some clues to jot down in her locked diary, and she made a
mental note to consider him a possible source. Today, though, she felt preoccupied with recurring worries that she would never be able to keep up
with Roxy, keep her as a friend, not with all the changes hurtling her best
friend forward into young womanhood.

She followed Hotshot past Grandemona's flower garden and the big-
leafed bouquet of a fig tree Kansas often hid beneath, enveloped in the
harsh smell of sun-dappled black dirt and juices of roly-poly bugs and
rotten figs, peering out at her world, at Pinky's house. In the fecund cave
formed by arched branches, Kansas marveled at the notion of Grandemona turning the hard, velvety-skinned fruit into the shimmering pre-
serves that wetly sugared LittleBit's buttermilk biscuits.

Once, last summer, she and Roxy hid beneath the fig tree in a night
game of hide-and-seek with Leo. The two girls crouched motionless,
muddy-toed and sliding sweat, for a short forever, thighs, shoulders, forearms touching and electric, shallow breaths filling the dampness with
summer. Roxy's deep red hair caught slips of moonglow oozing between
the leaves, her eyes wide with childish fear, and Kansas suddenly wanted to
kiss her. She leaned in, imperceptibly, drawn to the lips panting swift currents in and out, in and out, under the shield of midnight green. When she
was close enough to see, even in the earthen darkness, Roxy's front teeth
gently working her lower lip the way she always did when she was nervous,
Leo screamed. He snatched back a limb to expose them, making Kansas
feel naked and ashamed of the mystifying urges taking her to places she
dared not share with anyone, not even Pinky.

Until this year, summers had always been times for games and explorations, nighttime roamings, and thick slices of fun pulled from thin air.
The bond of childhood kept them open to whims, one to the other, and
they ventured into each other's imaginations with unchecked enthusiasm.
But not this summer. This summer the willingness to engage was uneven,
on all their parts. Roxy was 100 percent with them one evening, unwilling
to go the next; at times she joined in the night games with her prior sense

of delight, but sometimes became detached, as if she did not care, after a while, which direction the game took next. Leo was more sullen than usual, seemed confused by the new shell of his sister. And Kansas ebbed and flowed between anger and appreciation, as if Roxy now bestowed her time upon her friend as opposed to spending it with her.

Kansas had sensed the coming change last summer, the summer Roxy became so enthralled with the workings of the female anatomy, so intrigued by the differences between men and women. Kansas did not believe her, at first, when Roxy told her where the man would put his penis and how perfectly it would fit in such a small place, but she could not deny that she had seen Daddy Jack's squirrel dogs doing just that when she was much younger, out at the farm, and had since been aware of the animal kingdom in an entirely different light. She knew, with an innate sense of foreboding, things were going to be different.

The change came into focus back in December, right around the time she and her great-aunt stumbled upon a parade of colored folks in Albany, a line of somber citizens with a preacher named Martin Luther King, Jr., bringing up the rear. Just a few days later, Roxy showed her a pair of underwear bearing brown-red stains, evidence of the menstrual shift in their relationship to one another. Smug and confident, Roxy demonstrated how to wrap the thin ends of the pad through the plastic teeth on an elastic belt that fit around her waist.

"Does it hurt?" Kansas asked.

"Not the menstruating part," Roxy said. "It's the belt and all you have to wear that bothers you. You'll see."

You'll see. Not now. This is not for you to know just yet. Later, when you are older. Run along, now. Kansas felt her days becoming more and more full of waiting and looking ahead, with less and less time spent basking in instants of present joy. And even though she dreaded the coming change, she began to look forward to it and even long for it, but mostly because she simply did not want to be left behind.

On this day Leo was at the tree stump behind the jail with a hatchet, passing the time hacking sticks into smaller sticks, destroying things the way only boys could. Coy sat in the dirt, picking at scabbed-over mosquito bites, tempting impetigo. Roxy was nowhere in sight, probably inside reading a Cheryl Ames, R.N., novel, feeding her interest in all things medical. She had read *Not as a Stranger* twice already this summer and it was not yet mid-June. It was last summer that Roxy announced she would become a doctor someday, the first lady doctor to come out of Sumner, maybe to come out of all of Blackshear County, ever.

Kansas followed Hotshot into the jail, the six-inch skeleton key making hollow clicks and rattles in the metal locks. They walked down a corridor of cells, the concrete floor stained with years of tobacco juice, amber imprints of time served, prisoners' voices echoing across the divide to one another. Each cell door had a rectangular port in the bars large enough for the meal tins to pass through, and Hotshot always let Kansas deliver them.

"Mmmmm. I smell me some fried bird," one called Joseph said.

"Got a tin of fried bird," Hotshot said.

"You don't say."

"I reckon it's a busted wing up in there," Hotshot said.

"You ain't right, big head," Joseph joked.

"I'm crazy as a one-eyed dog," Hotshot said.

Another one, called Gabe, said, "Tell Miss LittleBit she sure do some fine cooking. I'm going to send my wife by to get her recipe for hoecake."

"Eeee, Law," Hotshot said. "Dog-gone luck."

And as Kansas distributed the tins, the prisoners all thanked her and didn't seem like criminals at all.

White prisoners were put on the far end of the corridor, but there were no white prisoners today. There was, however, a woman prisoner on the second-floor corridor whom Kansas did not want to see. Her name was Angel and she had been in the county jail for five months already, charged with first-degree assault for cooking up several bags of grits in a five-gallon pot and pouring them on her husband, nearly killing him, for running around on her. Both of them were badly burned, and one side of Angel's face and both hands and forearms were grotesquely scarred.

Kansas had only taken Angel's meal to her once, whistling her way up the narrow steps to a cell stacked with packs of Alpine cigarettes and movie magazines where its occupant sat and puffed the days away to the dazzling lives of the stars. Angel did not praise the food or thank anyone; she only looked at Kansas with her one good eye, the other draped in scarred flesh scythed like slick satin across the mahogany face.

"A whistlin' woman and a crowin' hen be sure to come to no good end," Angel recited, her eye finding secrets in the skinny white girl bearing food.

Kansas was ashamed and afraid to return. So when Hotshot headed up the steps with Angel's tray, Kansas went out to where Leo was still producing piles of sticks with his hatchet.

"You are one big, sure-enough time waster," Kansas said, as the hatchet came down with another loud thwack.

"I'm going to build a fort for my army men," he said, with another thwack of the hatchet, jerking his head to indicate two cellophane bags of soldiers, Confederate and Union, battle flags and artillery lined up across the ash gray dirt. "Go on, Coy," he said to his little brother, who laid his hand on the chopping stump and drew it away in a taunt.

"Coy, quit!" Leo demanded.

But Coy repeated the motion as the hatchet came down, before Leo's brain registered it, and the thwack reverberated with the pained shriek of the child and Kansas's scream of revulsion.

The child lay writhing on the ground, squalling an ear-piercing wail, clutching his bloodied fist. Leo could only move slowly toward the chopping stump, repeating a mantra of "Don't tell Daddy, don't tell Daddy, don't tell Daddy." Suddenly, with a rush of nerve, he picked up the amputated digit and hurled it blindly as far and as hard as he could. Then he bolted, never looking back.

A crash of iron announced Hotshot jingling and clanking from the jailhouse. When he saw the carnage, he shrieked, "Oh, Law! Oh, Law!" and covered his face with his hands. Then he took another look. "Oh, Law! Gonna come a thunder!"

By that time Victor Tolbert was there, pulling off his T-shirt, scooping up the boy just as Mrs. Tolbert and Roxy rounded the side of the building. Kansas could only stagger, heaving, through the chain-link gate, horrified by a gore the like of which she had never before witnessed. The leaves of the fig tree slapped at her face and arms as she passed, bound for her own back door, above which an industrial kitchen fan blasted a typhoon of noontime smells into the summer heat.

*

Miss Pearl sat tall but ghostlike at the dining room table. Her chair was to the left of where Daddy, her husband since she was fifteen, sat at the head of the table. Her voice was slow and apathetic, her eyes without a shade of hope. "She hasn't been the same since your mama died," was all Kansas ever heard by way of explanation of the woman's faint presence. It was simply accepted, and everyone, including the family, referred to her as "Miss Pearl."

"The nigras over in Albany are getting all tore up again," Daddy was saying. "It's likely there'll be some trouble."

"It's that Dr. Anderson and those Albany Movement folks," Miss Pearl said in her hollow drawl. "Marching and carrying on."

"Could be it's a thing whose time has come," Grandemona said.

"Why anybody would want to go to jail over getting a piece of dirt road paved is beyond me," Miss Pearl, ignoring her mother-in-law, said to her husband.

"It's a damn mess, is all," Daddy said, "whether it's right or not."

"You can't believe how Coy hollered when Leo chopped his thumb off," Kansas said. "There was blood all over—"

"Not at the dinner table," Grandemona said.

"Yes'm."

"Might have to make the jail available like we did last December when that Dr. King fellow came to Albany and got them to marching," Daddy said.

With the tines of her fork, Kansas carved a trench in a mound of mashed potatoes. It had been exciting, the parade of paddy wagons coming in to Sumner, delivering loads of colored folks to the Blackshear County Jail. "Mr. Royce over at the sheriff's office says it's the federal government taking over how we do things. Is that right?"

"Well," Daddy said, "sometimes the federal government has to step in, if the states aren't doing right, that's all."

"So the states aren't doing right?" Kansas asked.

"Maybe not," Daddy said. "I guess we'll see."

"We'll see is right," Grandemona said. "We'll see if fair is fair."

Miss Pearl sighed. "It's just so much fuss over a little bit of pavement. I cannot imagine going to jail for such a silly thing."

Kansas laid a snap bean in her mashed-potato trench. "Mr. Royce said, 'Next thing you know the niggers will be fornicating with white women all over the place.'"

Grandemona slammed her palm to the table, rattling glasses and sterling silver. "I do not allow that kind of language, and you know it!"

"But I was only quoting Mr. Royce," Kansas said.

"You say 'nigra' or 'colored' or nothing at all," Grandemona went on. "And nothing of fornication!"

"You need to not listen to Royce Fitzhugh's theories about race matters, Kansas," Daddy said. "They're a might skewed."

"Mr. Royce said, 'Next they'll be wanting to sit next to us at the doctor's office or the soda fountain, wanting us to buy them banana splits with whipped cream and nuts and a goddamn cherry on top.'"

"Good night alive, Kansas!" Grandemona hissed, as Miss Pearl's fork rattled to her plate. "Little girls do not curse God in this house either, young lady, and you know that, too. What's got into you?"

"It's those Tolbert creatures she runs with, Miss Lucille," Miss Pearl said. "They are wormy and full of awful ways."

"They are not," Kansas said, pushing back against Miss Pearl, with her words, something she routinely did of late.

"It is the awful influence of those little Tolbert creatures," Miss Pearl said, echoing herself.

Daddy shifted forward in his chair. "I hardly think it's fair to refer to children as crea—"

"Creatures," Miss Pearl reiterated, and something in her voice made her husband stare into his plate. "And it is their influence on Kansas that makes her mouth so filthy."

"No, it isn't," Kansas pushed back again. "Anyway, I didn't curse God. Mr. Royce did. I was quoting Mr. Royce."

"Then don't quote him," Grandemona ordered.

"But Daddy said to always get the quote right and direct, or the evidence for your case goes bad," Kansas said.

"All right, all right," Daddy said. "Let's just say Royce Fitzhugh is not worth quoting and leave it at that. But I appreciate your effort, Baby."

"Why does he work for you, then?" Kansas asked.

"Don't be impudent, child," Grandemona said, then, "but it is a question to consider." She glanced at her son.

"My daddy hired him," he said, "and I promised to keep him on, since he's a decorated veteran and all."

"Humph," Grandemona said.

"Thank goodness the nigras in Sumner don't carry on the way they do in Albany," Miss Pearl said.

Kansas thought about Pinky, how she always used to keep her money folded in her sock and a can of snuff deep in her bra. Her skin was like black leather; her arms must have been sinewy and sure as they held the white folks' babies she had tended in Cordele, alongside her own.

"What would be wrong with Pinky or LittleBit going to Crowe's Drug Store for a Co-Cola or a banana split, Daddy?" Kansas asked.

"Now, Kansas," Miss Pearl said.

But Daddy was laughing. "I know it seems like nothing, but it's a lot more complicated than that, and it's something you don't have to worry about. Go fetch the tea pitcher from the kitchen, won't you, Baby?"

When she stepped through the swinging door and into the warmth of the kitchen, she found LittleBit on the perch of a high stool, facing the door. Her bare feet rested on the wood, knees dropped outward, palms hanging down between them in the bowl of her white-aproned cotton dress. The fingers of her left hand dangled a Picayune cigarette and her eyes were narrowed. "So you want to know about thumbs, girl?"

The question was abrupt and, in LittleBit's way, not preluded by chitchat.

"Yes."

"Then go see Mr. Royce Fitzhugh again. Ask him to show you the one he's got."

"Show me what?"

"A thumb."

"A real thumb? Whose is it?"

"Real enough, I reckon." She drew on the cigarette. "And you can't tell your daddy not nothing about it, you hear?"

"I won't." Kansas was hit with a thrill of anticipation. "I'm fixing to go get Roxy to go look at it," she said.

"It's a treasure all right," LittleBit said, words bathed in sarcasm.

"But who did it belong to?"

LittleBit narrowed her eyes again. "Get on, girl."

Kansas turned, then looked back, catching a flash of gold across the left pocket of LittleBit's apron. "What's that?" she asked, realizing it was a thing she had noticed before but never asked about, assuming it was a safety pin Littlebit had stuck through the cloth to keep the pocket in place.

"I'll show you what it is," LittleBit said, reaching into the pocket, turning it inside out, revealing a heart-shaped medallion, suspended from a width of purple ribbon edged in white, ridged in the silhouette of George Washington flanked by the stars and stripes.

"What is it? It's beautiful."

LittleBit's stare bore into her. "It's a medal," she said. "It's my husband's Purple Heart for being wounded in the war."

"What happened to it, here?" Kansas pointed to a deep nick in the metal.

"That's just where I beat on it with the claw end of a hammer."

"But why?"

"Just in my grieving is all. Now you get on."

"But can't I look at it some more? How was he wounded? What happened?"

"Get on. I showed you this medal so you going to know, one day, when the sun comes up and shines light into this mess—you going to know what a fine man I lost to you and your people."

"I don't under—"

"And I ain't saying no more about it now, so get on."

"But I—"

"Get!"

Kansas threw LittleBit a puzzled glance as she pushed back against the swinging door, but LittleBit waved her on through it, and she rejoined her family with fresh curiosity about more and more half revelations.

"Not today," Daddy said, when Kansas set the pitcher down before him and asked to be excused to go to town. "We're all going for a ride here after I look at the news. Remember? I've got this surprise to show y'all."

Kansas wanted to beg him, tell him she wanted to look at Mr. Royce's treasure of a severed thumb, but instead she said, "But I want to wait and see what happens with Coy's thumb. And what would it matter if the coloreds in Sumner got tore up like the ones in Albany?"

"That is enough," Grandemona snapped, "about body parts and race relations. I want a civilized conversation at my dinner table."

The exhaust fan in the kitchen hummed deeply to the swish-swishing as LittleBit scrubbed pots. The grownups chatted an effortlessly empty chat, but all the while Kansas felt awed by the happenstance appearance of two severed thumbs in the midst of her thirteenth summer.

*

"Can the doctors maybe get Coy's thumb and sew it back on?" Kansas asked. She sat in the back seat of Daddy's Cadillac with Grandemona, the back of Miss Pearl's head straight and silent.

" 'Fraid not," he answered.

"Well I don't see why not," Kansas said. "They sew up cuts and that skin goes back together. I don't see why they can't fix Coy's thumb."

"I declare, if you don't hush about all that I'll go to heaving," Grandemona said.

"It's more complicated than just sewing it back on," Daddy said. "Things just aren't as simple as you want them to be."

"I think it would be awful to be without a portion of one's body—any portion—even tonsils or your appendix. I mean, wouldn't you miss it? Wouldn't it be like part of you had died?"

"Don't be morbid, Kansas," Miss Pearl spoke quietly, not turning her head.

Kansas sank back in the seat and turned to Grandemona. "But it is kind of like dying, isn't it?" she whispered to the old lady.

"We die a little every day," Grandemona said. "You don't have to get a finger chopped off to experience death."

Miss Pearl made a little choking sound.

Grandemona put an index finger to her lips and Kansas nodded. "What is the surprise, Daddy? How much further?"

"Only a few miles."

"Such a mystery," Grandemona said.

"I know two hints," Kansas said. "I got them out of him last night when I came in from the play-out."

"You didn't get them out of me," Daddy said. "You got them out of Evan Williams."

"Still. I have two hints. It has something to do with the dam on the Flint River and it has something else to do with playing where the fish are," Kansas said.

"Those are two very cryptic clues," Grandemona said, "but I will let you figure them out."

"At first I thought he was taking us fishing," Kansas said. "But that wouldn't be a big secret because we go fishing a lot. Then I thought we were going to Albany to that park where the goldfish pond is, but that wouldn't be a big secret, either. Then I thought, maybe it just has to do with water, so I thought we were going to the Tift Park pool in Albany."

"Kansas, hush," Miss Pearl said. "It is not a prerequisite that you figure out the surprise. Besides, the Tift Park pool has been ordered to be integrated."

"So?"

"Dear Lord," Miss Pearl sighed.

"Anyway," Daddy said, "I heard somebody bought Tift Park. It's going to be turned into a whites-only club."

"Am I on the right track with my guesses, Daddy?" Kansas asked.

"I told you, Kansas," Miss Pearl said in her tired voice. "You don't have to figure it out."

"But I want to," Kansas said. "I want to know all the answers."

The car rolled on, through the small crossroads of Warwick and beyond, and across Smoak Bridge. Just past the bridge, Daddy turned left by a cemetery clumped in sage growing switches around fallen headstones. It was then he revealed the secret: he had bought them a house on Lake Blackshear, a fishing camp, a summer house, a winter retreat where they could bring friends and have parties and reunions and fun upon fun.

Kansas knew without saying that the surprise of the river house was only the latest attempt by her grandfather to get Miss Pearl to express joy, that emotion he had tried to cull from her ever since their daughter's death. Daddy had bought his wife all kinds of things: a white Cadillac she rarely drove; a color TV that was the envy of a town that took its entertainment in black and white; enough window air conditioner units to cool the whole house—except the kitchen—in the suffocating South Georgia summers; trips to Aunt Frances's Apalachicola vacation home on the seashore; to Atlanta, to see and buy even more things she did not seem to want, not to mention all the expensive clothes and jewelry he had given her over the years, each time eliciting from her a portion of an obligatory smile and a "How lovely. Thank you, Sugar." That was it. And each time the disappointment showed in Daddy's eyes. Kansas hoped, for his sake, it would work this time, knew in her heart it would not, had, in fact, long ago given up trying to hope any happiness out of her grandmother, and was most of the time able to ignore her presence altogether.

But this house was worlds beyond Kansas's expectations. This house was huge and completely furnished, with a fireplace and two bedrooms downstairs and one large attic room, full of beds, a bathroom on one end of the big room and a den on the other. There was a screened porch running the length of the house and steps down to two stone patios, and more steps down to a lush green lawn with azalea-lined retaining walls, a tree swing, a boathouse with three slips Daddy said he intended to fill, and a long pier with a gate and steps down into the water. A separate little cottage sat a ways from the big house, a maid's cottage, Daddy said.

"Can I bring Roxy?" Kansas said. "Can't we come with LittleBit and stay the weekend?"

"Oh, I don't know if LittleBit can leave her mama much, but we'll see," Daddy said. "Besides, I have to finalize some things, so it'll be a week or so before we can come and stay." He glanced over at Miss Pearl. "What do you think of the place?"

She gave a portion of an obligatory smile. "It's lovely," she said. "Thank you, Sugar."

Kansas turned away before the disappointment crossed Daddy's face. She walked down to the pier and looked out across the dammed-up, slowed-down river. To the south on the opposite shore was the dam itself, the massive gray power plant like a smoke-spitting monster next to the placid face of the water. A herd of goats grazed on the grassy mound of earthen dam surrounded by slag, jutting from the right side of the power plant, while the locks in the concrete dam on the other side regulated the amount of water that, having drifted down from Americus, would now make its way to Albany and south, through swampland and farmland, inching its way west to the Chattahoochee River. She looked straight across now, maybe a quarter mile across, to where a patch of headless trees jutted from the stilled water, then to the north, where her explorations in the Boston Whaler Daddy would buy would take her up a little branch not far from the new summer vacation home. Scratchy Branch would become their hideout, hers and Roxy's, a place where they would trade the deepening confidences of their changing perspectives. And this one little stretch of clear water, sandy-bottomed and punctuated with sandbars, rich with a deep vein of unmined family history, would take Kansas into vagaries and beauty and the possibility of peace.

*

The next morning found Kansas, not at the sheriff's office studying a bit of bone and torn flesh, but at her great-aunt Frances's house. Since school had only just let out, Kansas had forgotten that Friday mornings in the summertime belonged to Aunt Frances and Miss Martha, not for the social visits she and Roxy often paid, but for the little chores Kansas was to do for the two ladies. On summertime Friday mornings, Kansas walked the four blocks, past the telephone office, past the Methodist Church and the high school and the library, and around the corner to Isabella Street where stately columned houses, framed in green lawns front-edged with sidewalks, stood as they had for decades, evoking a flavor of the turn of the century.

Aunt Frances was a retired telephone operator, the first operator in Blackshear County, back in the days of the party line. She had listened in on enough conversations to know every underlying connection in Sumner, but was principled enough to keep most of the information to herself. She told Kansas stories about the days when residents would ring up "Miss Frances" to connect them with the desired party. She took Kansas into the back room at the telephone office where the technician, Roger, worked on the big grid on the wall, a place full of clicks and clacks. Aunt Frances was sixty years old now, a fun-loving, laughing woman with a shock of short white hair combed back and shingled above the neck, who always preferred khakis and boots to the floral print shirtwaists she had worn during her years as an employee of the Southern Bell Telephone Company.

Her companion and housemate, Miss Martha, was in her fifites, a refined, soft-spoken lady, originally from Waycross. The two women had a curious friendship. They were easy and affectionate in their speech toward one another, in the privacy of the big white house on Isabella Street, but they never went anywhere in Sumner together. Miss Martha did the shopping and cooking. Aunt Frances ran errands and came to the Laceys' for a meal every so often, without Miss Martha. They were simply never seen in each other's company, yet they made occasional weekend trips to Atlanta and took two long vacations together each year, one during spring break, when they traveled to New York for a week, and another during the summer, when they visited friends Kansas had never met, down in Key West, Florida. Lots of weekends and some summer months, too, were spent at Aunt Frances's place at Apalachicola.

Miss Martha had taught fifth grade in Sumner for more than twenty years, had even taught Kansas, who still felt the self-conscious discomfort of a student toward a teacher known outside of the classroom. But Miss Martha was kind, never brought up how awkward and socially ill-equipped Kansas was in school, and baked Toll House cookies, stirred sugared lemonade in a cut-glass pitcher, and was solicitous of Kansas, Roxy, and Aunt Frances.

On this Friday morning, Aunt Frances had Kansas at work on the big screened-in side porch, painting a low wooden table. A heavy ceiling fan whined a rhythm into the hot air covering the morning like a layer of cotton balls. Sweet olive and azalea bushes nestled their scents against the screens while music played from the hi-fi stereo in the front room. Rosemary Clooney, Aunt Frances's favorite singer. "Come On-a My House." Kansas felt the familiar yearning for a beautiful name like Rosemary, a name to make up for the fact that she possessed no beauty, had instead a high waist, and legs too long for the rest of her. If her name were Rosemary, people would not notice that her chin was too prominent, eyes too close together, hair thick and noncompliant when it came time to be styled. She would be willing to give up her secretly sneaked name for that. She dipped the brush into a can of yellow oil-based paint while Aunt Frances sat in one of the willow rockers, reading the *Albany Herald*.

"I still can't believe your granddaddy went and bought that big house on Lake Blackshear," Aunt Frances said. "And you say it's not far from the Smoak Bridge?"

Kansas nodded.

"And you can see the dam from the pier?"

"If you look left," Kansas said.

"He sure as hell was close-mouthed. Didn't let on to anybody. But I can't get over where it is on the water, if it's where I'm thinking." She turned a page of the newspaper and shook her head. "Miss Pearl might not be able to take that location, if she figures it out," she mumbled.

Kansas felt the prickle of curiosity she knew so well, having developed a sixth sense when it came to potent references to what all lay buried in the foliage of the family tree. Aunt Frances's voice carried that kind of tone.

"What about where it is on the water?" Kansas asked, telling herself this was an exchange to be recorded in the locked diary.

"Oh, nothing. I was just thinking out loud. Ought to check myself," Aunt Frances said.

"Come on, Aunt Frances. What is it about Miss Pearl and the lake? Why are people always dodging me when I ask questions?"

"People?"

"Well, you, sometimes. And Miss Pearl. And—"

"Miss Pearl dodges everybody. Has for years."

"Why does she do that?"

Aunt Frances sighed. "Some folks spend all their energy hiding things they perceive as shameful."

"What's shameful about the lake?"

"You ask too many questions."

Kansas stroked the paintbrush down the table leg, the fumes thick and stinging to her eyes. "I just feel left out is all. Sometimes."

Aunt Frances closed the paper, folded it up on her lap, and looked at her a moment. Then she shook her head and sighed. "I'll be damned. You are growing up," she said. "It's as plain as anything."

Kansas felt her face flush. "I am not," she said.

"Sure you are. I can see your mama's prettiness about to bust out. You trust what I'm saying."

"You're trying to change the subject."

"No, now dammit, I'm not. It really did strike me just now that you're about to be a young lady. And all your people want to keep you a child, including me, I'm afraid."

Kansas laid her brush on the paint can lid. "Why?"

"Why? Because there are things you'll see and recognize as ugly and hard to look at. You'll ask questions that have to be answered, and we grownups get awful uncomfortable with such as that."

"But what about the lake house?"

"Let me tell you the background of the lake instead, and you file it away for future reference."

"Oh, Aunt Frances."

"Look at me." The woman's voice was firm, serious, a tone Kansas rarely heard from her. "You listen and file it away. Then, one day, we'll talk some more about it."

"Yes'm."

Aunt Frances took a sip from her coffee mug and lit a cigarette, sliding the filter into a tortoise-shell cigarette holder. "That lake was made over thirty years ago when the Army Corps of Engineers dammed up the Flint River, put that power plant there. Your mama used to love to go swimming there, take her daddy's motorboat out on the lake at night and go skinny-dipping. Of course it was a lot more secluded then than it is now."

Kansas's eyes grew large. "Really? She would swim naked?"

"I imagine she even took you when you were too little to remember." The older woman glanced at her, seeming uncertain.

"What is it, Aunt Frances?"

Her aunt shook her head. "Just wondering why I need to be so damn pussy-footish about this."

"About what?"

"I don't 'imagine' she took you to that lake. I know she did. She told me she did."

Kansas sat up straighter. This was new. Aunt Frances seemed to be giving up a lot of what little dodging she usually did when Kansas questioned her. "That makes it so much more special. The lake house. My mama took me out on that lake?"

Aunt Frances nodded. "You were only four. It was not long after your mama's granddaddy died."

"Heart attack," Kansas said.

Aunt Frances looked at her long and sad, then, "My God, we do keep our stories sterile, don't we?"

"What do you mean?"

"Nothing. About your mama. She wanted to take you up the little creek where you were conceived."

"Conceived?"

"Where your seed was planted. You know."

"Oh, but that's so… significant! Tell more."

"Well I am, it seems," Aunt Frances laughed. Then she leaned forward. "Your daddy was long gone, and she was grieving for your great-grand-daddy, and she said she wanted you to connect with both of them, but especially your daddy. I think she wanted to connect with him, too. She always thought he might come back to her. I knew he wouldn't."

"I wish I remembered more about my mama," Kansas said. "You and Pinky are the only ones who really talk to me about her. I mean, Hotshot used to try, but he didn't make any sense."

"Your mama was something."

"She was crazy wasn't she?"

"She was, but in a wonderful way, delightfully crazy, until so much bad got into her head that she couldn't see past it."

"Like when her granddaddy died?" Kansas stood and walked over to her great-aunt. "I don't remember going on the lake in a motorboat with my mama. But I kind of remember when her granddaddy died. Just barely, though."

"Tell me about that," Aunt Frances pulled her onto her lap. "You were so little."

Kansas nestled her head against her great-aunt's shoulder. "It's funny. I never really thought about it. But I remember something. I remember being in Pinky's yard and we were walking to the chicken house and mama came out the back door, and the screened door slammed and made the loudest sound. And she hollered, 'I'll see you in the morning, Precious,' and waved and blew me kisses."

Aunt Frances stroked her hair. "Then what?"

"Then she went back in and a little while passed and there was another noise, like a door slamming, only a million times louder, and Pinky picked me up and took me in her house and gave me cookies. And I heard my mama scream and I heard a siren and Pinky said something like this was bound to happen, that she knew that girl would do it sooner or later, and she gave me more cookies. They were oatmeal cookies."

Her great-aunt was rocking the willow rocker, slow and comforting. "Is that all you remember?"

"Yes. Except that Pinky was real upset. And I didn't see my mama for a while. And then Mama was different and strange acting most of the time."

"We were all upset," her great-aunt said, still rocking the chair. "It was such a violent way to go."

"Violent?"

"Yes."

"What do you mean?"

Aunt Frances kissed her forehead. "That loud noise you heard. It wasn't a door."

"It wasn't?"

"No. It was a gunshot. My daddy shot himself. He committed suicide, though mama insisted it was an accident. After a while it turned into a 'heart attack.'"

"Why don't they tell the truth?" Kansas said, hearing the loud noise, straining to identify it in her memory as a gunshot but unable to take her thoughts that far.

"They consider it a shameful thing. But then, anything that must be kept secret is a source of shame. Or it wouldn't be secret."

"I don't understand."

"No, you don't. And you can't, not now. You're too young yet. But you're getting very close."

Kansas let her thoughts come out loud. "I wonder if the thumb is a source of shame."

"Thumb?"

"I found out Mr. Royce has a thumb over at the sheriff's office. But it's a secret. I'm not supposed to tell. But you always keep my secrets, don't you?"

Aunt Frances took in her breath, and unchecked shock took her face. "What is it?" Kansas asked.

"Oh, nothing. I don't know." She shook her head. "Don't you worry. Your secrets are always safe here. You know that. But let's talk about something else. That thumb business is more than a little disgusting."

Kansas was afraid Aunt Frances was going to go on more about how she was growing up, when Miss Martha walked onto the porch with a tray bearing slices of lemon pound cake and lemonade. "You hop up from there, Sugar," she said. "Take a break from the painting."

"Hell, she just had a break," Aunt Frances said.

"Oh, hush and don't be such a slave driver," Miss Martha said as Kansas put the warm pound cake to her lips.

"And where's mine?" Aunt Frances said, reaching for the tray.

Miss Martha slapped at Aunt Frances's hand, and Aunt Frances laughed the familiar laugh, her mind snatched away from their serious conversation, but Kansas turned it over and over in her own head as she sipped cold lemonade and listened to the familiar banter of the two women, the sound that was so genuine and comforting to the five-year-old, freshly orphaned child who still, even all these years later, hid inside Kansas, listening for gunshots and other loud noises.

*

Mr. Royce Fitzhugh grinned as he held the small jar up to his desk lamp. Leo, Roxy, and Kansas were mesmerized by the gherkin-sized object floating in the chemical wash. The sheriff's office in and of itself was a mysterious, fascinating place. Kansas spent storm-gusty summer afternoons poring over the "Wanted" files and photographs of "armed and dangerous" criminals, talking to state troopers riding the Southwest Georgia highways, creating patterns of numbers on the ciphering machine, or typing notes to Leo and Roxy on the big black Royal typewriter on Daddy's desk.

Every great once in a while, she talked Daddy into opening up the evidence closet to show her guns, knives, and tire irons, instruments of assaults and occasional murders being tried in the upstairs courtroom. Once, he even let her sample a sip of shinny that was tested clean by state experts; it ran a trail of fire down her throat, sending her coughing and gagging out to the water fountain in the cavernous hallway. "White Only," the sign above the fountain said, and she was grateful, at that moment in particular, to be white.

"I got it from a fellow said he found it in a fox trap, like some poor fellow had a tragic accident. Kind of like Coy, I hear."

Leo looked down sheepishly.

"So it's kind of like a trophy," Mr. Royce boasted.

"A trophy?" Roxy said.

"Yeah. A rare thing. A treasure. A keepsake. Like that," Mr. Royce said.

"Like LittleBit's Purple Heart," Kansas said.

Mr. Royce made an abrupt shift in his chair. "The hell you say. Got her a real medal, huh?"

"It was her husband's. He's dead so she keeps it pinned inside the pocket of her apron."

"I'll be damned."

"Can I hold the jar?"

"Sure thing, girl," Mr. Royce grinned.

It was translucent, almost, veins and muscle like dwarfed spaghetti tubes inside the larger tube of the thumb, lightly spotted in places like some strange, bruised fruit. The thumbnail had settled on the bottom of the jar, but the place where it had once grown was definable, and Kansas felt a shudder ripple through her as she realized there had once been an actual person attached to this tiny bit of flesh and bone.

Mr. Royce laughed. "You got to have a stomach for it, I reckon. But a sweet little girl like you ain't never got worry over seeing such as this."

"I'm going to be a doctor," Roxy said, "so I'll see dead people all the time."

Mr. Royce laughed harder. "Ain't no such of a thing."

"She will, too," Kansas insisted. "She's going to Emory and be a baby doctor."

"Hell, Roxy's too pretty to want to go and do something like that." He winked at Roxy and let his eyes brush down her body, then come back up and rest on her chest.

Kansas's stomach went queasy like it did whenever boys, and now grown men, too, gave her friend the kind of look that put them inside a familiarity full of implications. "I said she will, too," Kansas repeated, successfully nudging Mr. Royce's eyes from plundering through the cups of Roxy's brassiere.

The deputy chuckled them out the door. "Ain't no girl going to be no doctor. Especially not no jailer's girl. Get on, now."

Two curved wooden staircases led up to the courtroom, where they regularly played Perry Mason or acted out bizarre murder trials concocted from the thick summer air. The trio sat on the bottom step. Leo set his chin on his knees and rubbed his bare feet. Kansas reached over and touched the swollen bruise on his left cheekbone with her fingertips.

"Does it hurt?"

"No." He shrugged her hand away.

"Where's Coy's thumb?" Roxy asked. "I want to cut it open and see what's inside." The younger boy was still in the hospital in Albany. His mother was staying there with him, and Mr. Tolbert, after spending the night at home, had gone back to Albany for the day. Hotshot was left in charge of the jailhouse and feeling very important in his prison guard suit.

"Don't know," Leo said, glancing a warning at Kansas.

"I looked all around the chopping stump. It would've been there, so don't be stupid. Kansas?"

Kansas spread out her hands and shrugged. "Maybe a squirrel ate it," she offered.

"Daddy's mad as hell," Roxy said. "I'm just trying to help you. If he comes across Coy's thumb, he'll probably whup you again. We should get it first." She gazed into her brother's brown eyes, her gold-flecked ones looking deeper until he buckled.

"I was scared of what Daddy would do, so I threw it away. I don't know where."

"You thought you could cover the whole thing up?" Roxy's eyes grew larger. "Are you a retard?"

"He panicked, is all," Kansas said. "Let's go hunt the thumb."

The grounds of the courthouse were greenly manicured, sidewalks bordered with monkey grass. At the northwest and southeast diagonal corners of the lawn were steps leading down to recessed toilet areas for coloreds. Leo spat into the stairwell as they walked past. "Nigger shit," he mumbled, and a tingle of dread prickled down Kansas's spine.

It was only after a half-hour search of the backyard of the jailhouse that Kansas caught the glint of the sunset on the high tin roof of the jail. The thumb lay where it had been pitched. They could make out the meaty end bearing blackened blood, and reasoned it must be wedged on a bent nail or a stob in the tin that prevented it from following gravity to the ground. They took an oath to keep its location a secret, to gather to view its decomposition each day, and to never tease Coy about his missing thumb or make him feel freakish in any way.

Later that night, tucked in the canopy bed with the locked trunk of her great-grandfather at its foot, Kansas would think about how wrong it would be to make not just Coy, but anyone, feel freakish because of an accident, a deformity, a quirk of nature. She would wonder about the monsters that must have lived in her great-grandfather's mind, to make him want to put a bullet in his brain; and wonder all the more about her mother, about the whys of her determination to die. They must have felt helplessly freakish on the inside, she would decide, the way she herself felt on the outside; and, before she fell asleep, she would hope against hope not to ever have to feel so weakened in that kind of solitude.

Royce Fitzhugh rolled the jar over and watched the thumb bob and move with the Royce-made currents. He held a universe in his hand, was a force, a mover of tides. He was startled at first by the children's knowledge of the thumb's existence and quickly ran a made-up story of its origination through his brain. Here, after all, was a small crowd to impress, and impress was what he loved to do. Being impressive was foreplay for intimidation, and foreplay should always be practiced and refined. He took the key to the locking desk drawer from another drawer in the same desk and reveled in the complete spellbound fascination of the children, though that girl-woman, Roxy, was anything but a child. She had the same kind of ready, in-your-face sexuality Elizabeth had possessed, only without Elizabeth's class or maze of a mind. That Roxy, as she aged, might become some kind of second-hand version of Elizabeth someday, and he might partake if he had the chance, her mother be damned.

He held the jar up to the fluorescent ceiling light, turning and tumbling the object inside. It was a beauty, all right, and he had already begun to use it to cultivate his status with the inner circle. Stewart Sams and Bo Thomas had damn sure been impressed when he brought it out after the last gathering of the Klan boys over in their neck of the woods, two nights ago, after everybody cleared out.

"You say it's a real nigger's thumb?" Stewart asked.

"Hell, yeah." He cut his eyes over at Bo. Bo was the one he wanted to impress. Bo had pretty much taken over when Dewey Fountain died three years ago and would be the key to getting him a county election next time around or two. He damn sure needed to impress Bo, and the foreplay seemed to be working.

"That's mighty fine," Bo said, his eyes coveting the little member that seemed to preen and bow in the jar.

They sat on the porch of Bo's rathole of a fish camp, an abandoned shotgun house that had been moved to his pond near Leesburg. The trouble in Albany was the hot topic of discussion that night, but conversations had buzzed like night bugs here ever since last fall, when it all got started. Now trouble was building all across the southwest corner of the state and beyond. Voter registration drives were popping up. There was even talk that the niggers had plans to defy segregation laws and just walk right into selected public schools this fall. It was the kind of swell of confrontation Royce relished, feeling his purpose come more alive, knowing it was in taking action that he could build up a base of political power and finally take charge, run for sheriff in one of the counties neighboring Blackshear County, the place where Jack Lacey would undoubtedly run things his watered-down Lacey way forever.

"Bet Calvin Craig his ownself ain't even got one of these. You reckon?" Royce said.

"Not that I've ever heard of," Bo said, his gaunt, fifty-seven-year-old face shadowed in the summer night.

"Shit," said Stewart, younger, closer to Royce in age and easier to impress than Bo. "He's the Grand Dragon of the Georgia Realm. He's bound to have a ear or something."

"Could be," said Royce. "All I know is, I got this. It was took off a nigger raped a white woman in Leary," he lied. "I was the one rounded him up and got him took care of."

"I ain't never heard nothing about that," Bo said with a suspicious squint. "And I pretty much hear it all."

"It's been a good long time ago," Royce lied. "Way before you took over. And the woman was a preacher's wife. Didn't nobody want it to get out how she'd done been rurn't and all. I ought not to have said nothing to you two, but I want us three to be on the same page when this shit really gets going in Albany."

"We on the same page," Bo said. "And it is fixing to heat up around here—in lots of ways."

Stewart snickered. "Been heating up for months. Now there's even more of them coming, staying in folks's homes, some staying up in the nigger churches."

"Them Snick folks?" Royce said. "Goddamn if they don't give out the biggest pain in the ass of the whole world of them people."

Bo broke the seal on a bottle of Ten High, unscrewed the cap, and took a drink. "Let them be a pain. I'm already hearing what plans is being laid." He passed the bottle to Royce, a significance that was not lost on Royce, the order of the passing, and he could feel that foreplay paying off, but good. "There's talk of a rally, the biggest one in a long damn time, sometime this summer, if the niggers push all this stuff that's getting talked about," Bo went on. "Craig'll be there. We'll get Bobby Shelton too, by damn."

Royce held the bottle out to Stewart with an air of condescension, feeling his upward mobility in the organization. "Rally's good, but there's going to have to be some action, too, and it's best to put it in the planning stages now."

"What kind of action?" Stewart asked.

"Well," Royce said, "if it heats up around here, which it is just before doing, then I say we fight heat with heat."

"Go on with it," Bo said.

"I got a sheriffing buddy over in Terrell County that says they already got the boys after the voter registration folks over there, you know, giving them some shit, nothing major," Royce said. "I told him you got to build it slow, bring it on up to a bubble and then a boil. Find out what churches are putting them up. Don't torch them all at once, do it gradual."

"I already know where some of them are staying. Got white kids staying with them, too," Bo said. "Ain't that some goddamn shit."

"Yeah," Royce said. "You let me get my hands on one of them white boys, by God, I'll be done skinned him alive."

"No shit," Bo said, holding the bottle up in a gesture of acknowledgement. "You all right, boy. We going to fix you up."

Royce took the bottle and toasted Bo with it. "Here's to taking the 'de' out of 'segregation.'" He grinned into the night buzz of crickets and con-gratulated himself on his new rising, like the sun into a day. He would be the big shit kicker. And he had Roxy Tolbert's mama, Jolene, to thank, at least in part.

It was because of his relationship with Jolene Tolbert that Royce had come upon the thumb. Jolene, who was raw-boned and real, who needed so much in the way of loving she would have traded off anything, had more than willingly passed the thumb on to him. But then, she had a deep degree of loyalty toward him, and he to her. In fact, Jolene was a regular part of his hidden-away life, the only woman he had been able to fuck with any success, since his one run and failure at fucking Elizabeth Lacey.

Jolene was an odd-tempered woman, quiet and intent upon anything she was doing at any given moment. She gave the same single-minded con-centration to her encounters with him that she gave to her unending house-work. He met her when her husband took over the jail years ago, came in contact with her regularly as an acquaintance, hardly even noticing her at first, on those occasions when he had to enter the jail through the front house. As far as he knew, she had no friends, did nothing of a day but an endless and unnecessary succession of domestic chores. Sometimes he saw her out beside the jail, hanging laundry and talking to the Laceys' cook, Lit-tleBit, but that was about all. He gradually began to make small talk with her, at first out of boredom, but she gave him her full-on attention and he liked it, the swell of pride it brought him. She warmed to him, slowly, then, over the past four years, up to a full heat, before he made to fuck her last summer.

He didn't give a shit if she was married. Besides, he didn't have any use for her husband, who ran with some of the county boys late at night, harassing the niggers and anyone else who needed a warning. Victor Tol-bert was on the outermost ring of the inner circle, where Royce had once been, long years ago, a hanger-on, a "hey, boy."

"Hey, boy, call up the Early County bunch. Tell them to be here at nine."

"Hey, boy, take this chain and my pickup and go yank Dallas's car out of a ditch."

"Hey, boy, make a whiskey run over the line, and be quick."

Royce had flat done his own duty as a "hey, boy," and it was now time
to come into his own. And he was, indeed, warming himself beside the
core of that inner circle, so it was easy to see Victor Tolbert as nothing
worthy of standing in his way to getting laid on a regular basis. Hell, Victor
was a Terrell County pussy who beat up on his wife fairly regularly, was
even only a half-assed jailer, so on top of not giving a shit, Royce felt no
guilt whatsoever. In fact, he would have felt no guilt even if Victor Tolbert
had been his best friend.

The bottom line was he would be willing to sacrifice any friend to be
able to fuck any woman. And up until Jolene agreed to part her legs, he had
never found a woman he could have sex with to his satisfaction, never
found a woman who would tolerate all he went through behind what happened with Elizabeth. He either couldn't get it up or, if he did, it would go
off too fast, sometimes right away, as soon as his partner gave a subtle sigh
or the tiniest movement, let alone the kinds of more enthusiastic sounds
and pushes most women were prone to. Royce needed a woman who
would be still and let him stay in his head, who would not judge or laugh
as a couple of them had done over the years, making him want to clamp
his grip around their necks until their eyes bugged out and their faces
turned purple. He needed a woman who would let him go through the
motions that had taken over his libido by degree until sex became pure
ritual. Jolene Tolbert was that woman.

Jolene was almost a decade older than Royce, had given up on the big
dreams of her younger years. But although she was simple in her wants,
she was not stupid and took direction well. And she was starved for affection, said her husband rarely laid a hand on her except to slap her around
anymore, that he went out with bar whores in Albany and she was afraid
he might get a disease because he didn't believe in rubbers. And Royce
found himself confiding in her, bit by bit. He ranted about how he
deserved a county of his own, how Jack Lacey was too goddamn clean to
run the county the way it ought to be run, how Jack Lacey's daddy had not
done right to let his son opt out of participating in the doings of the

county boys. Didn't he see what was coming, what was going on in Albany with that SCLC, SNCC shit? And Jolene would commiserate with him, give him neck rubs to ease his stress, and finally outright asked him if he would put his hands on her and make her feel good the way she could only do for herself anymore.

Her status as a married woman who had to keep her mouth shut to survive gave Royce the wherewithal to describe his unreliable penis to her, something he had never uttered out loud to anyone; here he sensed the possibility for a big payoff. She told him he shouldn't feel bad, that she didn't have to have any regular kind of lovemaking; she just wanted to feel good. So he made her feel good, took her direction and made her purr and groan and gasp for breath, then prepared to wait for the inevitable trade-off. That trade-off came much more quickly than he anticipated. Her longing and his obsession clicked together like the bracelets on a pair of stainless steel handcuffs being snapped shut. She would have done any-thing to keep him present in her abandoned desire and he knew it, so he told her more secrets than he had ever shared with anyone, let alone a god-damn woman. It all led to delicious moments of release gone missing for both of them for an eternity; and they began watching for those days when the children were out, Victor was gone, and Royce could get away from the office or make up a reason to go talk to a prisoner. They began plotting and arranging things to make the time open up. Jolene went on underground missions to manipulate her husband away. She disabled the vacuum cleaner or the refrigerator, making crucial a trip to Albany to pick up a part. She made sure Hooker's Mercantile was out of this kind of sink trap or that size washer or any old tank set, then she went on guerrilla missions to sabotage the kitchen sink, the bathroom john. She threw Victor's favorite boots in the trash barrel, where they were licked away by flames that yielded another afternoon when her husband had to go to Albany. She burned a gun holster and a turkey caller from a special hunting store in the city. She was dedicated. Royce had to give her that.

As soon as Victor set off on a trip to Albany, she ordered the children out to play with Kansas or to the five-and-dime or just out from underfoot until dark. Then Royce got the phone call and went directly to her front door as if he had business at the jail, brazen with confidence that no one would think a thing of his standing there on the main street of town, right in the middle of town, on Jolene's front porch. They went through the fronthouse living room and through the kitchen to a corridor that led to the jail itself. There, near the deep freeze, they went down the stairs and into a little basement room intended to serve as a home for any colored help the jailer cared to take on in addition to Hotshot, who had his own unlocked cell. There was a cot, a toilet, and a sink in their damp, dirt-floored box of a musty boudoir, and they had managed to visit it at least once a week, sometimes more, since the previous summer. And Royce's confidence had mushroomed with the resonation of a hydrogen bomb, now that he had a real, somewhat functional penis hanging above the balls upon which he set such store.

It was Jolene who, a couple of months after they took up, in the midst of one of her aggressive "cleaning out" days, discovered the thumb in a cubbyhole behind the deep freeze that guarded their interludes. She pushed the deep freeze away from the wall to sweep behind it, she told him, and showed him how a four-inch-by-four-inch square of beaded pine boards could be separated from the wall, how a drawer pull had been secured there to facilitate in the opening of it. What sat inside the little box in the wall was the jar, two photographs of a colored woman with pendulous breasts and spread legs, another small jar full of keys of all shapes and sizes, some ancient condoms, and an outdated map of the state.

Royce knew immediately what he had in the thumb. It was, for him, a trophy, the finest of prizes, and, with carefully laid groundwork, it would provide his entrée into the inner sanctum of that dim world he aimed to pierce and take hold of with his presence. Thumbs were rare, much more rare than fingers, at a ratio of two to eight. And the more rare the trophy, the more prestige it brought. Happening upon a finger would have been sweet enough, but this was beyond anything he ever imagined.

"You can't tell a goddamn soul, understand?" he told her. "We're leaving this other shit right here. But I'm taking the thumb."

"Who do you think put it here?"

"I got a pretty good idea. But you'd be better off not to even try to guess it. It might cause you some trouble."

"I don't understand," she said, in her muted, washed-out way.

"Just do like I say," he hissed. "Like you always do. All right?"

"Okay."

He took her by the hand then and led her down the steps to the little room. She was wearing blue pedal pushers and a blue-and-white-checked man's shirt that she came out of easily. Their semblance of a romance was new, and he was still learning how to touch her with the kind of finesse he eventually developed, making an even trade of his touch for her compliance. They already had a kind of trust, a trust that had mutated out of both their needs for discretion, for silence. He put his fingers to her skin and began, letting her guide him to the place that would soon make her bow her back and shiver a little before she let a small cry explode from her throat and pressed her fingers hard against his thigh.

As soon as she got her breath she stood, brushed back her hair, and walked over to the sink. She leaned her back against the wall and placed the sole of her right foot against the rust-stained porcelain, opening the way to the one time Elizabeth invited him in. He stood then, and walked over, his fist to his penis, coaxing it to life. She stared with a focused intensity, pupils dilated in the dim room, and tickled her fingers up her open thigh. He closed his eyes, working faster.

"Come over here," she said. "Come on over here and put it in real slow."

He stepped forward, keeping his eyes closed tight, blowing and gasping, working his hand faster. And he stepped into his own mind, conjuring up the presence of Elizabeth, how she had taken him by the hand, led him outside the courthouse and down into the colored restroom, for God's sake, one disappearing afternoon, the air glowing with the near fluorescence of dusk just before bleeding into dark. She had spent the afternoon lounging around the sheriff's office, sipping from an engraved silver flask of bourbon in her purse. She was twenty-four then, mother of a three-year-old daughter, and he had spent years as one of her few confidantes, all the while making subtle attempts at wearing her down. He dated around a little, but preferred to pick up a bar whore every now and then and be done with it. If only he could get next to Lizzie, though, all that would change.

Jack Lacey and the old man were out on a call that afternoon, and Lizzie was getting intoxicated, killing time, toying with him, gossiping, telling him about some of the things she liked to do with men, things that had grown crazier and more seductively perverse ever since that slickster knocked her up and cut out on her. "Crazy Lizzie" had come into her own since then, leaving Elizabeth's fragility and innocence, for the most part, in pieces. She still had that same musky pull, though, that drew Royce to her, and he basked in her the entire afternoon. The charm bracelets tinkled, the pint flask sparkled, her hair was matted and tangled—a metaphor for her mind—and her eyes held that fast-moving glance of hers, the one that said she was capable of anything, anything at all.

"One time," she said, "I asked a guy in a bar to let me lay one of my pubic hairs in his drink."

"Shit."

"Yeah. And he said sure, but only if he could get it off of me himself. The hair, not the drink."

Who wouldn't, Royce thought, if he could plunder in Lizzie's drawers.

"So I said okay, why the hell not, and he reached under my dress and got one."

Royce decided to go fishing. "That fast?"

"Well not that fast, and it was kind of tricky, with him reaching under the table and all. But that was the only barrier, if that's what you're wanting to know."

"Any barriers right now?" he teased, casting another lure into the weeds.

"Do you want to hear what happened next or not?"

"Yeah, so what did he do with the damn thing?"

Elizabeth brushed her hair back with her palm, her braceleted wrist making little rattles. "He laid it in his drink, and when the waitress came over he started funning with her, you know, about having a hair in his drink. It was funny for a while but then he got ugly about it. You know, taking the joke too far and too serious, got the waitress all upset, almost made her cry. So I didn't have anything more to do with him. And I never will. He is lost."

"Poor guy."

"'Poor guy' nothing. He was making the waitress upset. Some people—my granddaddy, for example—don't know where to stop with funning around, you know? Those people are lost to me forever, so I just give them over to the River Styx."

"Maybe you need to know where to stop with your doings, too," he said.

"What do you mean?"

"I heard about that state trooper you let look at it when he was trying to give you a fine."

Her eyes widened. "Really? How elegant! How'd you hear?"

Royce shook his head. She seemed exhilarated to have the speeding-ticket story out, making the rounds. "Hell, it came over the radio."

She shrieked with delight then, tipped the flask with a flash of the silver charms, rolled her eyes, then her head, the way she did when she was a little drunk. Royce did not tell her that what he heard over the radio was Latham Jeter, the trooper, reporting to his other buddies patrolling the roads that day, that he had "just got a look at Crazy Lizzie's pussy," and the short wave came alive with congratulations from other troopers and deputies.

"Elizabeth, you could have gotten in some trouble behind that. What if he had charged you with attempting to influence?"

"Aw hell, Royce, he knew who I was." Her eyes had the sleepy look of alcohol and potential. "Besides, it got me out of a ticket, didn't it?"

"Shit. Your daddy would've made that ticket go away."

She laughed. "I know. It was really an experiment. Just to see if I could get away with it. For future reference." She took a swallow from the flask, the bracelets on her arms jingling the sound that always heralded her presence. She threw her heels up on her grandfather's desk and her light orange skirt slid above her knees. She let it stay there. "I miss the guys from Turner Field," she said, fingering some of the trinkets on her wrist. "I've got tons of charms just from them. Engraved." Her voice was sad and small.

"I'll get you a charm, Lizzie."

She smiled. "Okay. Since you're a veteran I'll put it on this bracelet. I keep the charms from civilians in a box to put on another bracelet sometime."

Royce wanted her to just offer him the possibility of potential. He wanted to be one of those she might allow in, might even invite in. He let his eyes light on her thigh, bringing his perpetual in-her-presence arousal up to the next level, the one that would not let him rise from his desk chair. "What's the meanest thing you've ever done to a man?" he asked, urging more tales out of her.

She laughed. "Well, it's more like the meanest thing I've never done to a man. And it isn't too terribly mean. No, I guess it is. Fun-mean, though, nice-mean, not mean-mean."

"Spit it out, girl."

She laughed again. "Okay, but keep it to yourself. It might scare some away."

Not likely, Royce thought. Not likely at all. "Go on, then."

"So I choose a guy who is really, really taken with me. The kind of guy who gets all mumbly around me, you know, because he really wants to be with me." She winked at him. "Kind of like you, Royce."

"Come on, Lizzie, I don't get all mumbly," he said.

"But you have a deep desire for me, true?"

"I believe we've done established that."

"Anyway, so I take the guy somewhere private, like out back of the bar or out by some parked cars, and I show it to him."

"Damn girl, that's the kind of mean any man wants."

"Wait," she laughed. "I show it to him and he's right then even more beside himself, and of course he asks to put it in. And I say, 'sure but only if—'" She giggled and paused.

"Come on, Lizzie. What?" This story was getting too good, way more good than Royce had bargained for.

"Okay," she said. "He can put it in, but only if he does it real slow, not slow like usual slow, but slow like I hold his watch and tell him he has to take five whole minutes just to put it in."

"Goddamn, girl, you call that mean?"

"Well, I've only done it a few times and so far only nobody's made it all the way in."

"No? Not even one?"

She took another sip from her flask. "Nope," she said. "They all went too fast and I had to make them stop. And one poor fool let go of his wad right off the bat."

She had the sweetest pale skin, like some kind of frothy meringue, whipped and sugared with a brush of something like fine down that was the light hair of her forearms, and he couldn't help wondering about the tops of her thighs. Royce decided to at least give it a try. "Hell, I could do it. Easy."

She laughed. "You think so?" She cut her eyes up at him the way she did when she might actually consider a proposition.

"Hell, yeah. You ain't never seen me watering no corn row without plowing it real good."

"You're a big talker all right," she said. She tipped the flask back, all the way, one last time. Then she stood, swaying a slight sway, just enough of a sway. "But okay, I dare you."

"Seriously?"

"Sure. Get up."

"Here?" Even Royce wasn't sure about that. "In your granddaddy's office?"

"No, silly. Come with me. Get up."

You damn sure got that right, Royce thought, standing, surrendering to the jokes he knew would come next.

When she saw his khakis spotted with patches of dark, she giggled again. "See? You're already getting ahead of yourself."

Royce smirked.

"This is going to be too easy," she said. "Maybe we should just—"

"Uh-uh. No you don't. Elizabeth Lacey don't take back a dare. That's for cheaters."

She smiled again. "You're right. Let's go."

She led him out of the office, out of the building, into the dusk. "You want to let's take a patrol car?" he said.

"Don't be silly." She took his hand then and he didn't care where, did not even care when she led him down the steps to the cemented, cave-like, mounded-into-the-dirt hole that was a restroom hidden on the court-house grounds, hidden behind lush leaves of sweet olive. "Colored," the sign above the steps read.

She led him down the cement steps, and the light of sunset went away fast in the cellared bathroom. There was, had to be, a smell singed with urine, something, after it had aged there, becoming like the spray of a tomcat, absorbed into the concrete forever. But all Royce could notice was Elizabeth, in the almost dark, hoisting her dress, putting one foot on the toilet seat, back against the wall, bunching her skirts at her waist to reveal that no, there were no panties this night. So it was true, then, some of the stories he had heard, about what a state of readiness she was in at times, as if she had planned this whole scene before she left the house, just as she was dressing, and, with deliberation, not adding underwear to the mix.

That image had Royce at yet another level of arousal, one he did not recognize, but it had him fumbling with his belt, his zipper, letting loose all that was bound up, held-in wanting. She was mostly just a dim form there, but he could see enough of her, the outline of her, and the fact that he knew it was her, Elizabeth, was enough. Hell, if she were in the full light he probably would have lost it already.

"Come over here," she whispered. "Come over here and put it in real slow."

Royce lunged toward her, and she held out her palms to push back against his chest, her bracelets clattering their warnings along with her touch. "Slow, remember?"

"Yeah." He got it out as more of a breath than a word.

"Now I can't see your watch in here because it's too dark, so you're going to have to trust me to call the time."

"Okay," he breathed again, wishing she would hurry and let him lean into her.

She relaxed her arms. "Now do what I tell you, okay?"

"Okay," thinking, goddamn, goddamn.

"All right," she whispered. "Slow. Do what I say."

He stepped in to the touch of her, then, waiting for the signal to begin. She reached down and guided it to the innermost meeting of her thighs, guided it until it was unmistakably positioned, and aching, aching. Royce's breathing was quick and gusty.

"I think," she whispered, and he could feel the breath of her whisper on his face, smell the warm rush of bourbon, "that this is the best feeling there is. The best, you know? That moment right before, right before you press in, make that first little nudge in, don't you?"

"Yeah," he lied, wanting to drive into her, push her back hard against the cement wall. There was an echo of water trickling somewhere in the restroom, and the hollow sound of a car going by, outside, above, and he was just before putting it in Elizabeth Lacey's pussy.

"Now," she said, still in a whisper, always in a whisper. "This is the hard part." And she bore down on him just a little, just enough for the slick heat to tell him just how aroused she was, and he had to be in her, had to be, and he started to push, but—

"No," she said. "Don't move. Be very still."

"Please," he whispered.

"Shhh. You know I need this to be right. To be good. Spiritually."

He could almost see her eyes looking into his, but the light had gone down even more in the short time they had been there, and he was thinking about maybe kissing her, when he felt her grasp go around him again and oh, God, she started, sort of, nodding herself, the outer part of herself, and there was a muted, tongue-against-the-roof-of-the-mouth sound that seemed to echo through the almost dark cellar of a fucking shit-hole of all places, and she bore down a fraction of an inch more, and the sound came louder, and he felt his nerve endings telling him what was bound to happen, bound to happen, and the sound of her made him want her to swallow him. It was then he surrendered, falling into her, giving in, without thought, without considering the consequences, only wanting to be wrapped up in Crazy Lizzie's pussy.

"God," he breathed, pushing into her, vaguely feeling her push hard against his chest with her palms again, saying something, but fuzzy and far away, the clinks of the silver charms on her wrists muted, because, just as he pulled back to make for a second thrust, in spite of the palms pushing against him, his ears thudded a pulse, a humming pulse, as he spilled onto her, letting loose an aching moan, loud, a muffled echo in the cement room, then dropping to the toilet seat, breathless, gasping.

Her form stood in front of him, the skirt now dropped, hanging below her knees. He was glad he could not see her face, as his senses returned to tell him he had failed the test, failed miserably.

"You cheated, Royce," she said quietly.

"Elizabeth—"

"You cheated." She seemed sincerely shocked, full of deep disappointment. "I never would have thought you, of all people, would cheat."

"I'm sorry, Lizzie." He reached out to take her hand, something, but she stepped back.

"No, I'm sorry," she said, "for you. You are lost." She sighed and let the effect of her words sink in, like the piss in that urine-soaked sacrificial tomb of a restroom, before she repeated them. "You are lost. Empty, just like your mother."

And she turned then, making her way to the steps leading back to the upper world, leaving him there, with his spent desire, sitting on a toilet in a colored restroom, spoiled forever, knowing it would never be the same between them. And he somehow knew, in that moment, that he would never be the same when he made to encroach upon any woman, that Elizabeth Lacey had pronounced him "lost" and therefore it was to be, his sentence for having thrown away the trust he had connived and cultivated in her for so many years.

That was how it happened then, but now, with Jolene, it was he who was in control, making it last, at least in his head, making it a conjured-up, proper fucking, one that had Elizabeth begging him, pulling at him, telling him how good he was, how he was better than she ever imagined a man could be, until his ears hummed with the pounding of his pulse and the cadence of Jolene's scripted words, and it was over.

"You okay, Baby?" Jolene put her palm against his neck as he sat on the closed toilet, breathing slower now.

"Yeah," he said.

"You want me to get you a cold drink?"

"No," he said.

He watched her pull her clothes back on, the man's shirt, the pedal pushers. She was good to him, he thought, knowing he did not love her, could never love anyone that way, lost as he was. He watched her run her fingers through her hair, fixing it into place, watched her bring the tails of the man's shirt together and tie a knot at her waist. He sat there, on the closed toilet, his limp, emotionally mangled penis resting on the cool lid, wishing he had gotten another chance to show Elizabeth, have her pronounce that he was not lost, after all. It had been a mistake, his impulsive rush, and he could do some kind of penance to set it right.

Royce rolled the jar over in the palm of his hand, thinking how sly he'd been about getting the thumb, how it damn sure got him noticed with the county boys, how Old Man Lacey had to have hid it in that cubbyhole way back years ago, when it happened, when they strung up the nigger that had gone after Elizabeth Lacey.

Royce heard about the lynching the morning after it happened. A friend of Dewey Fountain's called to tell him about how some nigger had slipped up on, of all people, Elizabeth Lacey, naked on a creek bank with the goddamn slickster she'd been going around with, the one that would leave her in the long run and set off her sure-enough lunacy.

The fool nigger. Talk about a no-win situation. If the county guys had not gotten the nigger outside the law the same night, then Elizabeth's grandfather, Campbell Lacey, the old man, the sure-enough High Sheriff, would have seen to it later. The more he thought on it, though, Royce figured Old Man Lacey had to have been one of the bonafides that was brought in on it dead first, and a familiar, seething boil began to bubble in the broth of anger that was Royce Lucas Fitzhugh, Jr. Goddamn him. Goddamn Sheriff Lacey, who kept a low profile in the organization while exercising his clout. Hell, he didn't even bring his only son into any of the superfluous shit, let alone the inner circle, a fact Royce embraced, thinking it could only enhance his own chances of becoming Campbell Lacey's protégé.

Royce was in the little bathroom at the sheriff's office taking a dump when he heard them come in, the father and the son, in the midst of an argument, the continuation of a running argument, now colored by the fresh result of Crazy Lizzie's behavior.

"It's not a thing I'll have on my conscience," Jack said as the door slammed.

"It ain't on nobody's goddamned conscience, now is it? Anybody here?" Campbell Lacey yelled.

"Hey now!" Royce hollered back from behind the closed door.

The voices at once dropped, but Royce leaned forward on his perch, toward the keyhole, and rustled some newspapers as if he were perusing the headlines as he sat.

"He had a wife. He had folks depending on him," Jack said.

"Goddammit!" Campbell snapped. "I've tried to respect your mama by not bringing you in on all this, but I'll be goddamned if it ain't made you soft on the niggers. Is this how you'll be running things?"

Jack said something low that Royce could not hear, but Campbell's response was explosive. "No, the hell you ain't!"

"It's already done and it's the right thing to do. Elizabeth will want it, too. She ain't going to be right for a while behind all this."

"No, by God, you stop right there. I won't have it. I won't let that be the kind of example the Lacey family puts out there for the rest of the world to see."

"No one will know where they came from," Jack said. "And it doesn't matter if folks do know. All I know is I can't have that on my conscience either."

"I don't think you heard me, boy," Campbell said, in the tone Royce knew well, the don't-fuck-with-me tone that ate up other men's confidence like sulfuric acid. "I won't have it."

Jack sighed. "It's too late, Daddy. I already spoke with his widow, and Mama's taking care of it."

Royce smiled. Whatever it was, if Campbell's wife dug in her heels and said something went, then it went. As big and mean and tough as Campbell was, Royce knew whose pussy kept it all in check on the home front, and Royce would be damned if he ever would let any pussy, save maybe one, take hold of his own life like that. True to form, Campbell went quiet, but not before he took one last shot at the son who was taking a different path, the path of his mother. "It was a hell of a thing to see, they tell me. That nigger denying it all, trying to fight back like a damn fool," Campbell said, and then all Royce could make out was the opening of desk drawers, the rifling of papers, the crackle of the radio. He leaned back against the toilet lid, thinking how pissed he had been when he got the call that morning, right away pissed because he had not been included. But he also knew that only an inner, hardcore group was really bona-goddamn-fide, made the calls, gave the orders, and at that moment he aimed to be right in with it. He obviously was not in just yet, but he would be. And he would bring to the table a chip he knew he could ante up into quite a take when it came to running things: the badge of a Blackshear County deputy sheriff.

Over the following weeks, word of the lynching was passed through the concentric circles of those who were always close to such goings-on and rippled outward through Royce and beyond, on its way to becoming part of the folklore of the region's underbelly. He knew from his eavesdropping there on the john that Campbell Lacey had probably set it up and would now look the other way, as was expected, having given the signal to hush it up, but good. The whispers would begin to make it unclear whether it even happened in Blackshear County. And, true to form, some said the nigger was carried into Crisp County for the festivities—a bonfire, a beating, a proper hanging, some creative carving—so it was maybe out of their jurisdiction anyway. No matter. He knew neither the Blackshear County sheriff nor his son would mention a thing about it, because, aside from the protocol exercised in such Klan activities, their blood kin, Elizabeth, whose wild reputation, already sanitized by the prominence of her family, had to be protected at all costs. And he knew that this could even be turned to his advantage as he schemed to grow her trust. He could reassure her, offer her a shoulder, help her recover from the trauma of being stalked and spied on by a nigger who must have coveted that white flesh, maybe heard how she sometimes gave it out freely. The black son of a bitch might have even got wind of those barely whispered tales, the ones no one dared to believe, about crazy Lizzie and a couple of colored men, nameless men, the stuff of half-truths and outright lies on her.

He did not see her for over three weeks after the lynching, was told she didn't feel well and had taken to her bed. Her nasal-twanged Midwesterner was still around, though, but even he was quiet about the whole incident. It figured. Jack Lacey had no doubt made sure there was no loud gossip about it, that the slimy encroacher got enough cash to keep his mouth shut. The Midwesterner continued to peddle his wares, though, stopping by the bars for a beer or two of an afternoon, but without the cockiness he carried weeks before. Then he moved on, bound for Macon, Atlanta, Savannah, the Carolinas, then down the coast and over to Tallahassee before he would come back up their way and start the circuit all over again.

When Elizabeth finally did emerge from the big white house next to the courthouse where Royce worked, she was not weepy and vulnerable, as he had hoped. Instead she was hollow-eyed and pale, with an expression of surrender on that ephemeral, unreachably beautiful face. She sat in her daddy's office chair, swiveling it around left, then right, then left, repetitive and sad.

"What's got you down, girl?" Royce asked, opening the door for her confidence.

But she did not take the bait. Instead her words were disjointed, mirrors of thoughts skipping to places nobody but she understood. "It won't ever be enough," she said.

"What won't?"

"The purging. The reclamation. 'I am Alpha and Omega, the beginning and the end, the first and the last.' You ever read The Revelation?"

"Say what?"

She gave an odd, diminutive smile then, secretive, full of implications. "The Resurrection, too."

"Oh, like Jesus?"

Her eyes widened. "No, no, no. Not Him. I can't."

"Come on, Lizzie," he said. "Talk straight to me, okay?"

She narrowed her eyes then, changing moment to moment, and she spoke as with a deep secret. "Did you know that I can see in the dark like an animal? Did you know my pupils can get bigger than a regular person's and just swallow up anything hidden in the night?"

Royce sighed. He had heard her nonsensical observations more than a few times over the years, knew he couldn't piece her thoughts together enough to understand, so he just played along. "Sure, Lizzie, I knew that about you."

She continued her slow, back and forth swivel in the curved-backed, squeaky-wheeled office chair. "I can see things. Here." She pointed at her right eye. "It's kind of like the Third Eye."

"That's nice, Lizzie. I wish I could, too. I could damn sure use another eye." Goddamn, sometimes she acted crazy as hell, but it was a thing he planned to use to his advantage, go along, take charge, play her like a fish on a line. "Can't you tell me what's got you so down?"

"'And the fruits that thy soul lusted after are departed from thee, and thou shalt find them no more at all.' Babylon will be destroyed, you see?"

"What the hell is it, Lizzie?"

She brought the chair to a halt and whispered, "My grandmother says I'm never to speak of it or there'll be no more purging. And it will never be enough." She began the repetitive swiveling again. "You would like to be

close to me." A different kind of smile flared up on her face now, a hint of
the old Lizzie, but still in the context of her gaunt face, the tired, dark-cir-
cled eyes.

"Who wouldn't?" he said, in an attempt to coax her into the kind of
playfulness men wished for when she was around.

"But you especially." Her voice was not playful and flirtatious, though.
It was flat and without nuance.

"Sure I would, Lizzie." In spite of the fact that her tone of voice did not
match her words, he liked this turn in the conversation, even though it was
something she held out to plenty of men, the hope, however faint, that
they might be chosen, make the cut.

"You aren't considered a handsome man," she said, "but I think your
scars look rugged."

Royce felt his face flush with the reference to the puckers of acne scars
that had been with him since adolescence. "Shit," was all he said.

"No, really. I think any scars are good. Eula Lura's husband had a scar
on his side."

"Did he, now?" Royce knew Elizabeth was speaking of the family's new
cook, the darkie Jack Lacey felt responsible for, knew she and her mama
were staying in the servant's shack out back of the big house. But he said
nothing to indicate his knowledge.

"He got a scar in the war, fighting in Italy."

"I'll be damned." And Royce felt even more hate in his belly, that the
goddamned nigger had been one of those who saw action.

"Scars force other people to notice the wounds they don't want to see.
Some notice, some don't. Do you notice?"

"Reckon I do. My job is to notice things, you know," he boasted.

"Bet you don't always. But some people do. Scars are symbols." She
stood. "I'm going home. I can't come out yet. It will never be enough. Not
until the Resurrection."

"Of Jesus?" he said.

"No, I said no! Of Othello." She smiled again. That knowing smile.
"And there *will* be a resurrection. Don't let anybody say different."

He watched her step out into the hallway, feet bare against the cool stone floor. She was a sure-enough lunatic sometimes, and he hoped against hope he could one day get some kind of control of her, determined to wait her out.

What Royce Fitzhugh did not know was that her night of lovemaking on the backwaters of the Flint River would send currents of repercussions into his own carefully laid plans. That sweetly scented swell of flesh at the juncture of her pale thighs, that thing he had incorporated into his desire for status, that same thing she had shared with one lacquered-up, liquored-up outsider and any number of others who elbowed their way into her madness would never be his for more than a minute in life. What he did not know was that, try as he might over the next five years, and close as he would come—close enough that he had it offered to him in her frenetic, drunken way, when she took him to the nigger bathroom and fresh humiliation—he would only know it long enough for it to take his desire over the wall and into obsession, tainting all of his dealings with women and wanting and double-handed masturbation. And even a dozen years after that, long after she had been buried in the Isabella Street cemetery, he would still be clutching at his foiled plans and struggling to wash the smell of her away.

Royce held the jar up to the desk lamp again, and the thumb seemed dusted by liquid starlight. He thought again about Jolene, with her hard life and her desperate sexual appetite. Yeah, she would do anything for him if he would keep her feeling wanted. The next time they got together he would make sure she had bought herself a light orange, below-the-knee dress. And a charm bracelet or two. Jewelry. Then his mind went to LittleBit's Purple Heart, and a slow smile stretched into his pocked cheeks. A Purple Heart. Now there was a thing to be had. There was a thing that would give a little more credibility to his desired status. Yeah, maybe he would get his ownself a piece of jewelry before too very long.

Eula Lura sat in a straw-bottomed chair beside her mama's bed, wishing she could make the cancer go faster, let her mama be done with its unforgiving pain. Her mama was ready to meet Jesus; she had said so more than a few times, and yet she would not die. It was as if she simply could not, not yet. Eula Lura suspected that Pinky was only blowing smoke when she said she was ready; there were so clearly things to be taken care of, peaces to broker, maybe even a score to settle. And it was this she put before her mama as she sat at her bedside.

"Sweet Baby," Pinky said in her haggard tone, cheeks sunk with the pain Eula Lura could only ease at intervals, injecting her mother's veins with an illegal substance smuggled from Albany. She had just, in fact, prepared a syringe, having cooked the powder into a liquid that would make her mama a good bit easier. "You think I'm hanging back from the Glory waiting on me? You think I wouldn't rather be walking streets of gold and singing with a choir of angels?"

"I think you got more on your mind. And I think it mostly has to do with that young 'un you done raised."

"I reckon it's Kansas you talking about."

Eula Lura resisted the temptation to let her bitterness spill onto her mother's deathbed, did not for a second want to let fly all the bottled up envy and rejection she could not help feeling. She and her sister Pruella had been spectators at Pinky's rearing of other children, relegated to the kitchen and back yard while her mama tended to another woman's, a white woman's, offspring. She watched her mama raise the Pearson babies until

Eula Lura married Ned and made her own life, a childless one. She longed for a baby while her mama nursed other white children. And finally, with Ned's death, she was forced to watch her mama tend to the crazy white woman who was the cause of it all, the crazy white woman whom Eula Lura quickly came to love, in spite of herself. And if that were not enough, along came the crazy white woman's baby, and her mama had another child to bring up.

She felt ashamed for her jealousy, for hating the succession of white babies who had not one thing to say about the matter. She felt especially ashamed when she let herself know, at her heart level, how much she was loved by a mother who had to trade time with her own children for other children and for the sake of her own children.

Pinky put out her thin hand. "It's all my children I'm afraid to leave. Is that what you waiting to hear?"

"Yes'm, it is." And Eula Lura was relieved, finally, to have gotten Pinky to admit it, a portion of what was holding her back from death and relief. At the same time she was afraid she was hastening the hour when she would be, once and for all, without the mother she wanted to love so much better than she had been able to these last thirteen years.

"I want you to be good to the child. I'm all she has and I ain't long for here."

"Mama, you can't ask me to do that. You know what all I'm carrying in my heart."

"I know you blame a child that was born innocent, that means no harm to nobody, just like her mama meant no harm."

"I know Elizabeth meant no harm. I know that. But she did do harm, didn't she?"

"And it caught up with her mind. She's done paid with her life."

Eula Lura wanted to say it didn't matter that Elizabeth paid, because Ned was still gone, would always be gone; to say it *did* matter that Elizabeth was dead, because Eula Lura carried the weight of responsibility for that death. But Kansas was a different matter, and Eula Lura wanted to say that happy-mouthed daughter of Elizabeth's had no right to take Ned's nickname for her and place it back upon her. "LittleBit." She cringed when the white folks used his name for her, powerless to do anything about it but let it stew and simmer it with the rest of the mix of her resentment and loss.

"I ain't going to be able to die easy till you tell me you can try."

Eula Lura remembered how Kansas toddled behind Elizabeth, catching the crumbs of sanity while she waited out the times her mother was not right by clinging to Pinky. Yes, Eula Lura liked, then loved Elizabeth in full spite of herself, recognized the white woman's aberrant purity, steeped as it was in that off-kilterness that wrecked her after her grandfather's execution. And for that Eula Lura knew she would pay dearly when she went before Saint Peter her ownself.

"You'll die easier, too, you know, if you can be good to the child," Pinky said, as though reading her mind. "When your time comes."

Eula Lura knew her mama was right, that Eula Lura was far, far from an easy death of her own. She touched her mama's hand, fingertips pressing into loose skin draped over hard bone, flesh sliding like chicken hide across gristle. "Yes'm," she said.

"So you will try?"

"Yes'm." She thought about the years of her occupation, her taking of the Lacey kitchen like an invading army. Never mind that Jack Lacey had placed her there. She used her time to study them, know their weaknesses, take inventory behind a façade of stern detachment. Elizabeth was the only one who ever coaxed a smile out of her, made her laugh, in fact, when they sat in the kitchen, Elizabeth slipping her a pint of gin every now and again, the two of them getting tipsy together. Eula Lura tried to hate her, tried to see her as a temptress who set up her husband's death, tried to see Elizabeth's affection for her as nothing more than a bid for atonement, but in only a short while her instincts won out. Ned always told her she could read a person in a heartbeat, and she could not force herself to read Elizabeth wrong.

Elizabeth knew what her indiscretion had caused, knew a decent man was lynched for stepping into her realm, blundering into her storm. She came to Eula Lura early on, late at night, out to the backyard shack. She sobbed and begged forgiveness and talked nonsense. It was infuriating and befuddling, especially since Eula Lura had been given to believe that only Campbell, Jack, and Miss Lucille were aware of her connection to the dead man. Elizabeth herself had been shut in her room for days and days, incoherent.

"How do you know what that man was to me?" Eula Lura asked.

Elizabeth looked up at her, eyes swollen almost shut from crying, face splotched with pink. "I feel it," she said. "I felt it right away."

And Eula Lura believed her.

Elizabeth came to her in the night for a whole week of nights before Eula Lura crumbled, allowed herself to care for the young woman. She knew Elizabeth would never be able to bear seeing, every day, the widow she created unless there was a peace between them, a forgiveness. Even though she resented the way Pinky looked after "Crazy Lizzie,'" she found herself pulled along and into the currents of the woman who could only bear to see the light in the world and let all that was not pure and good take her into a dim despair apart from anything Eula Lura had ever seen a human mind suffer, white or colored. Before long their relationship was clear. Pinky was Elizabeth's caretaker; Eula Lura was her spiritual sister.

Eula Lura caressed her mama's hand. "I'll try to be good to the child," she said again.

"Will you try hard?" Pinky winced, putting her palm to her stomach.

Eula Lura reached for the syringe and began feeling for a vein.

"Will you?" Pinky insisted.

Eula Lura remembered the months of Elizabeth's pregnancy. All the while she watched Elizabeth's mood lift and go more and more ecstatic as her belly grew larger by the month. Eula Lura put her palm to it, many times, there in the kitchen, when the child made its first flutters of movement; and later, when knots of bumps jutted out against the skin of Elizabeth's stomach, they laughed, "It's a hand!" or "That's a foot, I bet!" or "That big thing must be its caboose!" Elizabeth would lay her pale hand over Eula Lura's dark one and say, "That was the only time I ever really did it, you know. It's practically a virgin birth, and their spirits passed through one another in the sky. Ned was going up and my baby was coming down, riding on the point of a star, sitting beside an angel. And that angel took Ned just as their spirits all touched."

Eula Lura believed it, too, resolved to think of it that way, and it did take a second of the sting out of her bitterness. Then, finally, nine long months into Eula Lura's new dead life, on an evening in May, Elizabeth went into labor, screaming at the top of her lungs while the doctor wrestled a girl child from her open thighs. And Eula Lura was there, assisting in the delivery along with Miss Lucille and Pinky, was as thrilled with the baby as Elizabeth was. In a sense it felt like a shared birth, and, in the beginning, she helped Elizabeth look after the child, but Pinky was so much more comfortable with the role of nursemaid that the child soon gravitated to that comfort. Then, with Elizabeth's death, the child clung to Eula Lura's mama, dredging up Eula Lura's memories of herself as a three, four-, five-, six-year-old, longing for a mama who would tickle her the way she tickled the white babies, would tell her she was precious and smart and pretty as a picture the way she did the white children. All Eula Lura could remember her mother saying were things like, "Get me a clean bottle to feed this precious thing," or "You and your sister run on outside so you don't wake Genevieve from her nap," or "I'm going to swat the hide off your legs if you don't stop giggling so loud." Those were the echoes in Eula Lura's head as Pinky turned her attention to Kansas.

"You was a grown woman when Elizabeth had that baby," Pinky mumbled, again reading her mind. "Ain't you shamed, to be a grown woman and jealous of a itty-bitty baby."

Eula Lura pressed the needle into her mama's vein. Yes, she was ashamed, knew everything she looked at was tinted with the emptiness that came behind her lost husband. She took in a sharp breath as her mama's eyelids closed. Soon, probably before the summer was out, she would be looking into her mama's casket, wanting her back, wanting to do everything over. At that instant it caught in her realization: she had never really mourned for Ned, never let her cries roll from her tongue, from deep in her soul, from the places keeping her heart at bay. She had gone to the funeral, yes—a hasty ceremony at the True Zion Baptist Church outside Warwick, thick with the floral scent of elegant sprays of blooms, some, she was certain, sent by Jack Lacey. Flowers had even been ordered all the way from Chicago, from Walter Lewis, Ned's sergeant during the war, the man so like a father to her husband, the man whose telephone number Pinky thought to look for as she went through Ned's things.

The simple pine box Jack Lacey paid for remained closed. Eula Lura sat ramrod straight, feeling the eyes on her, feeling the fear in the congregation, feeling their relief that it had not happened to them, speaking of the facts of the incident in hushed, secretive tones. Jack Lacey drove her out to see the headstone he had bought for Ned's grave, American flags unfurled in granite, "American warrior" inscribed beneath his name, just as Eula Lura had asked. She had to admit it was fine and elegant, that she would never have been able to afford a stone like that, if any, not unless she dipped into their savings, and she could never do that. Not yet.

She had not revisited his grave, suddenly wondered why, at once knowing why. Every bit of her focus, her will, went into occupying the Lacey kitchen, going through the kind of surveillance worthy of a true combatant, a true warrior like Ned. She took to pinning his Purple Heart inside the pocket of her apron, leaving her apron hanging in the Lacey kitchen overnight, as if to say, Ned is here, waiting for me to be as heroic as he was, waiting for me to take the kind of risk he did, and you stupid, no-'count crackers don't have the first idea. Someday, it will all come out. Someday will come the time for me to leave this place and speak out and, God willing, find justice for my man. But in the meantime, here I am, watching and waiting and learning.

Now she watched as her mama slept for a while, then stepped out onto the front porch, into the dark of a summer night, sounds of beetles popping against screens and mosquitoes humming past her ears. She thought of Ned's trek through the woods toward Scratchy Branch, the brush of the leaves, the hang of humidity in the blackness beneath the trees. She lit a Picayune and looked into the night, searching.

Eula Lura thought it was ridiculous at first, the idea of coming to work for this white family whose patriarch had ordered Ned's death, or so she had heard. But no one asked her for an opinion before they strung him up, certainly did not want one afterwards. When the deputy, Mr. Jack, came to her home that morning, she knew Ned was gone. It was in the white man's apologetic eyes, the way he stumbled and stuttered over the words.

"There's been some trouble. It's an unfortunate thing," and he produced her husband's carved staff.

The "unfortunate thing" that was her husband's murder took her deep into a place glimpsed in others who were more beat down and bitter than she ever had cause to be, made her heart crust over like it had been dipped in a batter and deep fried. She did not let Jack Lacey see her react, kept her bearing passive, her expression without feeling.

He gave her a morsel of the story that morning, just at daylight, long after Ned should have been home. The remaining details came to her, though, through the near-silent network of colored folks who knew what went on, passing it, in separate strands, down the line. She cut and pasted the story together, throughout the following days and weeks, as she eased into her duties at the Lacey home, as she began to observe and learn each of them.

Miss Pearl was one of those snooty white women she had always heard about but never worked for, a woman who was overly concerned with what kind of picture she presented, a thing that seemed at odds with the easygoing grain of her husband's demeanor. Miss Pearl was polite but spoke to her with condescension and set keen stares on maybe catching her at something, Eula Lura couldn't imagine what. It was clear she was not trusted on that front, so she turned to the older lady, Miss Lucille, who laughed more and chatted with her, seemed interested in how she was doing, went solemn and sympathetic in a genuine way when she told Eula Lura how sorry she was about the loss of her husband.

"You know," Miss Lucille said, "you might find it more comforting to put the incident in different terms."

"Ma'am?"

"I've just found that my own heartaches from the past are easier to carry when I couch them in different terms."

Eula Lura gave her a puzzled look.

"Oh. I thought Jack told you what you might say about the incident, if you are ever asked about it."

It sank in, then. The day she and Mr. Jack Lacey visited the new grave-stone, he had suggested the version of Ned's death he wanted her to adopt. "He was on a fishing trip and he drowned." It was the version that was in the newspaper: "Local Negro Drowns on Flint."

"I know it seems dishonest, but truly, this might make things easier on you," Miss Lucille said, and as jarring as the lie was, the white woman seemed to mean her concern.

Eula Lura did not betray her outrage, simply said, "Yes'm," keeping her focus on biding her time. She even took to offering that version of the story when questioned. "He was on a fishing trip and he drowned."

And so the myth of Ned's passing was born, becoming the replace-ment story told around town, until, over the years, it became fact. But Eula Lura never let it become fact in her own consciousness. She worked and cooked, sometimes staying in the little shack out in the backyard with her mama, other times staying with her sister who had moved to town with her husband and her new baby when Mr. Jack found her husband a job at Collins's Pecan Company on the highway to Albany. Eventually she moved into a little shack of her own. And so Eula Lura had a new life, a new dead life, without Ned. And she had no choice but to be brought into the Lacey family circle so that her family would have security, jobs, the most basic of needs met, while she bided her time. She kept the money she and Ned had saved sealed in a manilla envelope locked in a strongbox under her mama's bed; and, when the day came, when she had exacted her revenge and was in a position to expose them all, she would take that money, travel to Chicago, and find Walter Lewis, U.S. Army, retired.

In the meantime, there was one person she resolved to hate, silently but well, and that was the patriarch, Campbell Lacey. When they were in the same room, she could feel her dead husband pounding at her pulse, urging her to keep close, look out, get even. Campbell Lacey watched her through the squinted eyes of Old Scratch, as guilty as if he had butchered her husband himself, and she watched back. She watched his habits, his quirks, lying in wait for an opening, a way to either trip him up or do him in.

"Morning, Eula Lura," Old Man Lacey said when he came to the kitchen for coffee of a morning, and her back would rise like an angry cat's while she opened the refrigerator and set out the cream.

"Morning," she always said back. And that was bulk of their conversation.

Eula Lura's presence did not seem to ruffle him or inspire any notion of guilt in him, though she sensed he did not want her there, which only made her more determined to be a presence in his life every single day of that life. Let him wonder if she thought him guilty. Let him watch her over his shoulder. Let him question a stinging undertaste in his grits. Let him look on her towering silence and ask himself what she would say if given that luxury. Let him never again, in this life, be completely comfortable in his own home.

Before long she began to find a kind of cold comfort herself, though, in that feeling of hate that wanted to be scored and passed out to all those white folks who cut her husband down from an oak tree by the river and threw him in the bed of a pickup like a trophy deer, to be carried to the colored funeral home outside town. And she would pass out the biggest helpings of her hate to all those directly involved, did so now in imagined acts of retaliation, fantasies of revenge. She would spend long mornings frying up chicken or corn cakes, carving roasts, boiling fresh vegetables in pot liquor rich with ham fat, keeping a level gaze, a steady voice, never revealing a hint, but all the while serving up daydreams of sweet, sweet vengeance in her troubled mind.

*

Kansas could see LittleBit sitting in the dark on the porch of Pinky's shack, barefoot, smoking her Picayune, a small lamp from a bedside table within drawing moths to the screen. The woman wiped at her sweaty neck with her palm. As Kansas drew closer she thought LittleBit's face, light cocoa glazed with acorn-hued freckles, was unusually strong and beautiful.

"What you doing?" Kansas asked.

"What does it look like?"

Kansas felt her face flush the way it often did when LittleBit snapped at her or made her feel foolish. "Well, I see you're sitting."

"Yes, I am."

"Is Pinky asleep?"

"Why? You wanting to visit?"

Kansas walked over to the screened door and peered in. "I do want to talk some things over with her. Things on my mind."

"Have to wait till the shot wears off."

"I don't mind. I'll sit with her if you want to walk over to the Blue Goose," Kansas said. She knew LittleBit liked to visit the club just across the tracks, come back all mellow with beer and flirtation.

"You'd better get on before Miss Pearl sees you out here."

"It's okay. I told them Roxy, Leo, and me were going on a play-out. We go all over town on a play-out, and I don't have to go in until Daddy turns on the siren."

The town that was their playground was a two-block-square expanse of narrow alleys and stone buildings. Dougie Moore's Furniture Store even had swing sets and yard chairs along the sidewalk, their own private park. On summer evenings the three of them did night dances across sidewalk fields of darting palmetto bugs and squash-slaughtered cigarettes, finding adventures in store window displays or reflected in the shiny black marble of the bank building, often climbing the fire escape to the courtroom's open windows, filling it with new dramas.

"Go on. Really," Kansas said again. "Besides, Miss Pearl's been in bed all afternoon."

LittleBit stared at the dark a moment before rising, licking her finger, and tapping the fire off her cigarette and into the dirt yard. She put the remaining butt in her dress pocket. "I won't be but a little while, then," she said. The wood steps groaned under her callused feet before she turned. "Wait a hour before you give her a shot."

"Okay." Kansas watched LittleBit walk down the alley and across the pavement. Her thin yellow dress, held together at the waist with a safety pin, framed the sturdy form beneath it as she stepped through the hazy glow of a streetlamp and into the dimness on its other side.

She went inside and sat next to Pinky's bed, watching her chest rise and fall for a long time, wondering if Pinky really was going to die, hoping it was all a mistake. Maybe, just maybe, God would change His mind. Miracles did happen, she had always heard. She thought about the Methodist preacher, Brother Stryker. Maybe he would come and pray over Pinky. Then, on second thought, no. Kansas did not care for Brother Stryker, though she would never voice such a thing to her family. She felt a meanness in the preacher's stare and had never really trusted him ever since last winter, when he was accused of fondling fifteen-year-old Marietta Boligee in one of the vestibules. She felt sorry for Marietta because the congregation rallied around him so. No, she would never ask Brother Stryker to come and pray over Pinky.

She was wondering a lot more about God this summer. Sometimes she visited the Baptist church, and on those occasions she considered the Devil, finding it difficult to conceptualize such a place as hell. The Baptists seemed set on it though, while Methodists, she was realizing, leaned toward the "God is love" philosophy. It was all so confusing, and there were hundreds more brands of Christians, and then to take into account other entire religions made her dizzy. How could any one of them be right and the rest wrong? She considered herself religious enough, though she had never read the Bible all the way through. She should read her mother's Bible sometime, she thought. It occupied a place on a bookcase in her room, but she had never opened it, just kept it there on the shelf, flanked by the Junior Classics. She knew her mother was a virtual encyclopedia when it came to Bible verses, and she thought her mother must have been an extraordinary Christian, which didn't square with the wild reputation she continued to uncover, the bits and pieces of a life gathered after the fact.

"Do you think my mama went to hell?" she asked Pinky a while back. "Janice Rowe at the Baptist Sunday school class says she did because of her fast ways and because of how she died."

Pinky jutted out her chin, the way she did when she was sure-enough incensed. "Janice Rowe ain't got the sense God gave a cow patty if she thinking such as that. Your mama was full of goodness. You think the good Lord don't know that?"

"I didn't say it. Janice said it."

"She said your mama killed herself?"

"No. Just 'how she died.' But it seemed like that was what she meant. Is it a deadly sin to kill yourself?"

"Don't matter. Jesus says the onliest thing that matters is how you be treating folks. Your mama was good-hearted and kind to anybody she liked. Anybody she didn't like she just didn't have nothing to do with."

"Do you think she would like me?" Kansas asked, thinking of her clumsy attempts at being graceful, at becoming a young lady.

Pinky smiled. "Your mama is up in Heaven just a-beaming her pride down on you. Don't you think nothing different, you hear?"

Now Kansas looked at Pinky's thin face, the spindly arms all sharp-boned and skinny, trying to feature her up in Heaven with her mama, both of them looking down on her, both of them proud of what she was becoming. "Don't go," she whispered, wanting Pinky there always, to see her through, to tend her own children, the babies she would have when she was grown, transformed into something complete.

Pinky's eyes fluttered open. "Child," she breathed.

Kansas rubbed at the tears spilling down her face.

"Don't you be crying about Pinky."

"I'm so selfish," Kansas whimpered. "I'm crying about me. About how much I will miss you if you go away."

"Oh, Baby," Pinky said. "Pinky ain't going away. Just going to join your mama so we can sit up in them clouds and sprinkle angel dust down on you wherever you be." Her voice caught and she grimaced.

"You hurting?"

"It ain't bad as it can be," the old woman answered.

"Want a shot?"

Pinky shook her head. "Naw. Keep on talking to me. It takes my mind off the pain."

"Okay. Because there are some things I need to talk over. You ready?"

Pinky nodded.

"There's this: Why doesn't LittleBit like me?"

"Oh, Baby, she does."

"But she won't talk to me. She acts like all I do is irritate her. She can even be mean." Kansas fingered the edge of Pinky's bed sheet.

Pinky sighed. "There is some folks in the world done had such sadness in their life they can't show their love."

"Why?"

"'Cause love done cut them to the bone. Lost love."

"Lost how?"

"Lost to death."

"You're talking about her husband, aren't you?"

"Him and two little babies spilled out the womb."

"What do you mean?" Kansas knew what a womb was. Roxy had made sure of that, but for a baby to be spilled?

"You ain't ministrated yet," Pinky said.

Kansas blushed. "No."

"Well, that's the egg comes down once a month."

"I know that."

"And if the man's seed makes it grow a baby, it supposed to stay in there till the baby's growed to life."

"But it doesn't always stay?"

"No. A backup of more ministration can spill it out, kind of like water building back of a dam. That ministration busts through and washes everything out and then you miscarry."

"And it happened twice to LittleBit?"

Pinky nodded.

Kansas felt guilty then, to have been so thin-skinned when it came to LittleBit. "How did her husband die?" she asked, struck by the fact that she had never asked this question before. Everything about LittleBit's long-dead husband had felt out of bounds for so long that she always simply let it be an unanswered question.

Pinky shook her head no. "It's a thing only LittleBit can answer for you, and I don't recommend you ask no time soon."

"Why?"

"That man died a unnatural death, the most unnatural there is. That's all can be said about it by me, you hear?"

Kansas nodded.

"Now you talk a spell. Got Pinky talking so much she hurting."

Kansas rambled on about the lake house, about how cold Miss Pearl was when they looked it over, and about the things her great-aunt revealed to her on the big curved porch.

"Lord, Lord," Pinky breathed when told about the sound of the door slamming that turned out to be a gunshot.

"Why didn't you ever tell me about that?" Kansas demanded.

"You never did ask me."

"But you always knew?" Kansas pressed on, wanting more.

"I was there that day. Wasn't no way not to know he'd done been shot. All I was thinking about was getting you away from it all."

"I remember the sirens," Kansas said. "But I mostly remember the oatmeal cookies."

Pinky responded with a whisper of a smile. "Then I done my job."

"I don't remember much about him. I don't remember being all that sad when he died. Did he love me?"

"I reckon so. He left you alone, didn't mistreat you none."

Kansas started to ask Pinky what she meant by that, but the old woman's face was suddenly knotted up, eyes clenched.

"Pinky!"

"I'll have me a shot now," Pinky said.

"Bad, huh?"

"It's Satan's own fire."

Kansas opened the cigar box that held several syringes and vials, plus the mysterious beige-colored powder brought from Albany by a friend of LittleBit's. Kansas smiled, thinking how jealous Roxy had been to know Kansas had a for-real patient in her back yard. She held a spoon over a kitchen match until the liquid was ready. She tourniquetted Pinky's arm, then searched out a vein at her wrist. She drew back the plunger, carefully, filling it to the mark LittleBit and Pruella had shown her. The vein was stubborn, but in a moment took the not-too-gentle slide of the needle's point. Another draw on the plunger, a cloud of blood, then a push, and Pinky's eyes rolled back, black lids falling almost the whole way, pulling her into a silent fogginess while a solemn cadence of crickets and humming bugs droned dirges in the dark.

Another half hour or so passed with Kansas content to sit and look at a *McCall's* magazine and puzzle over all kinds of things, to be near Pinky while she could. She thought about how ready Pinky was to tell her about the past, let her have the pieces she was missing. And Kansas wanted them. She wanted the pieces to lay into a pattern of a larger story, but at the same time she was uncertain, fearful of what the story might be. After all, everyone put so much energy into keeping it unknown, as if the ugliness Aunt Frances mentioned might be unbearable. Sometimes Kansas filled in the spaces with her imagination, trying to conjure the worst scenarios possible. Maybe her mother was kidnapped by white slavers and gang-raped and Kansas was the conception, in spite of what Aunt Frances said, of that perverse violence. Maybe her daddy was a murderer and sat rotting in a prison cell right now. Maybe Kansas was not even the natural, biological child of Elizabeth, but rather, an orphan left on the doorstep by a passing prostitute.

She turned a page of the magazine to the Betsy McCall paper doll layout. Last year she had collected the paper cutouts, put Betsy's outfits on the flat image by folding little white paper flaps over the shoulders, at the waist, making up stories in her head: Betsy traveling to Thailand, to Poland; Betsy making friends with an Indian boy, learning about the Hindu religion; Betsy accompanying her parents, a mother and a father, to the seashore, where her father goes swimming with her, collecting shells from the sandy ocean floor. Last year she had made up stories in her head about a paper person; now she was deciding if she was ready for the real story of flesh-and-blood people, *her* people.

In a while Pinky was somewhat alert, after drowsing in an abbreviated sleep. The injection had her pain muffled enough for Kansas to sit on the edge of the bed and launch into more tales about new lake houses, the habits of the apes, the trouble in Albany, and severed thumbs. She had just described the thumb Royce Fitzhugh showed them when she glanced over at Pinky. Kansas gasped and drew back instinctively. The old woman's black eyes, expressive of sudden shock, surrounded as they were by the dark circles of illness, gave her face the ghoulish appearance of a deep brown skull.

Pinky reached out to touch her forearm. "It's all right," she said. "It's only Pinky."

"But what's wrong?"

"Just took by surprise. Seem like LittleBit going to try to show the way, maybe, after all."

"Huh?"

She gave a deep sigh that caught in her neck and became a wrenching cough. Then she spat in a Maxwell House coffee tin she kept on the bedside table. "It's just the thinkings of a old woman's thoughts come out the mouth." She ran her palm across her lips, wiping at white spittle. "You done said a heap just now. And a heap more to come, I bet. You be wanting the truth, just ask, like I done told you. I won't be dying with a lie on my lips."

Kansas drew back again at the words, words she had wanted to be offered so many times before, words becoming more and more familiar as Pinky approached her end. Death. Suddenly Kansas had another reason for keeping still, resisting the questions. After all, her questions would be an admission, to Pinky and to herself, that death was, indeed, close by and would, indeed, take Pinky soon. It would make the possibility, the certainty, of her death more real. It would be a letting go of the nearest thing she had ever had to a mother, since her own mother had deliberately embraced death. It might even give Pinky permission to surrender, once she unburdened herself. At once all the important questions caught in Kansas's throat, snatched back by the five-year-old child who would never let go, so she re-formed her words into other, less threatening questions.

"Do you think it's wrong not to tell where Coy's thumb is? So his mama can maybe bury it?" Kansas asked.

Pinky looked deep into her, a knowing look, and Kansas was afraid the old woman would push her to give her the truth. But Pinky only answered, "No, Baby. Coy's thumb ain't got no spirit in it. It's just a old shell, just like the ones them biddies leaves in your Grandemona's chicken coop. Just like Pinky going to be real soon. 'Course, some of Coy's spirit might be done leaked out that hole in his hand before they got it all sewed up. But he'll be all right."

"Leo's mostly scared of what his daddy's going to do," Kansas said, ignoring Pinky's death reference.

"Well, them children ought to be scared of they daddy." The words came sluggish and a bit slurred. "You stay slap away from him. He a evil somebody. He's done busted many a nigger's head, plus his woman's. And that girl child of his better be sly cause he humps the women prisoners, white and colored."

Kansas's face grew hot at the reference to sexual intercourse, the term Roxy had already shared with her along with the stark details.

Pinky gave a weak chuckle. "You old enough. Ain't no sense in keeping them thoughts away from Pinky. Just wait till you get the ministration. You going to be doing it your ownself before too long after that come."

"It's nasty!" Kansas spat out. Roxy had told her about the milky stuff that would fire out of the man's penis and into the woman. As much as she wanted to get her period, she could not imagine a penis inside her the way Roxy described.

"Well, it's how we all come to be," Pinky said. "It's how you come to be."

"Then how come LittleBit only did it two times with her husband? If she wanted another baby, I mean."

Pinky laughed with all the energy she could muster. "You don't get no baby every time. Folks do it cause they like it. You'll see one day."

Kansas took a relieved breath of trust, knowing she could go farther than ever in her quest to fill in the gaps of what she knew about her mother, and Pinky would not tell her anything without an invitation, even on her deathbed.

They talked on for a while, Pinky allowing that the trouble in Albany was bound to come and right as rain, allowing that she liked doing it with her husband and grieved for it when he went missing, pointedly allowing that she was not afraid to die. Kansas put out the light when Pinky finally slept again, just as LittleBit's bare soles slapped against the steps.

Kansas met her on the porch. "You have fun?"

"Such as it is," LittleBit said.

Suddenly Kansas was overwhelmed with love, for Pinky, for LittleBit, wounded by life. She felt it tumble through her like a random spirit invading her body, wanted to express it. She flung her arms around LittleBit's waist and pressed her cheek into the big woman's breastbone. "I love you, LittleBit," she said, feeling the sweat-damp of the thin cotton dress, smelling the Juicy Fruit gum LittleBit kept in her bra, the callused scent of Comet and fatback and hard work. She could feel LittleBit go rigid, but she squeezed against the resistance. "I love you," she said again, nuzzling against the thin yellow dress, feeling a trace of softness, a moment of give, when LittleBit pressed her palm against Kansas's shoulder, patted it gently and said, "Get on to bed, then."

Late that night, after writing down fresh thoughts in the locked diary, Kansas walked to the back porch and watched the dark face of Pinky's shotgun house, knowing LittleBit was sleeping in the chair by Pinky's bed, maybe feeling a shade more tender toward Kansas now that she had been offered her love. And when Kansas finally lay in the canopy bed where her mother once slept, where Kansas used to cuddle against her perfumed body, she knew Elizabeth Lacey could see her, was just this moment, even, sifting a whispering of angel dust down from the clouds.

II: iv

Frances sat on the pier at her brother's lake place, watching out across the water, marveling at her brother's gutsiness, at the way he had orchestrated it all, his being near the memory of his daughter. She reminded herself again and again that Kansas was not Elizabeth, after all. At some point Kansas would have to be told the complete family history, but she would surely take it in stride, not let it knock her down. After all, Kansas was a happy child, one who took what came at her, adapted, did not take herself too seriously, a chatterbox full of questions, but, at the end of the day, Frances was sure her niece's daughter would be all right. And how lucky the child was to be growing up in such a time of impending freedom! It was thickening in the humid air, a swell of justice, almost tangible. Most refused to see it; many would fight it tooth and nail; but Frances and Martha both knew a shift in mood was coming fast, most recently with the protests in Albany. Then she came back to the thumb, the one Royce had, wondering how he had gotten such a thing, since he had not been in on it, as far as she knew.

She thought about her old job at the telephone office, where she heard all sorts of things over the lines, where she had first heard about the lynching, the following day. Usually the calls were benign as Frances made connections and chitchatted with Blackshear County callers.

"Connect me with Ira Barker, please, Miss Frances," a caller might say.

"Oh, hey, Pauline. No, can't do it. He's gone to a livestock auction over at Tifton today."

"Has he, now?"

"Oh, yeah, told me about it last week when he was calling to check on his mama."

"Well, I reckon I'll get him later. So how are you doing?"

"Just as well as I wish," Frances said, "so I wish you well," her standard telephone operator line. She loved talking to folks, joking with them, being a part of their family news. She loved celebrating with them when they experienced triumphs, and she felt useful when she could help them through tragedies—send flowers, have Martha bake them a cake, offer consoling words of comfort, just be there. That was the luxury of her job as a rural telephone operator. She was a connection between folks, and it made her feel like she was doing something that really mattered, on a very human level.

The other side of the coin was that her job fed her sense of fun at having a private seat as audience to the little-known tales of Summer and its outlying regions. At the time of the lynching she knew, for example, that Scottie Hawkes was carrying on with Jeanette McGibbons, and Jeanette not three months married. She knew about Marian Cummings's husband being a secret drunk and a liar in his business dealings, while in public Marian called him the spine of the church community. She knew about the hard financial times the Clemmonses were having these days, and Mrs. Clemmons driving that brand-new automobile, living a precarious notch above their means. Frances had a front-row seat to hypocrisy each day as she listened in on conversations, party-lining her ears to unfolding dramas that, but for her discretion, would stun the residents of Sumner with scandal.

The downside of the flip side was the utter sadness of some of the stories, the isolation of others, and Frances's knowledge of how pervasive were those human failings she had always known existed, existed especially in her own life and family. Of all people, Frances Lacey understood the fragility of monogamy, the permeation of desire, and the spiritual desolation of greed, because she heard those themes played out in real-life stories every day, through the headset she wore, through the telephone lines. The news of the lynching, though, was by far the most disturbing thing she had ever heard, and of course it was inevitably tied to Elizabeth. Frances felt sicker and sicker with every conversation.

"They say it was because of what he seen," the words crackled into her headset.

"Well, hell yeah, it was because of what he seen."

"You reckon he followed them there before?"

"All the time, probably."

"Well Old Man Lacey took care of it like he ought to have."

"Good thing he didn't leave it up to that son of his."

"Jack Lacey don't act like no daddy that's had his girl violated if you ask me. I'd be done blowed the nigger's brains out my ownself if he messed with Lucy."

Frances remembered going through a half a pack of cigarettes as she listened that morning, stomach turning over, diving into itself, and a new wave of nausea with each batch of fresh details she picked up.

"That goddamn whore of a young 'un is going to bring down her granddaddy's office if she don't quit flaunting it."

"Shoot, she can flaunt it my way anytime. You don't want the bars to be without Crazy Lizzie, do you?"

"Ha. Guess not."

"Anyway, it was the nigger chased her down, not the other way around."

"Did they carve him up?"

"Yeah."

"Takers?"

"Yeah."

"Who?"

"The usual."

A half a pack of cigarettes and cup after cup of coffee had Frances wound up with her thoughts jumping all over the place every time she happened upon a conversation about the lynching.

"His family ain't likely to say a thing, just put him in a box and under the dirt."

"He ain't got no children. Only a wife. But she looks after her mama."

"How do you know?"

"I heard something about it."

"What's that?"

"Jack Lacey was the one went to talk to his wife. To tell her he was killed."

"That right."

"Yeah. And there's talk that Jack Lacey might give her a goddamn position of employment."

"Shit."

"You ever seen such a pussy when it comes to niggers?"

"Hell no."

"I hate to think how Jack'll deal with the niggers when he takes over."

"Like a big old sad, pink pussy is how."

"Speaking of a sad pussy, yonder comes my wife."

By early afternoon of that day, Frances had put a good deal of the story together. She knew not to confront her family about it, knew to hang back, act as if she did not know, then to go and visit Elizabeth, see how she was doing, see what was being spoken of and what was not, dreading what she might find. The dread came from her deep knowledge of her niece, a knowledge beyond anyone else's in the family. Elizabeth was unstable and rebellious, certainly, but she was, above all, kind. She was especially kind to those misfits and outsiders with whom she identified, fellow residents of a periphery they shared, not by choice but by circumstance and the estimation of others, of the larger society.

Even when Elizabeth was a child and Frances took her shopping in Albany, Elizabeth had approached any folks who looked as if they might be on that periphery. She babbled on with them in her delightful way, telling about the last funny thing she had done, like helping her grandmother make blackberry cobbler, then, her hands stained blue, going to town and telling a perfect stranger the blue stains were her birthmarks, that Jesus was trying to give her a matching set of blue gloves and botched the job, leaving her scarred, not in a shade or tint of flesh, but in color, glorious like the feathers of a peacock. Elizabeth spoke in near poetry to the little legless man who parked his plyboard cart near Crowe's Drug Store and held a tin cup out to the passersby, subtly challenging them to notice him, to drop him some change. Elizabeth sat beside him on the sidewalk and drank Royal Crown Colas with him, calling him "magic man," telling him there were coins in the clouds, she knew, because she had gathered them there and would someday wear them on silver bracelets. Frances always watched her niece, proud of how easily she connected with those who made little headway connecting with others, simply because the others were not comfortable enough in their own skins to acknowledge anyone who stood out for different. Yes, Elizabeth was nothing if not kind, and Elizabeth would not be able to bear the fact that a man was dead and she was the rationalization for it.

Frances visited her three days later, late in the evening, and found an alternately silent and incoherent child who whispered garbled words to her grandmother, seemed to want Miss Lucille's forgiveness. That forgiveness was granted along with readings from the Holy Bible, and admonitions: "You must rise above this, Elizabeth. Use it as practice for yet another hardship and another challenge."

Frances sat on the other side of the bed, her strong, suntanned hand covering her niece's. "You know, Mother," she said. "This is the time to bring in a special doctor, someone who can really help her."

"She will be all right," Miss Lucille said, as if saying it would make it so.

"There is a very good psychiatrist in Albany, named—"

"No. Jack says Pearl will never have the family put under a microscope. She simply will not have it."

"That's not what he does. You know that, Mother." Frances said. "Psychiatrists don't necessarily do that. I have a friend in Atlanta who sees a psychiatrist, and he's a tremendous help to her."

"Your friend might need the help," Miss Lucille said, "but Elizabeth will be fine."

"She's not looking so fine now."

Miss Lucille stood. "Frances Leigh," she said, reminding her she was not in a position to call any shots. "You may stay and visit with her if you like. But do keep your opinions to yourself. I don't want any talk about the family being circulated for the amusement of the whole town."

Frances smirked. If only her mother could have heard the phone conversations flying around the county over the last few days, conversations that had become mutated versions of the real story by now, and more whispered, more subversive, since it was, after all, not to be talked of. As it passed through to the wives, it became more absolute and more absolutely incorrect.

"She told them to hang him. Elizabeth Lacey did."

"No."

"I mean those boys were going to let it go with a beating, but she cussed them and called them pussies if they didn't hang him."

"I thought that boyfriend of hers was behind it."

"No, honey. My husband told me about it. He got it from Freddy Stout who got it from Mooney Dees. And Mooney Dees was there."

"Was he?"

"Oh, yeah. Mooney said Elizabeth was cussing and carrying on and told them if they didn't do it then her granddaddy would."

"I thought her granddaddy was there."

"Oh, no. Her granddaddy was in Apalachicola on a fishing trip."

"Well I say he should have been hanged. I know I'd want any nigger that tracked me like an animal to be drawn and quartered."

"I swanee, the rice is boiling over. Let me go, Sharon."

Frances leaned into Elizabeth's field of vision. "Lizzie, it's all right," she said, getting no reaction, only an occasional little sob like the gasp of a dying bird, barely there. Frances rose, her heart like a chunk of metal in her chest, and walked home, connecting the sidewalk's dots of light, glowed down from lampposts, with her footfalls.

She visited Elizabeth every day after work, and, over the days, observed the tiny, small-boned, middle-aged colored woman called Pinky being moved into the vacant little shotgun shack where her own childhood nursemaid, Samantha, and later Elizabeth's nurse, Jubil, had long ago lived behind the big house. She noted that Cleria, the former cook, was gone, and a giant of a woman, Pinky's daughter, had taken her place. Frances met her, and with each visit to Elizabeth or each time she joined the family for supper, Frances said hello and complimented the big woman on her cooking. They told each other several times with their eyes that they were aware of the strange situation, the circumstances of the new cook's and her mother's employment. And every day after supper, Frances found Elizabeth either sleeping or sobbing or just staring at the wall, until a dozen days had passed. Then, on the thirteenth day, out of the blue, Elizabeth was sitting up, mercurially different, in her out-of-the-blue way, eyes wide, with a whisper of a smile on her lips.

"Honey, this is so much better," Frances said. "You look worlds better."

Elizabeth tugged at the slick satin comforter at her neck. "I have a secret."

"A nice one?"

"The nicest."

Frances knew what was nice to Elizabeth was not necessarily nice in the realm of the Lacey family, so she proceeded with caution. "Have you told anyone?"

"No. Just you. Just now."

"What is it?"

"Since the night on the creek it's been a thought in my mind and I think it's coming true."

"What thought, Honey?"

"My period hasn't come."

"How late are you?"

"Two days."

"Good God, you scared me for a minute. Two days is nothing. It'll come."

"But I have to have his baby. I have to."

"Oh, God, Elizabeth. Not Eddie Frye's."

"Yes."

"You just get that out of your head. That man is a rounder and a ne'er-do-well. The last thing you need is a baby from the likes of him."

"No, Aunt Frances. I have to be pregnant. Don't you see? It's life out of death. It's the best thing I could hope for. It's the Resurrection."

"Honey, no. You can't think that way. Nothing will bring that poor man back."

"Yes, it will. It will make everything all right. I have to tell Eula Lura."

Frances wondered when and how Elizabeth, isolated in her room for so long, had connected with the new cook and why she would want to confide the suspected pregnancy in Eula Lura, but all she said was, "You don't have any idea what having a baby by that man would mean."

"Yes, I do. I see in the dark like an animal, did you know?"

"But you don't know—"

"Yes, I do. It means that Eddie and me will get married. As soon as he comes back through town in two weeks I'll tell him. And we'll have a beautiful wedding. And we'll live here with Mama and Daddy, and it will be like nothing ever happened."

Frances resisted challenging Elizabeth's vain hopes, and for the next little while, Elizabeth fluctuated between secretive, serene Madonna and uneven shadow of a Jezebel, the one Royce Fitzhugh said visited at the sheriff's office in subsequent days.

Frances thoroughly hated Royce Fitzhugh. He was a blowfly on the cow turd of life, in her opinion, a pawn of her own father's who skulked at the edge of her family, just waiting to pounce on Elizabeth. She knew, too, that he appealed to Elizabeth because of his inability to belong, to fully participate in polite society, or any society, with the kind of success he craved. Unfortunately, and uncharacteristically, Elizabeth could never bring out any beauty in Royce, Frances knew, because there was nothing of beauty there. Still, Frances talked with him when she needed to find out how Elizabeth was getting on, out there in a world where Royce and others like him waited to use her.

"If you're a friend to her, then keep watch, all right?" Frances said.

Royce lit a cigarette and smiled his conniving, crooked little grin. "You know I'll always watch out for Miss Lizzie," he said. "She's right steady a woman that bears watching."

Frances felt her stomach go sour, like it did whenever she thought of her niece wallowing on top of some Fitzhugh or another, some sleazy Eddie Frye, an optical illusion of an artist, with the insincere cockiness of a salesman. But it was something about Elizabeth that was as unstoppable as a river's current. It could be diverted at rare times, but it always eroded itself back on course, so Frances worked with that current as opposed to fighting it.

She knew her brother also had no use for Royce and his hungry-hound demeanor, but Jack had already promised their daddy that he would keep Royce on when the office was turned over to him, would keep Royce on until Royce might make a viable candidate in Early or Lee County. It was a nasty business, all this sheriffing and policing in the bottom end of the state. It was called the Velvet Corridor, this swath of deep black soil at the southwest corner of Georgia. The Velvet Corridor was such a beautiful name for the richness of the dirt, the huge wealth of the plantations like Nilo and Magnolia, the deep roots of those plantations tendriling out for miles and miles. But Frances thought of the Velvet Corridor as more of a heart of darkness than a place of beauty. It was a row of pickers stooped to the furrows, a barefoot woman with a rip at the shoulder of her shirtwaist dress. It was a place rooted in the past, where barrel fires flashed images of dancing devils around clumps of shotgun shacks at the edges of fields of cotton and soybeans. She despised what Royce Fitzhugh represented, the social order of the Velvet Corridor, the world of her father. She had despised Royce then and still did now. And now Royce had a thumb, a trophy from the lynching, she knew, because she had known her father so well.

Frances looked out over the lake, marvelling again at Jack's uncharacteristic assertiveness, even brazenness, in purchasing the place, wondered what he would think if he knew Royce had the thumb, what Kansas would think if she knew what the thumb represented, over a decade after the lynching.

She thought back to last December, the day she had driven Kansas to Albany to do some Christmas shopping. They went through every department in Rosenberg's, then walked to Crowe's Drug Store for vanilla cokes, sitting on stools at the fountain, watching the soda jerk dribble cola syrup over ice then fire a blast of carbonated water into the mix with a few dashes of vanilla flavoring. Kansas wanted a banana split too, so they took their time, watching folks dash in and out, agitated with the feeling of the coming holidays. Finally they piled into the Thunderbird with their packages and drove across Oglethorpe to a gas station. It was after that, as they rounded a downtown corner near Jackson Street, that the harsh blast of a police whistle jolted them alert and an officer held up his hand to stop them. Frances at first thought she had done something illegal. But then she saw the people approaching the intersection, a line of somber-faced Negroes, walking single file, silent, dignified.

"Oh, Kansas," she whispered, full of reverence. "You are looking at history."

"What is it?" Kansas replied in the same tone.

"Shhh. Just watch. Take every image in. And remember it."

The line of marchers, still single file, crossed the main street dividing the white and colored sections of town, to where a gathering of police cars and wagons waited to arrest them. Frances was struck by how they were all dressed in their Sunday best, the women in dark, lace-edged dresses and church hats, the men in suits. But most of the group was made up of younger people, teenage girls in dresses cinched at the waist, petticoated, and young men in suit pants and white shirts with ties. A woman wearing a pancake-brimmed black straw hat passed in front of the car, the sunlight catching the shiny weave of her hat, bouncing light back at them. At that moment Frances realized how deliberately the marchers were holding their heads dead level, not thrown back and arrogant, and at the same time not with eyes cast down and subservient. They all walked proud and steady and level and silent. Frances felt prickles of admiration and envy as she watched them. How liberating it must be to simply step forward to say, "This is me. I will be treated with the same respect you would give anyone."

She reached over and tapped Kansas's knee. The girl was just as swept up in the mood of the marchers as she was. Kansas leaned forward, arms on the dashboard, chin resting on her arms, watching the silent line move past.

"Look," Frances said. "Look there." She indicated the gentleman bringing up the rear.

He wore a fedora and a London Fog overcoat. His eyes glanced up and left, up and right, in a forced tempo of vigilance. Other than that he looked straight ahead, just as the others did. The sun was bright and a cold December breeze brushed the marchers, billowing his overcoat open, revealing a Scottish plaid lining as he passed in front of them.

"That is Dr. King," Frances said.

"The one on the news?"

"The very one."

"Mr. Royce at the sheriff's office says he's an outside agitator and he ought to be strung up because shooting is too good for him."

"What do you think about that?"

Kansas watched the line of colored folks move on up the street. "I think he has sincere-looking eyes. That Dr. King. I think they all look nice, but him the most."

Frances thought of that day now as she sat on the pier at Lake Blackshear, knowing it spoke to her grandniece's character that she could challenge the sorts of perverse attitudes that were shoved in her face all the time from the Royce Fitzhughs of the world, and worse. Kansas knew the difference between kindness and familiarity. Kansas knew the difference between goodness and charm. She had a way of seeing through to the heart of a matter, just as her mother had, but without her mother's spun-glass vulnerability.

Frances watched the water grow dim and cool in the afternoon shadows, watched the steam from the hydroelectric plant billow up to the fading clouds, let her eyes glance north to the opposite shore, where a little creek spilled its cold water into the expanse of the dammed-up river, a little vein of clear water trickling into the murky gray of the Flint. It seemed like nothing, a drop in an ocean, a breeze in a hurricane, but Frances knew, as she had known nothing so certainly in her life, that the smallest thing could turn the largest around. The weakest, most subtle tide could be just enough to stop a flood surge. There were different days approaching, and she knew it could only bode well for Kansas and, with any luck, for her own life, too.

*

The summer unfolded in lazy mornings and slow afternoons. Kansas, Roxy, and Leo wandered the streets of the town or loitered in the courthouse or threw rocks into Cane Creek from the bridge high above. They viewed Coy's thumb every few days, as if attending a visitation at Bridger's Funeral Home, respectful and silent. Soon, however, they began to play games with the thumb as an object, twenty questions as to what each of them thought the thumb resembled this week or that. Some of their perceptions included a miniature dill pickle, a piece of a little link sausage, a cigar chewed off at the end, a turd from a Chihuahua, a pine stick, a bit of jerky, a monkey pecker. No one knew what a monkey pecker looked like, but they all agreed it should resemble Coy's corpse of a thumb, which continued to waste, shrivel, dry up, shrink, hollow out, until it looked to be the crust of a cicada clinging tenaciously to the stob. They kept hoping for a strong wind or a thunderstorm to wash it down from the roof, but the days were still and only a few midafternoon sprinkles drifted their way, up from the Gulf of Mexico.

They walked to the city park some afternoons, Coy following along with Hotshot, who pushed him tirelessly on the miniature merry-go-round. Kansas, Roxy, and Leo sat on the swings eating hot dogs from the pool's concession stand. There was a wading pool, too, with a fountain in the middle of it, where nursemaids took their young charges to swim, and, while Leo went down the slides and swung on the maypole and hung on the monkey bars, Kansas and Roxy waded with the children, feeling big and helpful, even a bit like potential mothers. And all the while, Hotshot pushed Coy in continuous circles, drawing other children to them. "Push me! Push me!" and "Let me on, too!" the children sang out.

"Cranking up!" Hotshot called. "All aboard! Eeeee, Law!"

She visited Pinky a few times, usually finding her either sleeping or moaning loud, with the kind of pain Kansas could not watch, so she yielded to Pruella and LittleBit, raced off to find Roxy, to keep herself from thinking about Pinky maybe leaving her. Roxy's interest in Kansas was revived with the purchase of the lake place, most probably, Kansas thought, because there would be boats and boys involved in that scenario. Roxy was forever looking at boys and saying how cute they were. She listened to Elvis Presley records, had torn pictures of Elvis and Ricky Nelson and Brian Hyland from magazines and pinned them on her wall until her daddy ripped them down. She attributed the features of her rock 'n' roll heroes to any cute boys she noticed. "Oh, look! He has eyes like Ricky !"or "Can you believe his hair is just like Elvis's?"

Kansas usually went along with whatever Roxy said, did what she wanted to do, recognizing her subservient status with the girl who had taken her place in their two-person pecking order, Roxy making all the rules because she was the more mature-looking one, with the curves and the Kotex. Everything was different. Roxy grew more and more difficult and foreign to her. She teased her hair to look like Brenda Lee. She did her eyes to look like Natalie Wood. She talked about wishing a boy would kiss her, that she would even let a boy French kiss her.

Kansas slapped her arm. "That is nasty! God!"

"Oh, don't be such a baby," Roxy snapped.

"How can you want to feel something so nasty?"

Roxy sighed her I-know-so-much-more-than-you sigh. "Someday you will understand." And she put the finishing touches on yet another drawing of a penis, then slid it under Kansas's rug with all the other drawings.

Kansas seethed, but pulled out her ace in the hole. "I think we're driving up to the lake for the weekend." And suddenly Roxy couldn't be nicer, at least until she got her official invitation, heard with her own ears when Kansas asked her granddaddy if Roxy could come, too. He always said yes.

The last weeks of June found them more and more at the lake. Daddy filled the three boat slips as promised, with an aluminum fishing boat, a Boston Whaler, both of which he taught Kansas to operate, and a fifteen-foot Chris-Craft ski boat—sharp red with dark wood-paneled sides—that he used to teach Kansas, Leo, and Roxy how to water ski. It took Kansas exactly seventeen tries before she got up on the two wooden skis Daddy had bought at a marina by the north end of the lake, near Americus. She was afraid, at first, of the hugeness of the lake, the depths beneath her where mud creatures and river monsters lived, but the lure of the motor's drone grabbed her, and once she mastered the idea of letting the boat guide her up to the surface of the water, she was hooked. The sound of the glide and slap of skis across the river's face, the warm air hitting her water-cool flesh, and the feeling of power fueled her enthusiasm. Before long she was begging Daddy to take them skiing whenever they drove up to the big house on the water. Before long she was asking for a slalom ski, and it did not take long for him to give in. After only a few tries she was able to slip her left ski off and slide that foot in the strap behind the ski shoe holding her right foot and go like crazy. The single ski gave her much more speed and control, and she coached Roxy until her friend, too, could drop one. Leo was content to continue riding two.

They made the drive two or three times during the week, in the late afternoons, three hours of daylight remaining after Daddy got off from work. Most weekends, Friday afternoon until Sunday night, were spent skiing or lounging in the sun, the girls lying on towels on the pier while Leo lowered hook after hook into the water, stalking a big one. Sometimes they just sat in the Whaler, letting it drift around a dropped anchor, Roxy always noticing the boys in their fast boats, boys from Americus and Tifton and Cordele and Albany. The boys had crew cuts with bleached blonde bangs, butch-waxed straight up—defying the spray of the wake to take away the shape—and small-checked bathing suits and tanned shoulders. They waved at Kansas and Roxy, who left Leo on the pier to fish more and more as they ventured into the summertime world of the opposite sex, if only as far as flirtatious smiles thrown to passing boats.

Daddy puttered around the yard, weeding things, tending the scuppernong arbor, oiling hinges, and working on the lawnmower on weekend mornings. On Saturday and Sunday he took the girls and Leo skiing in the early afternoon, then again before dusk. In between ski time, the girls floated on air mattresses or inner tubes or anchored the Whaler in tucked-away sloughs while Leo snatched bream and catfish from the lake bottom and slipped them curving and flopping into the fish basket Daddy had tied to the end of the pier.

When Miss Pearl made the trip, which was not very often, she sat on the screened porch watching the birds and squirrels as she sipped her brandy, the sounds of televised baseball games drifting out from the big den where Daddy drank beer he got out of a separate refrigerator that held only beer, and ate boiled peanuts as he lounged in his recliner. After the late-afternoon ski run, he switched over to Evan Williams, and his face eventually took on the ruddy look that came after several drinks. By ten in the evening he was asleep in the recliner, Miss Pearl long gone to bed after she made a light supper for everyone at sundown.

More often LittleBit fried up some chicken or made Brunswick stew or roast and gravy for the family to take to the lake house. She came to stay once on a weekend, when Pruella was able to watch over Pinky for a long spell, and slept in the little servant's cottage on the edge of the property. She showed Leo her fishing technique, how to bob the cork just so, tempting the fish to clamp down her hook.

Aunt Frances visited, too, and sat on the pier to watch the sunset after she took a swim or went with them for a boat ride. Sometimes friends of Daddy's visited on the screened porch, having drinks and telling loud, laughing stories to one another. Miss Pearl rarely joined them, and when she did she had little to say, and only smiled her partial smile when the conversation called for laughter.

Daddy bought a map of the entire lake to keep in the glove box of the Chris-Craft and urged the girls to study it in case they should ever go too far or get turned around. As a map, the huge lake looked long and skinny, with little fingers of inlets and creeks snaking from its edges. The lake itself was about twenty miles long, curving up from Blackshear County and into Crisp County and northward to Americus and beyond. It was the map that made Kansas thinly aware of the place that grabbed her by the ankles one day and threatened to pull her under, though she didn't know why. Scratchy Branch was suddenly a presence, and instinct told her to file this away along with Aunt Frances's story of the dam.

She was skiing when it happened. She was out on the big water that overwhelmed her sense of security. She told Daddy she preferred to ski on the more narrow part of the lake, where the shores were in easy swimming distance, the houses close and nurturing. But sometimes Daddy steered the boat around the point of land facing the dam, out to where his house looked across a quarter-mile-wide band of water, which, on windy days, became a choppy mess it took concentration and strong legs to master. This day was a windy one, and overcast, the boil of clouds giving midday the look of twilight. The slalom ski slapped at the water, hard bumps threatening her balance. The boat, too, bounced and slapped at the chop, Roxy and Leo coming up out of their seats, squealing laughter. Kansas lifted her arm and pointed back toward the calm, close part of the lake, back toward Smoak Bridge, and was relieved when Daddy steered the boat in a wide arch of a turn. It was then she crossed the wake, not meaning to, but the pull of the boat's turn took her. The chop outside the wake was much worse than what she had been fighting and she knew she would not last. Her eyes caught the patch of tree stumps off to the right, ahead of her, toward the dam, and directly to her right, the mouth of a creek drooled its current into the stopped-up current of the river. That was when the whitecaps got her, as she was slung out from behind, then catching up, coming even with the boat. The wind-sharpened waves took her airborne, the tip of her ski dipping, foot snatching free, body skipping like an odd stone skimmed, then tumbling, taking water up her nostrils, going under hard. She surfaced gasping, the dark water lapping loud at her neck.

She waved her arms, an attempt to get Daddy to hurry, hurry, panic taking her. The largeness of the liquid space around and beneath her gave her the most piercing sense of vulnerability and danger she had ever known, and she pulled her knees up to her chest, pressing her thighs against the ski belt around her waist. She wanted to be out of the brown-gray water, but there was nowhere to go, and Daddy was taking so long.

She began to sob.

"Hey, you all right?"

She had not heard the boat idling at her back. It was an aluminum fishing boat, powered by a Johnson 40-horsepower outboard, an older, dark-haired boy at the throttle handle.

"That was a hell of a fall," another, younger boy, sitting at the bow, said in a tone of admiration. He had big teeth and a Band-Aid across his nose. "We were fishing right over yonder in the weeds and saw it. It was the best."

"You okay?" the older one asked again.

"Yeah," Kansas felt her face flush, caught in the act of being terrified, panic subsiding with the nearness of safety.

Daddy's big boat drew up beside her. "Roxy said you took a nasty fall. How are you, boys?" He put his hand down and helped Kansas up into the boat. "Ain't you Asa Jones's boys?"

"Yessir. She didn't look too happy when she came up from under the water, so we came over," the older boy said, eyeing Roxy.

"Your daddy still got a place upriver?"

"Yessir."

"Ain't he still lawyerin' in Albany?"

"Yessir. He's working for the city, though."

"What's your names?"

"I'm Asa, too. This here is my brother Sammy."

Daddy pointed to his big house. "That's our place, there on the point. Tell your daddy to come by."

"Yessir," Asa said. He was nice looking, probably around fifteen, and it was clear he had noticed Roxy.

"This is Roxy, Leo, and my granddaughter Kansas. You come to the house anytime, fish off the pier if you want to."

"Thanks," the boys said.

As Daddy pulled the boat away to pick up the skis, Sammy yelled, "That was the best fall I've seen in a long time!"

Kansas smiled and swapped glances with Roxy, who made her big-eyed "he's cute" face as the boat bounced across the wind-chopped water.

Later in the afternoon they sat on the pier, lowering fishing lines into the brown-gray water. The clouds had passed on over, mid-afternoon sunlight spilling across the lake, its malevolence gone, yielding to glittering reflections of the sky.

"Your granddaddy is rich," Leo said, out of the blue.

"He is not," Kansas said, baffled by the defensiveness that prickled beneath her façade.

"My daddy says he is. Says he got rich off the stock market buying up telephone company stock. And look at all the stuff he buys."

"Miss Pearl says it's not nice to talk about money," Kansas said.

"My daddy don't like your granddaddy," Leo said.

"Why?"

"Because he turned my big brother against us."

"Shut up, Leo," Roxy said.

"You shut up. Daddy says Jack Lacey talked my big brother Jay into leaving and going off to military school, said he should get a good education, offered to pay for it and everything, all the way through West Point so he can make a military career."

"That's crazy," Kansas said.

"Says your daddy is trying to get me and Roxy away from him, too, by carrying us up here to his fancy lake house."

"Shit, Leo," Roxy said. "Can't you keep your big fat mouth shut?"

"Didn't say I believed him," Leo said.

"Well you better not believe lies on my Daddy Jack," Kansas said. "He's never done anything to hurt anybody. Except maybe some old outlaws or something, and they had it coming. He wouldn't talk Jay into leaving his family." But even as she said the words, something felt wrong. After all, Jay *was* away, at Marion. And she wasn't so sure Victor Tolbert could afford such a thing by himself.

"I said I don't believe him," Leo repeated.

"He carries you up here fishing and all," Kansas went on, "because you're my friends and you have fun. He does all kinds of things for you. Don't you ever talk bad about him again."

This made Leo go all sullen and quiet, but Roxy used the opportunity to change the subject. "I think we should go explore up that little creek where you fell."

"I don't know," Kansas said. "It was creepy, sort of."

Roxy nudged her with a freckled elbow. "Oh, come on. Let's all go."

"Not me," Leo said. "I'm staying right here and catch a mess of bream." He lifted his line. "Sucked it right off the hook," he said, reaching for the container of worms from the Smoak Bridge store.

"Come on, Kansas," Roxy said again. "We might even see those boys again."

Kansas was at once struck with the notion that it was probably the boys, not the creek exploration, in which Roxy was interested, but she grudgingly gathered up a towel and the boat key, leaving Leo behind with his fishing pole and schools of little bream to nibble away the worms.

The creek curved back into the trees, and as they rounded the first bend they came upon a series of little sandbars surrounded by clear water. They followed the deepest currents around more and more bends for maybe close to a mile, until they came upon more sandbars leading to a natural spring near a steep, clay-gray bank. They tied up the boat and swam over to the clay bank, where they scooped the malleable mud into sculptures to leave there to dry: a bowl, a toadstool, a pie. Roxy said they should put on paint and pretend to be cannibals, and they streaked their faces with the clay, giggling at one another's suitability for such savagery.

They searched for smooth, flat rocks, then used them to spell out their names in the cream-colored sand on the opposite side of the spring. The creepy feeling Kansas dreaded was not here anywhere, was left out on a river that seemed to have disappearing boundaries, felt as if it were swallowing her when she fell. Here it was close, with woods all brush-stroked in shades of jade and emerald, leaves moist-veined, filtering any sunshine that was not directly overhead. She felt wrapped in warm air and life sounds and a longing she could not name, a piece of comfort just outside her reach.

"Scratchy Branch," Kansas said. "I checked the map. It goes way, way back to—well, to here. This spring."

"Does the spring have a name?"

"I don't think so."

"Well it doesn't matter. We can give it a name if we want." She manipulated the flat rocks in the sand, pressed them with her palm.

Kansas smiled. "Let's call it 'Liquid Obscurity.'"

"I like that. It's mysterious."

"It can be our place, okay?"

Roxy dug her toes into the sand. "What about Leo?"

"No," Kansas said. "Just us."

"Okay."

Kansas was relieved that Leo, who was becoming more and more of an annoyance, would not be in this picture.

"It's the most beautiful place on the river," Roxy said. She had spelled out her whole name, Roxanna Diane Tolbert, in a string of stones set in the sand. Another name for Kansas Lacey, who had no middle name, to envy.

"Why don't you put 'Dr.' in front of it anymore?" Kansas asked. This had been her friend's common practice for the past year, ever since she began reading the medical textbooks and planning to save little babies for a living.

Roxy shrugged. "It seems kind of silly now."

"Why? You're not about to believe Royce or anybody else that says a girl can't be a doctor, are you?" Kansas challenged.

"No. But it just seems immature to write it down until it's real."

"It's going to be real, isn't it?"

"Sure. Daddy won't let me talk about it at home, though. He says no Tolbert ever graduated high school, much less college, and he reckoned I'd have to pay my own way since jailers don't make squat, but to not talk about it anyway 'cause it sounds crazy."

"That's just your daddy being mean," Kansas said. "It's not crazy. Besides," and she shifted a little in the sand, "he's paying for Jay to go to military school isn't he?"

Roxy glanced down. "No. He doesn't have the money for that."

"Then who?"

Roxy sighed. "That's the thing. It's true what Leo said. That part, anyway. Your Daddy Jack is paying for my brother's school."

Kansas wrinkled her brow. She knew Daddy could afford it, but the why of it was confusing, unless… "Well, then he's doing it to help out. Like he knows Jay is real smart. You told me that before. About how smart Jay is."

"Yeah, he is. I just remember how he used to read to me all the time, before he went away."

"Well that's it, then. Daddy saw how smart he was and wanted to help out." Still it was a puzzle. She thought about how Jay rarely came home, how his mama and daddy used to drive to Marion to see him, how he would soon be going much farther away, to West Point, if the appointment came through.

"Yeah, that's it," Roxy said in a tired voice.

"You know that's it," Kansas challenged, though she wasn't sure why.

"I know," Roxy sighed.

They were silent for a while, trickles of creek water licking their toes.

"That Asa boy was cute wasn't he?" Roxy finally asked.

"He's older. Pinky says the older they are, the more dangerous they are."

"He has eyes like Paul Newman."

"He's still too old."

"I could pass myself off as fifteen or sixteen," Roxy said. "So really, in that way, we're the same age, Asa and me. Did you think his little brother was cute? I did."

Kansas did not want the conversation to turn entirely to boys, as it did more and more frequently. "Sure, they were cute. How's Coy's hand healing? Has he missed his thumb?"

"Oh, he thinks of it as a badge of honor. Leo's got him convinced that other kids will be jealous because Coy stood up to the pain of bodily mutilation."

"Hell. He screamed and cried like a loony tunes," Kansas said.

"I know," Roxy said, "but if we keep telling him he didn't, maybe he'll believe it forever." She leaned back on her palms.

"Your daddy hadn't ought to have beat Leo so bad for that. It was an accident."

"My daddy does whatever he wants to do and you know it."

"It's not right," Kansas said.

"Well what's the point in talking about it?" Roxy demanded. "Nothing will ever change. The only thing that will change is when I get the hell out of there. So stop talking about it and making it worse."

"God. Sorry."

Roxy stared into the woods, her forehead set in a crinkle of deep thought. "You can bet I won't stay there a day longer than I have to."

Kansas withdrew her feet from the water and dug her toes into the sand, wiggling them down to lift two mounds of sparkles that scattered like sugar crystals when she pushed her feet clear. "Let's go swimming."

"Let's go skinny-dipping." Roxy unhooked the top of her two-piece and slid the straps off tanned shoulders. Kansas could never help looking when Roxy took her clothes off these days, curious as she was about how her own chest might sprout out. Roxy's breasts were very round and full, set off by the scattering of freckles brushing across her chest, stark white where the sun had not hit, with light pink nipples the size of five-cent pieces.

"No! What if someone sees?"

"Don't be a coward," Roxy challenged. She stood and wiggled out of the bottoms. "Besides, if a boat comes we'll hear the motor."

Kansas sighed and stood, removing her own bathing suit, thinking of her mother, challenging herself to be more like her. "It's going to be cold as hell in there."

Roxy studied Kansas's body for a moment. "You know, I think you are going to be taller than me, and lean, like those high-fashion models."

Kansas blushed. "And all I want is to look like you."

"Look!" Roxy yelled, pointing over Kansas's shoulder, beyond her back.

"What?" With a quick pang of fear, Kansas searched the kudzu-swaddled tree trunks, fully expecting to see the unthinkable, such as boys, watching down on them. Then she felt Roxy's fingers around her forearm, heard Roxy's playful shriek, felt herself pulled then slung into the cold water of the spring, gasping with the surprise of it. Roxy jumped in and they both squealed with the shock of the water, so accustomed as they were to the river that usually felt like a warm bath by this time of day.

The little pool was deep, so they treaded water for a while, hands and feet sending gentle pushes of ripples into one another's skin; then they swam and chased and ducked each other under, baptizing the pure sense of childhood back into their spirits, laughing, kicking into each other, diving under. Kansas could feel the slide of Roxy's body next to her, as they wrestled, chests and shoulders tense, arm muscles taut, legs grappling, and the pit of her stomach erupted in prickly tingles. Her limbs grappled harder, the force of her enthusiasm taking her, surprising her with its exuberant mystery. And she giggled and laughed and pushed her friend under again, making to dodge, letting the catch of Roxy's hand take the calf of her leg, the sling of Roxy's red hair slap against her face when her friend emerged.

They swam back over to the clay bank, feeling free in their nakedness, walking as if they owned the little creek, as if it were their own Eden. They decorated their bodies with the clay paint, covering themselves with it, rubbing it on wet and slick like the gray-membraned amniotic sac around a newborn pup, then drawing designs in it as it dried. Roxy carved out lines spoking from Kansas's breasts, turning them into stars, and drew concentric circles around her own. She invited Kansas to decorate her back, down to the curve at her waist, and Kansas drew wavy grids interspersed with dots and felt the strange tickle in her stomach unfolding and unfolding, not having any idea what to do with it, knowing, somehow, that it meant something, had some purpose.

Then, after the air had the clay flaking and chunking from their flesh, they took one more swim in the spring, slow and shivery with the sun's dip. Kansas thought of the time she had wanted to kiss Roxy, beneath the fig tree, and now she wanted to touch her, but didn't dare do something like that, not in that way. So she settled for faint brushes of touches, watery flutters of current that rushed around her, her body inches from Roxy's, while they laughed softly and talked about whether the boys would come by the house for a visit, until the threat of darkness sent them home.

The boys did come over, the following day. They drank Cokes and swam around the pier. Asa splashed water at Roxy, flirting, pulling her under, and Roxy splashed back. Kansas envied the ease with which her friend interacted with Asa. She remained tongue-tied and self-conscious sitting on the pier next to Sammy, who finally wandered over to fish with Leo.

"Y'all want to come to the Tift Park pool next Thursday?" Asa asked as he sat dripping on the pier. Roxy rubbed suntan lotion over her shoulders, and Kansas couldn't help noticing the way the boy stared. "It's the grand opening," he said.

"But it's always been there," Kansas said. "How can it be the grand opening?"

"Easy," he said. "This man that owns the newspaper and the TV station bought it when the niggers said they were going to try to integrate it. He turned it into a private club. You have to be white to get in."

Kansas thought that was a dirty trick but only said, "Yeah, I remember my Daddy Jack talking about that."

"My daddy knows the man that bought it," Asa continued, "so I'm taking up admission. If y'all come you can sit with me in the booth until you want to go swimming. Plus you can get in for free."

Kansas did not care to go to such a place, created as a dirty trick, but Roxy was beside herself. After the boys sped away in their little aluminum boat, she begged Kansas. "Please, let's go, okay? I've never been there. And I know my daddy will never take me. You have to ask your Daddy Jack. Please? You're always going to fun places, but we never get to go. And I think Asa really likes me."

Kansas sighed. She always gave in when Roxy cited how little she had compared to the Laceys, stirring a strange sense of guilt in Kansas, of having more than her friend. "All right," she said. "I'll see if he'll get Mr. Royce to drive us in the patrol car."

It was the following Monday when Roxy appeared with the bathing suit. She had saved up her allowance for months, ordered it from a Spiegel catalog, and intercepted the mailman when he delivered the package.

"You can't wear that at Tift Park," Kansas said. "Your daddy will kill you."

"I'm not crazy enough to wear it at Tift Park. My daddy would be sure to hear about that."

"Then where?"

The two girls were in Kansas's bedroom, melodic strains of "Ramblin' Rose" coming over her mother's pink Bakelite radio on the bedside table. Roxy laid the bathing suit out on Kansas's bed—two pieces, a top and a bottom, but smaller than a typical two-piece, gingham-checked in bright blue.

"I'm leaving it here," Roxy said. "You take it to the lake next time we go. My daddy will never find out if I wear it up there." She unbuttoned her blouse, revealing the bra Kansas coveted with flat-chested envy.

"But my Daddy Jack will," Kansas said. "You'll be the only girl around in a bathing suit like that. Daddy will have a fit."

"So I'll wear it when he's not there," Roxy snapped. "When it's just us and LittleBit."

Kansas watched as Roxy put on the bathing suit. The top was cut lower than anything Lake Blackshear had ever seen. Roxy pulled up the bottoms, what there was of them. She looked like one of the girls on the calendar in Mr. Golden's feed store across the street, the skimpy bathing suit signaling the kind of woman who would pose for such a calendar. The bottoms were well below Roxy's belly button, a band of untanned flesh around her waist there, and more white flesh topping the push of her breasts. Suddenly Kansas felt a fierce anger take her.

"You're just showing off," she said. "And even Pinky would say so. Nobody will let you wear that."

"Then I'll wear something over it until we go out in the boat. Why do you have to be so stupid about it?" Roxy walked over to the full-length mirror on Kansas's bathroom door. She turned sideways, running her fingertips across her bare midriff. "I'll have to get my tan evened out. We'll have to go back up Scratchy Branch for that."

Kansas could feel her eyes stinging tears. "I'm not stupid. You're the one being stupid. Wearing that."

"I want boys to notice me," Roxy said. "Don't you?"

"They already notice you. All the time. Can't you tell? Mr. Royce even notices you, and he's old! You don't have to walk around naked to get noticed."

"You're just jealous," Roxy said.

"Of what?" Kansas felt foolish and exposed.

Roxy laughed.

"I'm not jealous of you. Take it back," Kansas fumed.

"Don't be. Don't waste your time being jealous of me. I'd trade places with you any old day. And don't be a moron about the bathing suit. Sometimes you act like such a baby." She studied herself some more in the mirror. "You'll keep it here, right? And take it to the lake?"

Kansas looked at her friend's perfectly shaped legs, calf muscles curving into the back of the knee, light hairs at the tops of her thighs where she did not shave them. "Are you going to do things with boys?"

"Maybe I already have."

"But you haven't told me."

"Maybe I don't tell you everything." Roxy peeled off the bathing suit and stood naked in front of the mirror. Kansas lay on her stomach on the bed, watching her look at herself.

"Have you done it yet?" Kansas asked.

Roxy began slipping back into her clothes.

"Have you?"

"That's silly." Roxy stood before the mirror again, buttoning her blouse, stepping into her shorts. She looked at Kansas looking back at her.

"What's so silly about that question? I thought we told each other everything," Kansas said.

Roxy watched the face in the mirror, then slid her eyes to the reflection of Kansas lying across the chenille bedspread. "Does anybody ever really tell somebody else everything?" she challenged, daring Kansas with her eyes to answer truthfully.

Kansas took in the adversarial gaze, thinking of how strange she felt, wondering about her mama and daddy, and about Miss Pearl's isolation, and Daddy Jack's feeble little attempts to bring her out of it. She wondered about whether Pinky was really not afraid to die or only said that to comfort those who loved her, and about why she was not allowed to go into Roxy's house, not ever. Then she thought of her own insides, the secret aloneness she kept in her heart, even when she was surrounded by family. "Maybe not," she said finally, knowing there was no "maybe" to it.

She mulled over the question all afternoon, after Roxy went home, and into the evening, wandering her thoughts around the idea of that private place, deep within the heart, where the true essence of a person was. She lay on her bed and thought of her own mother, of the why of her death, and wondered how much Elizabeth Lacey kept shut away. She reached back in her memory and relived the times she remembered, some on this very bed, when her mother painted Kansas's tiny fingernails and called her a china doll. She glanced at the bookcase, at the Bibles pressed next to the Junior Classics. Funny, she had read the set of classics over and over, but had never once thumbed through her mother's Bibles.

Kansas sat up on the edge of her bed and reached for the framed photograph on her bedside table. It was a picture of her mother, standing barefoot on a creek bank, head thrown back, hair illuminated by a backdrop of sunlight, laughing, cutting her eyes at the camera. How could she have been so beautiful and not passed one bit of it on to her daughter? How could she have put a gun to her head and squeezed the trigger, sending a blast of a shock to knock her so hard into death? How did she ever get to that, to a moment when she could leave her child behind, given over to relatives who kept their essences so thoroughly hidden? Kansas put down the photograph, stood, and walked over to the bookcase. And, rising on her toes, she reached for the top shelf, for the spine of the Holy Bible, a thick black one, then a smaller white one. She set them on her bed and wiggled down beneath the cool, crisp sheets. She picked up the larger book, laid it open against the bedclothes, and began to read.

Kansas, Leo, and Roxy stood in the backyard of the jailhouse, squinting up at the steep-pitched roof. Reflecting midmorning sunshine bounced random patterns of mirrored light from the tin. The thumb was nowhere to be seen.

"Maybe it finally rolled down from where it was," Roxy said, immediately beginning a search of the grass at her feet.

"Shoot," Leo said. "I bet a old blue jay come and took it."

"Why?" his sister said. "Birds don't eat thumbs."

"Maybe he thought it was a worm," Leo offered.

"I think a squirrel took it," Kansas said, but Roxy continued to search, dropping to her knees, groping, raking her fingers through the grass.

"I'm going to see Mr. Royce," Leo said. "I bet *his* thumb ain't lost."

"God, Leo gets on my nerves these days," Roxy said, as her brother walked away.

"And Coy's playing up his sore hand so much he's still got Mama running and fetching for him. You're so lucky to be an only child."

Kansas dropped to the grass and halfway helped Roxy with her thumb hunt. "I don't know. Being an only child is really lonely sometimes, especially when your real mama and daddy are gone."

"Mamas and daddies are overrated."

"What do you mean by that?"

Roxy stopped poking her fingers into the nap of the grass and sat down. "You know how my mama is. She won't stand up to Daddy about anything. Why would I think for one minute she would stand up for me?"

"About what?" Kansas did know how Miss Jolene was. She was strange, out of place. She stayed in the house all the time, like Miss Pearl did, but Roxy said she did odd things like clean the same room over and over again, or play the radio and stare at one page or one photo in a *Screen Play* magazine the length of time it took for a half-dozen songs to come on the radio. Sometimes Kansas saw her at the clothesline between the two houses, talking with LittleBit, and other times she knew Mr. Royce would go in the front house of the jail and not come out for the longest while. LittleBit and Mr. Royce seemed to be her only friends.

She glanced at Roxy, who was staring off into space. "I said, about what?" Kansas repeated.

Roxy gave a start. Then she stood. "Nothing. I'm going inside and read or something."

"Want to come over and play Chinese checkers?"

Roxy sighed and shook her head no.

"Don't you even want to go with me to see Pinky?"

"No." Roxy walked toward the side of the building, to the rut in the grass that led to the front door facing Kelly Street.

"Or to the five-and-dime?" Kansas yelled. "We can buy some stick-on nails and—"

"No!" Roxy called over her shoulder.

Kansas watched her disappear around the corner of the house, hating her. "She thinks she's just *it*," Kansas mumbled, saturated in anger and fresh frustration with her so-called best friend who loved her one day and wanted nothing to do with her the next. She rubbed her fingertips into the grass. If she found the thumb Roxy would be joined at the hip with her again. She would want to cut it and examine it and talk some more about being a doctor. Kansas began to search in earnest, crawling across the cool green of shadowed grass, feeling down to the dirt. But it at once occurred to her how ridiculous she must seem, doing a toddler creep on the ground like an idiot, hoping to get Roxy to pay attention to her. She stood and brushed off her legs, indentations of grass blades patterned in the skin of her kneecaps, and headed for Pinky's house.

It had been over a week since Kansas had last visited the old lady in her little shotgun shack, and in that space of time Pinky had grown thinner, her cheeks hollowed in even more, eyes discolored. The house held a different smell now, overlying the phantom scents of greens and fatback. Though Kansas could not name it, it was the ripening odor of decaying flesh, a petty thief, precursor of death.

She relayed her frustrating experiences with Roxy to the old woman, and Pinky nodded weakly as Kansas spoke. "I told you that girl child of Tolbert's best be sly. Look like she done begun to be sly," Pinky said. In spite of the look of her, in spite of a thready, raspy voice, this was a good day for Pinky. She was ready for company and ready to talk.

"But she'll get in trouble if she wears that bathing suit." Kansas sipped on a Coca-Cola as a heated, late afternoon breeze washed through the screen door and an oscillating fan stirred it around the room.

"Sure will." Pinky managed a part of a smile.

"Then how is that being sly?"

"You ain't ready to understand that," Pinky said, the slip of a smile fading.

"Understand what?"

"What goes on of a night. When windows is closed and folks is sleeping. No light but the moonlight. Only it's dark, and—" The familiar cough rattled through her chest and she put a handkerchief to her lips to catch the mucus.

Kansas picked up a soft rag and wiped away what collected at the corner of Pinky's mouth. "You mean bad things? Like the things Aunt Frances said I was bound to find out before long?"

"Your Aunt Frances a wise girl. Sly, too."

"I just don't understand Roxy, that's all."

Pinky shook her head, a look of sadness taking her face. "And you won't. Not from here on out."

"But why?"

"Child, that Roxy, she done come up in trashy ways. And now she done found a way to get even."

"For what? For all the times her mean old daddy beat on her and her mama? And Leo?"

"For that and then some. Going to get even. Can you feature having to get even with your granddaddy?" She coughed into the handkerchief again.

"No." Kansas was confused by the strangeness of the question. People did not get even with those they loved.

"That's a fact," Pinky said. "Your daddy ain't mistreated you none, has he?"

"No."

"So you can't understand that Roxy."

Frustration joined the confusion. Pinky seemed to be talking around the subject, just like the other adults in her life. "Can you?" she challenged.

Pinky drew herself up higher into more of a sitting position than she was usually able to assume. "The Lord knows I can," she said. "I had a daddy something like hers."

"Then explain it to me."

"Done told you you can't understand. Just know this. Getting even is revenge. And the Lord said, 'vengeance is mine,' and can't nobody get even their ownself 'cause it'll turn back on you." The sunken eyes were intense with the look of warning Kansas knew well.

"How?" She pressed the question with defiance into Pinky's cautionary gaze.

"I reckon you want to know. I reckon you're changing." She put out her hand. "Help this old woman sit up some."

Kansas stood and reached under Pinky's arms, pulling her further into a sitting position. The old woman moaned from the pain of it. "I'm sorry," Kansas said. She drew in some pillows to Pinky's sides, to help her maintain her posture.

"You was a easy child, all those years I tended to you," Pinky said. "Old Pinky ain't so easy, is she?"

"I don't mind," Kansas said.

"You going to be off from Pinky before long. Going to have so many things to do."

"No, I won't. I'll always come visit you." Kansas sat back down and picked up the Coke, an attempt to disguise the guilt she felt for avoiding Pinky of late. She finished it off and held the bottle up to read the name of the city written in raised letters on the bottom. "You want to guess the city?"

"No, Baby. I just want to tell you it's all right."

"What is?"

"It's all right if you don't come see me as much as you used to. It's meant to be that way."

Kansas slammed the bottle down on the table. "I'm tired of everybody telling me I'm changing and I'm growing up and acting like they know more about me that I do. And I'm tired of my supposed best friend acting like a know-it-all two-face." She felt tears spilling. "And now you."

Pinky held out her hand again. "Come here."

Kansas laid her cheek against the old woman's chest, knowing it pained Pinky to be touched too hard, but Kansas's hurts spilled out against the landscape of Pinky's embrace, feeble and comforting.

"Yes, you was a easy child," Pinky said again. "I asked Jesus to keep you that way and not let you come into your mama's ways, and He done right by me."

Kansas sat up. "Why did Mama kill herself?" She steeled herself for the answer.

"That what you want to know?"

"Yes. And I've been reading in her Bibles. I found things she wrote, but it's confusing."

Pinky sighed. "You keep reading them things your mama wrote. Read them again and again and maybe some of it'll come clear." She coughed and spat into her tissue. "But even your mama didn't know the real reason of why she killed herself."

"Why did she?"

"You sure you wanting to know this?"

Kansas took a deep breath. "Yes."

Pinky nodded, her discolored eyes steady in their fixed gaze. "Then here it is. Miss Elizabeth died because of vengeance."

"I don't understand. Was she getting revenge on somebody?"

"No, Baby. Somebody's vengeance come back on her."

At once Kansas heard her internal vigilance warn her against asking whose vengeance it was. She altered the line of questioning, keeping to the old dance of revelation so ingrained with the two of them. "And vengeance always comes back on you?"

"Yes."

"How?"

"All kinds of ways. Like this cancer that's eating me up from the inside out."

"You had revenge on somebody?"

"The worst kind."

"What was it?"

"I wished a man dead, and it came to be."

"What man?"

"Well I can tell you his name but not the story. Or I can tell you the story but not the name." She touched Kansas's hand. "Which one do you want?"

Kansas did not ask her why, did not begin to question the trust, somehow knew the question was significant. "Tell me the story."

"Give Pinky some water."

Kansas picked up a glass that sat on the bedside table and aimed the straw at Pinky's mouth. The woman's lips pinched a sip and a swallow from the end of the straw, then she wiggled herself up a bit. "I wished a man dead," she said again, "and it came to be."

"How?"

"I knew a lady that worked for the man. She told me how he liked to trick little children by sneaking and taking all the bullets out of his gun and putting the bullets in a pink crystal candy dish." A pause turned into a silence.

"Did he try to make the little children think the bullets were candy?"

Kansas coaxed, thinking Pinky might be changing her mind about finishing the story.

"No. He would put the gun to his head and pull the trigger. He would tell the little children he was going to shoot hisself."

"That's awful!" Kansas said. "It's mean. Were the children real little?"

"They was. They was babies on up."

"And it would scare them?"

"But it made him laugh to scare them."

"How could anyone do that to a little bitty child?"

"A evil heart can do anything. And my heart turned off evil when I wished him dead. 'Cause he did die, and my evil has come back to me in a cancer."

"How did he die?"

"The lady that worked for him saw him take the bullets out of his gun, so she knew he was fixing to pretend killing hisself 'cause that's the only times them bullets left that gun. And she hated him and what all he had done. And he sat down in a easy chair and in a while he dozed off, with that empty gun laying on the arm of that chair." She motioned at the water glass and Kansas helped her take another sip, then she continued.

"The lady that worked for him knew what she was going to do, 'cause like I say, she hated all the other evil things he done. So she tiptoed in that room where he was asleep in that chair and eased that gun up off the chair arm. And she tiptoed in the other room and slid every one of them bullets back in, real easy like."

Kansas's eyes widened. "She wanted to kill him? Why?"

"Just know that man was evil. Just know that, for now."

"But what happened?"

"She slipped back in to where he was sleeping and laid that gun back on the chair arm with no more sound than a butterfly's wings, and when he went to joke the one child in particular, his brains blowed out."

Kansas was dumbfounded. She could feel the blood throbbing up from her heart to her ears, felt submerged in silent water. She knew there was a point to the tale, a reason Pinky wanted her to know it, but she could not allow herself to think down any paths that would tell her why, needed to digest only this.

Pinky touched her hand again. "Don't fret too much, honey. But don't never wish nobody dead. Never. See how it come back on Pinky."

"But it's not your fault what happened to that man."

"I ain't pulled no trigger, but I put it on his spirit by wishing somebody would do the pulling of it."

"No," Kansas insisted. "Even then, it's not your fault."

"My thoughts wasn't pure."

"Jesus doesn't care about that one thing. He didn't send cancer to punish you."

Pinky stared at the ceiling. "It's a punishing thing."

"What? The cancer?"

"Yes, that, too. But mostly to have a baby that's hurt so bad."

"Your baby?"

"Yes, Lord."

"I know how LittleBit was hurt. She showed me her Purple Heart medal."

Pinky looked at her, surprised. "She did?"

"Yes. Do you think it means she'll talk to me more?"

But Pinky did not answer. Instead she was staring at the ceiling again, even harder, as if she were trying to look through it and up into Heaven. "It's a punishing thing," she repeated, and the tiniest trace of a tear rolled fast down to her ear.

Kansas held her hand and wondered at it all, thinking to go straight to the house and write it in her diary. "Is there more?" she asked, addressing the tear as much as Pinky.

"There's always more. But not now, Baby. Pinky got to rest now."

"But what about Roxy?"

Pinky gave her hand a faint squeeze. "You don't worry none about her. You just know that girl's right before doing some things that's going to turn back on her. She was headed to it all her growing-up years and she's fixing to bear out what's always done meant to be."

"What's meant to be?"

But Pinky only released and then patted Kansas's hand. "Where was that Co-Cola made at?" the old woman asked.

"Tupelo, Mississippi," Kansas said. She held up the bottle so that Pinky could see the bottom. "That's more than a whole state over."

Pinky sighed. "I done wore myself slap out."

"I'm sorry," Kansas said. "It's me that wore you out."

"No, Baby. You are life. You are the spirit of your mama."

"Can we talk more about her soon?"

"Yes, Baby. But not now. I got to have me a shot now."

The courthouse clock chimed four times into the slow afternoon. Kansas thought she could set more questions before Pinky, very soon, and not be afraid of what might be spoken. For a moment she even formed the words in her head and thought to just go on and ask, one more time, for the last time, the time she knew she would get an answer: Why did my mama kill herself and go away from me? But instead she opened the cigar box and set about preparing the syringe to ease the pain she knew she had drawn out in the old woman. In a while she closed the screened door and stepped across the dirt yard, picking her way around the white droppings from the chickens in Grandemona's coop. She closed the gate and walked toward the stark white walls of the Lacey home, where suppertime was the main concern at the moment.

She was relieved to find that she and LittleBit had the kitchen to themselves. LittleBit peeled the waxy, deep-green skin away from a bumpled cucumber with a razor-sharp paring knife. Her technique was so precise that a whisper of green, transparent and damp, was left behind.

"LittleBit, do you think Roxy will stay my friend all the way through high school?"

"That child ain't going to make it all the way through high school."

"She will, too. She has to. She's going to be a doctor."

LittleBit smirked in her dry, dry way. "I'll be done made a doctor before she does."

"Why is everyone against her?"

LittleBit stopped peeling. "Now you look here. Ain't nobody against her. Your people let that child and her brother just about live over here and at that fancy new vacation house. Even Miss Pearl lets you run the streets with Roxy, and she don't like it one bit. But your people know what kind of home them children come up in, and wouldn't no decent Christian send them children to their daddy for any longer than they got to be." She continued peeling, the long leavings piling on the tabletop.

"So you think I'm right to be worried we won't stay friends," Kansas prodded. It was the most sentences she had heard LittleBit string together in a long, long time, and she wanted it to last.

"You ought to be glad you won't stay friends. That girl is made for trouble and she'd be like to lead you down that path." She laid the cucumber on a wooden cutting board and began to slice it into paper-thin, see-through circles.

"What about Leo? Is Leo made for trouble?" It occurred to Kansas that maybe the hug she had pushed into LittleBit's arms, that night on Pinky's porch, had worked on her a little. Maybe LittleBit was going to warm up to her after all. "Tell me what you think about Leo."

The knife blade knocked against the wooden board. "No, he ain't made *for* trouble. He's made to *be* trouble."

"What do you mean?"

"I mean that boy is like to be giving it out instead of taking it. He's got a right hard edge to him. It's them hard edges in both them twins that's bound to keep them down."

"What about Jay, then?"

"Got it made, thanks to your daddy."

Kansas smiled inside at the fact that LittleBit was supplying information, much like Pinky did, in veiled, digestible chunks. But she knew not to make a fuss over it. "And Coy?"

Again LittleBit did not hesitate, did not hold back. It was completely different from the monosyllabic answers and fussy observations Kansas was used to. "That child puts me in mind of Hotshot. That Coy ain't never been right. And now he's crippled to boot."

"Then why doesn't my Daddy Jack help him out?" Just as the question left her mouth, she wanted to take it back. She wanted it back because a sudden thought, an unthinkable thought, had rushed across her speculation. It was a logical thought that came from a possibility—that she might not be the only child in the family, might have more kin than she knew.

LittleBit spoke as if she sensed Kansas's dread, turning the conversation into a new direction. "What you done took on them Tolberts for?"

"Just some things Pinky said."

"Mama be talking out of her head some days, you know."

"Not today," Kansas said, deciding to test some of the other waters, go even further. "She told me how she hated a man dead one time."

LittleBit's knife froze again, for a slice of a second, then she continued cutting through the cucumber. "Do say," she said, short, curt, more like the familiar LittleBit.

"Yes, I do," Kansas said, curt, to match LittleBit, pushing back.

LittleBit did not react but put the thin, white-seeded discs in a bowl and proceeded to pour vinegar into another bowl.

"Pinky told me the story. Do you know the story?"

"I do." LittleBit set the sugar canister on the table.

"I never knew anyone who was shot—well, besides my great-granddaddy, but I don't remember much about him."

LittleBit was staring hard into her. "Why you say your great-granddaddy been shot?"

"Oh! I didn't mean for it to slip out like that. Aunt Frances didn't want me to say anything. But telling you is different, sort of like telling Pinky."

"Your aunt told you that?"

"Yeah, about how my great-granddaddy committed suicide. You knew about it, didn't you?"

"I reckon so. It was me cleaned up the mess."

"The mess? Where was he?"

LittleBit still did not hesitate. She jerked her head. "Up yonder. In the living room. Miss Lucille told me to clean the floor and get that chair to the upholstery place and mostly to—" Here she stopped and dropped her eyes.

Kansas was afraid to press, afraid of making LittleBit skittish, but she gathered her nerve. "To what?"

LittleBit spoke to the bowl of vinegar. "To get rid of the gun."

"That must have been awful."

LittleBit shrugged.

Kansas pressed on, gently, vigilant. "What was he like?"

"Who?" LittleBit added some vegetable oil, then some sugar to the vinegar and stirred it until the sweet crystals disappeared.

"My great-granddaddy."

"He was a stern man. And he done all kinds of wrong in his life." She poured the vinegar mixture over the cucumber slices.

"Like when?"

"Don't you worry 'bout when. That's for another time."

"LittleBit, you're talking to me just like Pinky does. For the first time. Ever."

"Now you the one talking out of your head." LittleBit stirred at the cucumbers with a wooden spoon.

"No, I'm not. Just look at us. We've been talking and talking away. Having a conversation, a real one."

LittleBit said, "Shoot," and gave a hint of a sneer.

"It's true," Kansas insisted. "Just like me and Pinky. And you showed me your Purple Heart. And I told Pinky you—"

"You hush, girl," came LittleBit's angry tone. "I ain't none of Pinky. Ain't never going to be Pinky. And you can't wish it so."

"I know. It's just that—"

LittleBit slammed the spoon to the metal tabletop. "You don't know. You don't know I ain't Pinky. You want me to be but I ain't. She's been a mama to you, and I ain't going to be a mama to nobody."

Tears stung in Kansas's eyes. "That's not what I—"

LittleBit did not, had not, raised her voice, yet it simmered with more power than volume could ever give it. "Yes, it is. You just want a mama. Done had one to die. Can't find one in this house, so Pinky let you find one in her. But now that leftover mama of mine is about to give up, go to Glory, and you looking for me to be the next mama to you. And like I say, I ain't going to be a mama to nobody."

Kansas sat in a stunned kind of silence. There were tears, still, but something shrouded in LittleBit's words was beginning to dawn on her. She let it filter through the hurt feelings, wanting to understand. "LittleBit?" she asked, voice trembling.

"What?"

"Are you scared she's going to die soon?"

LittleBit looked toward the window that framed Pinky's shack at the far back of the Lacey yard, her face falling into a startling expression of sadness. "Child, when you're eat up with the cancer, and you start to talking about things done laid up inside you for too long, then you can't die soon enough."

Kansas let that sink in, then, "LittleBit?"

"What?"

"Do you hate me because Pinky loves me?"

LittleBit sighed and walked over to the stove.

"Do you?"

LittleBit took a cast-iron skillet from a wall hook above the stove and turned to face Kansas, arms loose, the skillet dangling from her hand, down the side of her thigh.

"Do you?" Kansas asked, one more time.

LittleBit squinted. "I reckon I do have some of that up in me."

Kansas felt a wave of hurt feelings that would not allow her to speak for a few seconds, and she sensed LittleBit's discomfort at the same time. Finally LittleBit spoke. "Don't mean I hate all of you all the time."

"It's okay," Kansas said. "Even if you did—even if you do, I still mean what I told you on Pinky's porch."

Littlebit shook her head, as if she could not for the life of her figure out this child. Then she turned, set the skillet on one on the eyes of the stove, and set about tending to supper.

*

The morning sun was brilliant, blades of grass still damp, down towards the soil, beneath her bare feet. Eula Lura draped a double-sized sheet across the clothesline between the sheriff's house and the jailhouse, and a cotton field of yellow rosebuds began to flutter in the faint June breeze. Damn that child, that Kansas, she thought. Damn her for dredging it all up yesterday, reviving the guilt Eula Lura lived with, always, the guilt that poured out from her settled score with Campbell Lacey. Not that she regretted his death. No, the guilt had nothing to do with his death, not one whit. It had everything to do with Elizabeth's.

"They got the prettiest sheets," Jolene said, joining her in the yard. "Just look at that." She attached one of her husband's T-shirts to the line with wooden clothespins. "I don't hardly got no sheets that match, let alone ones with rosebuds."

Eula Lura's impulse was to roll her eyes but she did not. Even though she and Jolene were friends to the extent that they could be, Eula Lura was always guarded when talk went to the Lacey family. She could not let on what she was up to.

She had bided her time in a quiet focus, so determined in her mission. She had observed, worn a forever-detached demeanor, and learned volumes about all of them—their habits, their idiosyncrasies, their weaknesses. She never put herself at risk of being suspected. She waited for moments when the house was empty and set about plundering through their things, gathering any and all the facts she could. She made forays to the jailhouse and even the sheriff's office, looking for anything, everything, finding a good bit more than nothing. During those first four years, though, the one in her sights was Campbell Lacey.

She thought of her visit with Kansas again, of the child's talk of her great-granddaddy's suicide, and an odd, twisted knot caught in her throat. Their conversation brought it all back, how Eula Lura made a decision that was bound to stir Elizabeth's madness, though to what extent she never could have imagined.

She knew exactly when the moment was dropped in her lap. She knew when he came in for lunch, on a winter Wednesday when Jack was at a state meeting in Atlanta, Miss Pearl and Miss Lucille in Albany shopping, and four-year-old Kansas, having already been fed, out back at Pinky's house, where she was to stay for the rest of the day. Elizabeth was in her bedroom, getting ready to go to a club for the afternoon, and into the evening. Eula Lura knew she had her perfect moment when she saw Campbell Lacey emptying the pearl-handled pistol of its bullets, rattling them into the candy dish that resided there on the sideboard, beside the silver candlesticks and sterling tea service.

As Eula Lura set one place for lunch at the long dining room table, Campbell chuckled, "Going to get her good," he said, one of the few times he addressed Eula Lura in complete sentences, ever. "Don't you go flapping your lips to Elizabeth, because I'm going to get her good today, while everybody's gone. She's shown out again and cracked up the truck out at the farm. Wasn't going to tell me, I reckon. You keep quiet, you hear?"

"Yes, sir," she answered, placing a folded napkin to the left of his plate.

He walked over to the liquor cabinet and poured a generous shot of Early Times. "And don't set the food out just yet. I got to put my feet up a while."

"Yes, sir," she said, as he went through the French doors and into the living room, where she heard him collapse into the easy chair.

There ensued in her head at that moment the greatest struggle she ever had with her own conscience. It was not a matter of convincing herself to replace the bullets; she had played out such a scenario in her mind many times over the years, was ever vigilant when it came to the gun. She had gone so far as to visit a pawnshop on Jackson Street in Albany, asked the Negro owner behind the counter to show her a similar gun, show her how it worked, how it opened, how to take bullets out and, most important, put them in, always hoping Campbell Lacey's sick joke would play itself into her hands. But now that the circumstance had presented itself, she was caught in a momentary trap. And it had everything to do with Elizabeth Lacey.

Elizabeth was already coming apart, behind that mess with Emmit Till. That, too had brought it all back, put it fresh in everyone's mind, but especially in Eula Lura's and Elizabeth's. Ever since she gave Elizabeth the

Jet magazine, Elizabeth had been steady partying, staying out all hours, sending Kansas more and more to stay at Pinky's house. It was her desperate way of holding on to a tenuous silk thread of sanity, just enough to keep out of that deep hole that was bound to suck her down for good, eventually.

Eula Lura almost decided to let this moment pass, wait for another one, when she heard Campbell's loud snores coming from the living room. Her mind formed pictures of Emmit Till, laid out for all to see up there in Chicago, battered and disfigured, laid out in public at his mother Mamie's insistence, to show the world what really went on, deep inside the belly of America. Then she saw Ned's face, how they battered him, how they tortured and defiled his body in the most gruesome ways, ways that brought the vomit to the back of her throat whenever she allowed herself to remember them. And Campell Lacey's snores let her remember them well. There lay the God-spurning white man who ordered her husband's death, who oversaw the distribution of the trophies, a thing she knew for a fact, having plundered so thoroughly. He was only a few feet away, sleeping, a gun at his side, just waiting for her to make his relatively easy death happen. She took a deep breath and tiptoed into the dining room.

"Eula Lura?" Jolene was saying. "Where you gone? You look a million miles away."

She was yanked out of her thoughts by the sound of her name. Jolene was just about the only person who ever called her "Eula Lura" anymore, and it sounded odd and intrusive each time she heard it. She looked down. She had stopped mid-gesture, and a floral sheet hung from her grasp, trailing down into the clothes basket. "Lord," she said. "I took a journey, that's for sure."

"What you thinking about?"

"Oh, nothing. Just what all I got to do."

"Is that all? You looked so serious. I thought you might be thinking about that thumb again."

"You ain't told nobody I seen it?"

"No. Who would I tell? I don't tell Victor squat. And Royce hates the thought of you and me being friends, so I make like we don't tell no secrets or nothing. Just talk about the weather and the house chores." She gave a punctuated laugh.

"That's a fact," Eula Lura said, seizing the opportunity to drive home a warning to Jolene. "If he thought I knew about that thumb, he'd be like to stop coming over to see you."

"Oh, I know," Jolene said, eyes large. "And I could never give that up. I swear I thought I would never get no loving again in my life, and I'll grant you Royce ain't much on doing it the regular way, but he does know how to touch me just right. You know what I mean?"

Eula Lura did know, could remember how Ned made her moan, but she tried not to think about it. She did not want to miss it enough to go find another man, get sidetracked on this mission of hers to make folks pay for their evil. Every once in a while, when she was out at the Blue Goose, she found herself getting a little wooed by this one or that one. A couple of times a year she even went out back with that one or the other one, kissed him hard, felt herself falling over a cliff of desire, until the moment passed and she remembered how it was with Ned, saw his ever-familiar face above her and at odds with the strange hands she felt sliding over her breasts or up between her open thighs. That was when she would be overtaken by shame, feel her disloyalty to her husband, having put her focus on something other than her secret quest, betraying him. She would push whatever man away and head for home, where she would soothe herself to sleep.

"That LittleBit," the men at the Blue Goose would say. "She don't never come through. But you got to give it a try ain't you? 'Cause she's a lot of woman."

"Royce makes me shiver when he touches me down there," Jolene was saying, "and he makes it happen so fast. I guess that's what comes of practice."

"Reckon so," Eula Lura said. She had heard it all before, knew everything about Royce and Jolene's strange affair, how twisted and perverse it was. She had actually learned quite a bit from Jolene, over the past dozen years or so.

It had been an odd coincidence, meeting back up with her co-worker at Sweetie Pie's Café, when she was first brought to Sumner by Jack Lacey, the man intent upon doing penance for Ned's death, the man still waiting for her forgiveness. As soon as Eula Lura cooked her first meal for the prisoners and heard Victor Tolbert's name, she knew she would find a valuable reconnection with Jolene. And she did. It was through Jolene she had been able to enter the front house of the jail and use the days she spent in Jolene's kitchen, ironing the Lacey's bed linens, to poke around in that structure, too. She knew that at one time the old man, Campbell, had lived there, long ago, before his children were grown, and he had been a consistent presence at the jail, too, throughout his career. Eula Lura had no idea what she might find, if anything, in the building housing the jail, but thought it was worth looking into. And her quiet persistence paid off in the biggest way possible.

"Ever since that thumb showed up he's gotten even more randy," Jolene said.

"That so?" It was easy to get Jolene to ramble. All Eula Lura had to do was insert the appropriate short remarks and the woman would babble till Kingdom Come.

"Yeah, I swear, ever since I got that thumb into Royce's hands he's strutting and preening like a peacock. He can't think of enough ways to meet up with me. And when he does he's horny as the devil."

"Reckon he likes that thumb, all right."

"Oh yeah. Told me he had done shown it to Stewart Sams and Bo Somebody? Bo Thomas, maybe? They're Klan, you know."

Eula Lura smiled to herself, filing the names away in her head. She knew Royce well, knew he would use the thumb to move up in his favorite organization, parlay it into some power. Jolene was invaluable in spilling Royce's secret dealings with the Klan into Eula Lura's lap, information that was bound to be useful someday, though she didn't know when. "You be sly, though," she said, using one of her mama's favorite words of warning. "There's some mean folks up in that."

"Oh, don't I know. Victor sure does wish he could be deeper in it. And Royce would flat sure kill me if he knew what all I tell you."

"Just be sly," she said again.

"Don't worry. I will. I wouldn't never let on how us two talk. I'd go out of my way to keep our friendship safe."

Jolene threw that word around frequently—"friendship"—as if their relationship could really be characterized as such. Jolene jabbered and Eula Lura listened, gathering information. But she certainly never confided in Jolene. Jolene had no idea why Eula Lura was brought to Sumner, only knew that Ned died in an accident, did not even pursue finding out any details. Eula Lura had a degree of affection for the woman, would always be grateful for the way she had read Ned's letters from the war. During those days, long ago, the two women did have something of a bond between them. But now everything, every relationship Eula Lura had with anyone white, anyone save Kansas, it occurred to her now, turned on how her bitterness could use them, how they could move her plan forward.

"I've come up with a way to see Royce even more," Jolene was saying.

"That so?"

"Yeah. Victor's got to where he likes to tote Roxy to Albany, to the picture show and such. He never says no when I suggest it."

"That so?"

"Yeah. He won't never carry Leo or Coy with them, though. But I just send them boys outside and lock the damn door. Me and Royce have hours on those afternoons."

Eula Lura saw them once, Victor and Roxy, in the old, dented-up orange Plymouth sedan out at the curb. Eula Lura was on the front porch watering Miss Lucille's plants when she heard the car doors slamming. She looked down from the front porch, down through the windshield and into the front seat. She could see Tolbert's hairy right hand massaging Roxy's left thigh, working higher and higher before he let go and cranked the car. Roxy stared out the passenger's side window the whole time, right up until her daddy backed the car out and drove away.

She wondered for a moment if she should tell Jolene what she suspected, what she knew Jolene's husband was doing to the girl. It was the right thing to do. It was what a very good friend would do, if she truly cared. But she knew at once the information would only rupture what she had in Jolene—a source to be used. Jolene would be angry with her for sabotaging her time with Royce, if she believed her at all. So in her head she simply wished Roxy well. That was all.

"What you going to cook for supper?" Jolene asked. All she ever asked Eula Lura about was meals, how Pinky was doing, and what chores Eula Lura had waiting back in the Lacey house.

"Got a roast. Fixing to put it in, cook up some new potatoes and some butterbeans."

"Lord, what would I give to have a cook." She stared at the sheets. "To think I could have had all that, could have had Jack Lacey, if it wasn't for his loyalty to that crazy wife of his."

"He set you up here," Eula Lura said, too much said too fast, she thought, wondering at her impulse to defend Jack Lacey.

"True enough. But it's almost worse. To be this close to it and not have it. All the beautiful things."

Eula Lura resisted the automatic impulse to tell her that no, she probably would have shown herself for the manipulator she was, that Jack Lacey had probably more than figured it out by now.

"But who knows what might come of me and Royce," Jolene said, lifting an eyebrow. "Just think if I was to find him another thumb," she giggled.

Eula Lura smiled. The thumb. Eula Lura found the thumb three years earlier, on one of her ironing afternoons in the Tolbert kitchen, taking advantage of Jolene's quick dash up to the drugstore for Kotex pads. She walked to the back hallway leading to the jail, passing by the deep freeze when an irregularity caught her eye, a crack in the beaded pine behind the freezer itself, a place she passed scores of times, never noticing anything out of the way. She used her strong arms to scrape-slide the freezer out from the wall, then opened the little cubbyhole, uncovering some photographs, a jar of keys, and the thumb, suspended in a jar. She did not allow emotions to sabotage her, stifling the reflex to scream and cry and flail and curse. She knew right away what she had, suspected that Victor Tolbert could possibly soon know about it, if he did not already, and her mind worked on it until Royce came into Jolene's life. That was when Eula Lura came up with a surefire way to get Jolene onto it. It was a damn good thing that white woman was such a cleaning fanatic and so easily maneuvered. In fact, it was simple enough for Eula Lura to lead Jolene around to thinking it was Jolene's own idea to pass the thumb on to Royce. Eula Lura smiled again. Jolene Tolbert had a thing or two to learn about manipulation.

Jolene picked up the empty laundry basket. "Well, I reckon I'm done finished."

"Uh-huh," Eula Lura grunted, picking up her own basket as well.

"You coming over later, to iron, aren't you?"

"Yes."

"Good. We can talk some more," Jolene said. She reached out and brushed her fingertips across the pink and green floral sheets, then the ones with the yellow rosebuds. "They are just so pretty," she said. "I wish Royce and me could lay on something so pretty. Wouldn't it feel nice then."

"I reckon," Eula Lura said, watching the thin, sallow white woman press the sheet to her cheek, nuzzling it, coveting it as if it were some glittering diamond, like the diamonds worn by Miss Lucille and Miss Pearl, like the diamond of a life Ned had shaped out for her, from his little cart of coal rolling down the streets of Cordele, Georgia. She reached into her apron pocket, to caress the medal she kept there, as she often did when she thought long on Ned. Her fingers fumbled against cotton, clutched against the back part of the square of material. This was strange. Her touch always went to it so easily. She looked down, pulling the pocket open, throat tightening, breaths shallow, then drawn in sharp and unbelieving as she realized it was gone, just like Ned. She could tell, by the stretched holes in the cloth, where it had once resided, but her dead husband's Purple Heart was nowhere to be seen.

II: vi

The morning warmth found Kansas, Leo, and Roxy sitting around the chopping stump gazing up at where the thumb had once been, deciding it would by now, were it observable, resemble a dark, shriveled up, miniature Vienna sausage. Leo drew circles in the dirt with one of his chopped sticks, the Civil War fort now only a vague intention. Roxy's upper lip was swollen and pink where her daddy had backhanded her the night before.

"It's not right," Kansas said. "It's just not."

"Someday I'm going to beat his face in," Leo said. "I'll get a baseball bat and pound his brains out."

"Why did he do it?" Kansas asked.

"Because she argued back," Leo said. "She's got to where she argues back when she ought to keep her mouth shut."

"Is that it?" Kansas asked.

Roxy rolled her eyes. "He said I was doing it with boys. He said I do it with boys when us three are on a play-out."

"But that's crazy!" Kansas kicked at some of the sticks. "You're with us. We're your witnesses."

"I want to do it," Leo said. "And I will."

The courthouse chimed four thirty, sending droves of sparrows out from under the dome in a frenzied flapping.

"I don't think Daddy and Miss Pearl do it," Kansas said, shuddering at the image.

"Sure they do," Roxy said. "All men do, anyway. Who else could he do it with?"

"I'm going to do it with one of the girls on Mr. Golden's calendar at the Feed & Seed."

"Don't be so silly," Roxy said.

"So what if I think about it?" Leo said.

"He thinks about it when he beats his meat," Roxy said to Kansas.

"What?" Kansas said.

"Shut up," Leo snapped, then he got up and walked over to where a baseball bat leaned against the chain-link fence.

"I saw him doing it one night," Roxy laughed.

"You shut up!" Leo threw a Confederate soldier in the air and hit it across the yard with the bat.

"I don't get it," Kansas said.

"I went in his room and he was laying up in the bed beating his little meat."

Leo snatched up another soldier and batted him across the yard. Roxy caught Kansas's confused look and said, "You really don't know?"

"No. Tell me."

"You know," Roxy said, making a fist, moving it up and down on the lap of her shorts.

"Oh, God, that's nasty," Kansas said, not letting on how tempted she was, sometimes, to take longer drying herself down there, because the rub of the terry cloth was so nice.

"Y'all leave me alone," Leo said, still batting plastic soldiers.

"But, Roxy, why don't you let me tell your daddy you were always with Leo and me?"

"Daddy says we're all liars," Roxy said.

"The hell with Daddy!" Leo strode across the yard and began banging at the chain-link fence with the bat, sending rattling shocks all the way down its length.

Roxy gazed down at her hands, tucking her left thumb under as though imagining what Coy's life might feel like from here on out. "It'll be strange," she said. "The three of us going to Blackshear County Junior High

School in September, being the youngest class. Seventh graders."

"You think any coloreds will ever try to come?" Kansas said. "Folks keep saying it might happen one of these days."

"Not as long as my daddy has a gun, they won't." Leo had tired of bludgeoning the fence and joined back in the talk. "And I'll personally kill any nigger that thinks he's going to sit in a class with me." The rawness of his anger shoved itself into the words.

"That won't happen here," Roxy said. "Maybe in Albany, but not here."

"Ain't no nigger going to my school," Leo said again.

"I'm not sure how Daddy Jack feels about it." Kansas sighed. "He says the federal government will decide."

Leo threw the bat hard against the fence. "I'm going to go look at Royce's thumb again," he said, slamming through the gate.

"Do you think we'll stay friends?" Roxy asked, and her gold-flecked eyes were incredibly sad. "It's such a big school. All those older boys."

Kansas felt her face flush with the shame of being so angry with Roxy the other day, about having conversations of betrayal with Pinky and LittleBit. She hoped Roxy could not see through her and attempted a convincing bluff. "Oh, Roxy, you like boys. Since when were you ever scared of anything?"

Roxy's front tooth worked on her lower lip. "Since forever." She stood. "I have to go in and clean the kitchen. Daddy said I can't go to the lake this weekend unless I do about a million chores."

"Want me to help you?"

"You know you're not allowed in the front house, Kansas. Let's stay out of trouble. If I couldn't go off to the lake with you, I'd go nuts."

"So you can't go on a play-out tonight?"

"No," Roxy said, her voice bathed in sarcasm. "I might go off and do it with some boys."

Kansas watched her step through the chain-link gate and walk up the side yard of the jailhouse, the afternoon sun playing the rich red of her hair beneath its glow into muted flames. She stopped abruptly at the corner of the front porch, turned around, and yelled, "I'll tell Leo to meet you at the fig tree at dark." Then she turned, took a deep breath, and forged ahead, her delicate hands coiled into tense, knotted fists at her sides.

Kansas meandered over to the fig tree, to the cave of the lower branches and the higher ones that naturally dipped down toward the dirt. Sitting on the ground, she leaned her back against a low limb, looking out at Pinky's house, picturing its rough wood floors, its meager little bathroom, its sad-looking, worn furniture. She thought about how nice it was to feel loved, and she wished a fervent wish that Pinky would not die, there was a mistake, the cancer was really just a bad bout of pneumonia in disguise. She thought of her mother, of the strange diary left behind, written in the margins of the Bibles.

Kansas had spent late evenings poring over her mother's big black Bible, reading the puzzle of notes, the starred verses. It was overwhelming, flipping through, seeing the frames of scribbles around the scripture. In the clutter that was Psalms and Proverbs, the notes were difficult to read, but Kansas transcribed some of the phrases and sentences into her own locked diary. The notes she transcribed from Psalms were especially sad in places: "'I water my couch with my tears.' They can't hear me when I'm quiet and they hear me less when I'm loud. Must do more must do more must do more—will they understand then? Maybe; March 1945—the world ends 'not with a bang but a whimper,' so Eliot said and it's so and I am whimpering still; 'Heal my soul' all black with canker sores and full of night terrors—October '55."

There were more than a few nights when Kansas cried herself to sleep in grief and frustration after reading her mother's unburdenings, some like pathetic gibberish: "Crazy crazy Lizzie Izzie living in her head; finding all the corpses' bones—the butchered flesh the dead; I want a pear, bite the fruit, spit it hard, hard, into his oh so holy face right there in the middle of Sunday service, drawn and quartered—I am wicked, icked, icked; dance, twirl, Ling, long, notes, float dust into the light, slips through the cracks, bleeds like I should, and my ears see it all through the pores of my bare breasts, beautiful breasts."

There were some references to the family, some to men in the bars, but

Kansas first zeroed in on those references to LittleBit: "Eula Lura is my soul, my strength, my best friend, but it came to be because I killed her. I can do nothing but destroy the ones I love the best, along with the ones I love the worst; E. Lura, E. Lacey, it is our child grown in my belly, the child of Eddie, who says he'll be back. I don't know. I don't know how to be loved after all the wickedness and death I've brought; Told E.L. *Prufrock* and *The Wasteland* and *The Hollow Men*—E.L. just laughed."

It was such a swirl of images and thoughts that Kansas had to put it aside from time to time, just to reacquaint her own thoughts with sanity; and the weight of that word was only now beginning to sink in. She had always taken it so lightly, her mother's "craziness," even when it was verified for her as a real feature of her mother's personality, beyond a playful joke about Elizabeth's rebellion. But now, after spending time in the margins of her mother's Bible, in the margins of her mother's reality, it was now, slowly, stealthily sinking in, what a thready grasp Elizabeth had had, all along, on life.

Kansas danced her fingertips across the fuzzy leaves of the fig tree and against the hard fruit, not near ripe, and looked again at Pinky's house, where she had found warmth and comfort and more love than she had ever felt in Miss Pearl's presence. Maybe her mother knew. Maybe part of the reason Elizabeth took her own life was so that Kansas would be thrust into the arms of those who could show her genuine, unbridled affection. Maybe, in a way, it was because of Kansas. Maybe an infant, a toddler, then a four-year-old were too much for Elizabeth to nurture, what with those fragments and dim corners in her mind. And, for the first time in her life, with a wave of the worst, deepest guilt she had ever felt, digging her fingertips now into the soft black dirt, and harder, and faster into the cool, cool dirt of her fig-leaved cave, Kansas thought: Maybe it was me, finally, after everything else. Maybe it was all my fault.

*

Frances was grooming Monty, her adored fourteen-year-old Boston terrier, offspring of Jaffe and Mary Margaret. Monty was sluggish and fat, had cataracts, and pant-drooled without end, but she treated him with the deference one would show an elderly relative. The poor old dog's health had gone steadily downhill ever since his sibling, Cleveland, passed away four years earlier, after being hit in the head with a baseball. It happened one day when Kansas brought the Tolbert twins over to the house. Leo was in the fenced backyard practicing his swing, while Roxy and Kansas visited with her and Martha inside. The vet allowed that the ball must have hit Cleveland just right and killed him instantly. It was a freak accident, Frances said, trying to reassure the boy, while Leo hung his head and kept his eyes to the floor. She grieved mightily over it, though, always had doubts about whether it was really an accident, but said nothing, even to Martha. Something about that boy was disturbing, even malevolent. She hated thinking that way about a child. Still, she was relieved when Leo stopped coming over with the girls, saying, they reported, that it was "too sissy to sit around eating little cakes with two old ladies."

She scratched Monty's ear and he grunted with pleasure. These days she put an inordinate amount of time into ministering to Monty. He was like her child. She bought him little outfits from a fancy pet store in Atlanta, brushed him, painted his little terrier toenails, boiled chicken livers to pour over his dog food, and doctored him incessantly. Martha teased her about all the medicines and treatments Frances gave him: vitamin pills, heart-worm pills, and stool softeners, as he had become more and more consti-pated as he entered his golden years. Once, when Monty was stricken with hemorrhoids, Frances even used Preparation H on him. She smiled, remembering how Kansas watched with appalled fascination as she dabbed the cream around Monty's puckered little canine anus. She scratched his ear again, just as her niece bounded up the steps and onto the porch.

"Another scented bubble bath for Monty?" Kansas asked.

"Of course. Nothing but the best for my baby. He's fresh out of the laundry room sink."

Kansas put her nose to his fur. "Mmmm," she said. "He smells pretty."

"So you've come to visit your backup friends," Frances said. "The second string, Martha and me. After all, it's not a Friday and I see you don't have Roxy with you."

"She's being punished," Kansas said. "Again."

Frances shook her head. "That poor, pitiful child." She rubbed Monty's legs with a towel.

"I'm bored, Aunt Frances."

"You're too young to be bored."

"But I am."

Frances fluffed the hair on Monty's neck, then picked up a leather dog collar that jingled vaccination and identification tags—both Monty's and Cleveland's.

Kansas spoke again. "Why do you say Roxy is pitiful? That would make her so mad."

"Oh, I can't really put my finger on it."

"Yes, you can. You're hedging again."

Frances laughed. "I suppose I am. Just keep on kicking me. Keep on reminding me you're not a baby any more."

Kansas lifted her leg and tapped her great-aunt gently on the rear. "Why do you say Roxy is pitiful?"

"No particular reason."

Kansas kicked her again, a little harder.

Frances laughed. "Oh, all right. I just don't think much of her daddy."

"That's funny. Somebody else told me Roxy should be sly around her daddy because—"

"Because what?"

"I can't. It's nasty."

"Goodness, Kansas, there is nothing you cannot say to me. Your mother told me all kinds of things." It slipped out without her even recognizing her brain forming the words, and Kansas jumped on it immediately.

"Nasty things? Mama?"

Frances felt her face flush, and she sat on the glider. "No. Not nasty things."

"You're all red, Aunt Frances," Kansas said. "I know you mean nasty things."

"No, I don't. Really."

"You said you'd stop hedging. I already kicked you. Twice. Why won't you—"

"There was nothing Elizabeth told me that was nasty because Elizabeth saw no nastiness in anything, until the end."

"But you thought it was nasty?"

Frances sighed at her niece's tenacity. "I admit I had some trouble with it, at first."

"With what?"

"The things your mother told me."

"But what?"

Frances furrowed her brow. Why did she resist sharing a bit of the truth with Elizabeth's daughter? Where else would Kansas get her questions answered directly? Yes, there was always Pinky, but not for long.

"What?" Kansas asked again.

Frances sighed. "How much do you know, Kansas, about the facts of life?"

"Well, Roxy's told me a bunch of things. She got medical books from the library. And drew pictures."

"I should have known as much," Frances said, squirming at the blush of Kansas's cheeks. "So you do know about your menstrual cycle?"

"Yes, but I don't plan to do that."

"And how will you avoid it?"

"Easy. The books say it stops temporarily when you're in water."

"Oh, you plan to sit in water for a week?"

"Sure."

Frances laughed. "I'm afraid I'll have to see that to believe it."

"I just don't understand why girls have to go through so much. In my mama's Bible she's got stuff marked about how women are cursed and commanded to suffer with pains and all that."

"Yes, I remember how your mother used to write in her Bible. What kinds of things did she write about?" Frances felt devious for a moment. After all, she had read Elizabeth's Bible soon after her niece's suicide. Still, she wanted Kansas to point the way this conversation should go.

Kansas looked away. "Just things. Most of it is hard to make sense out of."

"Maybe we could both look at it sometime. Maybe the two of us could figure it out. What do you say?" Frances could feel a new level of discomfort from her niece, wondered if she were upset. But Kansas glossed over the question.

"Do you believe it's God's revenge? What women go through?"

"Revenge for what?"

"I don't know. For Eve tempting Adam or something."

"No, Sweetie, I don't." She made one last pass down Monty's back with the towel, and the dog, recognizing the signal, began to wiggle and squirm until he was lowered to the floor.

"Then why?" Kansas asked.

"Why what?" She opened the screen door for Monty, who lumbered down the steps and began wallowing in the warm grass.

"Why do girls have it so much worse than boys?" Kansas asked as she and her aunt sat on the glider.

"I can tell you it's no curse from God, not at all. You don't have to believe in a God who curses people. And I'm not so sure girls have it worse."

"But look at—"

"No. Look at how they get treated, if they're nice. They get taken care of. And look at the miracle of birth. Men don't get to give birth."

"That's no miracle. It's a pain that splits you in two. That's what Roxy's mama told her."

"Oh, good Lord, Kansas. If it was that bad do you think folks would keep having babies? It must be worth whatever pain comes with it."

"Like the pain that comes with how the baby gets made."

"Pain?"

"You know."

"What pain?"

"You know what pain." Kansas lowered her voice to a whisper. "The man's penis." She shuddered.

Frances laughed. Kansas's demeanor was very other-side-of-the-coin compared to how Elizabeth would speak of sex.

"What's so funny?" Kansas demanded, and her eyes were large and full of fear.

It brought Frances up short. The girl really was afraid, was truly questioning God's motives, thought of the act as something filthy and painful. Frances was suddenly ashamed of laughing at her niece. "Oh, Sweetie," she said. "You have to remember all of these things have been going on since the beginning of time. And it is because they are lovely, loving things. Things of pleasure."

"How?"

"You simply must trust me. You will meet a man someday, when you are older. Much, much older," she smiled. "And you will be thrilled to have him touch you in every way."

"Aunt Frances?"

"Yes?"

"Have you ever had a man touch you that way?"

No, she had not. But Frances decided, quickly, that Kansas needed to hear that it was all right. "Yes, I have."

"But you didn't marry him."

"No."

"Why not?"

"It just wasn't meant to be. I think God wanted me to stay around to be a help to Elizabeth and now to you."

Kansas smiled, then, reminded again of her mother, asked, "What are the nasty things you won't tell me about my mama?"

There it was again. That word—"nasty." Frances sighed. "There are no nasty things. None at all. Your mama was a passionate woman. She loved flirting with men, dancing, making them happy. She loved them all, the soldiers."

"From the war."

"Yes, the war."

"She wasn't a prostitute or anything, was she?"

"My God! Kansas! What on earth?"

"It's just that, everybody is so secretive about Mama, like they're hiding something really, really bad. I'm just trying to think of the bad things it could be."

Frances felt the lump in her throat, warning her she might cry. She hated that Kansas had gone so far in fretting over her mother's life and death, and she decided at that moment it had to stop. "You look here," she said. "Your mama was a person everyone loved. And she saw the truth about good things."

"Like what?"

"Like," Frances took a breath of nerve. "Like sex. Like that."

"What about sex?"

"That it is a natural, lovely thing, a source of fun."

"Fun?"

"Fun. Now mind you, your mama was unusual. She had fun with sex and not a moment's worth of shame. That doesn't mean I would recommend any young lady to act out like your mama did. It was a function of her state of mind. It was how she held together as long as she did."

"What kinds of things did she do with the soldiers?"

"No. There are things I simply cannot go into with you yet."

"But you will tell me?"

"Yes. When you are older."

Frances was relieved that seemed to satisfy the girl, who asked, "The soldiers really loved her, didn't they?"

"The airmen called her 'Angel' and thought she was the most beautiful thing, the most worth-it thing to protect that they ever knew. Trust me, Sweetie, there is nothing nasty to know about your mama."

"Yes, there is," Kansas spat out, with more anger than Frances had ever heard in her voice. "It was nasty of her to kill herself, to do that to me. It was selfish and hateful and nasty."

Frances pulled the girl over and wrapped an arm about her shoulders. How wrong the Lacey family was, to think their avoidance of the truth could protect Elizabeth's child. She pushed the glider back and forth for a while, Kansas's head on her shoulder. Finally she spoke. "The only way your mama would have ever been able to do that, to kill herself, would be if her pain was so great she knew it would hurt you."

"Is that what she thought?"

Frances stopped the glider's motion. "She did. In her way."

"Tell me."

"I will. I am." She pushed her feet into the floor, moving the glider back and forth again. "You see, your mama was so sensitive and aware of things she thought she caused pain. She thought she caused your great-granddaddy to shoot himself."

"But why?"

"Remember she was ill in her mind. It is not logical, but your mama took on the hurt of anybody she cared about, even strangers halfway around the world, during the war."

"It's hard to understand."

"Just trust me. Not a week before she died she told me you deserved a better mama. It was New Year's Day."

"But she was a good mama," Kansas said, sitting up, eyes filling.

"Remember. You want to think with your kind of reasoning and logic. You have to try to follow her reasoning. She thought she caused bad to happen to others. She used her sexuality and her beauty to make others happy. Almost like that gave her the power to make others happy. Do you see?"

"Sort of."

"And she said the strangest thing to me, that same time, New Year's Day. Funny. I haven't thought about this in so long, and I always wondered what it meant."

"What?"

"The same time she told me you deserved better, when she said how she had killed her granddaddy by wishing him dead, she told me she was spiritually dead. That she had been dying that way ever since the night of her high school prom—the one high school dance she ever went to."

"Why would that be? And why did she only go to one high school dance?"

Frances stopped the glider. "There is so damn much you don't know, isn't there?"

Kansas nodded, tears spilling. "I've wondered if I caused it, if I was too much—"

"Oh, no, you don't. No, ma'am." Frances wiped her niece's face with her fingertips. "You will not take on misery like your mother did, and we'll just have to fix that right this minute. We'll just have to fix a lot of things. All right?"

Kansas nodded.

"But you know what? First I'm going to go fix us two big bowls of ice cream, and you're going to sit right here till I come back and tell you my story of the life of Elizabeth Lacey."

Kansas smiled, sniffling. "With the fun sex things, too?"

Frances tapped her on the top of the head. "No. It will be without the fun sex things, but it will be quite a life nonetheless." She would give her as much as she could. Not everything. Not the awful violence. Not the lynching. A great-grandfather putting a bullet in his brain and a mother following suit was quite enough violence, thank you very much. Aside from that, though, she would give Kansas the delightfully true picture of her delightfully rebellious lunatic of a mother. She stood and went to look for the ice cream scoop.

*

Kansas sat near the fig tree in one of Grandemona's curved-legged, metal yard chairs. She wondered if Victor Tolbert was yelling at Roxy, calling her a goddamn idiot the way Kansas heard him do more than a few times over the years. She wondered about Miss Jolene, his wife, how she could let him do her children that way. It struck her again that Miss Jolene was a lot like Miss Pearl, a presence in her family but not really there, fading in and out of the background. She wanted to ask Daddy if Roxy could come and live with them. Maybe then Pinky and LittleBit's ominous predictions would not come true, Roxy would become a baby doctor, and they would always be friends. They would be in each other's weddings, have husbands who were also best friends, and children who would start another generation of connectedness between them. They would go on trips to Europe and see the cathedral at Aachen and the Louvre in Paris and all kinds of exotic sights that would put the blandness of Sumner, Georgia, to triple shame.

She pondered the things her Aunt Frances told her this afternoon, about how her mother twirled her full skirts and danced alone until men begged her for a spin, how her clothes were never in style but always original, how the other girls envied her. Aunt Frances told her about the high school dance, how Elizabeth had worn her mama's lace wedding dress but must have worn it to a creek bank later, since it was found in the floor of her bedroom all wadded up and patched with dirt. Elizabeth had laughed, "You wanted me to have the best time of my life! And I did!" so no one was angry about the dress. Aunt Frances told story after story about a girl who did wild things and got away with them because no one could ever stay angry at her. And Kansas missed her mama more than ever.

"You should have brought us out a Co-Cola," Leo said, breaking into her fantasy. He was impressed by the fact that the Laceys kept cases of Cokes on the back porch, always had cold ones in the refrigerator in the back hallway, where surplus food was also kept, and he loved to use the heavy steel Coca-Cola bottle opener in the big kitchen. Kansas thought Leo probably went through at least a case of Lacey Cokes every week, but no one ever begrudged him this indulgence. The Tolbert children were not allowed to plunder through their own kitchen at home, could only eat when commanded to do so by their tyrant of a father, though sometimes their mama let them eat cookies when Victor was not around. There was a cake safe in the kitchen, though, that had a little padlock on it, and whenever Jolene baked Victor a cake, Roxy said, it sat in the cake safe for all the children to see but never touch, a torturous thing, not to be allowed more than a sliver or two of chocolate cake, for their daddy to eat huge chunks of it right in front of them, grinning a sticky, chocolate grin. Kansas reminded herself of that image whenever she hesitated to offer Leo a Coke or a cookie or a big, fat slice of Grandemona's six-layer cake iced in chocolate. She went inside and brought them each an opened bottle of the molasses-colored liquid.

They carried their Coke bottles as they walked the square block of the town, commenting on store window items and talking about nothing in general. Finally, Kansas had to ask about her friend.

"Is Roxy all right? Is he making her do everything?"

"Just the kitchen. Then he's taking her to Albany to the picture show."

"What? She said she had a million chores to do."

"Well, she did, at first. Daddy always does that to her lately. He tells her she has to do all this stuff, then, after she gets a little bit of it done, he says to come go with him to Albany."

"She never told me that. You're lying. Mr. Victor never has been good to Roxy."

"You're the liar," he said. "You said you didn't know about meat beaters."

"Shut up, Leo." She slapped him on the shoulder and some Coke spilled on the sidewalk.

"Hey!" He shoved her and she stumbled.

"Stop it!" She glared at him, but he met her gaze with an odd, cold one of his own, just for a split second the look of his daddy. Kansas backed down. "What do they do in Albany?"

"I told you. They go to the picture show. Or the drive-in. Or he takes her to the Arctic Bear for a hamburger and a sundae. He's done took her off about a dozen times, I reckon."

"Why didn't she tell me? Why'd she let me think he was nothing but mean all the time?"

"I don't know. She acts weird about it. She says it ain't no fun. But you don't see him taking me or Coy or even Mama off to get a sundae."

Kansas went silent for a while, trying to figure Roxy's reasoning. Maybe it was part of her general secretiveness, part of the way she seemed to want to keep some things to herself lately, but Kansas resolved to talk to her about it.

"Mr. Royce comes over when they go to Albany," Leo continued. "And Mama sends me and Coy away to town and locks the door. I reckon Mr. Royce is pokin' my mama."

"What?"

"I say I reckon he's pokin' her. But if my daddy finds out, somebody is going to get killed."

"Do you really think your mama is doing something like that?"

"Why else would Mr. Royce only come over when my daddy ain't there?"

Kansas could not think of a logical answer.

"I'm going to find out, though," Leo continued, and Kansas was amazed by his flat tone, as if he did not care one whit that his mama might be committing adultery.

"How?"

"I'm going to spy on them. I spied on Daddy before. Seen him poking somebody."

"God!"

"You don't believe me?"

"No, I don't. You couldn't catch someone doing that." She thought of the apparent absence of sexual activity in her own house, how they must be very furtive, if they did it at all, since Kansas never sensed anything like that going on.

"I reckon I did see it, too."

"How are you going to prove it?"

"I don't know," he said, "but I will."

"Anyway," Kansas said, tiring of the argument, "what are we going to do?"

"Let's go to the courthouse," Leo said. "Up to the courtroom."

"Okay."

They rounded the corner and cut across the street to the courthouse lawn. The fire escape that zigzagged up to the second floor faced the alley running alongside the Lacey property. They climbed the steps to the balcony and pushed open one of the big, unlocked windows. Leo found the light switch and the room was revealed, rows of church-pew-like benches for spectators, the gated area where the counsels' tables sat before the high desk of the judge. The stenographer's table was off to one side, the jury box off to the other. Ceiling fans began to churn the summertime humidity and stir musty air all over, while their footfalls on hardwood floors sent creaks and echoing pops up to the cavernous ceiling.

"You be the judge this time," Leo said. "I'm the guy that talks about the criminal."

"The prosecutor," Kansas said, taking a seat beneath the three flags, American, Confederate, and State of Georgia, hanging behind the judge's swivel chair. She picked up the gavel, smoothed with years of use, and rapped on a square of dark wood. "We will now hear from the prosecuting attorney, Leo Tolbert, in the matter of what, Mr. Tolbert?"

"In the matter to put Victor Tolbert in the jail."

"The State versus Victor Tolbert, then. You can make your case now." Kansas rapped the gavel again, for emphasis. "What has he done?"

"He beats his wife and his kids. And he gets drunk all weekend. And he beats on the prisoners, too, even the white ones, sometimes."

Kansas had heard the case against Victor Tolbert dozens of times. It was Leo's favorite case to present. If Roxy was here, she would be questioned and an imaginary jury would return a "guilty" verdict, then Kansas would sentence him to death by hanging or electrocution or whatever method Leo desired at the time.

"He gave me a black eye for cutting off Coy's thumb, which it was a accident. Even Mama said so and then Daddy popped her, too."

"Is there anything else?"

"There's lots more. He hates everything I do. Like I told him about Mr. Royce's thumb in the jar and how Mr. Royce said some fellow found it in a fox trap, and Daddy told me Royce was a damn lie but for me not to never say nothing else about that goddamned thumb. Not ever. And then he called Royce and cussed him out."

"Why?"

"I don't know. Something to do with the thumb. Just last night I asked him why it was such a thing that can't be told and he took his belt to me. See?" Leo turned around and lifted his T-shirt to reveal welted stripes of deep pink, some edged in bruised flesh, some bordered by thin scabs.

Kansas was blindsided by the abrupt revelation, could not speak for a moment, then could only utter, "God, Leo."

The boy pulled down his shirt and faced her again. "You can't be you. You're the judge."

"But Leo, this is bad. You need to tell my Daddy Jack."

"Shut up and be the judge!"

"Leo, look. We can—"

The boy at once picked up his empty Coke bottle and hurled it at the front of the judge's high desk. "Stop it! You can't tell nobody! You have to be the judge!"

Kansas sat back down. She had glimpsed Leo's temper, like today when he beat the fence with his baseball bat, and a while ago when he glared his daddy's look at her, but he had never directed any violence at her. Besides that, she was afraid for him, that he could be hurt even worse the next time his daddy went at him. "I find Victor Tolbert guilty of being mean and hateful to his wife and his children. How do you want him sentenced?"

"Ten years in the jailhouse where I can pick at him every day, then after that, I'm going to shoot lead in his belly and watch him die slow."

Kansas pounded the gavel. "That is my sentence, then. Court's adjourned."

She climbed down from the bench and picked up the Coke bottle. There was a healthy nick in the wood face of the big desk. Leo was sitting at the table, his head lying on his folded arms, and Kansas thought at first he might be crying, but he was silent. When he looked up, his eyes were all hate. "You can't tell," he said.

"I won't."

"He would kill us. He really would."

"I won't tell."

"I know one thing, though," Leo said.

"What?"

"Something about that thumb bothers the hell out of my daddy."

"It's weird, all right," Kansas said.

"Come on," Leo said.

Kansas followed him from the courtroom to the foyer, they switched on more lights, then descended the curved staircase to the wide hall, its floor set with hexagonal stones. "Where are you going?"

"Right here."

They stood before the sheriff's office, Kansas's grandfather's name stenciled on the glass. Leo pushed open the door.

"We can't go in here," Kansas said. "You know Daddy doesn't want us in here at night. He doesn't care if we go in the courtroom, but we can't go in here."

"I'm not staying long." Leo walked directly over to Royce's desk, retrieved a key from one drawer, then unlocked and opened the bottom drawer.

"Leo, are you crazy?"

The boy lifted the small glass crypt to the light of the hallway. The thumb nodded with the jostle of the boy's hand to the jar. "I have to take it."

"Leo, you are going to get us into so much trouble. I swear."

"You never get in trouble."

"I never stole anything, either."

"You ain't stealing it. I'm stealing it."

"Why?"

"'Cause if it bothers Daddy, I want it. And I want to find out why it bothers him."

"Please put it back, Leo," she said, pulling the drawer further open, an edge of ribbon beneath a small box of paper clips catching her eye, a medallion nicked at the side. She resisted the impulse to point it out, thinking Leo might steal it as well, and lie about it, and then LittleBit would never have it back.

"Told you I ain't putting it back."

"Please?" Kansas wondered why Mr. Royce would have taken LittleBit's medal, promised herself to come back, alone, and retrieve it. "Please put the jar back, Leo," she said again.

But the boy had already closed the drawer. "Come on," he said.

Kansas followed him back up the stairs to the courtroom. "Leo, we're going to get it."

"Damn, Kansas, shut up! It's mine to worry about."

Once outside, on the courthouse lawn, Leo thrust the jar at her. "Take this," he said, glaring.

"I don't want it," she said.

"You have to hide it for me, just for a while."

"Why?"

"Until I find out why it bothers Daddy. Until I know what I want to do with it."

Kansas shook her head. "I don't understand."

"I hate his guts," Leo said. "I can use this to get even with him, maybe."

"But he's your daddy, no matter—"

"Take it!" Leo glared his reservoir of hate at her again, and she felt a ripple of a shudder move through her. She took the jar, tentatively, sensing a shift in Leo's relationship to her, another change with all the other changes of the past months. This one gave her a feeling of deepening dread, as if she had discovered in Leo, a freckled-over pudge of a boy, the potential of becoming a man not unlike Victor Tolbert, the daddy he hated so thoroughly.

*

Eula Lura sat on the porch of Pinky's shotgun shack, smoking, trying to decide whether or not to go to the Blue Goose. Lately she had been feeling that vaguely familiar, inevitable rise of desire within her, knew she would be unable to follow through, yet again. So she sat smoking her Picayune, listening to Kansas and Pinky talking, just inside.

Kansas was sitting by Pinky's bed, where the old woman occasionally slurred her words, thick-tongued with medicine. The girl had been talking about her mother, making observations about Elizabeth that were so accurate it sent chills down Eula Lura's back. The child had obviously been learning a lot from somebody.

"I always wondered why Mama killed herself," Kansas was saying now, "and Aunt Frances helped me understand it a little better."

"Your aunt a good woman," Pinky said.

Shoot, Eula Lura thought, *she a man-woman.* But she was good to Elizabeth and doing right by Kansas as well, it seemed.

"Only the strangest thing happens. See, every time I find out more, another can of worms gets opened up," Kansas said.

"That's all right," the old woman mumbled. "You need worms to catch fish."

"But what if I catch a fish I don't want to keep?"

"You let it go."

A few moments of silence, then, "Okay, I'll ask you. Why did my great-granddaddy shoot himself?"

"Maybe he didn't."

What you talking about, Mama? Eula Lura thought, hoping the medicine didn't make Pinky too loose with her tongue.

"No?" Kansas asked.

"Maybe the gun just went off."

"Maybe it did. But if it didn't, if he had a reason to do it himself, what would it be?"

Lord, that child was full of questions. Eula Lura took a long drag off the Picayune and looked up at the night sky, its dark face freckled with stars.

"You know what the Ku Klux Klan is?" Pinky mumbled.

Again Eula Lura grew tense. Be careful, Mama. If you say too much you'll ruin my plan.

"Yeah," Kansas replied. "Everybody knows what that is. Only I never saw any of them, except on the TV."

Pinky's voice came clearer, with a bit of revived energy. "Oh, you seen 'em. See them all the time, dressed regular."

"I guess so."

"Just know you can't tell."

"What do you mean?"

"I mean a man might dress regular." Pinky took a short coughing spell before she continued. "Might dress regular. Then might go and butcher a nigger alive, or cut off his tallywhacker in front of his children, or drag him behind a wagon till he's skin't raw and pour gasoline—"

"That's too awful! Why would anyone do that?"

"Just know."

Eula Lura felt a wash of sadness over her heart. *Mama talking harsh now*, she thought. *Mama getting close to her time.*

"What does this have to do with my great-granddaddy?"

There was another long pause. Eula Lura strained to hear the answer. "Some folks die and the world don't miss nothing," Pinky said, feeble again.

"Was my great-granddaddy a Klan person?"

Her mama gave a long sigh. "Like I say, some folks die and the world…" her voice trailed off, weakly, before she added, ". . . don't miss… nothing."

Silence, this time for a very long time, this time long enough for Eula Lura to finish her smoke, light another, and smoke it halfway down before she heard the screen door's gentle squeak and Kansas's bare feet on the wood boards.

"She's asleep," Kansas said, dropping down to sit beside Eula Lura on the top step.

"Sleep keeping her away from pain," she said, not looking at Kansas.

"You heard what we talked about?"

Eula Lura nodded.

"I don't remember him. I don't remember him being mean to me. I don't remember him being any way to me. I only remember big boots and puffy pants."

"Then it's a blessing." Eula Lura still did not turn toward the girl.

"He was that terrible?"

Eula Lura nodded.

"But Grandemona loved him."

Eula Lura turned her face to the girl. "Did she?"

The girl looked confused. "She married him, didn't she? Why would you live with someone if—"

"Child, you got a lot of learning to do. Folks do that all the time."

Kansas rested her chin on her knees, then she sat up straight and looked up at the sky. There was a slip of a moon and the stars were brighter than usual. "Isn't the moon pretty? It looks like the edge of a silver dollar."

Eula Lura nodded, letting her thoughts tumble unchecked to her lips. "Your mama could hear the moon. She said it chirped."

"I remember that! I do! She would tell me to listen late at night. And she said it smelled like—"

"Strawberries and bananas," Eula Lura finished, spontaneous, without thinking.

"Yes! How do you know?"

Eula Lura took another step, now more hesitant, into this new arena. She wasn't sure why, but she followed her thoughts with the sound of her own voice. "She told me things."

"What things?"

"More things than anybody else she told, except maybe your aunt."

"You'll tell me sometime?"

Eula Lura shrugged and thumped her cigarette with her middle finger, sending it arching across the dirt yard like a shooting star.

"Will you?"

"Maybe. Not now, anyway."

"The things Pinky said about those Klan people. She was talking out of her head, wasn't she?"

"No."

"Those are the kinds of things they do?"

"Been known to."

"Roxy's daddy is a Klan person. Does that mean he's done those things?"

"Maybe. Prob'ly not. Most of them just like to talk. Bunch of cowards is all they really are."

"Roxy told me her daddy might take her to a rally near Albany this summer. What do they do at a rally?"

"Jump around and burn a cross or two and act a fool," Eula Lura said, "and then go looking for a nigger to beat on, or worse."

"I might go to the rally with Roxy. I want to see how they act for myself."

"Your Grandemona ain't about to let you do such as that."

"I won't tell. I'll say we're on a late play-out or something."

"Best not to get so close to evil."

"I'm just curious. I know they're mean, crazy—well, Grandemona says 'ignorant' is the word to use for folks that hate their neighbor."

"'Evil' the word to use. And you better be afraid of it."

"Why? They can't do anything to me."

"That evil can stain your soul if you ain't careful and watchful."

"How?"

"You just be careful and watchful, else that evil will spill into your spirit and take you down dangerous roads." She glared into the dark.

"LittleBit?"

"What?"

"Did you ever wish a man dead?"

"I did."

"Which one?"

"Same as Mama."

"Will that come back on you?"

"Don't care."

"Ever feel bad about it? Guilty, like Pinky does?"

Eula Lura shook her head no, not allowing herself to think of Elizabeth.

"Why not?"

Eula Lura gave her a hard, cold gaze. "Because the killing of some folks is so good you wish you could do it over and over again. Now you run on. I got to see to Mama."

"But she's asleep. And if you want to go to the Blue Goose I can sit with her."

Eula Lura stood. "I ain't got no use for that club tonight."

"Really, I don't mind. Go have fun."

"Said I ain't got no use for it tonight. Reckon I'll stay with Mama. I'll sleep on that cot your Grandemona put in there for me."

"Well," Kansas said. "I don't have to be in yet. I've got a couple of hours. Can I sit with y'all?"

"I reckon." Eula Lura stood and went into the house, Kansas following behind, watching as Eula Lura unfolded the cot and laid a pillow on it. Eula Lura adjusted a second oscillating fan, one Miss Lucille had sent over with Kansas, and the breezes from the fans crissed and crossed. She considered whether to mention the missing war medal to Kansas, then dismissed the notion, thinking that, too, would play out as it should. All secrets and misdeeds would come to light soon enough. She could feel it, deep down, the way Elizabeth used to feel things.

Eula Lura started to sit in the straight chair by Pinky's bed, but instead she went to the kitchen table and pulled a second chair out. She lifted it easily, then set it down next to Pinky's bed, and motioned for Kansas to sit.

"Thank you," Kansas said, joining Pinky's daughter at the old woman's bedside.

"Welcome," Eula Lura said, watching her mother's chest rise, fall, rise, knowing it would cease to do that before too many weeks passed, wishing for the kind of closeness Kansas sought with her and had with her mama Pinky, wishing, as she had when Ned died, for all kinds of second chances.

Kansas and Roxy sat on tall stools at the back of a long, narrow room with large roll-up aluminum windows across its face, the four windows backed by countertops, four more tall stools pulled up to the four windows, four cash boxes lined up along the countertop. Asa and three other boys sat on the stools, waiting for nine A.M., when they were to roll up the metal partitions and begin collecting admission money from folks at the grand opening of the new private club, a "whites only" club that had once been Tift Park. It had a new name now, but Kansas couldn't remember it. That didn't matter, though, because everyone still called it Tift Park, and it promised to be a busy day.

The girls arrived at eight-thirty and sat watching the boys, all of whom Roxy pronounced "cute," saying she couldn't wait to get a look at the lifeguards. "But what's wrong with you?" she said to Kansas, low and secretive.

"Why do you do that?"

"Do what?"

"Flirt with Mr. Royce. He's an old man."

"I think of it as practice. Besides, he's kind of cute," Roxy retorted.

"You think anything with testosterone is cute," she said sarcastically, throwing out one of the words Roxy had taught her. "And he looks at you like he can see you naked."

"So what?"

"It's icky. I mean, it's repugnant. He's *old*."

"No, it's not. It's a compliment. God, Kansas."

Kansas rolled her eyes.

"Come on, Kansas. Let's have a good time today. Don't act like this."

An older man, maybe the new owner of the place, the man who bought it from the city, came into the admissions booth and told all four ticket sellers to listen up. "If an unusual situation comes up, like if a nigger comes to the window to buy a ticket, all you have to do is say this, word for word: 'I'm sorry. This is a private club for whites only, and I can't admit you.' That's it. Don't say no more and don't say no less. Don't be cussing and don't go to fighting. I chose you boys because I know you ain't a bunch of hotheads. Going to follow the plan. Okay?"

"Yes, sir," all the boys mumbled.

"He sounds so serious," Roxy said.

"Oh, you don't think he's 'cute' then?"

"Come on, Kansas. Come on, okay?"

Kansas did not allow herself to smile, was not going to offer Roxy another chance, not yet.

The strong, stinging scent of chlorine drifted in from the pool behind the long building. The girls could already hear splashes and shouts from the three lifeguards, who had also arrived early, to make ready for the day. Kansas and Roxy wore long T-shirts over their two-piece bathing suits, and Kansas was self-conscious, dreading the unveiling. Too, she was still soured by irritation with her friend for what had happened in the car on the trip over.

Mr. Royce Fitzhugh had been enlisted to drive the girls to the park, where they were to meet up with Asa and enjoy the privilege of helping out in the admissions booth before they spent the day swimming and sunning. Mr. Royce pulled the patrol car up to the Lacey back door, and that was when Roxy got everything off on the wrong foot.

"Shotgun!" Roxy yelled, climbing into the front seat opposite Mr. Royce, who grinned and stared at her legs while Kansas grudgingly got in back. Then Roxy proceeded to spend the entire twenty-minute trip giggling and flirting with Mr. Royce, both of the front-seat riders ignoring Kansas until she felt like an inconsequential child. She slammed the door hard when Mr. Royce dropped them off.

"Come on, Kansas," Roxy said again, leaning forward, perched on the stool's edge, then losing balance.

Kansas caught her arm and could not help giggling as her friend got her legs back. "Okay, okay," she said. "But don't act like I'm invisible if a boy talks to you."

The boys on the stools had already noticed the curves of Roxy's body and were not discreet as they tried to get a better look. And Roxy was even covered up in that baggy, cotton T-shirt of her daddy's. Well, Kansas thought, at least she didn't wear that dumb bikini.

Asa brought both girls a Coke, being especially attentive to Roxy, as if he were showing off for the other boys. "If y'all get bored in here you can go ahead and swim," he said, "and I'll find you when the crowd slows down. That's when only two of us have to stay here at the windows. We're going to take turns all afternoon. Okay?" He smiled at Roxy, then glanced at Kansas, who knew he was only including her to be polite. The only reason Kansas was even invited in the first place, she figured, was that Roxy had to have a ride to Albany. Kansas was already feeling excluded, just as she knew she would.

In a while the man walked through again. "Roll 'em up, boys," he barked. "And remember my instructions, you hear?"

The metal windows made a thunder of noise as the boys lifted them, sending the aluminum up to the ceiling, rolling along metal tracks. Kansas and Roxy pulled their stools over next to Asa, to help him make change, as he had asked them to do. But what Kansas saw through the window took all thoughts of self-importance straight out of her head.

"Uh-oh," she heard one of the boys breathe.

"Shit," said another.

Outside Asa's window stood a line of colored teenagers, twenty-five or thirty of them. There were no white customers to be seen at first, then Kansas noticed knots of them further back from the windows, in groups scattered about the parking lot, as though they were waiting to see what was going to happen.

At the head of Asa's line was a tall, thin colored girl, sixteen or seventeen years old. She had pretty eyes and a flip hair-do, a wide, stretchy white headband set back from her bangs. She wore a yellow dress, full-skirted and belted at the waist, but she wore no shoes and had a towel draped around her neck. Several of the other colored teenagers also held towels and stood barefoot, but in street clothes, as if they did not really expect to go swimming, were only making the gesture of attempting to get into the park. But why? Kansas wondered. If they know they won't get in, then why did they come?

The colored girl's eyes met Kansas's for a second, but before Kansas could think to smile, the girl looked at Asa, and she was stone-faced, serious, and direct. She laid fifty cents down on the counter. "One admission, please," she said.

Asa's voice cracked a little as he delivered his scripted reply. "I'm sorry. This is a private club for whites only. I can't admit you."

The girl did not argue. She simply picked up her money, handed it to the boy standing behind her, and moved out of the way so that the next colored teenager could ask to be admitted. Kansas watched the swing of her full skirt, the way she held her head, level, just like the marchers she had seen with Dr. King in Albany that day last December. Then the girl did the strangest thing. She lay down on the cemented ground a few feet away from the admission booth. And the next teenager, a stocky boy Asa turned away as well, went and lay down beside her after handing the fifty cents off to the next boy. It began to dawn on Kansas that the whole line of them was going to do exactly the same thing, and she was riveted by the deliberateness and quiet of it all.

They each repeated the request, "One admission, please," very polite, not demanding, but at the same time not timid, either. They made full eye contact with Asa, but without either challenging or letting their gazes falter. Kansas wanted to talk with them, to know where they had come from, how they had arrived at this decision, what they thought of her, the girl on the other side of the counter. She thought of the lady in the black straw hat who had walked a few paces ahead of Dr. King, the line of marchers spilling a wake of dignified silence across the pavement, just as these teenagers were doing.

In a moment, though, the quiet disintegrated, as half a dozen police cars and two paddy wagons roared into the parking lot, the paddy wagons pulling straight up to the windows of the admission booth. There were no sirens, just the roar of the engines, the squeal of tires as they stopped, then a slamming of doors, policemen disembarking from their patrol cars. The moment the officers approached, the rest of the teenagers standing in line at Asa's window lay down on the pavement. None of them said a word. It was like a thing they had practiced, like a choreographed dance or a play, and Kansas was awed by it, though she wasn't sure why.

The policemen were quiet, polite even, not yelling orders, simply saying, "I need you to move on, now. Go home," then, "I need you to stand and walk over to that vehicle," pointing to a paddy wagon, "and get in." The teenagers continued to lie motionless on the pavement. That was when the officers, in pairs, went from teenager to teenager, one officer at the shoulders and one at the feet, and lifted the person, whose body would go limp, dead weight, from the concrete; the teenagers were carried over to the paddy wagons, where they were loaded like sacks of grain. Once laid inside, they would rise and quietly take their seats on low benches bolted to the inner sides of the vehicles.

"What the hell is going on?" a boy said, coming into the booth. He was dripping wet and wore a lifeguard T-shirt.

A second lifeguard followed him into the admission area. "What's shaking?"

"Shhh!" someone said, infected by the calmness of the scene.

A few shouts could be heard from some of the crowd in the parking lot. "Nigger, go home!" or "Burn in hell, nigger!" and other shouts Kansas could not make out. She was fascinated by the stoic protesters, by the officers carrying the limp-bodied teenagers—kids not much older than she was—to the open doors of the paddy wagons, by their limp forms coming back to life and taking a seat, compliant but proud. At once she envied them. Even with the slurs of the crowd, maybe with a lifetime of slurs, they were acting out an example, it seemed. They were trying to show folks how, in spite of fear, to behave with confidence, the kind of confidence

Kansas wished she had.

A couple of the officers stood by the girl in the yellow dress. The girl was silent, limp, heavy in spite of her thinness. She did exactly what the others did. As the policemen lifted her, the full yellow skirt hung down, sweeping against the asphalt. Then they carried her over to the vehicle and loaded her inside, stiff-netted petticoats like the folds of a white rose, nestled within the petals of her bright yellow dress.

"Gosh," Kansas said. "This isn't like the trouble my grandmother described."

"You mean like throwing bottles and knocking heads?"

"Yeah. This is almost as quiet as church."

Asa chuckled. "See, we beat them at their own game. That's how we beat goddamn Martin King last year. The police arrest them, real polite-like, you know? Then the newspapers and TV stations don't give them hardly any airtime or newsprint. Just like it never happened, see?"

But it did happen, Kansas thought, as the police cars and vans drove away. "Aren't the newspapers supposed to report what happens?" she asked.

Asa and some of the other boys snickered.

"You know that man that was in here earlier?"

"Yeah."

"He's the one that bought Tift Park, to keep the niggers out."

"So?"

Asa grinned. "So you know what else he owns?"

"What?"

"A big old newspaper, that's what. And a few radio and TV stations, too, from what I hear. He can have them say whatever he wants."

"But that's not right," Kansas said.

"Are you crazy?" Asa yelled.

"Hey," one of the boys said. "Is your friend a nigger lover?"

Kansas felt a threat in the question, did not know what to say. "It's just that—" she began.

All of a sudden came a huge commotion, shouts of curses from the third lifeguard, who had remained by the pool, and loud splashes, two of them, in quick succession.

"Johnny! Mark! Hurry!"

Even though there was a crowd of white ticket buyers gathering at the windows, the boys at the counters all ran to the doorway leading to the swimming pool, Roxy and Kansas following behind.

As they got to the pool area, Asa right off the bat shouted, "Get out of there!" and "Goddamn sons of bitches!" came from another of the boys. But by the time the other lifeguards dove in and began swimming to the far end of the pool, two very muscular, very black teenaged boys were scrambling out of that end, having swum the length of the pool, and were now rattling up and over the chain-link fence, now jumping into a waiting automobile, which sped away before anyone could think to follow.

"No, goddamn it! They didn't!" Asa yelled.

The crowd in the ticket line had gotten a glimpse of what had come out of the far end of the pool, and as word spread so did angry curses and shocked expressions. Kansas, though, was delighted. It was perfect. The distraction of the arrests, the timing, the boldness. They had scaled the fence before they were even noticed, diving into the deep end and swimming for the shallow, swimming hard and fast. Kansas wanted to applaud the guts it took, wanted to giggle at the crowd's dismay at being had. But she didn't. The boy's words came back at her: "Is your friend a nigger lover?"

Certain things were second nature to her, and she knew not to show her true response, knew a response like that, like delight at a couple of colored teenagers pulling one over on the whites-only club, would bring her mountains of grief, and even something of a threat. It was the first time she felt a bit of the danger of the society she lived in, the rigid code of the Velvet Corridor. So it was that, after her initial, internal delight, she felt rattled, then shaken, deep inside, a piece of her sense of security snatched away.

Some in the crowd wanted the pool to be closed and drained, but were finally convinced of the disinfecting, purifying properties of chlorine. Still, there were a few who refused to get in the water all afternoon. Most people swam, though, and the incident faded into the background. But it did not fade in Kansas's head. Roxy spent the afternoon ignoring her, wiggling her wet bathing suit top against the bare chests of the boys who wrestled with her, ducking her under in the pool. But Kansas didn't care. For once, it did not bother her that Roxy ignored her. It did not bother her that Roxy did not wear a T-shirt on the ride home with Mr. Royce that afternoon, that the *old* man could hardly drive for looking over at Roxy's chest. All Kansas could do was mull over that bit of security lost to her now, more curious than ever about the whys of it all, more impressed as the day wore on, impressed by the actions of the colored teenagers.

And that night, as she lay in the canopy bed, she kept reliving what had happened. It had not been on the news that evening, nor was it in Daddy Jack's afternoon edition of the *Herald*. Still, Kansas kept seeing it: their level gazes and their practiced, choreographed movements; the bath towels and bare feet; the boldness of the swimmers who breached the fence, dripping tainted water as they scaled the chain-link barrier. But the most vivid image stuck in her thoughts was that of a full yellow skirt fluffed about the legs of a thin colored girl, a skirt yellow as a lemon skin, its cotton fabric brushing across asphalt, revealing layers of white petticoats, all delicate netting, like clouds laced across the stars and the moon, against the tar of the paved lot.

*

"I think it's wrong," Roxy said.

"Why?" Kansas asked. She and her friend lay on the bank beside the cold spring up Scratchy Branch, bare skin against spread towels, discarded swimsuits in the sand.

"Simple. It's like my daddy says. The white race is the civilized one, and the only place it's bound to lead is to race mixing."

"Race mixing?"

"Yes, race mixing. My daddy says every nigger man alive wants to do it with a white girl, which is why they're all the time raping us and all." She shuddered. "Can you imagine?"

"When did you start thinking so much of your daddy?"

Roxy sighed. "That's not why I believe him."

"Then why?" Kansas rolled onto her side, her head propped on her hand.

Roxy was lying on her back, the lowering sun kissing light across her body. "I don't know. It's all I ever heard about it. And it does make sense."

"About being civilized? How is it civilized?"

"Somebody has to be in charge."

"You should look at my *National Geographics* and read about all the people out there in the world. They do just fine. They are civilized."

"What does that have to do with anything?" Roxy's eyes were closed, and Kansas wondered at how Roxy could be so smart about some things and unable to see others.

"It has everything to do with everything." Kansas was frustrated, searching for words, knowing what was in her gut but unable to give it any kind of eloquence.

"You're being dramatic." Roxy swatted at a horsefly that was buzzing past her ear, then dropped her hand to her stomach, against her skin.

"No, I'm not. Just read about all the people, the tribes, the clans, the— all of them." Kansas wanted to say there were too many kinds of people in the world for there to be such a fuss over keeping one kind down or another kind superior, but she was distracted by a gentle, liquid feeling in her own stomach as she watched Roxy's palm move across and down and rest again at her side.

"What does it matter?" Roxy was saying. "We live here. We'll never know any of them."

"I will," Kansas said. "I want to travel all over."

They were silent for a while. A small plane droned overhead. The creek water made trickly sounds against the muted backup of buzzing insects. Roxy pushed at her long hair, eyes still closed. "I told you my daddy is taking me to a big Klan rally this summer. It's going to be near Albany."

"Yeah." Kansas thought of her great-grandfather, was swept up in a feeling of curiosity about the organization with which he had been affiliated. She touched Roxy's hair, thinking she might braid it for her, just for fun.

"You should come with us."

"I know my Grandemona would never let me go to that kind of thing." She twirled her friend's hair around her fingertip, watching it undo in a ribbon-like auburn curl.

"So sneak off. Be your mother's daughter."

Kansas laughed, thinking of the wild hellion with the sweet, sweet heart.

"About those boys," Roxy said, out of the blue, opening her eyes.

"What boys?"

"Any boys. The ones at school. Or out on the lake." She rolled over on her side to face Kansas. "I never did it with any of them."

"Why are you telling me this now?"

"I just wanted to answer your question. You know. The one you asked a while back and I was being mum."

"Okay." Kansas wondered what prompted Roxy's sudden offer of such personal information. Maybe she felt sorry for a motherless child, an awkward girl.

"I'm going to do it with one of them, though. I made up my mind," Roxy added.

"But why?" They lay face to face. Kansas glanced down at her own body and saw it as a thing less lovely, much less lovely than Roxy's.

"Just because, that's all. I want to be the one to decide."

Kansas heard something in her voice, like a flavor of shame and half-truth. "Roxy, what have you already done with those boys?"

"Just kissing, you know," she said, twirling her hair around her own fingertip now. "And I let them touch me. But not down there."

"You would, though?"

"Yes."

"And you would really do it? Go all the way?"

Roxy pressed strands of hair against her lips. "I want to. I really do."

"No, Roxy. It's nasty."

"I used to think so, too."

"You'll get p.g. and never go to college."

"God, Kansas, there are ways to keep from getting p.g."

Kansas did not ask how one would keep from becoming pregnant, was looking deep into Roxy's gold-flecked irises, trying to see what she was hearing in her friend's voice, embedded in a tone at odds with her words. "It's nasty," she said again. "And boys will take advantage of you."

Roxy's gaze went angry. "They take advantage anyway." Then she smiled. "Plus, there's something else."

"What?"

"I was reading about it, all about it, you know, wondering how it feels," her voice trailed off.

"What? You know something new? Tell me."

Roxy blushed. "I'll tell if you'll tell."

"What do you mean? Just spit it out."

"Okay, okay," Roxy wiggled a little closer, secretive, and her voice dropped. "I know it feels good down there. Because I've done it to myself."

Kansas let her eyes go big. "Roxy, you're lying."

"No. Really. Lots of times. Haven't you?"

"No," Kansas lied. After all, there had been times when she lay in bed at night and let her fingers drift down to the borders of that place with which Roxy seemed obsessed.

"You must have done it to yourself, too."

"No," Kansas said again.

"But it feels so good."

The afternoon was taking the sun's intensity away from the sky and shadows were stretching toward the bank. Kansas rolled onto her back again and looked up at the sky, then back into Roxy's eyes, wondering if she should ask, and at that very instant blurting, "How do you do it?"

"God, Kansas. You just rub yourself wherever it feels good. I can't believe you've never done that."

Kansas did not tell her that she had put her palms to her breasts, thinking to massage some size into them, and the sensation stretched all the way down to her thighs. She did not tell Roxy about the times she had tried to go past the boundaries but only came up afraid, sensing its unknown potential. She rolled onto her side again. "No," she said. "I never have."

"But you have to. It's what everything comes down to. I mean, think about it. Babies come from there. Life comes from there."

"I'm scared to," Kansas said.

"I can show you," Roxy said.

Kansas hesitated.

"I can. Unless you're a coward. Or a prude."

"I'm not a prude."

"Let me show you, then," Roxy said. "Give me your hand."

"I can't."

"I promise," Roxy said. "It's good." She took Kansas's hand and guided it with her own to the tops of Kansas's thighs.

Kansas brought up the sole of her left foot, almost involuntarily, and along the towel until her knee was pointed skyward, exposing the place where Roxy's fingers guided hers. She wanted to say again, "I can't," but was already past speaking, knew she was going to know, finally. "See?" Roxy said in a while. "Now you."

Kansas hesitated again, but was drawn back by the feeling, until there was nothing in the world but her own touch, that ebbing and flowing swell of something rising in her, pushing to burst free. She let the feeling swallow her, until the place began to swallow itself, until flashes of light burst behind her closed lids. When it was over and she got her breath, her lids opened to Roxy's eyes, searching and reassuring.

"You see?" Roxy said. "It's so strong it makes me want to find out more about it. Does it you?"

"It makes me scared to find out more," Kansas said, looking up at the clouds.

"Well, then. I'll just find out more and tell you about it."

"I still say it's nasty."

"That felt nasty just now?"

"No. It felt good."

"So how can it be nasty?"

"What I'm talking about is doing it with a boy. How could you do this with a boy?"

"God, Kansas. I imagine it will be a hundred times nicer with a boy. Boys have strong arms. And they kiss."

Kansas said it before she thought. "We could kiss, too."

Roxy laughed. "It's fun, showing you how to do that. But if we kiss and all, we could turn lezzie like your Aunt Frances."

"What?"

"Don't look like that. Everybody knows they're lesbians."

Kansas sat up. "Take it back."

"I will not."

"You take it back, right now, right this second, or—"

"Or what?"

"Or you're not invited to the Fourth of July party."

Roxy sat up, scowling. "God, Kansas. What's the big deal?"

"You can't talk bad about my Aunt Frances, that's all."

"It's just the truth. You don't have to have a cow over it."

"Take it back!"

"Okay, okay, okay. I take it back. God."

Kansas watched her stand and step into her bathing suit bottom, and Kansas reached for her own suit. The sun was behind the trees and the material was cold against her flesh. She shivered and watched Roxy put on her top without flinching. "How do you do that? It's so cold."

"I can do lots of things. I just shut off my thoughts. If you shut off your thoughts, you don't have to feel anything you don't want to."

"You could walk over hot coals or lie on a bed of nails?"

"Probably."

"You make it sound easy."

Roxy picked up her towel and shook the sand from it. "It's just a thing I learned to do."

"How?"

Roxy snapped the towel hard and bit down on her words. "My daddy taught me." Then she twisted her towel, snapped it at Kansas, and said, "Last one to the boat is going to do it with a boy!"

Kansas kicked sand as she ran toward the tree where the Whaler was tied up, currents pulling its rope taut. She overtook Roxy and caught the sun's flicker in the corner of her eye, late afternoon light beaming through the tree trunks, and was relieved when she reached the boat. She slapped the hull with her palm. "Beat you!" she called to Roxy, happy that, even in a joking, make-believe way, she did not have to do it with a boy. No. That was a thing she could not comprehend. She untied the boat after she and Roxy climbed aboard and let it drift with the current around a few bends, then cranked the motor, making for the big river and home.

*

Grandemona and LittleBit cooked nonstop in the days leading up to the Fourth of July party at the lake house, and Miss Pearl even agreed to be there. Daddy was upbeat and full of laughter, but Kansas could not get excited over it all. She could only see the summer going into its second month without the familiar fun of previous summers, the nights of pretend and "swing the statue" and "Mother, may I?"

She spent more and more hours alone in her room, thumbing through her mother's diary of a Bible, picking over the marked passages, transcribing, decoding what she could, appreciating the lines that were possessed of clarity: "I want to be the music when I dance. Any moment can be a moment of perfection—I just have to let it happen"; and "February 1942—I feel such wonderful days coming and all I can do is savor the anticipation"; and "Angels ride and slide down to the earth on the points of stars, and their wings are bright beacons for the souls passing them along the way, back and forth and across the light of the moon." Kansas sought out the pretty, uplifting words to help temper the sad ones, the letters spelling out her mother's despair, which so often got tangled in Kansas's own thoughts, where she knew they did not really belong.

She was glad to have so much time to spend in her room, now that she couldn't really look Grandemona or Littlebit in the eye—not any of them, especially not Daddy, not since the afternoon on the creek bank with Roxy. She was afraid they would see something in her demeanor that would tell on her, show them the sin in her own eyes. Roxy said they were not lesbians because of what they did, but Kansas was not sure. She wished she had the nerve to tell Aunt Frances about it. Surely Aunt Frances would know if Kansas was a lesbian or not. Aunt Frances would tell her if it was normal, what she had done with Roxy, what she continued to do with herself.

She had done it alone lots of times since that day, in her bed late at night, air conditioners humming, or lying in the bathtub, hot water trickling to keep the warmth going. She let her fingertips touch a slow rhythm into a spiral of heat pinwheeling through her pores until she shuddered, out of breath, forehead trickling perspiration. Then she would have to face the faces in her life, her own face flushed with the pink coaxing of shame.

On top of the shame, she couldn't meet Aunt Frances's eyes, or Miss Martha's, either, not with Roxy's allegation simmering suspicion about the two women. Kansas argued with herself, telling herself the ladies could never in a million years be such things as lesbians. After all, they went to the Methodist Church. Miss Martha even sang in the choir. Aunt Frances looked for the good in folks, even the lowest of the low.

But Roxy was insistent about the accuracy of her take on the pair of women, living together for over two decades, no boyfriends anywhere to be seen. Kansas had to admit there was something strange about the arrangement. There had always seemed to be more to know, more than the why of a simple absence of boyfriends.

Roxy was focused on the value of boyfriends these days, flitting from one to the next in the space of a day, or less. It seemed that all of Asa's friends had Kansas's phone number, calling long distance between the appointed hours of one and four p.m., to be sure Roxy was there.

"Why didn't you give them your phone number?" Kansas demanded, when the jangling ring of the pink Princess phone in her bedroom intruded for what seemed like the hundredth time that day.

"Because you have your own line. It's private. Besides, you know Daddy won't let me talk to boys on the phone."

"Why not?"

"Same old thing. He says I'll go off and do it with them."

"That's depraved," Kansas said, borrowing one of Miss Pearl's favorite words to use in case of hints at sexuality.

Roxy shrugged.

"Why is that all he ever thinks about?"

Roxy shrugged again. "He's just jealous," she said, turning her attention to another phone conversation with one of the Tift Park boys.

The conversations went on forever, while Kansas picked through her mother's Bible, reading the starred and underlined verses: "'A merry heart doeth good like a medicine: but a broken spirit drieth the bones'; and 'All the rivers run into the sea; yet the sea is not full; unto the place from whence the rivers come, thither they return again.'"

"Do you think it's okay if Asa brings some of his friends to the party?"

"Sure." Kansas rolled her eyes. There was no telling how many high school boys would show up at the lake house, sniffing around Roxy like dogs sensing a heat.

"Great." She pulled out the neck of her blouse and looked down to study her skin. "You know what?" She tugged at her bra. "My tan's even enough for me to wear that bikini to the party."

"Are you crazy? There'll be a bunch of grownups there."

"I won't let them see. Just Asa, and whoever else goes out in the boat with us."

"That should be just about every boy in Dougherty County."

"Very funny. Hey—"

"What now?" Kansas did not like the expression on Roxy's face, did not like the plan to wear the bikini, a plan that could only end in disaster.

"At some point I want to go off with Asa. Just him and me."

"Yeah, just you and him and that naked bathing suit."

"Seriously. You help me get that one thing to happen and I'll do whatever you want to do for a whole week."

"I think I need to protect you from yourself."

"Seriously. We'll take the boat out and find a place."

"Where are you wanting to go in the boat? What are you going to do with him?"

"Nothing. Well, not really nothing. I like him. I want to see what it's like to make out with him."

"You mean more than kissing?"

"Yeah, but not everything. Come on, Kansas. I would do it for you."

"Let's just don't go up Scratchy Branch, that's all. Okay?"

"I wasn't planning for us to take him there."

"Well, let's don't. That's our spot, and it's a secret spot, especially the clay bank and the spring."

"So why would I go there? There's about a thousand little creeks and places to go on the river."

"Promise me we won't go up Scratchy Branch with Asa?"

"Sure."

"Cross your heart."

Roxy drew an imaginary X on her chest with her index finger, then leaned over and hugged Kansas. "Thank you," she said. "You are my very best friend ever."

"Come on, Roxy. I'm your only friend."

The two girls took a giggling fit, falling back on the bed, gasp-laughing. When Kansas got her breath she said, "I still feel weird about what we did at the creek."

Roxy blushed. "Just stop it. I was only showing you how to do it right."

"Because you're a true friend."

"A true best friend."

"You wouldn't tell anybody, would you?"

"Do you think I'm a nut?"

"Yes," Kansas exploded into fresh giggles as Roxy threw a pillow at her head. The laughter died down and Kansas said, again, "But you wouldn't tell, would you?"

"Of course not. We keep each other's secrets."

"Do we, really?" Kansas asked, looking deep into Roxy's gaze, sensing that her best friend's eyes had been invaded by something like resignation. Just a flicker, then Roxy giggled it away at the ring of the Princess phone.

*

There must have been more than a hundred people there, boats tied up at the dock and along the shore, kegs of beer and picnic tables loaded down with food. Small children ran squealing across the grass or splashed in the shallow water at the edge of the yard, toddlers guarded by colored nursemaids. The older ones tossed a football and did cannonballs and can openers off the end of the pier while Roxy and Kansas cleaned up the boat, waiting for Asa and two other boys, Mitch and Johnny, to come over and take them skiing. Roxy's fragment of a bathing suit was hidden beneath her T-shirt, but she had announced to Kansas that she would waterski in it, far up the river.

"I don't think we could get far enough away from here to keep it from spreading around that you wore that thing."

"Don't be silly."

"I'm not. Have you ever seen anybody on the lake in one of those?"

"Of course not. I will be the first."

"The first one your daddy kills, you mean."

"The hell with Daddy," Roxy said, suddenly vicious with anger. "He's not around today so I'm going to have the best time I've ever had in my life."

It was a different kind of tone than Kansas was used to hearing from her friend. It was defiant, more than intimidating. Kansas felt a twinge of fear, but that dissolved into shyness when Asa and his friends idled up in the little fishing boat. She had to admit to herself that the other boys were, in fact, cute, even before Roxy coded that word to her with her eyes. Kansas remembered them from Tift Park. Mitch was tall and lanky with a movie star smile, kind of a crooked, cheek-dimpled smile; and Johnny was shorter, with blonde hair and the deep, deep tan of a lifeguard.

"Ain't no niggers tried to crash your party yet?" Johnny asked, laughing.

"You going to do something about it this time?" Asa said. "Or are you going to dog-paddle behind like you did when they jumped the fence at Tift?"

Johnny replied by giving Asa a playful punch in the arm while Roxy began to giggle.

Kansas didn't think it was funny, the jokes about the colored boys, but she did not dare dissent from the humor. She felt nervous and awkward and afraid of being excluded yet again, so she laughed a hollow sound. "Y'all ready to ski?"

"We ready to ski, Mitch?"

"We are now."

Kansas turned. Mitch was loading an ice chest into the Chris-Craft.

Roxy lowered her voice. "Y'all got the beer?"

"Hell, yeah," Asa said. "Told you we would."

Kansas's stomach did a little back-flip. She should have known it wouldn't be simple. The potential trouble the bikini could cause was now compounded by two cases of Busch Bavarian beer, iced down in a big cooler, and there was nothing she could do about it but climb into the boat.

Asa was old enough for Daddy Jack to trust to drive the big boat and take them skiing, even on the Fourth, with the lake chopping the wakes of scores of motorboats hauling skiers and kids on inner tubes behind them. They decided to go upriver, to the less-populated part of the lake, and have their Fourth of July party there.

The unveiling of the bikini was every bit as dramatic as Kansas had dreaded and Roxy had apparently hoped. The boys whistled and applauded, Mitch sang "Itsy Bitsy Teenie Weenie Yellow Polka-Dot Bikini," and Roxy had Asa slicking her up with Johnson's Baby Oil in no time. The boy threw a significant glance at his friends, who couldn't help commenting on the daring it took to wear such a thing.

"Man, I ain't never seen one of those except on TV or at the picture show," Mitch said.

"I ordered it. You can't buy them around here," Roxy said coolly.

"I wish they'd catch on," Johnny said, "'cause it would sure as hell make my job at Tift a hell of a lot better."

"Shit," Asa said. "You already broke out in girls." He turned to Kansas. "Watch out for him. He looks sweet but he's a gigolo."

"What's that?" Kansas blurted, then blushed when the rest of them broke into laughter.

"Are you as innocent as you act?" Mitch asked her.

But she could only blush a deeper shade of crimson and was happy to volunteer to ski first, just to be away from them. There were enough boats on this part of the lake to make her nervous, but it was still more relaxing than worrying about how to act around a bunch of boys. She leaned back and let the spray from the slalom ski mist over her, a cool wet veil. She used her back foot to guide the slat of wood, "Cypress Gardens" in script across its face, and curved out over the wake, all the way out. The remnants of wakes spreading across the water from other boats created an irregular chop of woven-together waves, and it was difficult to remain balanced, so she maneuvered herself back behind the boat and relaxed there, deciding to just hold on and ski as long as she could last. At least she was not with the boys, trying to think how to act.

They spent a couple of hours skiing, taking turns, opening bottles of beer with the church key hanging from Asa's key ring. The beer was cold and fizzy and bitter, but Kansas liked it. She had sipped from Daddy Jack's bottle before, many times. When she was a child she would climb up in the easy chair with him and help him eat boiled peanuts chased by a sip or two of beer as they watched baseball games. The boys seemed impressed, too, that she did not flinch with her first sip, the way Roxy did.

By midafternoon they were all light-headed and silly, and ready to drop the anchor, eat from the mound of pimento cheese sandwiches in the girls' ice chest, and to sunbathe and swim. She and Roxy jumped in the water whenever they had to pee, not letting on to the boys what they were doing, knowing the boys knew anyway. They floated on seat cushions and ski belts, wrestled and ducked each other, and Kansas felt relaxed and included, even attractive. Mitch especially seemed interested in her, and whenever his arms slipped around her waist or his legs kicked against hers, there was a familiar tingle of anticipation, down low in her stomach, that made her even more giddy than the alcohol.

All the boys smoked cigarettes, and Roxy begged them to teach her how to smoke. Soon she was French inhaling and attempting smoke rings to the droning of passing motors, boats that slowed, passengers waving, then speeding up again, leaving them alone with their water party until the next boat passed.

Finally Roxy stretched out on the bow, and Kansas folded down the seats to make a long, flat cushion to lie on. The big, red boat floated in lazy circles, the transistor radio and a gentle slapping of waves lulling them into deep relaxation. The boys sat and scarfed down sandwich after sandwich before opening more beer.

"My daddy says Martin King'll be back in town soon to do his jail time," Asa said. "You watch. Them niggers'll go all to pieces over that."

"Won't be doing it up at Tift," Johnny said. "Boss man put barbed wire all around the top of that fence."

"Man, I thought last year was bad," Mitch said. "Now it looks like it's going to start again."

"Last year was a bitch," Asa said. "But my daddy says Pritchett showed them how much they could get by with."

"Who's Pritchett?" Kansas asked, trying to participate in the conversation without hooking into the spirit of it.

"Laurie Pritchett. Chief of po-lice. That son of a bitch knows just what to do with a bunch of crazy niggers."

"What's that?" Kansas asked.

"Kill 'em with kindness. Like that day at Tift. Cops were polite as hell."

"Hey," Johnny said. "You hear about Martin Luther King drowning?"

Mitch laughed. "What happened?"

"His wife took him out on a boat and told him if he didn't eat her pussy she was going to throw him overboard."

The boys guffawed and Roxy even laughed through her short drowse.

"Yeah, that's two things a nigger won't do: eat pussy and swim," Johnny said, reaching for another sandwich.

Kansas thought it was a strange joke. She thought of the colored boys who swam the length of the Tift Park pool before scaling the fence, leaving the white boys feeling foolish. It was then she noticed the boat, pulling past at idle speed, and heard the shouts, "Hey, Baby!" and "Show me some skin!" Then a chorus of whistles.

Roxy did not sit up, merely lifted her arm and waved.

"That bathing suit has been drawing boats like flies," Johnny said.

Roxy smiled. "Really?"

Kansas sat up. "Is that what all those slowed-down motors have been?"

"Hell, yeah. Folks staring and grinning and waving. I feel like Hugh

Hefner," Asa said.

"See, Roxy?" Kansas said. "I hope none of those people know my Daddy Jack's boat."

"Somebody's bound to," Mitch said.

"Yeah," Asa said. "We need to find a more private place."

Now Roxy sat up straight and Kansas gave her a look of warning. "I know the perfect spot, if Kansas will let us go there."

Kansas offered her a withering stare.

"Where is it?" Johnny said.

"Back up near the house. A little creek, but deep enough to take the boat up a ways. Only Kansas has the final say," Roxy said. "Can we, Kansas?"

"What's Kansas got to say about it?" Asa asked.

"It's a secret," Roxy said, begging Kansas with her eyes. "Come on. We'll just go around the first bend in the creek. Just far enough to get out of all the traffic."

Kansas shook her head, not believing what she was hearing, how easily Roxy's loyalty slid into oblivion when boys were in the picture.

"What do you say, Kansas?" Mitch asked.

Kansas had the feeling of being punched in the stomach. She was backed into a corner and did not like it one little bit. If she said no, the questions and haranguing would begin, then "party-pooper" status would follow. There was nothing else to do but give in before they turned on her. She forced a light, casual tone into her answer. "Sure," she said.

As they traveled the length of the lake back toward the dam, the hull of the bow slapping against little waves, Kansas told herself she could not cry, could not show her anger, could not act in any way that would make her appear foolish. At the same time she was disgusted with herself for holding in. Why not be herself? Why not lash out against Roxy and her betrayal? Why not tell the boys she had watched Martin King walk by, that he had a kind and gentle face? Why was she so concerned with how they saw her? Why did she let herself be swallowed up by their attitudes and their words?

People in other boats pointed as they passed. It was not the usual boating etiquette, a leisurely wave. Kansas's so-called friend was the topic of conversation today. More than that, Roxy was a spectacle, and word had been passed from vessel to vessel: watch for a red Chris-Craft with dark wood siding. There's a girl in a little bitty bikini on board, and she's got some kind of body!

She wanted the day to be over. She wanted to go back to the house and see who was still there, find out how many boats had come and gone, listen to the bluegrass quartet Daddy Jack had hired to play the afternoon into sunset. She felt groggy with beer and sunshine, and she wanted to take a nap. But she knew none of that was going to happen. The day was going to unfold the way Roxy intended. Kansas might as well appear to enjoy herself, save her confrontation with her former friend until later.

The boys declared Scratchy Branch to be "tuff as hell" and Roxy carried on like a tour guide, directing them further up the creek, way beyond the first bend, almost to the spring, all the way to where the water got too shallow to accommodate the boat. They carried the ice chests to a sandbar and spread towels. Kansas avoided meeting Roxy's eyes and did not speak to her as they got situated.

"You drunk, Mitch?" Asa asked.

"Getting there."

"I'm feeling warm and cozy," Roxy said, standing by the towels, hugging her shoulders.

"What about you, Kansas?" Asa asked.

"Sleepy," she said, rolling onto her stomach to keep from seeing Roxy and because she really did wish she could take a nap. She felt limp and apathetic. Brenda Lee was singing "All Alone Am I."

"You want me to rub some oil on your back?" Mitch asked.

"What about me?" Johnny said.

"Your back's too ugly," Mitch quipped. "Kansas?"

Roxy was right. Being a little tipsy felt warm. Her body felt like it could melt into the sand, she was so exhausted. "Sure," she said, closing her eyes, the slide of his palms against her shoulders chasing the energy of anger away. She was not the least bit self-conscious anymore. She let herself doze off, thinking of jumping the wake, rolling into the cool water of the river, letting the surface close over her head, slipping into darkness.

When she woke up, Mitch and Johnny were splashing in the current, chunking mud clods at each other. The sunlight was dimming, slipping further behind the trees. She wondered how long she had been asleep. Daddy would worry if they were past dark. She looked around. No Roxy. No Asa. That was not a good sign. Then she heard splashing further up the creek and uncontrollable giggling.

Asa tromped along the creek bed, over to where they were, Roxy leaning on his shoulder, stumbling, laughing, stumbling again, and landing sitting in the water. "God," she laughed. "Oh, Kansas, I am so drunk."

Kansas felt a jolt of panic. They couldn't go back to the house with Roxy like this. But Asa was helping her up, steering her over to where the boat was tied to a sapling, pulling her in.

"Come here, Mitch," Roxy called as Asa climbed out of the boat. "I want to talk to you." Her voice was unnaturally loud.

"It's okay," Asa said to Kansas, seeing how appalled she was. "We'll ride around for a little while and let the air sober her up some."

"We don't have a long time," Kansas said. "We have to take the boat in before it gets dark enough to turn on the lights. We're in so much trouble I can't believe it."

"Mitch!" Roxy yelled, and both boys waded over to the boat.

"Oh, come on, Kansas. Be cool. It'll be okay." Asa swayed a little as he spoke.

"You're drunk, too," Kansas said, not holding back, too afraid and furious to check herself. "What good are you if you can't act sober?"

"Shit," Asa said. "My daddy can't ever tell if I'm drunk. I do this all the time."

"Is your daddy a county sheriff?"

A glimmer of recognition darted across his face. "Shit. I guess I didn't think of that. But still—"

"But nothing. We have maybe forty-five minutes to take a boat ride, then we have to take that to my grandparents' house." She indicated Roxy, who was now pressing her body into Mitch, kissing him full on the lips, while Mitch, far from resisting, pressed back, running his palm down and inside the back of her bikini bottom. "And don't you care if your girlfriend is making out with another guy?"

"Hell, she ain't my for-real girlfriend," he said.

Kansas shook her head. "What do you mean?"

"She's just a girl that wants to have a good time. Can't you tell?"

"But she thinks you're her boyfriend."

"Okay, okay, I am. I don't mind being a boyfriend for a day. Shit, look what you get." He nodded toward the boat. Roxy had shed her top and Mitch was all over that opportunity.

"We're going skinny-dipping!" Roxy shouted, then started climbing out of the boat.

"Keep her in there, Mitch!" Asa called. "Go help him, Johnny."

"Don't mind if I do," the boy grinned.

For some crazy reason, Kansas had the urge to defend her friend. She'd had enough of playing along, keeping quiet. "You make me sick," she said to Asa. "Tell them to leave her alone. She's had too much to drink and she doesn't know what she's doing."

Asa laughed. "She damn sure does know what she's doing. Knows way more than girls way older than she is. Showed me a thing or two."

Kansas was not about to ask him what. "Shut up. You make me sick," she said again.

"I hear she's shown you a thing or two, too, hasn't she?"

Kansas's face burned like crazy then, and she wished she could sink into the sand, disappear, or be ignored, as usual. Roxy was wrestling against both other boys. "I want to get in the water!" she whined. "I want to go skinny-dipping."

Johnny laughed, staring at her breasts. "Come on, Asa. Can't we go skinny-dipping?"

"No! Just keep her calm."

"I'm calm," Roxy whined. "I really am. Like a little lamb." Then she began to sing, "Asa had a lit-tle lamb, lit-tle lamb, lit-tle lamb—"

Asa turned back to Kansas. "Yeah, I saw your clay bank and your spring. Roxy even showed me a little bit of what she showed you. How'd you like it?" He gave her a knowing smile and winked at her.

Kansas, face growing hotter, shoved both palms against his chest, full force, and he stumbled backward. "Hey!" he yelled.

"I said to shut up, shut up!" Kansas screamed. Then she gave him her meanest glare. "If you don't shut up right now and take us home, I'm going to tell my Daddy Jack all about how you got beer and got Roxy drunk, and he'll be mad as hell at you. Then he'll tell your daddy, and the Albany police and—"

"Okay, okay," Asa said. "Don't be such a tittie baby. We'll take you home."

"And tell them to leave her alone."

"What do you think? They're going to rape her or something?"

"I don't know." She walked over to Roxy. "Put on your top."

"But I want to go skinny-dipping, Kansas," she continued to whine.

"No. We're going home."

But all Roxy wanted to do was argue, pointlessly, without logic, all thick-tongued and sloppy. Kansas got in the boat but only managed to get her top on her after Asa yelled, "Goddammit, Roxy, you're going to get us all arrested." And Kansas thought to add, "And that means your daddy will know."

Roxy furrowed her brow. "Daddy," she mumbled, letting her arms go limp while Kansas tied the back and neck of the naked bathing suit. Then she pulled the T-shirt over Roxy's head.

"You ought not cover that up," Mitch said.

"Shut up," Kansas snapped.

Roxy looked at him, through intoxicated eyes, and slurred, "Yeah, shut up."

Johnny had gathered up their things, leaving the ice chest of beer and the empty bottles behind on the sandbar, just in case. Kansas would not let Asa drive the boat, saying they would look much more convincingly sober if an actual semi-sober person maneuvered it into the boat slip. She steered the boat to the mouth of Scratchy Branch and looked across at the house.

Faint strains of bluegrass drifted across the water. There were still several boats tied up to the pier. As she approached the opposite bank, the music grew louder and she could hear laughter. A couple of little kids did dueling cannonballs off the end of the dock. Closer still, and she could make out her Daddy Jack up on the patio, sitting with a group of men, smoking cigarettes, probably talking politics. Nearing the boathouse, she saw her Daddy Jack stand, motioning to Grandemona, who joined him. Miss Pearl rose from where she sat alone, across the yard in a white Adirondack chair. She carried a glass. By the time Kansas had the boat in the slip, all three adults were there to meet them. She glanced over at Roxy. Her former friend's head was lying on crossed arms, on the edge of the boat.

"We were wondering if you were ever coming back," her granddaddy said.

"No," Grandemona said. "We were needing to clear something up."

"Not now, Mama."

"Yes, now. I need for Roxy to stand up and show me what she is wearing."

"Why?" Kansas demanded.

"You need not ask me why. But we've had folks in and out all day talking about this boat and a scandal of a swimsuit, and—Roxy!"

Roxy looked up, wobbly-headed.

"What's wrong with her?" Miss Pearl drawled.

The boys had been all silence up until now, but Asa acted fast to divert suspicion. "I'm sorry, Mr. Lacey. We just went up Scratchy Branch and got the boat motor hung up in some vines and things. It took a long time to get everything untangled. I'm really sorry."

But Daddy Jack was not listening. His full attention had gone to Miss Pearl, whose hand clutched at her neck, all color drained from her face. "Where did you say you all went?"

"Up Scratchy Branch," Asa said. "That's where we got—"

Miss Pearl interrupted him, turning to her husband. "How could you?" she said, voice breaking but full of bitter anger. Then, with an expression of such disdain as Kansas had ever seen on a person, her grandmother flung out one more word before turning to leave: "Liar."

Kansas was shocked by the display, much more extreme than anything she had ever seen Miss Pearl do or say. She started to ask her grandparents what was wrong, but at that moment Roxy leaned further over the side of the boat, retched, and vomited the remnants of the day—murky beer, pimento cheese and vanity—into the shallow water of the three-slipped boathouse.

S he could feel it coming, like an end turning in on a beginning. Her mama's little shack was permeated by it, a gathering whisper of circumstances, sure to rise and curl into all the lives Eula Lura tended in her watchful way. It had been building with the summer, with the doings in Albany, with the questionings of a white girl named Kansas, and with the taking of her husband's Purple Heart, that theft becoming a challenge, a dare, with the makings of some kind of showdown, though she didn't know what form it would take.

On the day before the Fourth of July, after cooking for the prisoners, with the Laceys gone and the kitchen clean, she joined Jolene at the clothesline for a midmorning chat, wondering if the white woman might give her some clues about where her medal could be. Ned's war medal had been years in the Lacey kitchen and she had shown no one except Elizabeth and now Elizabeth's daughter; and when she showed Kansas, the way was opened for someone to take it. Eula Lura spent days and days mulling over who it might have been. She knew it had to be someone in and around the Lacey household—one of the Tolberts, maybe, or that fool Hotshot, or even Miss Pearl, who never liked her anyway. She eliminated Kansas as a suspect, decided the girl would never sink so low as to steal, particularly from her, and particularly a thing that was such a treasure to her.

"You ever miss your baby?" Eula Lura asked, reaching into her laundry basket.

Jolene pinned a damp towel to the line. "I did at first. And I know this will sound just terrible, but after a while, after he went off to boarding school, I started to think of him as mostly Jack's baby. Kind of like it was a thing that was meant to be."

"But you don't hate Mr. Jack for taking him away?"

"How can I? I have one young 'un that has a chance in life. Lord knows what's going to happen to the rest of them."

"Still, I reckon it's like a lost treasure, ain't it?"

Jolene thought a moment, then reached for another towel in her clothes basket. "Yeah, I reckon so."

They hung the laundry in silence for a while, then Eula Lura spoke. "I got a lost treasure my ownself." She cut her eyes at the white woman, who betrayed nothing. And as she told Jolene about the missing war medal, it became apparent that Jolene Tolbert was completely in the dark. She was an easy one to read, and Eula Lura was satisfied Jolene knew nothing about who the thief might be, was fixed, instead, on her own miseries.

"Here's an awful thing," Jolene said.

Eula Lura was a little annoyed by the white woman's lack of sympathy for her own loss, but kept her voice even. "What's that?"

Jolene's washed-out, pale eyes were large with a sad, surprised look. "When I think of lost treasures, I think of Jack Lacey, not about Jay."

That *is* an awful thing, Eula Lura thought, to choose a man over a baby, but she only said, "Regret's a hard thing to live with."

"Yeah, it is. Sometimes I let myself hope, though."

"Hope what?"

"That he'll come back to me. That maybe that sot of a wife of his will kick on off and he'll come back to me."

"Has he ever said such?"

Jolene sighed. "No. He's never hardly talked to me over the years. Once, in the beginning, I tried to get him to kiss me—to touch me. But he told me he'd put us all out if I ever did that again."

"Lord."

"Yeah, made me feel like a piece of trash, you know? Said he done wrong by his wife and it wouldn't never happen again."

"But you ain't give up?"

"No. I just added more hope, that's all. Hoping if Jack don't save me, then Royce will."

Eula Lura shook her head. Royce Fitzhugh was a no-count cracker. She'd hated him from the start, even more after all Elizabeth told her. And with Jolene's recounting of the man's bizarre sex habits over the months, Eula Lura had come to think of him as flat crazy.

"I know," Jolene said, as if hearing her thoughts. "The demeaning things a woman will do for a man."

Not me, Eula Lura thought. I had me a good man that treated me nice and took care not to hurt my feelings, and stood tall. She picked up the empty straw basket at her feet and headed back to the quiet kitchen.

She loved it when the family was gone, when she was all alone with her thoughts, at home with the echoes of kitchen scents: Crisco and the last meal's lingering. On the Fourth of July, though, the quiet was demolished.

It began when Miss Lucille delivered a very intoxicated Miss Pearl from the festivities at the lake house. Miss Pearl was stumbling, sobbing, and cursing Jack Lacey for all he was worth.

"Help me get her in the tub, won't you, LittleBit?" Miss Lucille looked very old at that moment, tired, almost feeble.

"You go on to bed," Eula Lura said. "I'll take care of Miss Pearl before I go tend to Mama."

Miss Lucille gave her weak smile, then a look of utter surrender. "Grief is an awful beast when it's not tamed."

Eula Lura drew some bath water and sat with Miss Pearl, who, between slurred mumblings and periods when she nodded off from the alcohol, sketched a picture of what had happened at the lake that day, how her husband had bought a house overlooking the place where Elizabeth had killed herself.

Eula Lura studied the white lady, passed out in the tub, tinted hair tousled and damp, arms limp in the water, steam rising. She had always thought of Miss Pearl as a heartless woman, but at this moment she could not help feeling a seed of compassion. She looked at the thinning hair between the woman's legs, the aging stretch marks creeping across her stomach. Miss Pearl always kept herself shut off from life, did not know how to live, was as crippled as Hotshot in her own way. And when she lost her only child, she was forever frozen in that shut-away despair. Yes, Eula Lura thought, reaching for the drain plug, then making to get a towel and a nightgown and put the pitiful thing to bed, grief is an awful beast.

*

That slut of a girl had really done it, finally, just like he always figured she would. Not only would she never live up to Elizabeth Lacey's potential, but Jolene's daughter had also revealed herself as a cheap piece of ass, just like her mama, just like his own mama. And in the ensuing maelstrom, Royce had reason to believe that Victor Tolbert was onto him.

He was in the jail talking to a prisoner when he heard the ruckus from the Tolbert residence, such a commotion of cussing and crashing he felt he had to check it out, as an officer of the law if not for satisfaction of his own curiosity.

Jolene sat at the kitchen table, Coy's head buried in her lap. Leo hung back in the doorway, eyes wide as his daddy hollered at the girl, Roxy, who sat on the floor, where she had been thrown, no doubt. Victor's leg was reared back to kick her when Royce made his presence known. "You ain't going to beat that girl."

"You got no business here," Tolbert snarled. "Get the hell out."

"Nope. Can't let you beat that young 'un no more."

Tolbert gave him a look, up, down, up, eyes narrowed. "You ain't got no business here. You done took what's mine already, and you know it."

Royce sensed a look of brought-up-sharp fear from Jolene but did not dare make eye contact with her, decided to play it hard and tough. "You're full of shit."

"Am I?"

"Full of shit and crazy to boot," Royce said, wondering if Victor knew about him and Jolene.

"You know what you took and I, by God, aim to have it back."

"You ain't making a damn bit of sense. I ain't done nothing to you. But I'm damn sure taking that young 'un out of here if you don't leave her the hell alone."

"Or what?"

"Or I go get Jack Lacey, have him take another look at your suitability as an employee. Then we'll lock you up in your own goddamn jail." Royce let the significance of the words sink in before he added, "Unless you stop pounding on the girl, that is."

"Listen to him, Victor," Jolene said, faint-voiced and trembly.

"You keep your opinions to yourself, woman!"

She shrank back in the chair. Coy emitted some little sniffling sounds.

Royce made to defend her, but stopped, thinking the gesture would only confirm for Victor the relationship Royce had with his wife. "Should I go after Jack now?"

"I ain't afraid of Sheriff Lacey. You think I give a care?"

"I think you'd give a care if you had to go looking for work right in through now."

Victor stared at him, a jaw-working gaze full of spit and venom, for seconds piled upon seconds. For a moment Royce expected him to strike, and he felt his arms tense, ready to strike back. "What's it going to be? Do right or do unemployment?" Royce asked.

"Goddammit!" Victor drew his foot back again and drove it into the Sheetrock next to Roxy, who let out a scream. Then the jailer snatched up a set of car keys from the table. "I'm going out," he said, loud and defiant.

"That's a good idea," Royce said. "You go cool off, huh?"

"Maybe I will," Victor answered. "Or maybe I'll go pound on something else." He gave Royce a significant look. "Something like what you done took from me." Then he slammed out the side door, revved the engine of the Plymouth, and thundered it down the narrow driveway.

Leo leaned on the door frame. "I hate him," he said.

"Hush up talking about your daddy thataway," Jolene hissed. Coy stood and went over to the counter, opened a bag of Sunbeam bread, took out a slice, and pressed it into a ball. He began to lick it, grinning.

Royce looked at the girl. She still sat on the floor, knees drawn up, head down. He mulled over what in the hell her daddy meant by the vague accusations aimed at him. He glanced at Jolene and noticed for the first time that she held a knot of material in her fist.

"That it?" Royce asked. He had already heard the tale. It had been circulated through the courthouse that Thursday and spilled out across Sumner, how the jailer's girl had worn a bikini bathing suit up at Lake Blackshear, how she had gotten drunk and gang-fucked a bunch of older boys.

Jolene nodded, holding up the two flimsy pieces of the blue gingham swimsuit. Then she dropped her hands back to her lap.

"Girl, you ought to know if you put on a thing like that, it's going to draw trouble."

Roxy looked up at him with an impassive gaze. Her forehead was bleeding and her left eye was already swelling up into what would be a hell of a shiner.

"I want you to go next door and get yourself tended to. Leo, you get on out of the house, go to town or something," Royce went on. "Take your brother Coy round back and get Hotshot to carry him up in the clock tower for a while and watch the gears. But you," he said to Roxy. "I want you to go over to the Lacey house and get somebody to tend to your cuts."

"My mama will do that," she said. "Won't you, Mama?" Her voice came out small and childlike, like she was pleading for something, something faint and faraway he could not identify.

Jolene looked at Royce, then Roxy, then back at Royce. All the while her fingers tickled the fabric of the blue bikini. "Royce?" she finally whispered.

"You do like I say, Roxy," he said. "Go to the Laceys'. They'll tend to you. I got some things to talk over with your mama. Run on, now."

When Roxy stood he could see more skinned places on her body, across her knees, where she had been slung into walls, onto the floor. She wore only a white bra and panties, did not try to cover herself. She stood for a moment, staring at her mother, something like surrender taking her eyes. Her shoulders seemed to drop, just a faint fraction of a degree, as she turned and walked out of the room, Royce watching her move, enjoying every inch of her flesh, every curve. Finally he spoke. "You reckon he knows?"

"I don't see how," she answered, still fingering the bathing suit.

"You got yourself one crazy husband."

She sighed. "I wish it was anybody but him. I wish it was you."

"Shit. I ain't a husband kind of a man. Got no use for a wife all the time underfoot."

She looked wounded for a second, then a slip of a smile came to her lips. "You're probably right."

Royce thought about the girl, Roxy, how damp her body had been the day he drove her and the Lacey kid back from Albany, how full and soft those breasts promised to be. He thought of her standing there in her white panties, and the faint taste of Elizabeth's lips came to his, a pulse of desire to the rhythm in his chest. He walked over to Jolene, took her hand, and pressed her palm to his khaki pants, to the beat of his pulse. "Well?" he said. "Ain't you going to put that thing on?"

She nodded. He clasped her hand with his, pulling her to her feet. Then he led her through the doorway and down the back hall to the little cellar. He latched the door behind them and turned to her, standing before him in the dirt-shrouded room, where roots and cobwebs mingled their tendrils in damp corners where the stone walls met.

*

A week after the Fourth of July party, after Roxy temporarily wrecked their friendship, Martin Luther King, Jr. was back in Albany, just as Asa said he would be, to serve jail time for the march back in December. The black community was in an uproar, Miss Pearl said, injecting a new bitterness into everything she saw. And though he did not speak with an angry tone, Kansas's Daddy Jack said he did not think the jail sentence would pass without incident. He said the law enforcement officials in Albany expected several marches that might not unfold as calmly as previous ones had. But they would probably be calmer, Kansas thought, still awash in humiliation, than the repercussions following the Fourth of July holiday.

After the lot of them clambered out of the boat, Daddy Jack had walked Roxy up to the house with Kansas following behind, the adults clustered in little groups, whispering, throwing them shocked and disapproving glances, some wearing outright stares of condemnation. As if that were not bad enough, Roxy steadily yelled at them, challenging their judgment of her.

"Why are you looking at me?" she yelled at no one in particular, while Daddy Jack shushed her in his gentle way, which did no good whatsoever. "I can wear anything I want! I can be anything I want! I can be as good as you! I'm going to be a doctor!" She yelled all the way to the house, where she disintegrated into a drunken crying jag before spending the rest of the evening on the upstairs bathroom floor, Kansas charged with seeing she did not choke.

The boys' parents were called, punishments to be meted out, but Daddy said he would wait and tell Roxy's daddy when they went home the next day. In the meantime, the girls were to go nowhere near the boat, were to clean the house and yard after the party, and as for any future plans, well, we'll see.

The second major repercussion of the holiday was Miss Pearl's slip into a strange new nothingness tinged with anger. It started, however, with uncharacteristic acrimony—with a rare and tempestuous argument and Daddy Jack's refusal to be her indentured servant any longer. And Kansas overheard it all, rooting for him the whole time.

Immediately following the bikini incident, Miss Pearl had Miss Lucille drive her home. Kansas did not see her until she and Daddy Jack got home the next day, and Miss Pearl launched into a screaming fit as soon as they walked in the door.

"How dare you take me to that place? How dare you when you know that was where Elizabeth took her life? How could you put me through that yet again? You are the most self-centered, inconsiderate, cruel—"

"That's enough, Miss Pearl. Kansas, go outside." It was an odd tone of voice Daddy Jack used, much more commanding than the deferential one he usually offered his wife. Kansas walked out onto the front porch and closed the door. Miss Pearl's bedroom window butted up to the side of the porch, though, and she could hear every word, clear and cutting.

"You are a deceptive man, Jack Lacey. To put me in the proximity of that tainted place."

"It's just a place, Miss Pearl. And it's not tainted. It's just a very significant place. Elizabeth—"

"Don't talk to me about Elizabeth."

"She was a joy. She was tormented, too, just like—" He hesitated.

"Me? Just like me, you were going to say? You think I did it to her, don't
you?"

"No one did it to—"

"Stop! Don't speak of it! Just tell me why you deceived me into being
near that place."

"I didn't mean to be dishonest. I just thought you would be more
receptive to it if you didn't know where we were in relation to—"

"Liar! I will never forgive you."

Kansas let her back slide down against the wall, dropping into a sitting
position.

"Try to understand."

"Understand lies? Understand deception?"

Silence, then, "Understand me."

"You are my husband. I thought I did understand you."

"Not enough, Miss Pearl. I need you to understand more. I've kept it
to myself for so long."

"What? What in the name of Jesus are you talking about?"

"About how much I've missed my little girl."

"Don't speak of it."

"I have to."

"Why?"

"You have to try to understand, Miss Pearl. You've never even been to
the cemetery with me. Mama and I tend to her grave, keep fresh flowers on
it. You haven't been there since the funeral. It's been all these years."

"Why does it matter? Do you not care what it does to me, to be in a
graveyard? I feel as if those places want to swallow me up."

"It matters to me that we acknowledge her together."

"They wait for me. The dead. They snatch at me. They want me. They
want to swallow me under."

"It's just a place, the cemetery. Where I wish you would go with me."

"I cannot put myself through that pain."

"To see—to acknowledge our girl."

"It hurts too much!"

"She was *our* girl. Not mine. *Ours*."

"I can't!" Miss Pearl screamed.

"And I understand that, Miss Pearl. I do. And I thought the place—the lake place would be a way to—" He seemed to be struggling for words. "A way to—acknowledge her, with you beside me—without you having to be aware. Without the pain. I hoped you—I didn't ever think you would know the name of that little creek."

"But I had it thrown in my face, didn't I? And you did put me through the pain of it. You did it, all over again."

"Miss Pearl, I'm so sorry. I've always tried to do right by you."

"Have you?"

"Tried to do right by you, and right by any other obligations I owe."

"Do not speak of that, either!" Another screaming tone. Kansas drew her knees up to her chest and leaned her head back on the wall.

"I'm sorry, Miss Pearl. But I have tried to do right by you, even with this lake place."

"Then why?"

"I don't know how else to say it. I need to feel that you are with me, that we recognize Elizabeth's presence together, have someplace to go to where I can feel a little bit of that. That need won't go away. It hasn't in all these years."

"It might not go away, but I want that lake house to go away. Immediately."

There was a long silence then. Kansas held her breath, thinking, No, Daddy. That is a place I can love with you. I'll recognize my mama with you. Maybe, one day, we can even talk about her, together. Pinky always said Miss Pearl was a cold woman, and it was never more apparent to Kansas than right now, hearing her grandmother demand that her grandfather give up a way he had found, a way that gave him comfort and even pleasure, to be near his only child.

"I'm afraid I can't do that. I won't ask you to go up there with me, but I hope you will sometime. I hope you will come to that decision."

It was the first time Kansas ever heard Daddy Jack refuse Miss Pearl something, and the next sound she heard was of shattering glass and the most venomous, shrill-toned shriek she could imagine. "Get out of here! Don't ever come back in this room!"

More silence, then footfalls. Kansas sat still and waited until the footsteps left the bedroom, went through the living room, then the dining room, then down the back hallway and out the screen door. That was when Miss Pearl let out a great, anguished howl, slammed the bedroom door hard enough to rattle the pictures on the living room wall, and began to wail the most guttural, moaning cries Kansas had ever heard.

As if that were not enough, Roxy came tapping at her own bedroom window a short while later. Kansas was in her room writing about the bitter argument when she pulled the curtain back to see Roxy's battered face. All the resentment and intentions she had of punishing her friend went right out of her. She ran out the back door and around the side of the house to see about her, knowing exactly what had happened.

LittleBit took Roxy into the black-and-white-tiled bathroom and doctored the cuts on her face, allowing that no man ought to do such a thing to a child, no matter what.

"I hate him," Roxy said.

"Hate will suck the life out of you," LittleBit said as she dabbed peroxide on the girl's forehead.

"That's what Pinky says, too." Kansas sat on the edge of the bathtub, watching. LittleBit's hands were gentle on the bruises, and Roxy hardly flinched at all.

"And Dr. King," the woman said. "'Love your enemies' is what he preaches, just like Jesus did."

"How is Roxy supposed to love her daddy when he treats her so bad?"

"I don't know," LittleBit said. "But I'm coming to see there's a victory in it."

"I want to fight him back," Roxy said, "but he would kill me."

"Then rise above," LittleBit said. "Make something of yourself."

"I will. I am." But Roxy's voice did not have the conviction it carried the previous summer.

"Don't be saying one thing and doing another, girl."

"Nobody believes me."

"I believe you," Kansas said, even though her feelings were all shifted around.

LittleBit put a Band-Aid on the cut, gave the girl an ice pack for her swelling eye, and they went in the kitchen for Popsicles. Kansas sucked on a cherry-flavored one. "Scratchy Branch is where my mama shot herself. I overheard Miss Pearl say so when she was yelling at Daddy Jack."

"God, Kansas," Roxy gasped. "That's so weird. That explains how you felt creepy when you fell that day."

LittleBit smirked. "Your mama ain't the only ghost in them waters."

Kansas leaned forward. "What does that mean?"

"Y'all take them icicles and get on out from underfoot."

"Come on, LittleBit. You can't dangle things out there and snatch them back."

"Yeah," Roxy echoed.

"I reckon I can, too." LittleBit picked up a fly flap and slapped at their legs. "Now get on."

The two girls ran giggling from the kitchen and into Kansas's room, where they spent the afternoon listening to records, talking on the Princess phone, and pretending nothing whatsoever had happened to change things between them. And the Lacey family did the same, going through the motions, the routines, the same conversations. They ignored the change in Miss Pearl, glossed over it by living life as usual. It was strange, Kansas thought, how her folks hid behind dinner-table talk, not acknowledging that Miss Pearl was drunk or mumbling or stumbling to her room, not reacting to the harsh way she spoke to her husband these days.

"Pinky said the trouble in Albany was bound to come and right as rain," Kansas said, as the family sat in the dining room, eating supper, discussing the matter over roast beef and asparagus tips.

"Maybe it is," her grandfather said.

"Of course it is," Grandemona said, "but it should at least be kept civilized."

"Why?" Kansas asked. "When they're civilized, like at Tift Park, they get hauled away and then ignored. I liked those boys that went over the fence. That's the way to get your point over."

Grandemona chuckled. "Maybe so. But I don't mean things like crashing swimming clubs as all that uncivilized. I mean acts of violence."

Miss Pearl had not said much, had instead been sitting in silence, staring at her plate, groggy-eyed. LittleBit said she was on some kind of medicine to calm her, but it only seemed to make her mood move from detached to irritable and back again. "But that is their nature," she mumbled, reaching for her glass of brandy, taking a wobbly sip.

"Do you want to lie down, Miss Pearl?" Kansas's grandfather asked his wife.

"They are from the jungles," Miss Pearl continued, "so it is in their nature to carry on like savages."

"My goodness, Pearl," Grandemona said. "You don't mean that."

"Pinky and LittleBit don't act like savages," Kansas said.

"Let's hope nobody acts that way in the next few days," Daddy Jack said, "because the Dougherty County sheriff's office told me to have jail space available just in case. Got several county jails lined up."

"Really?" Kansas felt a surge of excitement. She wanted to run and tell Pinky about the guests LittleBit might be feeding in the coming days. Pinky would be pleased about that.

"It's just more of the same strategy the Albany folks use," Daddy Jack said. "The protesters will assume they can wear down the city by filling up the jails to the bursting point, keep marching in waves. But with all the jails they got lined up, like mine, won't none of them fill to overflow. And the press won't cover it much, either."

Kansas sipped her iced tea. "That's what Asa said, and it's not fair. Why don't they just go ahead and put pavement on those roads like the colored folks want?"

"I'll tell you who's a savage," Miss Pearl slurred. "Those Tolbert children. All four of them." She stared at her husband. "All of them. And their mother. And that Eula Lura. All savages." She reached for her glass and knocked it over, a splash of brandy washing over her plate.

"Goodness, Jack," Grandemona said. "Get her to bed."

"I don't want to." Miss Pearl slurred.

Kansas watched as her husband took her by the arm. "Come on, Miss Pearl. You've been into a little too much brandy today."

"I'm not intoxicated," Miss Pearl slurred. "And you may not sleep with me, not in my bed."

He helped her stand. She swayed and looked at Kansas. "Elizabeth, look what you've done," she said.

"Ma'am?"

"Look what you've done now."

Kansas watched her grandfather lead his wife out of the room, heard the bedroom door open, a swish of blankets, the hum of the air conditioner. "What's wrong with Miss Pearl?" she asked Grandemona.

The old woman sighed. "Having a bad day. And more bad days coming, I'm afraid."

"What do you mean?" Kansas pressed.

"Nothing, Sugar." She put her fingers to her temple and rubbed small circles for a moment. Then she sighed. "You want some more roast, Sugar?" she asked.

Kansas suddenly felt closed-in and suffocating in the large dining room, all the sad feelings of her relatives wrapping around her. Kansas loved them because they were blood, the blood that was passed down to her mama and into her, yet she did not feel a strong connection with them. It was Pinky and Aunt Frances who held her spirit safe. And maybe LittleBit would, too.

"I want to go outside," she said.

"You haven't let Miss Pearl upset you?"

"No. I just want to be outside. I'm going on a play-out."

"All right. Just don't be past ten; I don't believe your daddy is going to blow the siren tonight. He'll probably go to bed soon."

"But not with Miss Pearl," Kansas said.

"Kansas, that's not very—" She sighed again. "No. Not with Miss Pearl." Then she stood and began collecting the dishes.

Kansas wandered out on the back porch. She should go visit Pinky, lay her head on the old woman's chest and talk it all over. She felt bad that she had not visited her since before the Fourth of July. She would go over in a while, she told herself. For right now she just wanted to be by herself, just sit in the shade of the fig tree, the womb of branches and leaves that had hidden her with her wonderings so often, her place of security.

She lounged beneath the limbs for a long time, while the sunset took the air into gradations of grainy dimness. The damp scent of black dirt made her think of the places underneath Pinky's house, where Kansas and Pinky's granddaughter Bernice had played when they were very small. Bernice had been dimpled and giggly, full of energy and squeals of glee as they played. She tried to remember why they stopped being playmates around the age of nine or ten, and decided it was simply that they drifted more completely into separate worlds, that there were unspoken rules to be followed, just like the way she had felt at Tift Park.

She watched as Hotshot walked out of the jailhouse carrying the tins and trays he would rinse off with cold water from the hose pipe before carrying them to the jailer's kitchen, where he would wash them with soap, then set them on the back porch of the jail. Then the routine would begin again, when he would bring the tins over to the Lacey house to collect the next meal. There was a certain comfort in the routine, the predictability, the lack of a thing out of left field knocking you senseless.

She thought about Roxy, how hard it must be to live with that mean daddy of hers, mean one day and nice the next, carrying her to Albany to the picture show. Roxy did not have a comfortable routine. Maybe she shouldn't be too hard on Roxy. Maybe Roxy was struggling to do the best she could. Maybe with Kansas's help Roxy could prove all the adults wrong, the ones who said she would get pregnant and never amount to more than a baby maker.

"I want to show you something." Leo caught her hands, pulling her from where she sat beneath the fig leaves.

"What?"

"Just be quiet," he snapped, "and come with me."

They crept through the dark that was just past dusk, toward the jail-house yard.

"Where—" Kansas breathed.

"Shhhh!" He motioned her to follow as he entered the back stairwell of the jail through the door that remained open during the summer's hottest heat. A few steps up to the first barred door, they heard the male prisoners' conversations humming and lilting through the iron slats. Leo flattened his back against the opposite wall of the stairwell, easing up the brick steps. He put a finger to his lips and she followed his lead. The stairs zigged, then zagged, toward the second floor. Just as they zagged, she could hear it, a heavy, rhythmic, grunting exhalation, as if one were being punched repeatedly in the stomach, and a slapping, sucking sound. She hesitated, but Leo clutched her wrist, eyes warning her not to cry out. The grunting came louder and quicker now. They stepped up the last increments of the bricks.

Angel's cell was angularly framed by the doorway, steel bars slashing the picture into six-inch segments. Yet the picture they saw was clear: Angel, the perpetrator of first-degree assault, who had burned her husband with grits and scarred herself as well, lying naked on her back on the unyielding bunk, Victor Tolbert on top of her, knees cocked, pounding into her with all his strength and speed, groaning raspy growls into her neck. And all the while, Angel's arm, draped over the side of the bunk, a burning cigarette clamped between two fingers, never lifted to her lips. And her one good eye, the other being scarred into blindness, riveted into a blank nothingness from an expressionless face.

Kansas stumbled back down the steps, feeling sick, finding herself standing in front of Hotshot's unlocked cell. He was sitting on his cot, tapping a rhythm on his thighs, humming a beat with his breath. He looked up at her and grinned. She thought of a hamster inside a wheel, little legs scampering, cage rattling, while the tiny rodent turned the wheel around and around and around as it ran, never arriving, always spinning. Stuck. She heard Leo's feet on the concrete behind her, so she turned to the back door of the building, wanting Pinky.

When they emerged from the jail, Kansas punched Leo three times in the back. "Why did you take me in there?"

He whirled around and punched her back, hard, on her upper arm, then into her chest, connecting with her left breast and a searing flash of pain. "I told you I would prove it to you," he yelled, "and I did!"

"Prove what?" she demanded, slapping him again.

"That I know what it is. I know Mr. Royce pokes my mama just like my daddy was doing that nigger." He drew back to punch her again.

"Stop it!" she said, crossing her arms across her chest, protective but determined not to be intimidated by him any more. "I don't care about that. It's nasty. And don't you lay a hand on me, Leo Tolbert." She narrowed her eyes into her meanest look and he dropped his fist. "Your daddy might beat you and he might beat your mama, but don't you ever touch me like that again."

"What'll you do about it?"

"I'll tell my Daddy Jack, and he'll come and see you."

"My daddy is right," Leo spat out. "All you Laceys think you're better than everybody, but you're a bunch of looneys."

"Shut up, Leo."

"Like your crazy whore of a mama."

"Shut up, Leo!"

"Now you see what she done. Just like that nigger whore up there in the jail."

Kansas shoved him aside. "I hate your guts, Leo."

"See if I care." And he picked up a handful of small pebbles and began to hurl them at her, one at a time, as she ran toward the Lacey home, then past it, to Pinky's house, where the lights were unusually bright and a small knot of ladies from Pinky's church whispered to Pruella.

"Pinky gone, child," Pruella said in a gentle tone. "Gone home to Jesus. LittleBit inside tending to her."

Kansas stood helpless, arms dangling at her sides, a fresh bruise on the inside walls of her chest taking her wind. She gazed at a girl on the porch she knew to be the Bernice of her childhood, Pruella's daughter, blood kin to Pinky. Kansas nodded to the girl and the girl nodded back, then went inside to where LittleBit's form threw long shadows against the wall as she sponged off her mama's body. Kansas turned, lifting her face to look up at Grandemona's big white house as she approached it, her home, a crypt for the lifeless and the leavings of the dead.

LittleBit and Kansas watched the paddy wagons roll into town the next day—three of them, loaded with folks arrested in the Albany march and in scattered incidents around the city. It had come over Sheriff Lacey's shortwave that morning: a batch of prisoners was on the way to Blackshear County. Mr. Jack was calm, determined to go by the book, he said, and do right by the demonstrators; Miss Pearl was mortified and carried a bottle of peach brandy to her room to be alone with her outrage and her shame; and Miss Lucille was having palpitations over the prospect of a full jailhouse of hungry folks.

LittleBit and Kansas were standing out back of Pinky's house, watering her flowers. LittleBit wanted to keep them fresh and full-bloomed so she could arrange some bouquets for her mama's funeral in five days. Pinky's body had been carried by the undertaker to Cheatham Brothers, the colored funeral parlor, early that morning, and LittleBit was trying to fill the day with small chores related to her mother's passing, when she heard about the approaching prisoners. She knew right away what she would do.

Kansas was quiet and subdued, and LittleBit knew she would be grieving hard for Pinky, the mama they shared. Kansas had grieved hard for Elizabeth, too, burrowing her way into Pinky's bed, snuggling her way into Pinky's heart, giggling her way into Pinky's soul. But as much as LittleBit resented the girl over the years, she couldn't help feeling for her now. After all, LittleBit had herself a mama for all these years, and Kansas only had Elizabeth for five years, on and off, depending upon Elizabeth's state of mind. She'd had Pinky for only twelve-plus years. It was bound to be a spirit-breaking thing, unless there was some kind of strength offered to her. LittleBit wanted to comfort the child in some way but did not feel equipped, did not know how to give such a thing. So she asked Kansas to water the zinnias.

As they stepped around to the back of the house, spraying the hose pipe into the clumps of orange and hot pink blooms, Kansas pointed. "Look there!"

A police car led each of the three paddy wagons down the paved road that wound around to the back of the jail. Blue lights flashed. Zinnia blooms nodded in the spray.

"It's the Albany folks," LittleBit said. "A mess of them."

"Daddy said just yesterday he might have some extra folks in the jail."

"Looks like he does," LittleBit said, running grocery lists in her head like crazy. She had never cooked for more than a dozen prisoners at one time, and even that was a rare case. Here there could be no telling how many.

"Yesterday seems like such a long time ago," Kansas said, her voice trembling.

"Today's what's going to be a long time. Looks like I'm going to need to go fetch some food."

"But LittleBit, you have to go tend to Pinky's funeral arrangements. You can't stop to work on something as big as this. I bet Grandemona can find somebody else to help her."

"Arrangements done been made," LittleBit said. "Just waiting for the wake to make up. A few folks coming in to town."

"It wouldn't be fair to ask you to cook so much right now."

"It's a blessing," LittleBit replied.

They watched across the yard as the paddy wagons emptied their cargo. Royce Fitzhugh was there. He and Victor Tolbert showed the Albany police officers where to take the prisoners. It was quite a group, over twenty, LittleBit figured. It was mostly young men, including one white one, and a few colored girls.

"Them babies must be scared," she said. "Toted off to another town to be put in a jail."

"Why did you say it's a blessing?"

"It's a blessing to me, to have a thing like this to fill the time. Mama would want me to feed them young 'uns good."

"So you'll be cooking all day?"

"Long as they're here. I'll cook twenty-four hours per if it's called for."

"What about Pinky's wake?"

"Girl, don't you remember what Pinky said about the Albany doings?"

"Said it was bound to come and right as rain."

"You think she'd want me to let them eat weenies and peanut butter and jelly sandwiches?"

"No."

"Then I need to go and help Miss Lucille make up a shopping list."

"Will you let me help you in the kitchen?"

"I reckon." LittleBit looked down at the girl. Lord, she was an awkward thing, but with the potential for prettiness. In fact, here was a thing LittleBit had not noticed all summer, so maybe it had just now sprung into the spirit of Elizabeth's daughter. "I see the look of a young lady in your eyes," she said to Kansas.

"Really?"

"Yes, I do."

"Maybe it's just sadness," Kansas said.

"Pinky don't want you to be sad. She's with Jesus."

"I know she is, but—"

LittleBit threw her a sharp glance. "You ain't going to talk misery are you?"

Kansas looked deflated. "No."

LittleBit groped for something more comforting to say. The girl seemed wounded by her sharp words. The best she could do was, "You want to help me make that list?"

Kansas nodded, went over to the water spigot, and turned it off. Then they walked toward the big house, watching the lawmen one backyard over ushering the group of young people into the jail.

"We might help Hotshot deliver these meals," LittleBit said. "Deliver them in person."

"Pinky would like that," Kansas said.

"Yes," LittleBit replied. "She would. She damn sure would."

As they walked toward the kitchen door, the back of her hand brushed against Kansas's much smaller one. Again, LittleBit felt the urge to reach out to her, to honor her mama's wishes that she be a help to the girl. She strained to think how to take the girl's hand, pull her up next to her, and let her grieve however she wanted to. Kansas was a good child, after all, seemed to mean well just about all the time. It was wrong of her to begrudge Kansas her touch, the extension of Pinky's soul, so needed. She tried again to will her hand to catch hold of Kansas's hand, there on the back porch of the big, dreary-feeling Lacey home. She imagined her fingers curling about Kansas's palm, soothing her hurts, maybe soothing both of their hurts. But it was a thing that was, for the time being, out of her grasp, and the screen door smacked shut on that solitary, elusive moment.

*

The cooking was nonstop, and Miss Lucille was tired out in no time, but LittleBit was in a culinary frenzy. It was, indeed, her way of honoring her mother, Kansas thought, so she fell in beside the big colored woman she loved, not as an extension of Pinky, and not as a substitute, but as one she sensed had a wounded heart that might be able to love her back eventually.

Pinky had gone peacefully, LittleBit said. She seemed to know it was her time, and asked for Pruella and LittleBit to sit with her until the death angel came, at twilight. "I seen the life go right out of her body. It's a thing you can see. And she was smiling in her sleep, right up until the breath was drawed up in that angel, the one that carried her home."

"I wanted to see her again," Kansas said. "I was going to visit her."

"That's all right. Pinky knew. She could see everything, right into your heart, in her last bit of time. She allowed as much."

"She asked for me?" Kansas hoped Pinky had not asked for her and been disappointed. The image of Victor Tolbert on top of the scarred prisoner strobed in her head.

"Said to tell you to be the lady you was born to be, in spite of your folks. Said she would let love rain down on you from heaven."

Still, Kansas felt prickles of guilt rush over her. "But I didn't see her enough."

"You ain't going to do that, ain't going to feel bad."

"But—"

LittleBit spoke sharply. "No, you ain't. We've got too much to do around here. If you want to mope, go mope in your room."

"I don't want to mope. But I can't help it."

"You can help it by helping me. What you going to do?"

And Kansas knew LittleBit was right. Pinky would want her to help and to celebrate what they were doing, a thing of value, so she joined in all the tasks. They hurled themselves into the chores. They rolled dough, sliced onions, patted mounds of ground beef into loaves, and mashed potatoes, making ready for Hotshot's mountain of empty tins. LittleBit hummed and smoked Picayunes and showed her how to dust the biscuits with a dry mist of flour, how to glaze the meatloaf with ketchup dashed with molasses.

The family ate early, and the late afternoon faded into evening, but Hotshot's footfalls did not drift up from the back porch. Daddy watched the five o'clock news, and what little coverage the Albany Movement folks got was about bottle-throwing Negroes and acts of violence. In a while Miss Pearl stumbled to her room and Miss Lucille was bound for bed as well. The food warmed in the oven and still Hotshot did not come.

"What done got into him?" LittleBit complained. "These loafs is going to be all dried out and not fit to eat."

"You want me to go get him?" Kansas asked.

But before LittleBit could answer, they heard a pounding of feet and deep-voiced moans and whimpers. The back porch door slammed and the house shook as Hotshot ran up the back hallway.

"What in the name of Moses?" LittleBit said.

"What's going on?" Kansas's Daddy Jack came through the swinging door just as Hotshot stumbled in from the hall, his mouth pouring blood, face all knuckle-cut from an awful beating. He collapsed onto the floor, leaning his back against the refrigerator.

"Lord Almighty," LittleBit breathed. She wet a dish towel and squatted down beside him.

Hotshot began to sob, wincing when LittleBit dabbed at the blood on his face, and again, when she lifted his shirt to examine his rib cage. Daddy Jack took his gun out of its holster and fed some bullets into the chamber. "We got trouble at the jail?" he asked Hotshot.

The man on the floor nodded.

Kansas kneeled. "What happened, Hotshot? Who did it?"

The man did not answer, only sobbed, "I told him. I told him."

"Who?" Jack asked. "Victor Tolbert?"

"Mr. Royce," Hotshot blubbered. "I told him to please don't whup that white boy."

"Goddamn that sorry son of a bitch," Daddy Jack thundered, stomping out of the kitchen, toward the back door.

Kansas had never seen her grandfather lose control of his temper, and her expression must have said so. She felt LittleBit's hand on her arm, as if to say it was all right.

"Hold this on your mouth, boy," LittleBit said, "and stay put. I'm going to tend to you in a spell. But right now me and Kansas are going to fetch them trays and feed them poor folks up in the jail."

Hotshot's eyes were full of fear. "No! Mr. Royce!"

But LittleBit slid an orange Popsicle out of the freezer and pushed the icy treat through its wrapping. "Mr. Jack will be done settled him down by the time we get there," she said, smiling at Kansas. "Don't you worry none about it. Just suck on this here icicle till I get back. The cold will feel good on that busted lip."

Kansas let LittleBit's smile comfort her, calm her, immediately feeling a surge of excitement, anxious to get to the jailhouse to see what was going on, even though, "Daddy Jack might get mad if—"

"Shoot," LittleBit said. "I might get mad, too, if them folks don't get their food."

"Why would Mr. Royce hurt Hotshot?" Kansas asked as they walked fast across the backyard.

LittleBit breathed an angry laugh. "That man ain't nothing but meanness, all the time after your mama."

"To court her?"

"To use her the way men do girls, sometimes."

"I don't like the way he looks at Roxy. And Leo said he thought Mr. Royce was poking his mama."

"That a fact?"

"Yes."

"Then Leo's smarter than I ever give him credit to be."

"It's true?"

"Shh!"

Angry shouts drifted from the first floor of the jail as they approached, and LittleBit held Kansas back at the door. "Wait till the fuss dies down."

"He come up in my jail to get a piece of the boy," Victor Tolbert was saying. "Don't nobody run this jailhouse but me."

"Shut your goddamn mouth!" Royce yelled. "If I didn't do it, you was going to later. You said as much."

"No such of a goddamn thing!"

Kansas peered through the screen, looking down the corridor between the rows of cells, each cell holding four or five prisoners, teenagers and girls, plus a couple of older gentlemen and one elderly lady she had not noticed before, all of whom watched the scene play out in silence. The cell at the far end of the corridor, to the right of the corridor, was open. That was where Mr. Royce and Victor were, a blood-stained piece of clothing at their feet. Three colored boys stood near the open cell door, and a blonde-haired white boy sat on the bunk, shirtless, his mouth bloodied. The prisoners all looked like they could be football players, broad-shouldered and muscular. One of the colored boys, in fact, wore a football jersey that read "Tuskegee Institute."

"Who opened the cell?" Daddy Jack demanded.

"I did," Victor said. "To put Randall there back inside. Goddamn

Royce had him out here on the floor, whupping him good."

"And the only reason you pulled me off is so your boys could have him later!" Mr. Royce yelled.

"You a lie!"

"Shut up!" Daddy said. "Tolbert, close the cell door. Now."

"Get back," the jailer said to the colored boys, then slammed the door shut and turned the key.

"You, there. Randall?" Daddy spoke to the white boy.

"Yes, sir."

"We'll take care of you in just a minute. As soon as I figure out what these goddamn fools are talking about."

"Yes, sir."

Kansas studied the white boy, envious of his conviction, his willingness to break the unspoken rules, wishing she were more like that. She wanted to be brave and confident, to speak up for herself, to do something that mattered.

Her grandfather spoke again. "So, Victor, you had plans for Randall yonder?"

"Naw, Sheriff, all I was doing was—"

"Yes, you goddamn sure did!" Mr. Royce yelled. "Said you was bringing the Early County 'hey boys' up to work him over and for me to get the hell out of y'all's way!"

"That true, Victor?" Jack said. He stood with his back to the door, hand resting on the holster. Kansas noticed through the screen that his gray hair was thinning.

"Hell, no! Royce is a goddamn lie. Ain't never been no more than a goddamn lie."

Mr. Royce bowed up at Victor but Daddy Jack stepped toward the two men. "I'm just before throwing both of you in a cell. Now goddammit, settle down or I will!"

Kansas put her hand around LittleBit's forearm, afraid of the threatening words, afraid her grandfather would be hurt and then what? She looked again at the folks in the cells, and her gaze caught a few returned glances. She thought they must be terrified, especially the elderly woman, who was probably someone's grandmother who went to church and knitted and never had a minute's trouble with the law. She thought of the lady in the black straw hat walking up an Albany street last December. Then she thought of Pinky.

"He's a thief, too," Victor went on. "A motherfucking thief done took something of mine."

"Who's the liar?" Mr. Royce said.

"The one that's a thief, that's who."

"Piece of shit," Mr. Royce spat.

"Took my goddamn thumb. I know he did! He—" Victor stopped himself then, and a look of caught-in-the-act took his face.

"What's that?" Daddy Jack said.

"You goddamn lying moron," Mr. Royce said.

"What's that you just said?" Daddy repeated. Some of the prisoners whispered and murmured to one another. Kansas thought she heard one of them sigh, "Lord Almighty."

Kansas gripped LittleBit's arm tighter, continuing to watch the back of her grandfather's head. "This is a thing we're going to get to the bottom of, right now," he said.

"I ain't took nothing, Sheriff."

"Goddamn sure did," Victor spat out. "Leo seen it. It's in his desk drawer."

Leo. They had slipped up the staircase and seen his daddy on top of a colored prisoner. And the woman just lay there, as if it were a thing she had learned to wait out, disengage from, until the next time. Kansas felt the same nausea she felt the night before. Victor Tolbert was nasty, and she would tell her Daddy about it, ask LittleBit to help her find the right words. Then her attention went to Mr. Royce, whose face was red with rage, the knuckles of his right hand split. She noticed then that his belt was off and he held it snaking down at his side. Had he been whipping the white boy, the one who sat pale and shaken on the cell bunk, with his belt? Had he been snapping that length of leather against the skin of the boy's back?

"He's lying, Jack," Mr. Royce said. "And if you don't believe me, we'll go to the office right now, and you can look for yourself."

"You hid it, then!" Victor said.

"Ain't done it."

"Sure as hell did!"

"No, he didn't." The words spilled from Kansas's mouth before she stopped to think. Her grandfather whirled around to face the two shadowy forms at the screen door.

"What are you doing here?" Jack demanded.

"We came to get the tins for supper," Kansas said.

"You better get back to the house, right now. Just stay put till I straighten this out."

"I can help you, though." Kansas let go of LittleBit's arm and opened the screen door.

"LittleBit, take her on back to the house."

LittleBit shook her head. "She's saying what's so. The child is saying what's so."

Daddy looked dazed for a moment. There were more vague whispers from the cells. Kansas and LittleBit stepped inside the door and Kansas was suddenly aware of all the eyes on her, cells full of eyes, watching her. At that moment she was afraid, and she felt herself draw back. Then she felt LittleBit's hand on her shoulder.

"Say what you know, girl," LittleBit whispered.

"Shut up, woman, and go on," Mr. Royce said. "Get on out of here and take that kid with you."

Daddy Jack gave Mr. Royce another warning look, then turned to Kansas again. "What do you mean?"

The eyes watched her, and LittleBit squeezed her shoulder again. She took a deep breath. "I know Mr. Royce didn't hide the thumb."

"How's that?"

"Because I have it."

"What the hell—?"

"I took it out of Mr. Royce's desk drawer," she said, covering for Leo, wondering why she would cover for him, after what he had forced her to see last night. Then she glanced at Victor Tolbert and knew exactly why she had to cover for the boy. If Victor would beat Roxy so badly, there was no telling what he would do to Leo.

"You took it?" Daddy Jack demanded.

"Yes, sir."

Daddy Jack's face clouded over. "Then you get straight on back to the house, right now. We've got some serious business, you and me."

"See?" Victor said. "He did steal it from me."

"Lying bastard," Mr. Royce said.

"I don't know where he got it," Kansas said, "but it's true that Mr. Royce is a thief. That part's true."

"Ain't no little snot-faced kid going to call me that!" Mr. Royce shouted.

Jack leaned into Mr. Royce's face and narrowed his eyes. "You hear me good. Show your ass one more time and I throw you in a cell with—how about that bunch there?" he asked, indicating Randall's cell where the three muscular teenagers stood. "Reckon they'll look out for you after what they seen you do to Hotshot and Randall yonder?" He indicated the white boy and let a silence emphasize his words, then turned again to Kansas, studying her, speaking more calmly. "Tell me what you mean, Kansas."

"Royce stole LittleBit's Purple Heart."

Mr. Royce looked dumbstruck. LittleBit gave an amazed sort of sigh and said, "Thank you, Lord."

"The girl's making that up, Jack. I won that Purple Heart in the war. Besides, what's a nigger woman doing with a war medal?"

"Her husband got it because he was wounded when he was in Italy. Her husband Ned was a hero," Kansas said.

"Shit."

"It'd damn sure more like to be a nigger's medal than yours, Royce. You a coward," Victor said.

But Jack held up a palm, silencing him. The groups of cell mates exchanged glances. "Since when you got a Purple Heart, Royce?"

"I should have known," LittleBit said in a near whisper.

"Shut up, woman. I'm a veteran, too, you know."

"But it's LittleBit's medal," Kansas said. "It belonged to her husband."

"How do you know it's LittleBit's?" Mr. Royce demanded.

"Because it's scarred where she hit it with a hammer when she was grieving over her husband." Kansas's voice broke.

"That ain't no kind of proof," Mr. Royce said.

"I'm sorry I didn't tell you, LittleBit. I was going to tell you but I was scared. I thought if I told you, then Mr. Royce would know I saw in his desk drawer. And he would know that I took his thumb."

LittleBit slipped her arm around Kansas's shoulders. "Shh."

"Exactly where is the medal scarred, Royce?" Jack said.

"All over. It's old."

"See what a lying bastard he is?" Victor said.

Kansas continued talking to LittleBit. "I felt so bad. I was trying to think of a way to tell you. I thought about stealing it back, but Mr. Royce went to locking the office at night and I never had a chance during the day."

"It's all right, Baby. I'll have it back now, because you been brave to tell all this, ain't she, Mr. Jack?"

Daddy Jack did not answer. He was wearing the saddest expression Kansas had ever seen him wear, much sadder than the sad reactions to his wife's own lack happiness. He shook his head. "There has to be an end to all this."

"What do you mean?" Kansas said. "An end to what?"

"It's not right."

"Daddy?"

Daddy Jack sighed and looked at Littlebit. "It's worn on me like nothing else, all these years. It's worn me down all kinds of ways."

LittleBit squeezed Kansas's shoulder. "I know," she said.

Kansas looked up at the tall woman. "What is it?"

"Your mama used to say, 'The getting of treasures by a lying tongue is a vanity of them that seek death.' She would quote the Bible like that, you know," Daddy Jack said.

Kansas nodded. "I know."

"So for now the medal belongs to me," Daddy Jack said. "Just as soon I get things sorted here and get over to the office to fetch it. But I have a feeling I'll be passing it on to LittleBit as soon as I examine it."

"What the goddamn hell?" Mr. Royce exploded.

"Because if we're giving everything back to their rightful owner, then I figure we'll be giving the medal back to LittleBit."

Mr. Royce mumbled a curse under his breath.

"Not only that," Daddy Jack said. "That thumb you got. Wherever you got it from, it belongs to LittleBit, too."

Kansas took in her breath. "How can that be?"

But her grandfather went on. "And I'm wanting your badge back, Royce. You can go after another county. It's what you want, ain't it?"

Mr. Royce did not answer. Victor grinned.

"Ain't it?" Jack repeated.

"Yeah," Mr. Royce said finally, smooth and nasty sounding at the same time. "But I ain't done here."

"Won't be no threats made," Jack said. "And you can pass that along to your hard legs out the highway. Don't throw no threats my way and keep clear of Blackshear County. Now give me the badge."

Mr. Royce unpinned the silver shield and placed it in Daddy Jack's palm. "Now get on," Daddy Jack said.

As Mr. Royce walked past Kansas and LittleBit, though, he did leave a threat, aimed at the big woman. It did not consist of words, but Kansas could read it in his eyes and she was certain LittleBit could, too. LittleBit had gotten the best of him, and Mr. Royce's eyes told her she would pay, one way or another. It was the coldest look of pure hate Kansas had ever seen passed from one person to another.

"You, Victor," Daddy Jack said to the jailer, who still grinned at his one-upping of Royce Fitzhugh. "You tend to Randall, make sure he ain't hurt. And I better not hear nothing about you being less than polite to these good folks, let alone about any further whuppings and such. I'm wanting to be shed of you just as bad as Royce."

"These good folks need a decent meal," LittleBit said, nodding at the prisoners. "Let's fetch the tins and go see about Hotshot." She glanced at a couple of teenaged girls. "Y'all like meat loaf?" she asked, and the girls smiled back at her. "Yes, ma'am," they said.

Kansas walked over to her grandfather, and put her arms around his waist, trying to pull the affection out of him, the way she had pulled it from LittleBit. And she felt it, felt his arms tighten back around her, as if finding in her some of the thing he had lost, something like a daughter. "Daddy?" she said.

"What, Kansas?"

"Why does LittleBit get the thumb?"

He squeezed her a little more and breathed out. She could hear it rushing through his strong chest like a comfortable wind. "I think that's a thing you should hear from LittleBit. And I reckon it's a thing she's likely willing to tell you."

LittleBit picked up a stack of tins and held them out to Kansas. "I'm willing," she said. "And it's past time, too, but I ain't been very easy with myself."

Kansas released her grandfather's waist and took the tins. "So you'll tell me about it?"

"Yes. I will. But right now we got things to take care of."

*

It was late in the evening when the kitchen was cleaned, the dishes dried and in the cabinets, the pots scrubbed, the stove wiped free of grease. Kansas and LittleBit sat at the white metal table sipping lemonade, LittleBit dribbling a trickle of gin into her glass, "like I used to do with your mama," she told Kansas. Hotshot had been tended and reassured that Mr. Royce would not be around, that Victor was hanging on to his own job by the skin of his teeth and likely to practice civility for a time, at least. Jack walked Hotshot back to his little cell and looked in on the prisoners from Albany, was satisfied they had been well fed. Then he phoned Dr. Deariso, who came round and tended to the welts and cuts across Randall's back. There would be folks bailing them out all week, Daddy told Kansas, and in the meantime they would be treated like Miss Lucille expected any prisoner to be treated at the Blackshear County Jail, since way back during the Depression, when folks were hungry and scavenging for food, like Hotshot was, once upon a time.

Now the family was asleep, the house quiet, air conditioners humming. It was then that LittleBit told Kansas a story. It was about how her husband Ned went fishing up Scratchy Branch one warm summer night some fourteen years earlier. It was right near his favorite spot, near a scattering of sandbars, that he stumbled upon a white couple having sex on the bank, the glare of the moon against their skin turning them the color of catfish bellies. The white lady spied him before he could slip off, but not before the white man spied him as well and went hell-bent on running him down with a pistol. By the time the rumor ran its course, the tale had LittleBit's husband deliberately sneaking up to watch, "just to see a naked white lady get her eyes fucked out," LittleBit said.

Ned's body was recovered the next morning, strung up from a longleaf. Nobody was ever charged, and nobody ever took official credit for it, but it was said to be Klan. Ned had been beaten, hanged, and castrated. Strangest of all, every one of his fingers and toes was missing, and some said they were passed out among the Klansmen as souvenirs, but LittleBit knew for a fact that the man who ordered the lynching, the woman on the creek bank's granddaddy, kept most of them for himself, demanded them given to him lest they ever become some kind of evidence of his crime. "And the woman on the creek bank?" LittleBit said. "Nine months later she give you life, and I was with her to see you born."

Kansas listened as both Pinky's and LittleBit's truths came full circle, and she tried to envision the ripples ringing her conception in the smooth sand alongside Scratchy Branch. She thought of the shell of Pinky's body, lying out back in the tiny shotgun last night while LittleBit bathed her for the colored folks' undertaker. She wondered if the worn flannel gown was still in Pinky's bureau. There was no one to be ingrown with and it was lonelier than she ever imagined. She put out her hand to LittleBit, who took it in hers.

"Did my mama see it happen?"

LittleBit shook her head. "No. But she saw enough. She saw Ned stand up to them men. He ran, because he had to. He had to take that chance. But once he was caught, he was a warrior, and he fought back. Maybe that's why they done him so bad."

And LittleBit went on to tell about the small cubbyhole she discovered in the back hallway of the jailhouse, near a little cellar door, where a severed thumb was found. And that was the thumb she manipulated into the hands of Royce Fitzhugh, "where I'd always know right where it was," LittleBit said, allowing she figured Victor Tolbert had already found and coveted the thing, and she feared he would give it to some higher-ups or move it someplace out of her reach.

"And this is another thing," LittleBit said, "was found in that hiding place of your great-granddaddy." She opened a long utensil drawer next to the stove and raked through the mess of potato mashers, strainers, basters, and pancake turners, bringing out a small key. "There was a whole mess of keys in that jar up inside that cubbyhole, and I took them one at the time, whenever I could lay a hold of one. It took me a half dozen years just to get through about two thirds of that jar."

"What did you do with all the keys?"

"I tried them, one at the time, then I'd put them back, one at the time. I'd write down a picture so I'd know which keys I'd done tried. And all the time what I was set on was finding the key to that trunk in yonder."

"At the foot of my bed?

LittleBit nodded. "Your great-granddaddy's trunk. There's some more things in there that belongs to me."

"How do you know?"

"I told you. I was hunting a key that worked to open it and I found one. My aim was to look inside. And that's what I done."

"When?"

"When wasn't nobody here to see what I was doing."

Kansas admired LittleBit's long years of patience and persistence, was awed by the deliberate steps the woman had taken to unearth the legacy of

Campbell Lacey. "What else is in it?"

"A whole heap of stuff."

"Can we look?"

"Some of it ain't fit for a child's eyes." She paused, then smiled. "But you ain't a child no more, are you?"

"No."

*

LittleBit raised the lid of the cedar chest. The two of them sat on the floor and peered inside at a jumble of file folders, photographs, and a hodgepodge of keepsakes. Among the treasures were a Confederate uniform cap along with a stack of Confederate bills; a helmet with a pointy thing on top that LittleBit said must have come off a German in World War I; a box of old coins from all over, from places like Germany, France, Poland, and Russia; a woman's lacy red garter and some frilly red panties; a small bag of arrowheads; some manila folders; and a brown shoebox. In one of the manila folders were some photographs LittleBit would not let her see, saying they were nasty sex pictures of women, many of them colored women. In another of the folders were lists of names on yellowed paper, names written in script on dozens of sheets of the aging pages. "Lee County Klavern" was written at the top of one page; "Blackshear Klavern" headed another.

"I'd like to take those lists," LittleBit said.

"What are they?"

"Just names of folks. But some of them names are like to be who murdered my Ned."

"Ku Klux Klan people?"

"That's right. Your mama told me this trunk was sure to hold something I could use. That's why she asked your great Grandemona if she could keep it in her bedroom after he passed."

"Shot himself," Kansas corrected.

LittleBit gave her an odd look, then continued, "Elizabeth's daddy wanted to prize the trunk open, but Elizabeth said no, said it was only right for it to sit until it needed to be opened, and he finally agreed. I think he always wanted me to take this off his conscience."

"He didn't help them? The Klan people?"

"No. You can rest easy about him. He's a decent man. Your mama told me about a couple of other men, though. Ones that wasn't decent."

"Who?"

"That preacher, Stryker, for one. He was a man that did her bad, so bad, on the night of her high school dance."

"I saw it in her Bible," Kansas said. "I wasn't sure, but he—?"

"Yes. He did. He took advantage of her. She wouldn't let me tell. She was so afraid of what it meant, all mixed around in that mixed-up head of hers. She thought she was full of demons. I reckon that's what she thought after your own daddy was done with her, but her mind was all in a jumble then. It was hard to get much sense out of her on those times she was of a bent to talk about it."

Kansas let out a breath, not knowing what to say, not knowing how to feel about it all, not yet.

"Your mama told me a heap about Royce Fitzhugh, too, how she didn't trust him, how he turned on her."

"I'm glad he's gone. But he's mad as hell at you. I saw that look he gave you."

"I ain't afraid of no peckerwood like Royce Fitzhugh, but I ain't long for here, so I won't be thinking about him atall."

"What do you mean? You can't leave. You wouldn't."

"I reckon I can, and I am. I got all I need to carry up to Sergeant Lewis in Chicago." And then LittleBit told one last story, about Ned's war buddy, the one Pinky contacted when Ned was murdered, the one who called, begged her to move north, told her she could stay with him and his wife in a nice neighborhood with a nice church, until she found a nice place of her own. Finally, though, when she was so insistent about gathering every scrap of evidence she could find, Sergeant Walter Lewis counseled her to be cautious, be vigilant, and call him collect every month to let him know what she had found, just so someone else in the world knew, just in case.

"He and his wife are people who will help me when the time comes to put the truth out. When the time comes and when the time is right. And it will come, Lord willing, before I pass."

Kansas laid her head on her knees, knowing how selfish it would seem to beg LittleBit to stay. And how futile. LittleBit had been wronged in the worst way possible, and she deserved to see all those years come to something. Still, Kansas felt her shoulders shaking, heard herself sobbing, outside herself, coming from a loss deep inside herself. She wanted Pinky. She wanted LittleBit to be near. She wanted to be ingrown, connected, soul into soul. "First Pinky and now you," she heard herself say through ragged breaths.

And then she felt something strange and new. It was a touch full of determined care. It was LittleBit gathering her up, pulling her over and into her strong arms, holding Kansas against her shoulder, soothing and unrestrained. "Child, it's going to be all right," she said.

"But she's gone," Kansas said, ashamed of her tears, wanting to show LittleBit she could at least try to match her strength.

"She ain't gone," LittleBit said. "Just like Ned ain't gone. He kept me going all these years and now Mama's fixing to help him keep me going from now on. Right along with Elizabeth."

"My mama helps you?"

"Yes, she does. In spite of everything."

Kansas lifted her head from LittleBit's shoulder. "What do you mean?"

LittleBit flinched, then took a breath. "In spite of me not being there when she needed me so bad, and me the cause of it to begin with."

"I don't understand. The cause of what?"

"Lord, help me," LittleBit said. "Don't nobody but Pinky know this."

"Will you tell me?"

LittleBit sighed a deep, heavy sigh. "She come to me, that night."

"My mama?"

"Elizabeth. She left a pint of gin on the kitchen table over at my place across the tracks."

"But you weren't there?"

"No. I was out at the Blue Goose, trying to keep from thinking about what I'd done."

"What was—?"

"And I never would have left that gun—your great-granddaddy's gun—lying around if I thought Elizabeth would find it, but she did."

"Oh, no, LittleBit. No."

LittleBit nodded, yes.

"But you couldn't help that. They told you to take the gun."

"And get shed of it. Which I ain't done. No, I kept it like a prize, so full of myself, kept it in plain sight all the time, in those weeks after he shot hisself. I never would've thought..." Her voice trailed off and her eyes went to another shade of deep pain.

Kansas wanted to ask for more, but couldn't bring herself to exploit what LittleBit was giving her, so she only said, "LittleBit, can Ned look over me, too? With Mama and Pinky?"

"Your Daddy Jack throwed that gun in the river," she mumbled, "when they found her. And it's a funny, funny thing," she said, in a tone of sudden, somber amazement. "He never said a word to me about that gun. Never laid no blame at my feet."

"LittleBit?" Kansas asked again, offering her own kind of forgiveness. "Is it all right if Ned looks over me, too?"

LittleBit smiled a weak, appreciative smile. "Sure he can, Baby. Sure he can."

Kansas leaned her head on LittleBit's shoulder again. "I think I am lucky," Kansas said, "to have a heroic warrior looking over me. Don't you?" She looked up and thought she saw LittleBit's eyes fill with tears, but the woman quickly turned her attention back to the trunk. "You want to get that thumb for me now?" LittleBit asked.

Kansas hesitated. How could LittleBit bring herself to look at it? How could she remain so brave in the face of such vicious sadness?

"Go on," LittleBit said, taking the shoe box out of the trunk. "Get it for me."

Kansas stood and went to her closet, retrieving the jar from where she had hidden it away with her diary, in the Buster Brown shoe box. When she held it out for LittleBit to take, she gasped. LittleBit was holding another

jar, a larger one, a small mason jar like the other two left in the shoebox in
her lap, a jar full of liquid and a half-dozen fingers and toes, the same kind
of faded washed out flesh, devoid of pigmentation, as the bit of a thumb
she held in her own jar. LittleBit was sitting, cradling the jar in her palms,
shoulders slumped, staring at the pieces of him, at the cellophane-like skin
covering chopped bits of bone.

Kansas approached her, but LittleBit jerked her chin up and stood. She
put the jar back in the shoebox, along with the small jar Kansas had given
her. Then she put Campbell Lacey's lists of names in the bag. "I reckon I
got all I need now," she said. Her eyes looked wild, though, like she was
becoming aware of a frightening truth, too frightening to face, as if she was
an animal cornered and fretted into an adrenaline-induced frenzy. "I got
to go to Pinky's," she said, clutching the sack to her chest, hands squeezing
her shoulders.

"But don't you want—?"

"No!" It was whispered, but more intense than Kansas had ever heard
anything uttered. LittleBit walked from one side of the room to the other,
breaths shallow, eyes wide, whispering, "Oh God, oh God, ohGod, ohGod,"
over and over. Then she looked at Kansas one more time, and the reflection the girl caught in the woman's eyes was an unearthed recognition, raw
and primal and decimating. "I got to go to Pinky's," LittleBit said again,
and hurried out the bedroom door, a gathering sound deep in her throat
cutting into her shallow breaths as she strode down the back hall toward
her mother's home.

Kansas did not follow her, sensed she was not needed yet, some vague
recollection of her mother's death telling her to be easy, don't push, be
respectful of that pain. She did not follow even when she heard the guttural cries echoing across alleys and summer streets, or when she heard the
name cried out, beseeching and defeated: "Ned!" Kansas waited, for a long
time, fingering the perverse treasures of her grandfather, wandering
through her mother's biblical notations, listening for the courthouse clock
to strike one, then two, after the silence settled on Pinky's shotgun house.
She would wait another half hour, she decided. Then she would tiptoe into

the darkness as she had when she was five, and she would climb into the squeaky iron bed. She would put her arms around LittleBit and curl her body against LittleBit's spine and comfort her with the sort of soothing sleep that would keep them forever ingrown, no matter how many miles between them.

II: x

The first Wednesday in August was bright and blue and clear, white eruptions of clouds buoyed by the sky's depth of color. It was a jewelry-box day, a day as multifaceted as a diamond, a day glittering with reflections of the sun, a day, Kansas thought, that should be in a movie, the backdrop for the part where the man and the woman ride off into the sunset, or where the little lost puppy makes his way home, or where two long-lost friends find one another once again. It was not a day for departures, for sad endings, for letting go of needs so that another could find her way to a brand-new life. Yet here Kansas stood, on the platform at the Sumner Depot, preparing to tell LittleBit goodbye, a goodbye she feared might last forever.

LittleBit looked prettier and more feminine today than she ever had. She had on a new outfit, a brilliant green dress with a black Peter Pan collar and a wide black patent leather belt cinched at the waist. She wore a green and black straw hat with a small brim, bunches of black cherries nestled along the hatband, and her patent pumps matched her handbag. She carried gloves, and that gave her an air of refined sophistication, like Jackie Kennedy, and Kansas told her as much.

"Shoot," LittleBit said, but Kansas could tell she was flattered and proud by the way LittleBit said it.

LittleBit also carried a large manila envelope and clutched a small round vanity case with the same hand that held the clear plastic handle of her handbag, an intricately carved staff of some kind beneath her arm. Two large suitcases were on the platform beside her, brand-new luggage, new and not inexpensive, new, like the outfit. She had finally, she told Kansas, spent some of the money Ned left her, finally felt that she deserved it. Too, she had continued to work hard and live so simply after his death that she had been able to add a modestly tidy sum to his nest egg.

"I reckon I'm fixing to see some of the sights. Lord. I ain't never been past Macon," LittleBit said.

"Will you write?" Kansas was determined not to cry, not to even begin thinking about it.

"It won't be a pretty thing, but I'll do it." She smiled. "It's prettier than it used to be though."

"You practiced?"

"Practiced a good bit. Matter of fact, I left your Daddy Jack a letter telling a thing or two he might need to know."

"About me?"

"About lots of folks, but only good things about you." A train whistle sounded, far off but inevitable. LittleBit turned to a couple standing near the ticket booth. "Yonder it comes," she said.

Kansas glanced over at the couple, a distinguished-looking colored man and an attractive, plumpish colored woman, his wife. They nodded at her and Kansas nodded back. She had met them, Mr. and Mrs. Lewis, at Pinky's funeral. They had come all the way down from Chicago to see to LittleBit and to escort her back, and Kansas couldn't help feeling a slight resentment, as if they were taking LittleBit away from her.

"It's good to have folks in the world to help you out in hard times," LittleBit said, as though she were hearing Kansas's thoughts.

Kansas blushed. "I'll miss you, that's all."

"Hush that talk."

Kansas felt the train now, through the soles of her feet, and the whistle came loud and long and sad, like a howling stray. "The funeral was nice," she said.

"Yes, it was. Did it up just like Mama wanted, right down to the white lilies and the children's choir. And your granddaddy ordered up a fine headstone to put beside Ned's. A fine, fine stone."

"We'll take care of it, too," Kansas said. "Ned's, too. I already told Daddy and he agreed. And I told him I'd start helping him tend my mama's grave."

LittleBit smiled. "That's a right sweet thing to do."

The clackety-clack of wheels on the rails grew louder and slower.

"Please don't forget about me," Kansas said suddenly, and her throat tightened.

LittleBit sighed and put her hand on Kansas's cheek. "Lord, Child. How in the world could I ever forget about you and your mama?"

"You could get us confused with the bad things."

"No," LittleBit said, dropping her hand. "I'm leaving all the bad things behind, not going to dwell on them. Starting a new life, just like me and Ned planned. Like I told your mama about."

The train's whistle drowned out what LittleBit was saying. The big engine of the Man o' War rolled by, hissing and squealing.

"What did you say?" Kansas asked as the noise faded.

"I said, it's a funny, funny thing. But your mama was really the closest friend—pretty near the only friend I ever had."

Kansas tried to wish her the best. "I want you to make lots of friends in Chicago. I want you to have fun."

"I believe I'll do just that," LittleBit said.

"Maybe even a boyfriend?"

LittleBit threw her head back and laughed. It was a lovely sound, a sound Kansas had never heard her utter. It was like a fresh melody, and the girl stood in amazement, and watched, and listened.

Mr. Lewis and his wife approached, and Kansas's amazement fizzled into the urge to latch onto LittleBit, to tell them to go away, that they could not have her. She would beg and cajole and cry until LittleBit relented, moved into Pinky's house for good, and—

"You ready to get aboard?" Mr. Lewis asked, lifting the two large suitcases. "I already checked our bags. I'll go take care of these." He looked at Kansas and said, "It was nice to meet you, little lady."

"Yes, sir. You, too," Kansas said, nodding as she had earlier. She and

LittleBit would cook and garden and talk over all kinds of problems. They would sip sweet tea on the sagging little porch at the front of Pinky's shotgun, and in the evenings they would pop Jiffy-Pop and watch *Thriller* and *The Twilight Zone*.

"Don't you worry about Eula Lura," Mrs. Lewis said. "We'll look out for her, all right?"

Kansas nodded, her fantasy shattering, her false hope collapsing.

"You go ahead," LittleBit said to the lady. "I'll be on in a minute."

The train's whistle sounded. "Better be quick," Mrs. Lewis said. Then she turned to Kansas again. "You are a lovely girl."

"Thank you."

"'Bye, now."

"'Bye," Kansas said.

LittleBit struggled with her handful, then unclasped her pocketbook and withdrew a handkerchief. "I told you I didn't want to see no tears."

Kansas took the handkerchief and wiped her cheeks. She had not realized she was crying. How long had she been crying? "Sorry," she said, handing the handkerchief back to LittleBit.

"You can have any of the things in Mama's house. Pruella's done got what she wants, and I packed a few things to carry to Chicago."

The whistle blew a few short blasts and a porter called, "All aboard!"

"Well, then," LittleBit said.

Kansas threw her arms around LittleBit's waist, felt the woman's powerful embrace. One more time. "I love you, LittleBit," she said.

"I love you, too, Baby." And Kansas felt a kiss pressed to the side of her head.

A porter helped LittleBit step up into the car, but when she got inside she said, "Oh, Lordy!" and turned back to Kansas. "I forgot. This is for you." She handed down the manila envelope.

"What is it?" A sparkling flash caught Kansas's eye. A diamond ring on the third finger of LittleBit's left hand. "And what is that? Was that from Ned?"

"I like to pretend it was," LittleBit grinned. "But really it was a gift from Elizabeth. She gave it to me when I told her how Ned called me his diamond, how he wished he could afford a truckload of diamonds, just for me."

"I never saw it before."

The train began to roll. "All right," said the porter.

"I couldn't wear it around your folks or Miss Pearl would've had a conniption fit."

Kansas walked alongside the open car. "But what is this?" She indicated the envelope.

"Just some things of your mama's. Things she gave me a few days before she—did that. Made me promise to give them to you someday."

"Got to close up," the porter said.

Kansas made a face at him, then grinned at LittleBit. "Bye!"

LittleBit waved. Just as the porter began to close the door, Kansas shouted, "Please don't forget about me!"

She caught a sad expression rushing across LittleBit's face as the woman nodded no, mouthing the words, "I won't."

The train began picking up speed. Kansas stood and watched it roll away from the station, car after car, until she was watching the red caboose, wishing LittleBit was standing on the back of it, waving goodbye, just one more time. Just one. "Don't forget about me," she whispered.

The envelope was wrinkled and whatever was inside felt padded. Kansas sat on a bench near the depot, tore through the sealed paper, and reached inside. Her hand came out with one bracelet, then another, the charm bracelets she remembered from when she was small. One was all silver, with a bit of copper here and there, a collection of coins from all over the world, many like the coins she had seen in her great-grandfather's trunk, and she liked the idea of wearing bits of the world on her wrist.

"Bits of the world on my wrist." It came like an echo, far back in her thoughts, then grew stronger and clearer. They were her mother's words, not Kansas's. "I just love wearing bits of the world on my wrist. You want to count the pieces of the world your mama's wearing now?" They were her mother's words, coming from a lost well of words. Maybe it was exactly those words, she now thought, which had been the seed of her interest in the lands outside Blackshear County, Georgia, beyond the borders of the

United States of America, lands that found their way onto the pages of *National Geographic,* and into Kansas's curious hands.

The second bracelet was thick with silver and gold charms of all kinds: a kitten, a cross, a spinning wheel, a mermaid, a pair of dice, an ashtray with a cigarette resting on it, a cluster of music notes, among others. There were silver and gold discs and hearts, too, engraved with dates and events and messages: "Marry me! Love, Robert 9-19-42"; "For Angel, from the 45th squadron, January 1944"; "Angel: The most beautiful magnolia in the south. I love you, Chuck." Kansas fingered the trinkets for a long time, studying each one, vaguely remembering a few, sharply recollecting others as she encountered them.

There was a magazine in the envelope as well, a small *Jet* magazine, pages yellowing, and a note inside, in the center, marking the place where the magazine featured photos of a dead boy named Emmit Till. The note itself was strange and disjointed, written in ink on typing paper from the sheriff's office, with Campbell Lacey's letterhead at the top. His name was circled and an arrow was drawn from there down to a notation: "Look what I've done." There were other brief notes and odd verses, written in varying degrees of legibility: "Peace is a treasure, a diamond—'Oh, that I had wings like a dove! for then I would fly away, and be at rest'"; "Tell them not to hate me, please, please not to be disappointed." Some seemed to be directions: "Stay clear of Brother Stryker," and "Don't take any wooden nickels. Ha!" But Kansas did not see her name anywhere on the front of the paper.

Finally, in the middle of the back of the paper, a note addressed to her: "Kansas, I want you to be always the sweet child you are now, and beautiful, through and through. I love you more than anything—can't do what everyone wants me to do. Can't ever be genuine to them—I'm fractured notes in a minor key. They expect something I can't be, a concerto, a symphony with movements that hang together like the acts of a fine play, I, II, III and so on, a formula. I am all dissonance and clatter and flats and missed chords. Eula Lura will give you my favorite bracelets and Chen Ling's beautiful shirt. He was supposed to will it to me, but of course I had to steal it—all because of the horrors, the cruel things—but, oh, my baby, it is the most beautiful shirt in the world. Love, Mama." Then, at the bottom of the page: "P.S. It is a forever shirt."

She reached into the envelope and brought out the shirt, which was beyond beautiful, was so much like she remembered her mother, delicate and exotic, with the appearance of fragility but a deceptive strength, a strength that did last for a time, lasted until her tenuous mental strength gave way to surrender. Her fingers brushed against the smooth coolness of the satiny fabric, raised pastel flowers embroidered in prolific patterns. Kansas put the shirt next to her cheek, then against her nose, hoping to find her mother's scent, and she thought she caught the perfume of something familiar, something long ago pressed into her consciousness, an imprint, forever there, just barely reachable on the borders of sparse memories.

She put the treasures back in the envelope and stood. It was too much to take in. She needed to talk it over with someone, had to talk it over. She started for Pinky's house before it dawned on her, she was yet so unused to the death. The realization shocked her for a moment. She couldn't talk anything over with Pinky. No. She had said goodbye to Pinky, just three days ago, at the funeral, when the old woman was tucked into the earth, a blanket of rich black soil to keep her covered, an afghan of green-bladed grass thrown across her bed. And, while Kansas certainly aimed to have LittleBit as a pen pal, these things—the note, the shirt, and the bracelets—these were things begging to be discussed right now, this minute.

Then she thought of Aunt Frances, of the glider on the side porch, and the whining drone of the ceiling fan, familiar and comforting. Why had she let Roxy convince her there was something to fear at Aunt Frances's house? Why had she avoided going to visit? Maybe her aunt *was* a lesbian and maybe Kansas would even ask her about it, but why would their talks have to be any different from how they had always been? Maybe their talks could get even more to the bottom of things, now that Kansas had put so much of the puzzle together. Maybe Kansas would apologize for being such a turncoat and promise not to think ill of Aunt Frances, ever again, no matter what.

She crossed at the light and headed for Isabella Street, and while she walked she let the feeling of the town soak into her pores—the familiar, the routine, the familial spirits. She glanced up at the shimmering dome of the Blackshear County Courthouse, where her childhood was rooted in the settling wood and crown molding of the sheriff's office, the sparrows that set a great flapping when they soared from beneath the eaves, the hexagonal stone floors of the high-ceilinged hallway tunneling from front door to back. She loved the core of her hometown, the parts of it she roamed at night, the parts of it she kept in her imagination. The ugliness was what she planned to discard, the unwritten rules, the white-knuckled manners, and the cheap hypocrisy of those who claimed to love the Lord while they spat on folks not good enough, in their eyes.

She walked down the sidewalk that would curve into Isabella Street, stopped, fumbled in the envelope, and took out the bracelet of coins. She slipped it around her wrist and closed the clasp, feeling the taps—of Brazil, of France, of India and Russia and Morocco and beyond—against her skin, nudging her, prodding her with their jingling caress. And with every step, every glance, pore by pore, she felt a sense of purpose taking her, a knowledge that she would, indeed, as she really always knew, follow the coins on her mother's bracelet to magical places around the globe, determined to school herself in the ways of those other places, places with a different attitude, an opposite perspective. And those places would lead her to places in the spirit, where she would find the best of herself, the best of her mother, the best of every significant person she had ever known and would come to know. And she most of all knew, more completely than ever, that she could come through anything, any hard times the dice wanted to roll for her, very much and unalterably, at worst, intact—and, very much and with fluidity, at best, changed for the better.

Kansas would rediscover her thirteenth year in never-ending loops throughout the landscape of the rest of her life. She would return to it as surely as the moon cycled the currents of the earth in rhythmic bands of currents. She would, in fact, watch a man stand on the moon in 1969 and wonder if he could hear the strawberry-banana scented chirps her mother had listened to, late at night, across a chorus of insects and chattering tree frogs. In her memories she would crouch beneath the fig tree for quarter hours at a time, studying Pinky's empty house and Miss Pearl's equally empty one. She would throw herself into the changes swirling her through the decades of her youth, remembering Pinky's flannel nightgown as she snuggled beneath the quilts and into the curve of the old woman's embrace; and she would often imagine LittleBit's strong hand clasped around her own, showing her where to walk, while brave spirits protected her from a blind of clouds in the midnight sky. She would love and honor her family, but always at a distance, aching for her mother, but letting her aunt hold that chamber of her heart's longing, the bond between the two of them becoming fierce and unbreakable. And she would forever have vivid pictures in her head: of LittleBit's hands, wrists relaxed, resting on her aproned knees; of the back of her Daddy Jack's strong, tan neck, and the reassurance of his touch; of a skinny Negro girl in a lemon-yellow dress pushed full by white net petticoats beneath the starched cotton; and of Liquid Obscurity, gushing clear and cold, into a winding creek.

By August of her thirteenth year, Night Riders just up the road in Lees-burg and Dawson would fire shots into several homes of voter registration workers, churches would be burned to the ground, and Albany would never be the same again. By September there would be a nationally covered Klan rally just up the highway, attended by the Tolbert family and hundreds of others who wanted all the niggers to go back to Africa, and her friendship with Roxy would come to its natural close. Kansas would think back on South Georgia's gathering swell of violence when Schwerner, Goodman, and Cheney turned up dead in the morally desolate Mississippi grown out of Emmit Till's final summer.

Then she would think of her mother's slip into madness because of the cruelty done in her name, to defend her encoded, false honor. Kansas would decide, as she grew older and richer from a life lived fully, for continents traveled, for people experienced, that Elizabeth Lacey was solid and brave, in spite of the unwinding spiral of her mother's mind and the poise of a pistol barrel at her temple. She would think of her mother as the point of a star, the turn of a moment into honesty. She would think, too, of Eula Lura's Ned, the warrior, and of his severed thumb rolling in liquid, weightless as a man stepping across the face of the moon. And she would know the kind of peace most merely hope for or pretend at.

In the late afternoons leading into September of Kansas's thirteenth year, leading to school and the permanent parting of their childhood ways, Leo, Kansas, and Roxy roamed Sumner's streets and alleys, kicking rocks and bottle caps into the silence grown between them, serenaded only by the chimes of the courthouse clock, entertained only by diversion from one another. One rainy Thursday afternoon, they followed Hotshot up into the dome of the courthouse and watched him crank the heavy gears that clicked out the minutes and the hours while thunder boiled black clouds across the sky outside. On another day, the atmosphere stilled by the white heat of midsummer, they took refuge in the air-conditioned Bijou Theatre and watched a *Tarzan* double feature two times in a row, while children in the colored balcony above giggled at the African natives on the big screen. And one desolate Sunday, Kansas and Roxy put pennies on the railroad tracks, and, as a thundering string of freight cars mashed the money into thin copper puddles, Leo tossed slurs and track gravel toward the rows of shacks beyond the Blue Goose.

The bank's black marble façade threw reflections of the three of them behind the Feed & Seed, Leo poking poultry corpses with a sharp stick, the girls shuddering at the odor of stale chicken droppings, feathered carcasses, and the decaying eggshells of newly hatched biddies. And while Roxy stood back, masked impervious and unwilling, with her splintered spirit and dreams surrendered, Kansas, wearing Chen Ling's beautiful shirt and her mother's sun-glinting charm bracelets, stomped the mounds of shells with her bare feet, defiant, practicing the kind of expression that might make a dent in the world. She marched across the little hills of shell, bracelets tinkling in time, knees raised, one then the other, smiling as her feet compacted the reproductive remnants with delicate little crackles, feeling the give of possibility. The drying embryonic spittle stuck bits of eggshells to the summer-toughened skin of her soles, razor-thin shavings zipped stinging slices into the tender, gestating secrets between her toes, and she knew an entire, starry-skied universe of crystalline potential was waiting, just for her.

ACKNOWLEDGMENTS

What began as a novella became such a huge, fast-moving project that it never would have been completed in such a relatively short time without a whole lot of help. Joe Formichella provided encouragement and an eye for the big picture, help with answering the big questions, research, windows, and lots of maps. Having Sonny Brewer in my corner as friend, mentor, and editor is, as always, a huge support; and other editors such as Jason Wood, Suzanne Barnhill, and Jay Qualey did much to further refine the story. All the MacAdam/Cage staffers, in fact, who added their suggestions were invaluable. Thanks also to Catherine Simmons for giving it a read and responding as a reader more than an editor, and, as usual, to Stephen, Ben, Booda, and Gene for technical and historical help. Tasha, JP, Pat, Dorothy, Scott, Melanie, et al: you are amazing. Finally, nothing happens without David Poindexter, who breaks the mold when it comes to being a "publisher." At a time when numbers and trends and bottom lines determine so much of what folks read, he acts out of love for the words. Thank you, David, for offering unconditional support of this book.